Dear Reader,

The novels you've enjoyed over the past years by such authors as Kathleen Woodiwiss, Rosemary Rogers, Johanna Lindsey, Laurie McBain, and Shirlee Busbee are accountable to one thing above all others: Avon has never tried to force authors into any particular mold. Rather, Avon is a publisher that encourages individual talent and is always on the lookout for writers who will deliver *real* books, not packaged formulas.

In 1982, we started a program to help readers pick out authors of exceptional promise. Called "The Avon Romance," the books were distinguished by a ribbon motif in the upper left-hand corner of the cover. Although the titles were by new authors, they were quickly discovered and became known as "the ribbon books."

Now "The Avon Romance" is a regular feature on the Avon list. Each month, you will find historical novels with many different settings, each one by an author who is special. You will not find predictable characters, predictable plots, and predictable endings. The only predictable thing about "The Avon Romance" will be the superior quality that Avon has always delivered in the field of romance!

Sincerely,

WALTER MEADE
President & Publisher

LINDA P. SANDIFER

TYLER'S WOMAN

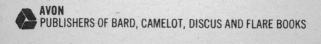

AVON
PUBLISHERS OF BARD, CAMELOT, DISCUS AND FLARE BOOKS

AVON BOOKS
A division of
The Hearst Corporation
1790 Broadway
New York, New York 10019

First Avon Printing, October 1985

AVON TRADEMARK REG. U. S. PAT. OFF. AND IN OTHER
COUNTRIES, MARCA REGISTRADA, HECHO EN U. S. A.

Printed in the U. S. A.

WFH 10 9 8 7 6 5 4 3 2 1

To Van, whose encouragement and love
have never faltered.

TYLER'S WOMAN

Prologue

August 1854

TYLER CHANSON LET HIS SHOVEL rest in his callused hands while he relaxed against a fence post to better watch the sway of Carlotta's hips. Her brightly colored skirt moved in cadence to her provocative, yet natural, light and happy steps as she came across the yard toward him. She carried an earthenware pitcher in both hands, and he silently blessed her; it was just what he needed to break this California heat and spell the monotony of the corral building.

She smiled broadly when she was still fifty feet away. "Señor, do you care for a drink of cold water?"

His brown eyes shifted to her young, full breasts that were nearly concealed by cascades of black, freshly washed hair, and he thought about how soft those raven strands would feel if he were to touch them. Instead he removed his hat, releasing his thick, dark hair from its hot confinement. Squinting against the sun, he wiped his brow with his shirt sleeve. "Sí, Señora Chanson. Could I resist something so tempting?" He mocked her heavy Spanish accent, smiling

1

in the secret way that told her he wasn't necessarily referring to the water.

When she was at his side, he took the water and, after draining half the contents into his parched mouth, set the pitcher on a post. With his other hand he pulled Carlotta into his embrace. Her melodious laughter brought a deep smile to his face and a warm joy to his heart. His lips possessed hers easily.

He felt content with her as his wife. She had brought new meaning to his life in just the short time they had been married. And soon there would be even more joy, for she would be giving birth to his child in about seven months.

The kiss successfully stirred his ever-present love and need for her to a glowing pitch, as one would stir the embers in a fire to enhance the flame. She was no longer naive to the silent words in his eyes and the way he tilted his smile when he desired her lovemaking. She laughed and pushed him away, but still remained at the length of his arms.

"You are like your papa's stud horse, Tyler Chanson. You never seem to tire. What will you do when your son is out to here"—she motioned with her hands—"and it is no longer possible?"

"I'll wait," he replied nonchalantly. "But there's nothing between us now."

"You are impossible!" she exclaimed. "I have dinner ready to be sat on the table. Your father and brother will be returning soon."

"We can hurry," he suggested playfully.

"It is easy for you to say!" Her accent became stronger and he knew his bantering was putting her into a fluster.

He pulled her closer to his leanly muscled body.

"They *are* returning. I see them on the rise. But tonight, my sweet Carlotta, we'll finish what we've begun and I'll show you once again how much I love you."

Tyler put his arm about her small waist, standing over her by a foot, as together they waited for the riders to dismount. "Did you find the horses?" Tyler asked.

"No." Orin Chanson pulled his horse to a stop next to the corral and swung to the ground. Like his four sons, he was a tall, broad-chested man, but hard work had kept away the slightest trace of excess weight. The deepening lines in his face and the dark hair now salted with gray gave away his increasing years, but he was still vital, and he did not complain of the extra pains in the mornings and the shortness of breath he experienced when he tried to keep pace alongside his boys.

"I swear that horse has just up and disappeared. Can't even see sign of him," Orin continued as he loosened the cinch on his saddle. "Maybe you and Kit can go out this afternoon and do some more hunting, but I've got a sneakin' suspicion we've got us a case of horse stealin' here."

"About all there is around here is miners," Tyler said.

"Yeah, but there's a lot of crooks biding their time in the goldfields. A fine piece of horseflesh would replace a few days with no gold." He turned to Carlotta. "I can smell your cooking clear from here, girl, and it smells mighty good. What do you say we give it a samplin'?"

Carlotta laughed in her usual lilting way and moved ahead of Tyler toward the house, but suddenly she stopped short at the sight of a group of riders cresting the nearby rise.

"They're the same ones we saw down on the river," Kit said. "They must have followed us here."

"Wonder what they're wantin'." Orin asked the question they were all thinking.

"Carlotta," Tyler said softly, "go to the house. We'll see what they want."

Instinct and experience had taught the Chansons that strangers could not always be trusted in this lawless, young land. Their hands were ready on their rifles as the group, consisting of over a half dozen men, drew near.

Kit stepped closer to Tyler. "I don't care for the looks of those boys, big brother," he said lightly. "About now I wish I'd gone for supplies with Keane and Rayce."

"They're a bunch of lowlives, for sure." Tyler tried to sound nonchalant, but there were times when a man smelled trouble, and this was one of those times.

Orin Chanson moved a step in front of his sons, silently declaring his authority and seniority to the advancing group, but almost simultaneously he felt the presence of his sons on either side of him. He held his rifle ready but loosely in front of him. The riders brought their horses into a ragged line fifty feet away.

Orin spoke lightly. "What brings you fellows out this way?"

From the center of the bunch an apparent leader emerged. He was a man who sat tall in the saddle, a handsome man if it weren't for the dangerous apathy glowing in his eyes and the malicious curl twisting his lips. "It all depends," he replied, raking a heartless gaze over the three and letting his head turn slightly back toward the house like a dog wanting to get to a bone he is smelling.

A foreboding feeling quivered momentarily through Tyler. He nervously wished he had told Carlotta to bolt the door and get the shotgun. He made a mental note of the riders' faces and their horses. He saw the malevolence in each. They would do what their leader said. He could take them directly through the gates of hell and not one would turn back.

"You can water your horses and yourselves, but I'm afraid that's about all we have to offer." Orin Chanson still spoke with forced friendliness. Only his sons could sense his dislike for the situation.

The leader allowed himself an oblique smile. "I had something a little more rewarding in mind. Something like some gold."

Orin Chanson's forced smile turned cold. It was too much to hope that these men might have been friendly travelers. In a lawless land, a man readily acquired the ability to pick the good from the bad, almost as easily as picking rotten apples from a barrel. "All you'll find here is cattle and horses."

"Don't lie to us, old man. We saw you and your kid riding the river. We all know there's gold in that river. My guess is you've got what we want in those saddlebags tied on your horses."

"Take a look," Orin Chanson offered tightly. "You'll find nothing."

The leader inclined his head to his left. "Tuttle, go see if he's telling the truth."

The rider next to him nudged his horse from the group and meandered forward. Tyler never took his eyes from the spokesman. Only his peripheral vision caught any movements from the others. They all waited, tense and ready. They had come looking for action and they watched eagerly. Tuttle checked out the bags and found nothing but a little food, ammunition, and spare clothing. He moved cautiously back to his group.

"Where is it?" The spokesman demanded.

"We have no gold," Orin replied evenly. "We're ranchers, not miners. I suggest you go work for it like the rest of 'em."

"I think you lie." Again the leader's eyes mirrored his thoughts as his gaze strayed to the house. "If you won't tell us, then I'm sure, that with a little persuasion, the woman will." He turned his horse to the house. The others followed, but a deadly voice and the click of a rifle hammer stopped them in their tracks.

"I think not," Tyler said. "You boys had best turn back the way you came. Like we said, we have no gold."

Silence reigned for several seconds. The leader looked back over his shoulder at the smoldering fury of the big man who held the Sharps carbine aimed at his head. The other two had drawn their rifles casually upward, their barrels pointed indiscriminately at two of his men. He hadn't expected a fight. Most men backed down when the odds were obviously against them. It was plain to see these three were different. It was also plain to see that even though they had no gold, they had a woman they wished to protect.

The leader smirked at the rifle barrel pointed at him. "My name is Walt Cotton, but it'll do you three no good to know it. You can't kill us all before we kill you."

"Maybe not, Mr. Cotton," Tyler warned, "but my first bullet has your name on it. If you savor your life, you'll find yourself some easier prey."

Walt Cotton's horse shifted nervously beneath him. The smirk faded from the man's lips. "A man can't argue with a bullet, now can he?" He mockingly touched the brim of his hat and jerked his horse around roughly. "Come on boys, let's go."

They headed out the way they had come, quietly but exchanging words among themselves. The Chansons felt Cotton had backed down too easily. In seconds their misgivings were realized. The bunch whirled in unison, pistols blazing. Tyler, Kit, and Orin dove behind a pile of poles, the only cover available. A barrage of bullets flew freely in both directions. Tyler found Cotton in his sights and, just as he had promised, gave him his first bullet. The man fell from his horse, just as Tyler spontaneously felt a bullet burn into his left arm from an unknown source. In less than a space of a second he felt another.

Tyler counted two men down as he drew a bead on another. The lead was falling around their flimsy barricade like hailstones. The renegades rushed in, circling them, pinning them, seemingly having little regard for even their own lives.

Suddenly Kit went down, a circle of blood growing larger on his chest. In only seconds Orin was dead, a bullet through his head. Tyler dropped two more men before a bullet pierced his shoulder, close to his heart. The rifle snapped uncontrollably from his grip and clattered over the poles. He groped for it, but everything went white and he followed it in a death-tumble to the ground.

The loud blast of a shotgun jarred Tyler back to consciousness. *Carlotta.* The memory of her surfaced in his groggy mind. He had to get to her and help her, but his hands and body wouldn't answer the commands of his brain. He clawed at the dirt, dragging himself around to the end of the pole pile. The house was there in his blurry vision, but it seemed so far away.

Again the ground shook with the report of Carlotta's last shell. A man flew backward from the open doorway of the house, but like a rumpled rug he was cast aside as the three remaining men trod over and around him and into the house. Carlotta screamed again and frantically he tried to reach her, but had to watch helplessly as they dragged her from the house while they laughed and pushed her from one to the other. He searched for his gun in the dirt but couldn't find it. Their maniacal frenzy grew.

"Where's your gold?" they demanded.

"I don't have any!" she cried. "Please leave me alone."

"Carlotta." Tyler's word was barely a whisper. She couldn't hear him. His body was numb and bleeding, useless from the wounds in his shoulder and arm. He called out to her again. "Carlotta."

"Tell us where you've got it hidden if you want to live!"

One man pushed her hard. She cried out in terror, stumbled blindly through her tears, and fell to the ground. She scrambled to get up. A dirty hand reached out for her and jerked at her blouse. It ripped and fell open to reveal her breasts. Desperately she tried to cover herself.

"She's too damned pretty to kill, Tuttle."

"You're right, Ingram. What do you suggest?"

"We'll have our fun and then we'll kill her," came the reply.

Hatred churned acidly inside Tyler. He struggled

to rise and protect her. Like hungry wolves on a wounded deer they closed in on her. The sound of her tearing clothing ripped into his mind. Her screams intermingled with their laughter, branding his memory forever, the same way their faces would not be forgotten.

Tyler faded in and out of the void of consciousness, each time helplessly aware of the men violating his young wife. It seemed it went on for hours, but he had no way of knowing. Rage boiled inside him but his battered, bloody body would not respond. He continually struggled to move. He would see them brought to justice if it was the last thing he ever did.

His numb hand felt from somewhere the solid wood of a rifle stock and the cool trigger slipped beneath his fingers. Only his mind and his hand were alive; he felt no other part of his body. He hung suspended in a disjointed pocket of mental revenge.

"She . . . she won't . . . want to . . . to . . . live . . . Ty."

Tyler recognized Kit's weak voice. Feeling no pain now, only the intense fury and venom, he turned his head just enough to see his brother lying in a pool of blood. At the end of his hand was the rifle. He had managed to push it as far as his hand would reach. Kit had only an ounce of life left in him; his eyes were already in death, but he pleaded mercy for Carlotta, not himself. "End it," he whispered. "For her."

Tyler stared numbly at Kit. He couldn't kill the one thing he loved the most. Yet he could end her suffering no other way. He had no bullets to kill her attackers, nor could he succeed before they killed him, and then he could never help her.

He drew his last strength and what he felt would be

his last breath, but he had to hold on. He pulled the rifle beneath him in painful slowness. He rolled to his side, lodging himself against his brother to help steady his aim. He drew the gun to his shoulder. He had failed her so miserably when she had needed him the most.

And then a man moved into his sights. Tyler adjusted the rifle until the man was in full view at the end of the barrel. His vision blurred. Weakness swept over him, threatening to take his mind again. He lifted his eye from the sight. Carlotta was looking at him, begging, pleading with her dark eyes, but did she plead for life? Or did she plead for death? He had no way of knowing. Her outstretched hand tore at the decision he had to make.

Suddenly she screamed, a maddening torment that echoed through the valley bursting any ear that could hear. It sounded over and over again, a piercing plea for release from her suffering.

Tyler shook the dizziness from his head and gripped the quivering rifle tighter to his bloody shoulder. The sure crack of the report quaked repeatedly in its savage fury, finally fading away on the distant hills. Her screaming stopped, but Tyler couldn't open his eyes. Even more agonizing than the sounds of her pain was the stillness that now engulfed him as it settled deeply, and forever, inside his mind.

Chapter 1

September 1861

THE MOMENT THE BUGGY HALTED IN front of the Texas ranch house, Roseanne McVey gripped the folded newspaper tighter in one hand and, gathering her skirts with the other, she stepped gracefully to the ground without assistance. The vaqueros who accompanied her on trips to town now dispersed themselves back to the corrals and their work. Singlemindedly Roseanne hurried to the house, her dress hoisted up past her ankles lest it interfere with her progress. Her usual calm expression was stricken with fear and apprehension, yet the house welcomed her with open arms and a protective warmth.

From the alcove off the living room she heard her father, William McVey, and her Uncle Jack conversing in indiscernible words but in a tone that indicated serious business. Was it possible that they had already heard the news?

She hurried across the living room, discarding her wrap on a chair, and brushing stray strands of her dark hair away from her oval face. The men gave her their attention immediately, but obviously hoped her interference would be brief so they could get back to their discussion.

With sapphire eyes she glanced from one to the other and then rushed forward with the news. "Hatteras Inlet was captured by the Union Navy in late August." She thrust the newspaper at her father. "It's all on the front page."

Hatteras Inlet, on the long islands off North Carolina's coast, was the best entrance to North Carolina's sounds—Pamlico and Albemarle—and it was also a haven for Rebel privateers, as well as blockade-runners bringing supplies to the Confederate Army in Virginia.

Now a Federal amphibious assault had taken the inlet. The Confederacy's earlier high spirits and confidence from the victory at Bull Run was now waning under this Union seizure.

Her father digested it silently just as he had in April when the Union surrendered Fort Sumter and four more states seceded. There had been men who had thirsted for war, but her father had not been among them. Like many others, Roseanne included, he had hoped for a peaceful resolution to the problems. He had not favored secession, but he would stand with the South now that it was done.

Roseanne felt bleak. The war had taken a bad turn for the Rebels, and here at home their financial situation was almost beyond recuperation. There was no market for the cattle, and her father was getting increasingly quiet and pensive. He was afraid of losing everything he had spent his life building, but he knew he was not alone in the situation, and there were many much worse off.

"What are we going to do, Dad?"

McVey released all the air in his chest in dismal resignation. He sat down heavily in his big leather chair.
The lines on his leather-tanned face deepened while
the light from the window seemed to draw out the
silver hair at his temples.

"We can't stop the war single-handedly," he said,
remembering himself as a young man in 1836 when he
and other volunteers had thought they had that power.
And they *had* been successful in avenging the slaugh-
ter of the Alamo at the bloodbath of San Jacinto, there-
by winning Texas her independence from Mexico. But
this war was so much bigger and so far-reaching, and
he was an old man who couldn't fight the way he once
had.

He shook his head and stood up. "We can try to
keep our senses intact and do what we can for Texas,
the Confederacy, and ourselves until, hopefully, this
mess clears up. It's a funny thing about war—whether
you're fighting in combat or not, the most important
thing is staying alive. The armies will pay their troops,
but no one will pay my vaqueros but me. Now, if you
will come with me, Roseanne, I have something to
discuss with you, and I need to get out of this damned
house." He turned to his brother. "We'll finish our
conversation later, Jack."

Roseanne watched her Uncle Jack leave, no longer
feeling the resentment toward him that had been present when he had arrived five years ago on their doorstep with a family to feed and not a penny to his name.
Her father had unquestioningly taken them in and immediately included Jack in the operation of the ranch,
something Roseanne had, for many years, hoped he
would ask of her as he would have done a son. Her father had even taken away her job as teacher for the

hired hands' children, giving it to Jack's wife so he could give the two of them more financial aid without it looking like charity. He had wanted Roseanne to go to one of those Eastern schools for young women and see something besides the ranch, but she had refused, preferring to settle for what was left of her duties— keeping the household and school budgets in order, tending to the sick, and handling the other daily chores that revolved around the house.

Still, it didn't keep her busy. Even the cooking was done by their one servant, Lolita, but Roseanne felt no antagonism toward her; she was more like a member of the family than a servant. Gradually, however, Roseanne had come to accept and like Jack and his family. She had also accepted the fact that she could not have her father completely to herself. He had needed his brother, just as she had needed him, and now she had to admit that Jack's coming to the ranch had helped her father get over her mother's death more than anything else had done.

Her father had not been trying to be cruel when he had deprived her of useful work. He had simply never believed that a woman's role should include ranch work. And, because she was his only child, he had always wanted the best for her. He had put her in her mother's place, never realizing that her restless nature, unlike her mother's, craved more excitement and challenge.

So it thrilled Roseanne now that her father wanted to confide in her on matters of the ranch, although he would discuss it all with Jack later.

She followed him into the yard and to the buggy still standing where she had left it, the faithful horse cropping grass near the roadside. "Get in," her father pointed to the conveyance. "We're going for a ride."

He helped her into the buggy, climbed in next to her, and took up the reins. They left the yard and turned onto a faint trail leading through the trees and down toward the old Chanson place that was also built on the Guadalupe River. He seemed to take the direction from habit and Roseanne didn't mind since it had always been one of her favorite places when she wanted to leave the confines of their own ranch. They rode in silence. Her father would talk when he was ready.

The meadows still sprouted some late summer flowers, the sky was blue, and the sun was hot on her face. On this tree-shaded road it was easy to forget the war and remember, instead, all the good times she'd had as a child with the Chanson boys—Keane, Tyler, Rayce, and Kit—who had once lived here and shared life on the two-owner ranch known then as the CM, standing for Chanson and McVey.

But in 1848, when she was nine years old, the McVeys had bid their good friends, the Chansons, good-bye, and it seemed she grew up swiftly after that. Vividly she could still see and hear it all.

"Don't let the news of that gold discovery in California make you lose sight of ranching," her father had kidded Orin Chanson while his sons loaded down the packhorses, and she and her mother had stood by watching.

Orin snorted and readjusted his hat against the sun. "You know damned good and well my mind was made up to go to California long before that damned news broke out about the gold. You know me, Bill. Things are getting too easy and civilized here."

Roseanne had heard all the stories about Orin Chanson and her father. Together they had killed Indians, Mexicans, rounded up stray longhorns, even rustled a few to get the CM ranch. But at the time, she hadn't understood why Chanson was leaving and selling his share to her father to go to some place called California.

Orin Chanson had looked up the hill where they had buried his wife Cassie just a year before, and where her own mother was now buried. He said, "Take care of her grave, Bill. Don't let some damned farmer plow it under."

And Roseanne had cried. She sobbed against Tyler's legs, the second oldest of the brothers, and then looked up at him so tall above her. "I don't want you to go. I won't have any more big brothers."

Tyler, nine years her senior, brushed the wetness from her eyes with a gentle finger. "Don't worry. I'll never forget you."

He was always so kind to her, but he had never been wise enough to know that she had loved him in her little girl way. "I'll never see you again, will I?" She had tried to be brave.

He smiled. His answer had been so confident and reassuring, thirteen years ago. "Yes, Roseanne McVey. I don't know when, but you will see me again."

But now she knew that promises are made for the moment, and suddenly she didn't want to see the Chanson place again. She asked her father to go upstream as they neared a fork in the road that had once been so well traveled. He obeyed without question.

When the horse emerged in a clearing bordering the river, Roseanne and her father alighted from the buggy, letting the horse graze without restraint. Mc-

Vey nervously picked up pebbles and tossed them into the water and Roseanne found a fallen tree and sat down on it, watching him, wondering what he was going to say and if it was something she would want to hear.

Finally he cursed and sat down with her, picking up a stick to give his hands something to do. "You know ranching here in Texas has always been half a business, even when the land belonged to Mexican and Spanish ranchers. If it wasn't for the horses, we'd go belly up. Those damn longhorns are bursting the seams of this state, yet we can't sell them. No one wants to eat them. They just want to grind up their hides and fat for soap and tallow candles."

This negative talk from her father made her nervous. He hadn't been so depressed since her mother had died. "We'll manage," she said, trying to reassure him.

"Yes," he agreed, "but there's no demand for beef locally with everyone gone to fight the war. New Orleans is blockaded by the Union Navy; we can't trail north on the Shawnee Trail any more; and our sustaining horse trade business with the Western U.S. Cavalry post is lost now that the troops have been pulled out to fight back East."

"Leaving the West virtually undefended against Indians," she added.

McVey tossed the stick into the water. "It does look like we're hemmed in tight. We may not die in battle, but the core of our livelihood is being bombarded. Still, we can stay afloat. There's got to be a solution."

McVey studied his daughter, knowing she was trying to think of that solution. At twenty-two she was any man's dream. Her petite figure was womanly; her smile quick and sincere from perfectly formed lips; her dark hair glistened in the sun, sparkling like her temper and her blue eyes. Yes, she was beautiful, and he knew that it wasn't just through his eyes. It troubled him at times, though, that she was still unmarried and seldom interested in any of her suitors. Yet, he was glad of that, too. He didn't really want to lose her, at least not to any of the men she had met so far.

Maybe he was just getting old, but he wondered lately what would become of her if he should die. He felt he had to do something to assure a home for her until she found the man she was searching for. And that home was this ranch. She could run it with the help of the vaqueros. She had a head for business and could make the decisions. He knew she wanted to, yet he had never let her, thinking that the work and the men were too rough to have her exposed to either.

She twisted a blade of grass as she considered their plight. "We could trail to Mexico—at least get enough to trade for supplies. It'll get rid of the overstock. Can we sell to the Confederacy like Richard King and some of the others?"

Texas was helping the Confederacy by handling trade with Mexico, and British shipments were making their way from the Bahamas and Mexico onto swift blockade-runners, which in turn were slipping the supplies onto Southern soil, where some of the ranches were acting as clearinghouses.

McVey shook his head negatively. "The Union's after King's head. Even though he's got his steamers under Mexican registry and Mexican flags, they'll be trying to put an end to his activities. What little we could get through to the Confederacy wouldn't be worth our time. King might make some money, but the rest of us won't.''

Roseanne nodded in agreement and McVey sank into silent thought as he looked out over his land. He had been through so much to claim it and scrounge a living from it, and now the war could take it from him as easily as the wind carries the dust.

When he was young, growing up in Tennessee, he had heard that Texas was heaven for a man and hell for a woman, but he had come anyway because he hadn't had a woman at the time, only a mighty big hankering for adventure. Now, looking back, he knew he would change none of it, not even the hardships. Sometimes that was all that kept a man going, kept him battling, kept him proving he could win.

And this was a hardship now—but there was an alternative, be it a gamble. Yet it would be worth it if it meant saving the ranch. Suddenly he spoke. His voice was calm. "I want to take a couple thousand head of mixed stock to Colorado Territory next spring, but this fall I'll have to take a preliminary trip up there to check out a trail and try to find a buyer or two. Jack will stay here and help Diego keep the ranch in order during my absence. There's money in the goldfields and there's always a need for cattle. Now''—he looked at her with scrutinizing, serious eyes—''what do you think of my wild idea?''

Roseanne's heart suddenly pounded in excitement. She too had heard the news seeping from the goldfields in the Rockies. There was talk that cattle or oxen were going for as high as one hundred dollars a head when here a longhorn *might* bring $3. Realistically, though, she knew the grand figure was exaggerated. But if they could sell a herd they could probably get as much as $25 a head. A fair profit and definitely worth the trip. Still, there was a risk. There were many dangers between here and Denver.

She knew his decision did not hinge on her approval, but she was happy he had asked her opinion anyway. And she agreed with him. She had always been one to take a chance. "We can do it. I say we give it a try."

Chapter 2

November 1861

THE COLD NOVEMBER SUN SLIPPED unnoticed behind the Front Range of the Rocky Mountains, leaving a faint opalescent glow on the wings of the snow clouds silently gathering over the young town of Denver.

Tyler Chanson rode in from the west and paused at the South Platte River to let his big bay horse drink and to let himself study the layout of the huddled array of buildings spread before him. The town was basking in a prewinter lull, but it would soon be noisy and busy when the miners tumbled out of the mountains, seeking warm refuge for the cold months ahead. Everything was quiet. There was no visible sign of danger, but he had learned caution in his travels. There were always Indians seeking scalps, and outlaws seeking trouble.

The bay snorted at the frigid water, taking only a swallow. A cold breeze ruffled the horse's black mane and he brought his head up abruptly, his alert eyes searching for the source of the elusive disturbance as if he, too, sniffed for danger. Water dripped from his mouth as he shifted restlessly, anxious to be moving again.

Tyler gave the bay his rein and it stepped into the cold water. The Platte was wide, its breadth taken up with sandbars, islands, rocks, and tree stumps. The strands of water were low this time of year and interspersed with the land that gave it the nickname, "braided river."

The bay crossed confidently to the opposite bank where a small band of Arapaho Indians were camped in the cottonwoods that lined the river. Once on dry ground the horse pranced nervously past the village, casting leery eyes at the barking dogs and gawking children. The younger Indian women glanced shyly at Chanson, then giggled and scurried away with their heads down.

The older squaws moved methodically about, involved in the daily chores of dressing skins and cooking meals. The braves talked and drank whiskey, and the children played, unconcerned about the white people who now shared the area.

The Indian tribes had seemingly accepted this new infringement upon their lands and carried on as usual, but now they could buy whiskey and trade with the whites. Denver excited itself occasionally with the rumor of a possible Indian attack, but so far the worst things the Indians had done were pilfering clotheslines, begging for biscuits, and demanding sugar from the women of the town.

There were several bridges now crossing Cherry Creek, but Chanson directed his horse to ford the small stream. He followed its course farther into town. On his right across the creek was a hotel. On his left was the Louisiana Saloon. The miles had taken their toll and dulled his edge of alertness. He needed a bath and a soft bed, but a good whiskey to warm him up sounded better so he stopped his horse in front of the busy saloon.

The interior was dark and Chanson had to let his eyes adjust. It put him at a disadvantage if the man he hunted happened to be inside. He moved away from the door but kept his back to the wall.

It was a shabby, crude little establishment filled with disreputable men, an element of society that was always abundant in a gold town. He moved to the bar, inconspicuously scanning the sea of faces. Most had gone back to their drinking or game playing, paying him no further mind. None were familiar, but still he did not relax.

The barkeeper moved toward him down the length of the rough wooden bar. "What'll it be, mister?"

"Whiskey," he replied tersely, being of no mind for conversation.

The barkeeper poured the drink and Chanson tossed its fiery contents easily down his throat. He placed the glass beneath the poised bottle and allowed the tender to pour him another.

"Want the bottle?" The barkeeper asked.

Chanson made a quick assessment of the man behind the bar, not particularly liking what he saw in the small, close-set eyes. His dark gaze shifted again to the crowd. "No." He reached into his pocket and tossed sufficient coins on the bar to cover the two drinks.

The barkeeper's nimble fingers lifted the coins then retained them, studying them. "Don't see much of anything around this town but gold in some way, shape, or form. Figured you were new to town."

The man's innocent comment went beyond mild curiosity in its implication. "I'm not a miner," Chanson replied simply and truthfully. He could feel the barkeeper's questioning eyes, but he gave the man no further information. Chanson knew better than to trust his kind. Over the years he had learned to pick out the honest ones from the dishonest as easily as gold dust was separated from dirt.

The barkeeper leaned against the bar, determined to force conversation. "Are you in town to stay?"

Since Tyler had been hunting the men who killed his father and brother and raped his wife, he had been uneasy about giving out personal information to strangers lest word of his whereabouts get back to those whom he had sought to bring to justice. "No," he replied.

"Denver's growing," the barkeeper continued doggedly. "A lot of people are finding it a good place for more than just mining."

Denver had progressed from the rough gold rush town of 1859 when he had first seen it, but it was much quieter now. The gold had eluded many and they had left for a secure and safer way of life in the States. And now that the War between the States had decreased westward migration, many of the men had gone eastward to fight, abandoning their claims, their businesses, their ranches.

Tyler Chanson sipped at the whiskey, enjoying the heat it created on its way to his stomach and the warm afterglow it left. It had been a cold ride over the mountains.

"Where you headin'?" The barkeeper insisted, unmoved at Chanson's lack of response to his previous comment.

Tyler wondered if the barkeeper was staking out his wealth so he and some cohorts could rob him later when he left the saloon. He had known places where such activity was common. Chanson sipped at the whiskey again and lied, "Kansas."

"Going to the war?"

"Maybe." How was the man to know he was fighting a war of his own? Yet, he knew the war was a hot issue here in this isolated town. He had already picked up pieces of gossip floating about the room. Denver was obviously not entirely pro-Union either, despite the fact that Lincoln had made Colorado a territory just this past spring to ensure its support and its gold for the Blue.

A man stepped up to the bar, brushing shoulders with him and scattering his thoughts. He realized his attentiveness was dropping badly; he hadn't seen where the man had come from and such lapses could be deadly. It was definitely time to get a room and get some sleep.

But he needed some food first. He put the shot glass to his lips and felt the liquid heat burn them, then he finished the contents. Temporarily relieved of the barkeeper's chatter, he glanced through the dim smokiness of the long, narrow room and found a table of rowdy-looking Mexicans who lit off a memory inside him. One even looked like Diego Padilla, but it couldn't be. It had been thirteen years ago. It was only wishful thinking and the longing for a familiar face.

Liquor-satisfied, he walked from the crowded Louisiana Saloon into the cold, cloudy twilight. He untied his horse from the hitching rail and led it behind him down the hard-packed street.

Already in the early evening, music from the dance

halls and nickelodeons drifted down the streets, but he was only interested in a small, unpretentious building up ahead with a sign that simply stated, Restaurant. He wrapped the reins around a hitching rail, savoring the aroma drifting through the flimsy wooden door that did little to keep anything out, or in.

The interior was lit with coal oil lamps on the tables. It was surprisingly warm, or maybe it just felt that way to him because he had been under the stars for years now, or so it seemed. There were a number of people in the room, but Tyler sought out a corner table and found one, settling himself wearily with his back to the wall and his eyes on the door. It was the way he had survived for seven years now; it had become second nature.

He removed his hat, laid it on the far corner of the table, and ran a hand through his thick, dark hair, realizing it desperately needed cutting. His moustache was getting long, too. Maybe tonight he could spruce up a bit. He had fit much too easily into that squalid crowd at the Louisiana Saloon.

The proprietress came to the table, wiping her hands on her apron and looking harried. She told him what he had to pick from—venison stew, or venison steak. He settled for the latter. God, but he yearned for a good beefsteak—even a tough old longhorn would do. He planned to have one as soon as he got to Texas, his ultimate destination.

A chair scraped against the plank floor. Across the room, a man of medium height rose and tossed some coins onto the table to pay for his meal. Tyler felt that he should know the man, but the hat brim pulled low onto his forehead made it hard to make out his face in the dimly lit room.

In a habitual movement Tyler rubbed his forehead. He suddenly realized his "hallucinations" were simply indications of how tired he was. It showed in his voice, in his eyes, and in his actions. He wasn't sure, though, if the cause of his fatigue was his years in the saddle or mental exhaustion. Regardless, it was beginning to take its toll on him, and the lines deepened in his face nearly every time he looked in a mirror.

In the years that had passed since that fateful day in California, he, Rayce, and Keane had searched for the three men who had gotten away. They had seen Ingram and Tuttle hanged by the hand of the law for their many crimes, including the one against the Chansons. Only Walt Cotton remained, the leader and most devious and elusive of the three. Tyler had only wounded him that day, but the bullet had caused him to lose the use of his right arm. He was a cripple and, from the information Tyler had gathered, he was a very bitter man because of it.

Tyler, Rayce, and Keane had searched for the men together. But when there were no leads, they made a living by working on ranches, panning for gold, driving freight wagons, or whatever jobs they could find, always with the plan that when the last man was caught and tried they would find a place and start another ranch of their own.

Then the war broke out. Rayce and Keane left to fight for the South, but Tyler had been reluctant. A lead on Walt Cotton took him to Utah Territory. It looked like the man could be heading toward Colorado's new goldfields, for it was his habit to go where the easy money was. But there Tyler had lost track of him again.

Up to then, he hadn't been sure what his own action

would be concerning the war. He hadn't wanted to see
the South secede, yet he understood why those Southern states felt they must leave the Union. Theirs was a
different world, and, because of that, the governing of
the North was not always applicable to the South.

However, he had spent so many years in the West
that the States seemed like another world. But he felt
tied to the South by his past, though he knew the indi-
vidualistic ideals of the west were too much a part of
him to discard.

He had, with this last defeat in tracing Walt Cotton,
decided to fight for the South—for Texas. It was his
homeland and it had always represented pride, liberty,
strength, and prosperity. Over and above this he had
his own personal battle, his own war, and there was
something else he had to do first.

Memories of old acquaintances and bygone times
had occupied his mind with increasing frequency of
late. The circuitous road of revenge had taken all personal meaning from his life. Now, with inexplicable
urgency and overwhelming need, something pushed at
him, quickening his pace, beckoning him onto a path
of purpose to seek the stability he thought he might
find again if he returned to the place of his youth and
his roots. He was going to Texas, to what remained of
the CM ranch, to visit the grave of his mother, to find
the humanity he had lost through the years of hate, and
ultimately, perhaps, the will to crush the desire for revenge and begin a new life. He felt good about his decision, yet he remained wary, for he might come
across Walt Cotton at any time during his travels and
he knew he would not pass up the opportunity to finish
the job—if it presented itself. But for the first time, he
wasn't really looking for it. And all he wanted right

now was a decent meal and a good night's sleep and the strength to finish the journey.

After the meal, Tyler found a livery for his horse and a room for himself at the Tremont House where he had stayed before.

Once inside his room, Tyler unstrapped his gun belt, laid it on the bed, and waited for his tub to be filled with hot water by two hotel employees. When he was finally alone, he shed his clothes and gratefully sank into the bath, staying there until the water was cold.

Later, after a shave, he crawled into the comfort of the bed, and began thinking once again of Texas, the McVeys, and wondering about the changes in the state and in the other people he had known there. Roseanne would be about twenty-two now, but it was hard for him to visualize her as a woman. All he could see was her hair in braids and her blue eyes spitting fire in vexation.

Glumly he reached up and turned the wick down until the room was black. The darkness was bringing its memories as always, but maybe more so tonight.

The sound of a voice brought him upright in bed, groping for the Navy Colt revolver at his side. He felt the metal beneath his fingers. Shivering from a cold sweat, Tyler stared momentarily confused into the semidarkness, reliving once again the murders of his family, but all that confronted him was the empty hotel room and the torture of his own mind.

Slowly he got out of bed, slipped his pants on, and moved to the window. It would be daylight soon. He fingered the Colt, remembering the first time he'd awakened from the nightmare. Keane was standing over him and immediately forced his bandaged body back into the pillows with a firm hand.

He had learned that the doctor hadn't given his brothers much hope that he would live. And he hadn't wanted to live, knowing Carlotta was dead. But at least he knew it hadn't been his bullet that killed her. He had killed the man in his sights, because at the last second he hadn't been able to do what Kit had told him to do, no matter what she was suffering. The doctor had tried to save her, but she bled to death due to complications from losing the baby.

So it had been the end of one phase of his life and the beginning of another.

He now moved back to the bed and found the oil lamp. He lit it and packed his few belongings into his saddlebags as the first light of day crept upward into the eastern sky. Texas waited. He was going home.

Chapter 3

December 1861

ROSEANNE MCVEY PUT THE FINISH-
ing touches on the Christmas tree with less than a holiday spirit. It was midafternoon, Christmas Eve, and
still her father had not returned from Denver. Friends
had stopped by off and on all week but today had been
relatively quiet. Most everyone had elected to stay
home, the holidays having brought sober thoughts of
the men fighting in the war who would have no Christmas.

Roseanne knew many of the men who had left
Texas to take up arms for the cause of the South, but at
the moment her main concern was her father. Anx-
iously she placed the gifts she had collected under the
tree. She could hear Lolita in the kitchen preparing
food for Christmas Day, but the woman was not singing as she usually did, which meant that the joys of the
occasion had forsaken her, too.

Roseanne had managed to find small things to keep
her busy but nothing kept her mind from her fear, and
pressing her slender fingers to her forehead she mas-
saged the tightness that had been there since dawn.

She glanced around the house, seeing that everything she had intended to do had been done.

An involuntary shiver ran through her. What if her father did not come back? She couldn't help but wonder if ill fate had struck him in his journey. He should have returned by now. She hastened to the fireplace and put another log on the diminishing fire. Perhaps it would take the sudden chill out of the room.

She wandered to the kitchen thinking Lolita might need some help, knowing full well the woman preferred no one else in her kitchen. The Mexican woman's preparations for any unexpected afternoon visitors were strewn about on the large table. In her fifties, Lolita Alvarez and her husband Pablo had worked for William McVey since Roseanne's mother had died. They had their own small house on the ranch and had raised several children who now worked for McVey or neighboring ranchers. Although she had been in the kitchen all morning, she still looked fresh. Her black hair was pulled severely from her face and coiled expertly into a bun at the back of her head. Her working pace was always furious and she never slowed down. She was always very efficient but apparently never exhausted.

"Is there anything I can do?" Roseanne asked, even though she knew cooking would only frustrate her more.

Lolita never broke stride as she replied, "I am fine, señorita. Do not worry about the food. Perhaps you should go for a walk or sit by the fire and read."

What Roseanne really wanted to do was saddle the gray and go for a ride, but since the war had started and so many men were gone, the Comanches had begun raiding again and it wasn't safe to be out alone.

The vaqueros were busy and she didn't want to take them from their work to act as her escorts. Besides, she really needed to be alone. Desire overruled her better judgment and she decided to go anyway, without an escort. There hadn't been any rumors of raids in the immediate vicinity and she would only be going down the river a ways.

"Yes," Roseanne finally replied, not telling Lolita her intentions lest she alarm her. "A walk sounds good."

She hurried upstairs and quickly changed into a simple skirt, blouse, and jacket. Back East they would be horrified at her riding clothes and her flat-brimmed hat, but out here there was no fashion, at least not on the ranch, and this was one time she wished to avoid the cumbersome habit.

Outside at the corrals, she caught the gray and saddled him, but before she could board she was intercepted by Diego Padilla. He had been with her father since the beginning, and in her father's absence he assumed the role of her guardian even though her Uncle Jack was at the ranch.

"Do you wish for some company, señorita?" he asked as he helped her onto the sidesaddle.

She straightened her skirt and gathered the reins, keeping the anxious gray in check: "No. I'm only going to the river," she declined politely, hoping he wouldn't be insistent. "I just need to get out of the house and be by myself for a while."

Diego held the reins beneath the gray's neck and subtly checked the horse from moving. He squinted up at Roseanne, despite the wide sombrero that shaded his black eyes from the winter sun. "You know it is not safe for you to be out alone, señorita."

She appreciated his concern but there were times when a person needed to be alone, and for her that meant *completely* alone, away from the ranch yard. With the increasing intensity of the war, it seemed everyone, including her, was feeling their previously secure existence slipping away. And her father's late return brought new worry.

"I'll be fine, Diego. Maybe Dad will be coming home. I can always ride back with him."

Diego questioned her wishful thinking with silence, but she saw the doubt in his eyes. His words belied those thoughts, however. "You are right, señorita. He will want to see your pretty face when he crosses the Guadalupe and steps onto McVey land. But I will come with you and two of my vaqueros. It is for your protection."

For the first time all day a smile touched her perfectly shaped lips and lightened the worried expression on her classic features. His concern was so chivalric. She brushed back a long, curling tendril of hair, which she knew she should have put into a bun, but preferred this way, and smiled fondly down at Diego. She had come to know him quite well over the years, and she was aware that, in this, he would not be deterred. "Very well, Diego, but don't expect me to be very good company."

Diego released the gray's reins and grinned, fully understanding her moods.

When her protectors were mounted and ready, Roseanne touched her heel to the gray and he strode out on a fast walk to the river, quickly making distance between himself and the others who continually had to trot to keep up. He was one of the best horses on the ranch—a gift her father had bestowed upon her several years ago. Her father had wanted the swiftest, strongest horse he could find for his daughter in case she ever had to outrun the Comanches. He prided himself on his horses. He bought stock from Kentucky and crossbred them with small mustangs to achieve a larger animal with even more stamina and endurance. He had somewhere around two thousand head, and the demand for his horses not only applied to saddle and work horses, but to pack animals, racing, and breeding stock.

In the lead, Roseanne followed the leaf-strewn path. She sat straight in the saddle, her square shoulders tossed back always a bit defiantly, as though she challenged even her thoughts to weaken her. Two of the vaqueros rode silently behind at some distance, but Diego made his horse keep pace a few feet to her right.

Roseanne expected it when he untied his lariat from his saddle and began twirling it above his head and then below his boots. It was something he did when he was riding and had no cattle to work. Occasionally he would toss the rope at some brush or a stump, then he would lean down and remove it from the captured object and coil it again into his hand. His horse paid no attention to this activity.

The Mexican cowboy, or vaquero, had invented and perfected the use of the lariat, and there were very few white men who could equal the roping ability of a veteran vaquero, or even his horsemanship, for the vaquero never walked if he could ride. He took great pride in his horse, his gear, his costume, and in the simple fact that all of it together made him a *caballero*, or horseman.

Roseanne stopped the gray at the wagon crossing on the river. The Guadalupe ran cold and clear on the

chilly December afternoon. Grass, burned russet in
winter's repose, bent close to the ground along the
water's peaceful curves, and shadowing it all were
tall, thick trees, the remains of their reddish-brown
leaves crackling in the gentle breeze.

It was getting late now and there was no sign of her
father. Sighing regretfully, worry creasing her young
face, she gave one last look up the length of the quies-
cent river to where it became lost from view around a
bend.

Diego's melodic voice interrupted her thoughts as
he nudged his horse up next to hers. "I do not think he
will come now, señorita. We should be getting back.
The sun—it is almost gone, no?"

Her prior concern took precedence again as she
studied the river and listened to the quiet land. "I'm
worried about him, Diego."

"He will be back. Perhaps not today, but you worry
needlessly." Diego folded his arms across the saddle
horn and glanced at the sun slipping behind the tips of
the tall trees. Normally he would have blamed her
anxiety solely on the war and her father's late return
from Denver, but today he wondered if it was caused
by even something more. He aired his thoughts, for he
and Roseanne had always been able to speak freely.
She had never held herself superior to him or the other
hired hands. "What bothers you so, señorita? I think
the matter is more than just your father's late return."

Furrows creased her smooth, flawless forehead.
"It's my life, Diego. Other people come and go, but I
remain the same in the same spot. I want to live my life
instead of watching it go by."

Diego chuckled, his face brittle with creases now,
not so much from age but from his life in the hot Texas

sun. "You are so young, señorita. Why do you worry? A woman's life was not meant to be the same as a man's. If it were, we would not need each other."

Roseanne glanced again at the afternoon sun making its journey ever closer to the western horizon, and Diego wondered if she had heard what he had said. "It is getting late, señorita. It will be nearly dark by the time we get back to the ranch."

Finally she consented to Diego's request and turned the gray away from the water and onto the path that led home. Dry leaves crunched beneath the gray's hooves as he moved into the trees, but the sound of a brittle limb popping brought him up short of his own accord, his small ears pricking forward and backward to catch the sound again. Roseanne tensed, nervously scanning the area for the cause of the gray's alarm. The vaqueros had also stopped their mounts, for the sound had not come from the group's immediate vicinity.

Roseanne turned in the saddle to look back at the Guadalupe flowing undisturbed. There was no one in sight. She nudged the horse nervously, but he clearly did not want to heed her command; instead he was trying to reverse his position. Then suddenly the clatter of rocks brought them all up short again. Through the trees they saw riders emerge from the river's opposite bank, skidding their horses into the chilly water as they urged them across in a shallow spot. Exultation replaced her momentary fear. The man in the lead was her father. The others were the vaqueros that had gone with him, but there was one, a stranger, who drew her immediate attention.

As Roseanne and the vaqueros directed their horses back through the trees to the river, she studied the stranger from the distance. Even in the saddle she could easily see he was a tall man. His hat was pulled low over his eyes and dark hair escaped from around it. There was something disturbingly familiar about him and memories caught at her heart. She pushed them aside, feeling foolish. It was impossible, just wishful thinking, for there was also a quality of danger about this man that caused her pulse to quicken in wariness. He could not be who she had thought.

Her father and the stranger reached McVey land and Roseanne called out as they emerged from the water. "Dad! Over here!"

William McVey brought his mount to a halt beneath the trees and waited for her to join them. She hurried to his side and hugged him as best she could from across their horses. "I was beginning to think you had been struck with gold fever." She made light of her worry, never wanting him to know that he had caused her any distress.

McVey chuckled. "No, my dear, but I did manage to talk a man out of this." He dug deep into his coat pocket and extracted a shiny lump of pure gold. "For a price, of course," he concluded.

Roseanne took the nugget in a slim, gloved hand and rolled it over several times. "I've heard some men will kill for the likes of this. You shouldn't have taken the risk of carrying it all this way."

Despite her words she was thoroughly entranced by the lustrous metal. Tyler watched her, searching for changes in her personality, but he saw the same Roseanne, grown into a beautiful woman. She was still slight of build, nearly dwarfed by the big gray horse she rode, but the short, waist-length jacket hugged her figure and left no doubt to male eyes that she was a woman. Her long, dark hair he remembered so well still cascaded freely in wild disarray over her shoulders. And apparently she hadn't recognized him.

"Some men will kill for the sake of killing, Roseanne," Tyler said quietly. "The gold is only an excuse."

She met his dark eyes then for the first time. Pleasure sprang to the depths of hers and she spoke, still disbelieving. "Tyler? My God, it *is* you. But where did Dad find you, and what are you doing here in Texas?"

McVey moved his horse ahead so that nothing separated them. Tyler nudged his horse up to Roseanne's and the years he had been gone were erased. He was absolutely the same—and yet, there was a difference. Roseanne saw something in his eyes that told her he was fully aware she was no longer a child. Instantly she knew he would never be her big "brother" again; that relationship was no longer possible.

He spoke, softly flattering her. "I had to see if the Belle of San Antonio was still as pretty as I remembered."

She knew instinctively he referred to her and she became slightly flustered by his smoothness and the dark brown eyes seemingly consuming her, but a lilt tipped her voice. "And is she?"

"More so," he assured her in the same persuasive voice. "If I had known you were going to be so beautiful, Roseanne, I would never have left Texas in the first place."

Before she could respond he leaned over and kissed her lightly on the cheek. The shock that resulted from the contact startled her. How many times had she been pecked on the cheek by how many men, both young and old? Too many to count or even remember. Yet none had ever set her heart racing before. She glanced up at him from beneath the sweep of her thick, black lashes and eyed him cautiously, but she could not tell what he was thinking as he, too, studied her.

Luckily her father saved her from the uncomfortable moment as he gathered his reins to ride. "We can jaw here until dark, but I'd much rather do it in front of a fire from my easy chair. I've been on this horse too long. Let's get on home."

The ranch, nestled in the folds of the hills, was weathered but otherwise unchanged by the years. At the corrals, McVey and the vaqueros were met by eager ranch hands and Jack McVey wanting to hear all the news about Colorado. McVey, Tyler, and Roseanne left their horses with a young stableboy and after spending a few minutes talking with the others, broke away and went to the ranch house with Jack.

Roseanne clung to each word and bit of information. As the four of them walked to the house, she learned that the two men had, by coincidence, run into each other at a livery stable in Denver on the morning they were both leaving for Texas.

When they stepped into the living room, Lolita appeared, her eyes glowing at seeing the ranch's *patrón*. "Señor McVey, it is good to have you home. We have been very worried these months."

"I should have been back sooner, but I have no excuse." He laughed mildly, knowing his daughter would not have let him know of any concern over his extended absence. "Everything went well. I think Roseanne was correct when she accused me of contracting gold fever."

"It is beautiful, señor? This Colorado?"

He nodded. "Yes, very. And there's a market for

the cattle." He moved to his easy chair by the fire and settled gladly into it. Roseanne sat opposite him on the sofa and Tyler found a place near the fireplace, one foot on the hearth.

"Then the drive's on?" Jack McVey asked.

"Yes. There are several men up there who would like cattle for a starter herd, plus there is a healthy market for the meat."

"Dad," Roseanne interjected quietly. "Will it be worth the risks?"

"I can't answer that for sure. We do have something on our side, though. We have experience in trailing cattle, and we have the vaqueros, the best horsemen available. The drive from here, for the most part, contains plenty of water and grass. As for the Indians and outlaws, there is always that risk.

"When I first came to Texas it was also a very wild country. I'm no stranger to what lies ahead on this drive, but that won't make the hardships any easier. There are the ranchers up there eagerly waiting for the cattle, though, so we don't have to worry about the market falling out from under us before we can get there."

Roseanne sat quietly thinking while the three men continued to discuss the spring cattle drive and the problems. Sometimes she forgot all the things her father had done in his life. Of course William McVey was capable of doing this. If it were impossibly absurd, he would be the first to realize it.

She studied him with a question that had been on her mind since they had first discussed the possibility of a drive last September. She wanted to be a part of this adventure, to do this thing that would help the ranch and, consequently, all those who worked here.

"I have something else to ask you, Dad." When he said nothing, she rushed on. "I want to know if I can come on the cattle drive with you."

McVey shot out of his chair, shaking his head, his face turning a pale shade beneath the leathered skin. "Denver! A cattle drive! I should say not, my dear." He pushed a stray strand of hair back that had fallen onto his forehead. "It's much too dangerous for a woman. You can't be serious."

Roseanne tried to stifle her frustration and her anger but she wasn't successful. She too came to her feet, facing her father, her back ramrod straight with defiance. "Am I to shrivel up and blow away, confined to this ranch for the rest of my life simply because I'm a woman? I can ride as well as any vaquero. I can hold my own, and you know it."

McVey gathered his argument. "I'm sure you can, Roseanne, but that's beside the point. A cattle drive is simply no place for a woman. It'll take weeks to get to Denver. There's no privacy, no accommodations for a woman with a bunch of men. It's much too dangerous anyway. And as for your shriveling up on this ranch, well I'm sorry you feel that way. Maybe you should have gone to that Eastern school as I suggested."

"Yes, I could have," she replied, "but I didn't, and now I'm a little too old. I don't regret it anyway. After all, that world is too far removed from this one to be beneficial."

"You could always go to New Orleans or Charleston and volunteer your services in the hospitals to help our fighting men."

"Damn it! I want to go on this cattle drive!"

Jack and Tyler had been forgotten. Jack simply acted unaffected, calmly waiting for the spat to subside. Tyler was amused by Roseanne's temper. No, she hadn't changed at all. She would be a formidable foe. He spoke calmly, trying to be a buffer between the two. "Why do you want to go, Roseanne? You know the cattle drive will be grueling."

Roseanne turned on Tyler. He either held no opinion on the matter or he had it cleverly hidden. "Why? Well, why not? Just because I'm a woman is no reason to make me stay behind."

Tyler was apparently noncommittal about her desires, but McVey felt as though he'd been struck across the face. How long had this insanity been festering in his daughter's head? Why would any woman who had a comfortable home and a secure life want to leave it to indulge in the miseries of a cattle drive across a thousand miles of Indian- and bandit-infested country? God, it was beyond him.

Despite her argument, McVey was adamant. Roseanne was ready to retreat to her room in a fury when Lolita rang the dinner bell. Tyler caught Roseanne's arm before she could scurry away. At his touch she was startled out of her rage into a subdued submission. His hand was hot on her arm, even through the fabric. It ignited feelings inside her that she had been unaware of, new emotions that were frightening yet exciting.

Jack quietly announced he would be going to his house; his wife would have his supper on, and William McVey left the room for the dining area. Tyler looked down into Roseanne's dark blue eyes, fringed with sooty lashes. Her skin was beautifully textured with a natural glow enhanced by the sun. He couldn't help but wonder if her entire body was flawless, but he knew he shouldn't be thinking that. She was Roseanne—little Roseanne. Still, her lips were full and inviting, and he had to fight the sudden urge to taste them. Instead he said, "Your father is worried about you, Roseanne. He knows what Comanches will do to women captives." He did not bother to mention all the lawless white men attracted to places like Denver for the gold, and the beautiful women they might find along the way, women who had lost their innocence long ago.

A finely arched black brow rose as amusement surfaced in her eyes; the argument with her father was put temporarily aside. "I have also heard, Tyler, that there have been some women taken captive who, when given the chance to escape, would not leave their Indian braves, so adroit were they at lovemaking."

He could not contain his smile although he was trying to be serious. "That could be *one* of the reasons they choose to stay with the Indians, but like white men, I'm sure those braves are not all so pleasing to their squaws."

She inclined her head in agreeable admission. "Possibly, but it doesn't change my mind about going to Denver. I need to get away from here, Tyler, but then you probably don't understand that any better than Dad does."

He placed her hand on his forearm and led her to the dining area. "I do, Roseanne, but getting there via a cattle drive is not the way a lady should take."

"Then perhaps I'm no lady," she said through gritted teeth. She accepted the chair he offered and then continued. "What is Denver like? Is it as rowdy as rumor has it?"

When McVey made no attempt to reply, Tyler did, giving an answer that McVey was obviously displeased to hear at first. "Not at all, Roseanne. You'll find there are an increasing number of females in the town and the place is getting some civilization and even some culture. I'm sure your arrival there would be hailed, as it is for all unmarried women. My guess is that some old miner would have you married off within a matter of weeks.''

Then McVey smiled, seeing Tyler's subtle attempt to discourage Roseanne. He leaped on the wagon. ''He's right, my dear. It may become quite a chore to fight the men off, but maybe you'll find one who has hit a mother lode and can make it all worthwhile. Now that all the eligible men have left Texas for the war, Denver may be just the place for you to do your husband-hunting.''

''Please.'' Roseanne spread her napkin over her lap, refusing to let their bantering affect her determination. ''My desire to go on the drive has nothing whatsoever to do with finding a husband. Whatever made you think I even wanted one anyway, Daddy? I can have my share of men right here in Texas if I were inclined to marry, which I'm not.''

Lolita brought the beginnings of the meal and the discussion came to a close, to Roseanne's relief. But long after Tyler had focused his attention away from her and onto his plate, she knew he had been amused over her last statement. He hadn't believed it, and for him to think she might be desperate for a husband was unbearable. She was thankful when Tyler initiated small talk about the ranch, the cattle, Texas, and the war. At least it took everyone's thoughts off her. She did not get the opportunity to ask her questions concerning Tyler's activities over the past thirteen years, but there would be time for that later.

As soon as the meal was finished Roseanne excused

herself to help Lolita prepare water for the men's baths. She heard her father and Tyler talking, but most of the words were unclear. William McVey excused himself shortly afterward and retreated to his room. The long miles of the trip were showing on his face and Roseanne knew that he probably wanted to avoid any further discussion of her going on the drive.

She joined Tyler in the living room, bringing with her a tray holding coffee, sugar, cream, and some slices of cake Lolita had made. "How about some dessert?"

Tyler leaned forward in the chair toward the small table where she placed the tray. "I think I can find room for some."

She poured the coffee and after she had seated herself in the chair opposite him he gathered up his plate and handed her the other. For a few minutes they ate in silence. "You know," he confessed to her, "I haven't had a piece of cake for years. I'd forgotten just how good it is." He glanced around the comfortable room, warm and cozy with its Spanish accent. "I guess I've forgotten how good it feels to be in a house, too."

These strange comments aroused her curiosity. She voiced her immediate thoughts. "What sort of life have you been leading, Tyler? Didn't things work out in California?"

He swallowed the last bite of cake and had been thinking of having another, but now he was no longer hungry. He set the plate and fork aside, and gathering up his coffee cup and saucer, he took a sip of the hot liquid to give himself time to compose answers to her questions that he had inadvertently induced. There were times he had wished they had never left Texas; none of it would have happened then. And there were so many times he wished he could simply wake up and discover that the incident hadn't happened at all. He momentarily closed his eyes and sighed, then he looked into the fire and told her the basics about that day. He told her his wife had been killed, but he didn't feel that discussing the rape was appropriate.

At his conclusion she was numb. Kit dead? Orin dead? And with them their dreams, gone so easily and much too quickly. It might have happened seven years ago for Tyler, but for her it was happening now. The reality came to her slowly but with strong impact. With suddenly weak, shaky hands she placed her fork on her plate and set it on the small table next to Tyler's. She could not look at him. Tears formed in her eyes while she clasped her jaw tightly in an effort not to cry.

Tyler stood up, took her clenched hands from her lap, pulled her to her feet and into his embrace. The action was the consent for her tears and, like that child so many years ago, she cried into his shirt.

Finally the tears subsided and she gradually became aware of Tyler's body pressed so close to hers. His arms were gentle yet powerful, and she could feel his muscular biceps beneath her slim fingers. Touching him in such an intimate way made her lose sight of her remorse and what it had been for. A shortening of breath in her chest made her realize he was exciting her in a physical way that she had never felt before. But he, no doubt, would be thinking of her as he always had—a neighbor, a friend, Bill McVey's little girl.

With that thought she took a step away from the comforting chest and his hands slipped from her. She glanced upward, but even though he met her gaze, she had no clue to his thoughts. "I'm sorry, Tyler, but all these years we had no way of knowing. It comes as such a shock. I used to play with Kit."

"I should have written." It was not so much an apology as a realization of something he had failed to do.

"I'm sorry about your wife, Tyler," she managed, although she found it unsettling to know he had even been married. "Tell me, what have you been doing since this . . . since this all happened?"

He read the deep concern in her eyes, and her womanly voice hinted that she guessed he had done nothing worthwhile. He turned his back to her and propped a booted foot on the hearth. Then, needing more to do, he busied himself with adding a log to the fire. "Nothing much, Roseanne. Keane and Rayce and I have just been wandering, doing odd jobs around the country. They've gone to fight for the South." There was no reason to detail the rest. What would be the point.

A worried look came into her eyes. "Is that where you're going now? To the war?"

Finally he seemed satisfied with the placement of the three logs he had added to the dying embers and turned to face her, standing over her by nearly a foot. Her eyes scanned his broad shoulders and rested on the dark hair curling just at his collar and barely over his ears. She had the urge to feel its softness, even lose herself temporarily in his arms again.

Tyler tried to explain to her the way he felt about the war and hoped she wouldn't think him a coward for not going with his brothers to fight. He didn't want to tell her about his search for revenge; there were so many people who couldn't understand it or the way he felt when he saw his wife raped. He concluded by saying, "If I join up, it will be with the Confederacy."

"So many men are dying," she replied softly and in a manner that did not demand a reply or an explanation. It was merely a statement that revealed her regret and her helplessness.

"Maybe that's the reason your father is trying to prevent you from coming on the drive, Roseanne. He only wants to protect you from harm. And death is not only where the battles are being fought. It is out there on the trail. He knows; he has seen strong men perish on cattle drives."

Roseanne's defenses came up. "I'm not a child any more. I don't need to be protected the way a child is." Her words were hard and bitter and her tone disallowed any argument on the question of her maturity.

"You wouldn't be the first woman to risk her life by leaving home and venturing into the wilds. Most of us men simply don't like to see our women suffer, but oftentimes the women don't look at it that way and are stronger than the men give them credit for."

"Then you're not siding with Daddy?"

"It isn't my place, Roseanne. As you said, you're an adult. I should think the decision would be yours."

Lolita entered the room. "I am sorry to interrupt, but the water for Señor Chanson's bath is now hot."

"Thank you, Lolita," Roseanne replied. "You may go home to Pablo now. I can heat the water for my own bath and help Tyler fill his tub."

Lolita beamed as she looked from one to the other as if she read something into their relationship that was not evident to them. *"Gracias."*

Tyler and Roseanne followed her into the kitchen. When she had gone home out the back door, they each took a steaming kettle of water from the stove and into the adjoining bathroom where the tub had been cleaned after McVey's bath. When all the water was in the tub, Tyler helped Roseanne fill the kettles again from the barrels on the back porch and return them to the stove. They were heavy but Tyler noticed Roseanne was stronger than she looked.

He offered to let her take the newly heated tub but she declined, saying she wanted to read for a while and then would relax when the house was quiet and everyone else had retired.

"Roseanne," Tyler drew her attention as she cleaned up some spilled water from the kitchen floor. When she looked up at him, his words caught momentarily in his throat at the beauty of her and at the warm honesty in her eyes. Finally he managed to continue. "I guess you know I'll be going with your dad on the return trip to Denver with the cattle."

She got up from her knees and placed the dirty cloth on the counter. Delight curved her lips and lit the depths of her deep blue eyes. "Then you'll be staying for a while? Oh, I'm so glad. I just thought you . . . would be passing through."

"We've got plenty of time to catch up on things," he replied. "I want to ride over to our old place tomorrow. Would you come with me?"

Roseanne thought of the grave and the weeds that would surely have grown up around the homestead, and now she wished they had kept the house and yard up. "Of course," she replied, feeling responsible for the neglect. "I'd love to."

She left him to his bath and curled up with a book in front of the fire, but the pages went unread. Her mind was on the cattle drive, the gold, the war—and Tyler Chanson.

Roseanne had expected Tyler and her father to sleep in since they had been on the trail for so long, but they were there at the breakfast table the next morning having coffee when she entered the room. It was her habit, in her father's absence, to take breakfast in her robe. Now she was intensely aware of her appearance in front of Tyler, but rather than draw attention to her discomfiture she moved gracefully into the room and accepted the chair Tyler pulled out for her.

"We waited breakfast for you," William McVey said. "We thought you'd like to open your Christmas gifts before eating."

"Gifts?" She eyed them both dubiously. She had not thought about Christmas at all. The holiday had been successfully overshadowed by her father's return and all the talk of the cattle drive.

"Did you think we'd forgotten Christmas?" Her father reached behind him and handed her a large package that had been sitting on the table.

"But when did you go to town?" she asked as she quickly ripped the paper from the box.

"We detoured south to San Antonio yesterday. Tyler had some things to buy, namely a new set of clothes. A few miles is of little consequence when you've gone a thousand."

The gift was a dress of the latest design and made in an expensive blue silk. Roseanne gasped in delight and leaped to her feet to hold it against her. "Oh, Dad! It's beautiful. I'll put it on."

Like a child she hurried from the room and in only minutes was back. The dress fit her perfectly. She subdued her urge to swirl about the room because of Tyler's presence, but she couldn't resist rustling the skirt just a bit.

"You look very lovely," William McVey said.

"It'll look much better with petticoats and all the accessories," she happily announced.

"Perhaps this will go well with it," Tyler said, drawing a small box from his shirt pocket and placing it in her hesitant hand. She looked up at him skeptically. He quietly explained, "It's been a long time since I bought a Christmas gift for a beautiful woman."

"You shouldn't have, Tyler, but thank you."

After another second's hesitation she quickly removed the simple wrapping from the tiny box. Inside, dangling from a delicate gold chain, winking brilliantly, was a sapphire cradled by two small diamonds. She caught her breath. "Tyler! It's beautiful!"

He reached for the box. "Let's see how it looks with the dress." He removed the necklace and while she held her hair off her neck, he fastened it.

She fingered it and then looked up into his smiling eyes. "It's lovely. You and Dad have made my wait worthwhile and my Christmas very happy, but"—she apologized and frowned—"I'm afraid I don't have a Christmas gift for you, Tyler. I wish I'd known you were coming."

He considered her plight for a moment, then seeing a simple solution he said, "I'd settle for a kiss."

Her laughter lilted upward. She stood on her tiptoes and placed a light, friendly peck to his cheek. As she lowered herself, his lean fingers gently cupped her chin, drawing her back to her tiptoes. "That wasn't exactly what I had in mind."

With no regard to William McVey's presence he lowered his head, pausing only for a second to study the curve of her mouth before he covered it with his. When he stood back, seconds later, Roseanne tipped unsteadily toward him. He caught at her waist to steady her.

She stammered as she risked a glance into his pleased, twinkling eyes. "I . . . I have a gift for Dad." Tyler's lips flickered into a hint of a smile and he released her.

After breakfast he reminded Roseanne about their riding date, but she was extremely wary of being alone with him. She wasn't afraid of him, just highly aware of the way her body seemed to come alive of its own volition when she was near him. All the warnings of her proper upbringing were not powerful enough to obey in the face of that seductive feeling.

But once again she changed her clothes, putting on a black skirt, white blouse, and a jacket to ward off the chill. She topped the outfit with her flat-brimmed hat and did not bother pinning her hair up.

While she dressed, Tyler caught and saddled the horses. He was waiting for her outside by the corrals when she emerged from the house. As they rode away from the ranch, they spotted a carriage with several outriders. Roseanne hastily looked for a quick exit, but as she had feared, the man in the carriage had already spotted her.

"Hello there, Miss McVey!"

"Maybe we picked a bad day to ride," Tyler said as the carriage drew near. "I forgot about company coming to visit on Christmas day."

"We weren't expecting him," Roseanne said irritably, "or anybody for that matter, although Lolita always fixes plenty just in case we end up with dinner guests."

The carriage came to a stop next to them. The man inside was about William McVey's age. He sat stiffly, businesslike, even on this apparent social call. His unsmiling, unemotional eyes shifted suspiciously from Roseanne to Tyler, where they hesitated a scrutinizing moment before moving back to Roseanne. "You're not leaving are you, Miss McVey?"

Roseanne's back stiffened; her previous smile disappeared and a scowl took its place. "Yes, I was, Mr. Kline. I have a riding date with Mr. Chanson. Perhaps you should have sent word to expect you."

There was no warmth in her voice and she glared at the short, barrel-chested man. Mr. Kline seemed unmoved by her curt response. He continued passively. "Has your father returned yet?" As he spoke, his fluid, dull eyes, their color unsure, rested on Tyler again, openly critical of him and his association with Roseanne.

She disliked Albert Kline immensely from the top of his bulbous head to the bottom of his small, scurrying little feet. He was a rancher who lived south of San Antonio but spent most of his time in the city on the pretext of business. He was well known around the ladies' circles, but his feelings about her had been made clear from the beginning; he wished to marry *her*. Why, Roseanne had no idea, since he seemed to enjoy his activities with the willing ladies in the town. There was many a widow or spinster who would have gladly taken his hand and his money. He was also self-centered, greedy, and frugal to the point of being stingy. He always rode in his carriage with drivers and bodyguards, no doubt to preserve his life from his many enemies, and word had it that he was mean and unfair to those unfortunate enough to be in his employ. He tolerated no shortcomings in anyone and expected that his wishes be carried out, no matter what they were. He also expected that Roseanne should be more than willing to marry him simply because he desired it. He was sure she was only being coy and shy.

She debated as to how she should answer his question. She didn't want to tell him her father was home because then he would have an excuse for staying, yet she couldn't lie because he would find out the truth easily enough. "Yes," she finally said resignedly. "He returned yesterday."

Albert Kline spread the tip of his tongue over the tight line of his large mouth and looked once again at Tyler. Heavy brows hung down over his eyes and it was impossible to guess at any time what was roaming through his head. Large ears protruded from beneath his hat and beneath it his thinning hair was parted far too low on one side and combed over the bare spot. The memory of his hand on hers made her suddenly shudder involuntarily.

It was plain to see, as he glanced at her and Tyler, that he was weighing his decision of whether to proceed to the ranch and wait for her, or return to town. She knew he had not come to talk to her father for he much preferred to call on her when she was alone. His visits had become entirely too frequent since her father had been in Colorado, just one more reason why she was anxious not to be left behind when the cattle were moved out in the spring. She would take her chances with the miners in preference to this boor.

"Will you be out long, Roseanne?" Once again his gaze shifted to Tyler.

Finally Tyler spoke, much to Roseanne's relief. "Roseanne and I will be gone most of the day. I don't foresee us returning before nightfall."

Kline's mouth twisted from side to side as the wheels appeared to move sluggishly through his mind, yet Roseanne knew he was a highly intelligent man. If he weren't he wouldn't have amassed his wealth in such a short time. "Very well." This time his attention focused on Roseanne and mainly on the curve of her breasts beneath the tailored jacket. "Perhaps some other time. Merry Christmas."

Without awaiting her response he motioned the driver. The carriage was turned in a tight circle and, with his bodyguards, Albert Kline hurried away back to San Antonio on a trot.

Roseanne dug her heel into the gray a little harder than usual, but she wanted to get away from Kline in case he should come back, and she also wanted to get away from Tyler's curious eyes. But from behind her he spoke and her mouth went dry.

"Who is Romeo? Or do you mind me asking? I suppose he's just one of your many suitors?"

Roseanne was a little surprised at the hint of disapproval in Tyler's voice, but Kline had a knack of putting everyone who came into contact with him on the defensive. "I don't want to talk about him if you please. He is a loathsome creature and I am so thankful Dad is home."

"Has he been bothering you?"

"You could say that. Almost continuously since he discovered Dad was gone."

"Could he possibly be one of the reasons you want to go to Denver with us?"

"Him and a few other old men like him. Since the war broke out, they've moved in like buzzards. I guess they think they'll have a better chance if the younger competition is out of the way, but I'm afraid I'll have to resort to something drastic if Kline finds out Dad is leaving again."

"Does he want to marry you?"

"Unfortuantely, at least, that's what he says, but he has an incredible reputation with the women in town, although I have no idea what they see in him."

Tyler chuckled and Roseanne half-turned in her saddle to flash him angry eyes. "What's so funny?"

"He may not be much to look at, but there are many women who only see a man's pocketbook."

She turned back to the narrow trail leading through the trees. "Money or no money, Albert Kline turns my stomach."

The trail widened and emerged onto the road that led to the Chanson place. Tyler brought his horse up next to hers. "Kline's society doesn't require that a man and woman be in love, or even that they be compatible in bed. He would have his mistresses and his wife could have her lovers. Although I'm sure if he were married to you, he would prefer you over any courtesan."

She shot him fiery blue eyes. "I'm afraid I would kill the man if he ever came near me."

Tyler laughed again but dropped the subject, much to Roseanne's relief, and they rode in silence. It was the middle of the Texas winter, but still it was relatively warm and only occasionally rainy. The day was clear and with no threat of moisture. All they waited for was the spring grass on the northern range, then they could head the cattle for Colorado. Her father was anxious; the three months until April would be long ones.

As they rode Roseanne had questions for Tyler, but she knew instinctively there were secrets in his past he coveted. She was leery about trying to step into that realm of his private world.

As they emerged into the clearing where Tyler had spent the greater portion of his childhood, he rode his horse up to the house and sat in the saddle for several silent minutes looking at it. Then, apparently seeing no need to go inside, he reined his horse in the direction of his mother's grave. Roseanne stayed behind, not wanting to intrude on his memories.

At the grave, he dismounted and removed his hat. He remained in the meadow for several minutes, suddenly looking very tired and unable to hold his shoulders back. Then, leading his horse, he walked back across the meadow and joined her. In his eyes was an irrevocable sadness.

He reached up to where she sat on the sidesaddle and encircled her small waist with his hands. "Let's walk for a while. I'll help you down." Effortlessly he lifted her from the horse and placed her on the ground. He led the way behind the house, past the outbuildings and corrals, and down to the river—the lifeblood of the McVeys and the Chansons and many others who had been lucky enough to claim land along its banks.

"My brothers and I used to fish and swim every chance we could, and we got into trouble a lot of times for shirking our work to cool off here in the heat of the day."

Roseanne found a seat on a large rock and Tyler sat

next to her, his shoulder rubbing hers, igniting pleasant, warm sensations inside her. His eyes revealed the desolation he was feeling and the pain, and the understanding of death that only comes with time and experience. Still, after a fleeting moment, he veiled all those emotions expertly with the subtlety of a smile.

"The water in Colorado hardly ever gets warm enough to swim in, but the miners will stand in it all day trying to get the gold. I've seen them sick with pneumonia, but they work until they drop. There's no lust greater than the lust for gold."

Then he continued on a different note. "There are things in our lives that we have to do, Roseanne. Sometimes we have no reason as to why, but I would say if you want to go to Denver you'll find a way."

The solid strength of his body touching hers made Roseanne feel weak. Her thoughts became scattered and unfocused, a combination of his nearness and the desolating knowledge that her father would probably never allow her to go on the drive.

Suddenly she stood up, and moved agitatedly to the edge of the water. She was stunned by her sudden thought that this increasing need to go on the cattle drive might have something to do with Tyler. She knew it would be foolish to become interested in a man who, no doubt, did not consider her as a woman he could become romantically involved with.

Nervously she picked up a stick and began twirling it in her fingers, trying to convince herself that she *did* have good reasons for wanting to go. Reasons that had nothing to do with him. Reasons that were her own. Reasons that *someone* should know and understand. He apparently didn't disapprove of her going and that

was what she had hoped for. So maybe he would listen
and not suppress her ideas as her father so often
did.

"I want to go on the cattle drive because I want to
feel like I'm doing something important toward saving
the ranch. But I suppose there's more than that to it.
It's the simple desire to move, to feel something else.
To maybe experience some of what men are able to experience instead of knowing my life will have no
course but that of a woman—staying home waiting for
God-knows-what, cooking meals, having babies,
feeding chickens, scrubbing clothes and floors until
my fingers bleed, while my man is out riding over
mountains and prairies and sleeping under the stars."

"Don't you mean, running from Comanches for the
sake of his scalp, sleeping on the hard ground with rain
or snow falling in his face, having nothing decent to
eat but jerky and dry biscuits and bitter coffee, and
having an old wool blanket instead of the comfort of a
woman's soft body to warm his soul?"

Roseanne knew he wasn't trying to be facetious.
What he said was the truth, but she was fretful and at
the moment anything looked more exciting than her
existence. Perhaps it was the war making everyone
restless. It only accentuated the fact that the world
was moving, doing, going, and she was standing
still.

He left his position on the rock and stood behind
her. "It's not that great, Roseanne. A man's home is
his castle, and it's a woman's too. You would change
your mind if you had a small taste of what you think
you desire right now, and if you had your own home,
children, and a man you truly loved."

She jutted her chin out defiantly. She wasn't sure

why this conversation was making her feel so argumentative. "You must like the rambling life, contrary to what you say," she insisted. "You've obviously had no desire to settle down."

He felt his anger rising, but he swallowed it. She didn't know the truth behind his seemingly aimless wandering. "I've seen a lot of country, but it gets tiring, and I frequently think about the life I had here before my mother died. Her dying changed our lives, but we never suspected it would have such an impact on us the day we rode out of here. We thought we were heading into a promised land, at least us boys did. I think Dad probably knew that life wouldn't be any better there. He just had to get away from Mom's memory."

"And what of your life, Tyler? You and your brothers. It seems out of character for Chansons to take up wandering."

Tyler knew she was right; his family had always put down roots. After some thought, he decided to explain. "We've been hunting some men, Roseanne. There are people who would not approve of what we have taken upon ourselves to do."

It was easy for Roseanne to figure out who the men were. "I assume they are the men who killed your family? But tell me, Tyler, are you doing it for bounty?"

Flames leaped into his brown eyes. How could she possibly think he would kill for money? Angrily he told her how he and his brothers had set out after the killers and how they had been on their vast search ever since. He told her about the one man who was left, but still he did not find it tasteful to mention the rape of his wife. It was not a subject people talked about, and especially in mixed company.

When he concluded, Roseanne found herself wanting to put her arms around him, for she sensed he needed comfort. But she remained motionless and tried to comprehend the person he had become, the person fate had forced him to become. Of course on the outside he was the same Tyler she remembered, only older and even more handsome. His young-boy good looks had been replaced by a maturity that could turn women's heads and make men take him seriously. But now there was a dangerous quality about him, a certain cautious restraint. Someone who did not know him might be intimidated by the inexplicable coldness that occasionally surfaced, even though momentarily, in his eyes.

"I'm sorry Tyler," she said glumly. "At least there is only one of those men left. Why won't the law try to find him?"

"Even if they did, small town law officials often let renegades go for lack of evidence. They won't really try to prosecute for something that didn't happen in their town, or something that happened so long ago. So they are set free to kill again. They become another sheriff's problem in another town or another state."

"Why did you come to Texas then? Honestly." She still felt his venom so she spoke carefully, quietly. "Surely it wasn't just to help my father drive cattle to Colorado."

He pushed his brooding hatred of the past aside and turned to her. A smile appeared and all the pain disappeared. He taunted her with his reply; it was the old Tyler she saw now. "Because I made a promise thirteen years ago to a certain young lady and I came to fulfill it. Don't tell me you've forgotten about it?''

His words were flattering, but she wasn't so gullible as to swallow them. Was he really down here looking for that man? She smiled at him fondly. The way he was looking at her brought butterflies to her stomach, but it also made her happier than she could remember being of late. "Of course I hadn't forgotten that you said you'd come back, but as I grew older I became wise enough not to hold you to it."

"Then you don't know me as well as I thought you did. I always keep my promises, Roseanne. That's something you can count on."

The dark glow in his eyes was suddenly so intense that she was forced to look away or be scorched by the heat. Why was he looking at her that way? It was vaguely unnerving. She focused her attention on Tyler's bay cropping grass at her feet, his ears twitching as he listened to the tones of their voices. If Tyler kept good on his promises, she wondered, what about the one to his dead wife?

Suddenly she was unwilling to see him go away again, possibly to get killed on his crazy manhunt. "What will you do when you get back to Denver, Tyler?"

He knew she wouldn't approve of his response, but he felt she already knew, or guessed at, the answer. "I've made a commitment to myself and to Pa, Kit, and Carlotta. I'll complete it, and when I'm done I'll take roots somewhere."

The lines around his solemn eyes enhanced his thirty-odd years. They indeed told of the trails and the towns that had hardened him. He was leaner, tougher, more alert than the day he'd left Texas so long ago, and now she knew the reason for the changes. It all fell into place. It was because of Carlotta, and suddenly Roseanne found herself strangely jealous of this woman who no longer lived, but held the key, nevertheless, to Tyler's heart and life.

Chapter 4

December 1861–February 1862

WILLIAM MCVEY SAT NEAR THE FIRE in the vacant living room and slapped the folded newspaper on the arm of his chair. The war was indeed having far-reaching effects, and now Colorado's economy was in trouble. If the present conditions prevailed when it came time to move the herd, the trip might not even be financially feasible. He could find himself in Colorado with two thousand head of cattle and no one with the money to buy them.

The problem had started many months before and now was coming to a head. In the West, the Confederates had had their eye on the golden mountains of Colorado and California for good reason. Pro-Southern sentiment had been especially strong in New Mexican Territory, and in March, at a meeting in Mesilla, a group of settlers declared the southwestern portion of the territory, known as Arizona, as a part of the Confederate States of America. If this kind of reaction continued, Southern sympathizers might be able to bring the entire Far West to the South, and with it enough gold and silver to win the war.

To give even more encouragement to this Confederate plan, the Union had ordered so many Western troops east to fight that there were only tiny detachments left to guard the scattered forts and the entire Far Western frontier. Confederate Colonel John R. Baylor, seeing a golden opportunity, had moved into New Mexico Territory in July, and struck Fort Fillmore across the border from El Paso. With luck and a poor maneuver by the Union commander, Baylor and his volunteer troops had succeeded in taking the fort. His next goal had been Fort Union in northeastern New Mexico. It was all that stood between them and a Far Western conquest.

However, Colorado's territorial governor, William Gilpin, had feared this very thing from the beginning of his appointment in May. Gilpin was many things: a geologist, a soldier, a man of action, and an intellect.

In his efforts to divide the territory into counties, set up a civil government, and organize a Unionist army, he had acted with neither instructions nor sufficient funds. In his fear that the gold mines would be seized for the Southern cause, he had issued drafts to buy guns, open recruiting stations, and finance a lead smelting foundry at Boulder for ammunition. The bill to set up house for his soldiers came to $400,000 in drafts on the Federal government, with the local merchants expecting payment.

When they were presented to the U.S. Treasury in Washington, however, they were deemed worthless, since they had not been authorized. Not only did this little incident, conducted with good intentions by William Gilpin, put the man to shame, but his mistake had plunged Denver into a financial depression. As was expected, Gilpin had been summoned to Washington to explain his actions.

McVey was jostled from his glum thoughts when Tyler entered the room and sat in the chair across from him.

"What's troubling you, Bill? Anything you'd care to talk about?"

McVey sighed and handed the paper to Tyler who only had to read the article headline. "Oh, yes. I know all about the mess Colorado's in, but there's always a need for beef in a gold town, Bill, although the profits may not be as healthy if everyone up there is broke from Gilpin's excessiveness."

McVey stood up and propped a foot on the hearth. "At this point I think the buyers are mainly interested in the cattle to build their herds; the meat market will come later."

"It takes a while for the news to reach us. The problem may be solved."

McVey nodded. "Yes, but you know how slow the government can be. It could take months to come to some settlement."

The crisis proved to be short-lived, however, and about as close as Denver came to being a war casualty. Congress finally approved Gilpin's spending, realizing the importance of his army, and paid all his bills. With the merchants no longer facing bankruptcy, it wasn't long before Denver was thriving again. Roseanne had rushed to San Antonio to do her shopping, for the good news meant the drive was on again.

Now, on her return, a winter breeze pushed at her back as she unloaded her purchases from the buggy and turned to the house. The yard was empty, thankfully. Now if she could just get to her room without Lolita asking to see the contents of the huge paper-wrapped parcel.

With her arms loaded, the walk to the house seemed unusually long. It was a one-and-a-half-story white frame structure, set back away from the yard on a small knoll, with a wide veranda running the entire length of the front. The wide double doors of the entry opened to a "dog run," or hall, that ran through the center of the house with rooms on either side, and served as a cool retreat when prevailing summer winds were allowed to enter the house. Now, in the last breath of winter, the doors were closed and the hall was used for additional living space.

The ranch was a small community within itself. Besides the corrals, stables, bunkhouse, and wagon sheds, there was also a commissary, blacksmith shop, houses for the married vaqueros and their families, and a one-room schoolhouse for the children. Above all this was the watchtower, where the vaqueros kept an eye out for marauding Comanches.

Inside, Roseanne heard Lolita in the kitchen at the back of the house. Quickly she hurried up the stairs to her bedroom, dropped her purchases on the bed, and closed the door. There was no lock, but she knew no one would enter without permission. Weeks ago, she had started collecting clothes and supplies for the trip to Denver in the optimistic hope that the trip wouldn't be called off. She had put the things in a large trunk so when the time came she would be ready to follow the herd.

Now she tore the paper off the large parcel and excitedly picked up the large sombrero. Of course it was a man's hat, just as were all the clothes she had put together, but it was all part of her plan—her disguise.

Quickly she coiled her hair on top of her head and placed the sombrero over it. The storekeeper had believed her when she said she was buying it for one of the vaqueros who had lost his to the horns and hooves of a longhorn. Close up, she doubted she could convince anyone that she was a man, but from a distance the hat would conceal all, as would the baggy pants, shirt, and serape. Now all she had to do was begin her subtle raiding of the kitchen, a task that would be no easy feat under Lolita's watchful eyes. For even though Lolita left each night for her own family, she would notice any change in the food supply.

Roseanne heard the supper bell and put the small items in the trunk, then wrapped the paper back around the sombrero and slid it under the bed. She had no fear of being discovered; Lolita did not clean her room. Feeling pleased with her secret, Roseanne left her room and descended the stairs.

From the kitchen window Roseanne saw Tyler and her father coming across the yard. While she carried on small talk with Lolita, she helped set the table and do some last minute preparations for the meal, but her eyes kept straying to the two men.

Tyler had stayed so busy since Christmas that she had seen very little of him except in the evenings and on an occasional ride together at his request. He had rescued her every time Albert Kline had come around and had even shown a romantic interest in her in front of the older suitor until Kline had gotten visibly angry on his last visit.

The way Tyler had responded so attentively to her had filled her with an excitement and anticipation that she did not, in her inexperience, fully understand. But it pleased her, and she wondered if he truly did it as a game, or if he actually felt a romantic inclination toward her, as she did him.

Regardless, she hoped Tyler's attentions could dissuade Kline permanently; but on the other hand, she thought it was also possible that Kline might become more determined and wait until Tyler was gone to pursue her again. She simply could not let that happen. Tyler had said she would find a way to get to Denver, and now she had. She would follow behind the herd at a safe distance, and with any luck, she would not be discovered until she presented herself in Denver.

Tyler and her father stepped onto the back porch, hung their hats up and discarded their gloves. After washing up in the large basin set up out there, they entered the kitchen and both settled wearily onto hard chairs, her father obviously more tired from the day's work than his younger counterpart. Still, he had a smile when he spoke to Roseanne.

"Hear tell there's going to be a big dance down in San Antonio Saturday. It's been organized to raise money for the war cause."

Roseanne placed a bowl of steaming food on the wooden table. A dance? It had been months since she had been to any social function. The war had successfully brought everything to a standstill, at least in her life. But with so many of the men gone, how could it be successful? Why hadn't she heard about it before now? Why hadn't she been invited? She was sure Kline would have sought her companionship—of course she would have declined if he had. Still the news was disquieting. She tried to cover her disappointment. "And who will you be taking, Dad?"

William McVey started the food around the table by giving himself the first helping of the biscuits. "I don't know as I'll go, but I might donate some money to help the cause. You know me, I've always preferred a good old barn dance to a ball."

"If they can raise some money to help the South, then I suppose it'll be a good idea." Roseanne had hardly any appetite as she took the bowls of food Tyler passed to her. He was extremely quiet and she felt his gaze on her from time to time. But she couldn't look at him. The idea kept running through her head that she would like it if he'd ask her to the dance, but she didn't want him to see that in her eyes.

When the meal was over, she helped clean up the dishes, then bidding Tyler and her father good-evening, she retired to her room. She was not tired, she felt dejected. She took the blue silk dress from the closet and laid it out on the bed. It was such a beautiful creation. It would be perfect for the ball. And she would probably never have the opportunity to wear it. Damn the war! It had disrupted the flow of everything. The only bright spot in the whole confusing mess was the dance. God, how she would love to go.

She fingered the dress until the urge came to try it on again, and she slipped out of her clothes. Suddenly a knock sounded at her door and she sighed heavily as she reached for her robe. What could Lolita possibly want? She should have gone home by now. Carelessly she jerked the door open.

"Tyler!" Hastily she grabbed the front of her robe together.

Mildly amused, he smiled at her discomfiture, but made no indication that he had seen her nearly-bare bosom. His glance took in the dress on the bed, then came back to rest on the sapphire necklace around her neck. It pleased him that she had never taken it off.

He leaned casually against the doorframe as if he intended an extended visit, but he got right to the point. "I'd like to take you to the dance, Roseanne—unless, of course, you'd rather wait for Albert Kline's invitation." A mischievous smile curved his lips. "If you would, I'd understand completely."

She couldn't help but smile at his bantering and felt inclined to play along. "It could be a difficult decision, Mr. Chanson. Although you are much more handsome than Mr. Kline and would surely make me the envy of all women present, a woman of my status must consider a man of financial well-being to secure her future. Kline's a very wealthy man and although you are a very charming rogue, I fear you are penniless."

He nodded his head in agreement and added, "Yes, that's all true, my dear Miss McVey, but perhaps you could take pity on me just this once and consent to my request. Besides, I'm determined to go to this dance, and I'd like to have the most beautiful woman in San Antonio on my arm. If she chooses to be on the arm of Mr. Kline, I'll just have to stay home rather than settle for second best."

She laughed, a lilting sound that lit his eyes in delight. Forgetting her robe, she suddenly placed her hands on his shoulders, and raising on tiptoes, kissed his cheek. His arm went around her waist in a natural response, its heat burning her skin even through the cloth of her robe. She looked up into his eyes and saw the smoldering glow in the brown depths. His hand tightened on her waist and the slight movement drew her the remaining inches to his chest, a hard wall that pressed into her nearly-bare breasts, drawing forth pleasant sensations that emanated from a central core and spread consuming tentacles throughout her body. A physical need inside her urged her to press closer to him for some satisfaction it recognized, but that she did not fully comprehend.

Danger flashed inside her brain then and she collected her senses, smiled, and gently pushed herself away from him, at the same time clutching her robe to her bosom again and feeling a flush rise to her cheeks that she hoped he wouldn't notice.

"I assume your answer is yes?" His dark brows rose questioningly.

"Of course." Roseanne glanced over her shoulder at the dress. "I was just wishing I had someplace to wear it."

Tyler's gaze was on her and he smiled at her gaiety. She had been quiet at the table. He had guessed the reason, but now he knew for sure. To see her in that dress again would be worth a night of suffering with a bunch of society stuffed shirts. It would mean he'd have to go to San Antonio and get the proper togs, but yes, it would be worth it. He would enjoy doing something that made her happy; he supposed it had always been that way between him and her.

"Well." He moved into the hall. "I'd better go." He swept her with approving eyes, then suddenly pulled an envelope from his pocket and handed it to her. "This nearly slipped my mind. I've been carrying it around for a week, I'm afraid. I do believe it's a formal invitation from Kline requesting your company at the ball." His smile broadened. "I'm afraid you'll have to decline now. Until Saturday. Good night."

Roseanne waited until the door had closed behind

him and then she squealed softly deep down in her throat and hugged herself. Wasn't it just like Tyler to pull a nasty little trick like that? Albert Kline would, of course, never forgive him. She tossed the invitation aside without looking at it. Butterflies began floating in her stomach. It had been so long since she had been to anything like this and never had she been on the arm of such a handsome man. Temporarily she might just be able to forget the cattle problem and the war, and even Tyler's revenge. His first wife still held the ties of bondage over him, she reminded herself, and once he left Texas there would be no reason for him to return. His feelings toward her were strictly of a brotherly nature. Yes, that was all. But it didn't matter. She had never felt like this before in her life and she was going to enjoy Saturday night come hell or high water—both of which were common in Texas.

Roseanne and Tyler left Saturday morning for San Antonio, taking Lolita along to assist Roseanne and, for William McVey's peace of mind, to act as chaperon.

They took adjoining rooms in the hotel, Roseanne and Lolita sharing one. When they had their evening wear and personal belongings arranged in their rooms, Tyler and Roseanne went about San Antonio in the buggy, sight-seeing, shopping, browsing, and having a light, early meal to sustain them until the dance. Lolita had requested that they drop her off to see some relatives and pick her up on their way back to the hotel.

As the hour drew near, and Roseanne sat before the mirror, Lolita clasped her hands together at her full bosom. "Señorita Roseanna, you are so beautiful.

Señor Chanson will be the envy of all the men at the ball, and"—she sighed dramatically despite the twist of a smile—"I fear the women will all hate you very much."

Roseanne laughed at Lolita and studied her reflection. She was not a vain person by nature, but she had to admit that she looked very nice, and yes, possibly even beautiful. Lolita had styled her dark hair in a becoming fashion atop her head. The woman was an expert and not one strand was amiss.

Roseanne turned to Lolita and took her hands in a friendly squeeze. "Thank you. It looks lovely. I never could have managed on my own."

Lolita chuckled proudly. "That is why your papa has hired me, Roseanna. He needed someone to look out for you until you find the right man." A knowing look lit her eyes. "Perhaps it will be Señor Chanson, no?"

Roseanne smiled in a wistful way. Even as a child, she had had this strong feeling for Tyler, when she was not even aware of the physical needs and desires of men and women. And consequently, over the years, her dreams of a mate had always demanded those qualities she had seen in him but never found in any other. His presence created a heaviness in her heart that she knew now could be lightened only by his smile and his touch. But they could have no future. He was bound to his past, and she was not yet ready to admit that he alone was the one she wanted. She was not strong enough to make him stay. Lolita's romantic notion was pure wishful thinking. She put it out of her mind, determined to enjoy the evening and not think of what was to come.

She gathered up her shawl and turned to the Mexi-

can woman. "Are you sure you won't be lonely here?
And promise me you'll order a meal."

Lolita smiled. "I will not be lonely, my child. You
do not know how good it will be to have the peace and
quiet. It will do Pablo good to have to tend to the cooking without me. Maybe he will come to appreciate
what I do a bit more, eh?"

"Very well. At least now I won't worry about you.
Go to bed early and enjoy your vacation." With sparkling eyes, Roseanne hugged Lolita. "I hope this will
be fun."

"It will be, señorita. It is your desire."

In the adjoining room, Tyler waited by the fireplace, a glass of whiskey in his hand. He was extremely handsome in the black suit, and Roseanne's
pulse suddenly quickened. She had wondered if he
would be uncomfortable in the dress attire, but she
needn't have worried. He appeared as relaxed as he
did in his work clothes. If she hadn't known better, she
would have thought he dressed in such a fashion every
day.

His approval of her appearance was evident in his
eyes. He set the glass aside and came forward.
"You're more beautiful in that dress than you were at
Christmas, Roseanne, and I didn't think that possible."

She flushed at the compliment, but felt he sincerely
meant it. It wasn't Tyler's way to flatter or say anything he didn't mean. She laughed gaily and said, "I
told you then that it would look much better with petticoats and all the trappings."

With her shawl draped softly in the crooks of her
arms, Roseanne moved to the door with Tyler's hand

on her back in gentle guidance. "Don't wait up,
Señora Alvarez," he said. "We may be out until dawn."

Roseanne caught a spark of devilment in his eyes as
he teased the Mexican woman with intent of worrying
her, but Lolita had grown accustomed to his bantering
ways.

"It is you who will have to face Señor McVey, not
I," she replied good-naturedly.

Tyler laughed and led Roseanne into the hall and
outside where he had McVey's carriage ready and
waiting. After helping Roseanne in, he went to the
other side, moving a blanket out of his way. "I
brought this along in case it's chilly on the way back,"
he explained.

"I hear it's terribly cold at night in Colorado in the
springtime," Roseanne commented, not really caring,
only concerned at the moment by how warm it was
being close to him.

"Yes, it is. If you should convince your father to let
you come with us, you'll have to learn to like the feel
of wool underwear against your skin because it's what
you'll need to keep warm at night."

"I suppose that under your noncommittal exterior
you agree with Dad—that it's no place for me."

He hesitated to answer, remembering her temper.
He didn't want to set off sparks and get the evening off
to a bad start. "At some other time I would be whole-
heartedly for it, Roseanne, but moving with a bunch of
cattle is no pleasure ride. It'll take several months to
get there. I'm afraid you'll wish you'd never heard of
Denver before it's all behind you. That silk dress suits
you much better than homespun and wool anyway, although you'd be pretty in anything."

She was flattered by his compliment, offhanded as it

was, hoping he really believed it. "I still see no legitimate reason to keep me from going to Colorado."

He shrugged and looked straight ahead at the narrow roadway and the black horses never breaking stride. He knew when not to argue with Roseanne McVey.

They arrived at the dance shortly and Tyler kept Roseanne at his side as they went around talking with people Tyler remembered and people Roseanne introduced him to. They were not aware of it, but behind their backs everyone was admiring them, saying what a handsome couple they made. Already rumors were flashing that it looked as though Roseanne McVey had finally found herself a serious beau. And Albert Kline turned his back on them, which pleased Roseanne immensely.

As the party loosened up, the men got up their courage and began asking Roseanne to dance. It wasn't long before Tyler found himself on the sidelines more often than not. Yet he could understand their infatuation, for she was easily the most beautiful woman at the dance—possibly the most beautiful woman in all San Antonio.

The dance was well attended and it looked as though the money collected for the Southern cause would exceed the committee's expectations. Most of the younger men were away at war so the group consisted mostly of older men and women, and those young women temporarily alone in their husbands' absences. There were a good number of teenaged boys and girls, and a handful of soldiers on leave, or stationed in the vicinity. Their presence led most conversations toward war talk and what was happening not only back East but in Texas. Their favorite talk was about the 8th Texas Cavalry, now fighting in the East, and the fellows comprising the Frontier Regiment in Texas, who were fending off Indians on the home ground. Roseanne listened intently to this talk, since she knew many men in the 8th Texas Cavalry.

After an hour or two, Tyler found himself on the sidelines almost all the time watching Roseanne dancing with other men. He realized he was a bit jealous; he wanted to keep her to himself. He wasn't sure what he expected after all those years away, but Roseanne's beauty and sensuality had taken him back a step or two. She fit into the curve of his arms naturally and gracefully, almost as if she had always been there. Together they danced as though they had been partners for years.

When the clock neared midnight, Tyler decided he would reclaim what was rightfully his. He led Roseanne to a dimly lit corner for a rest that she obviously needed. "Are you ready to leave yet?" he jested, knowing full well she wasn't.

"No," she laughed, out of breath. "I thought you told Lolita we'd be out until dawn."

"Only if you want to. You're so popular I'm afraid you may collapse from exhaustion."

Before she could respond, the clock struck the hour, interfering, and subsequently hushing all participants momentarily with its melodious chimes. As Tyler looked down into Roseanne's sparkling eyes, he gave in to the one thought that had been on his mind all evening. He drew her into his arms and whispered, "The day will go better if it is begun with a kiss."

Roseanne was powerless to resist his descending lips, nor did she want to. She had danced with more men than she could remember, but only when she had danced with Tyler had she felt that special tingle. His fiery kiss easily ignited her subdued desires. His lips moved gently at first, a bit maddening, then hungrily they claimed hers in a possession she would not soon forget. Beneath her hands she felt the thud of his heart, and she knew it matched the tumultuous beat of her own.

When she was thoroughly drunk, he lifted his head. His thoughts were invisible in the darkness of his eyes, shadowed further by the candlelight, but she was learning to recognize his look of desire and she saw it in the deep brown depths and in the rigid set of his jaw. But there was more, if only a fleeting inflection, and then he suddenly appeared disturbed and looked away toward the crowd.

"The music has started again." He placed a hand on her waist. "Shall we dance?" He didn't wait for her reply, but led her to the floor and into a waltz.

In his arms again, she was satisfied, although she suddenly felt as though she were walking on needles. With the other men she had no great desire to hear what they had to say, except out of politeness, and there was nothing about them that contained a mystery she felt she must solve. She was fully alive when she was touching Tyler, perhaps *too* conscious of everything she did and said, while feeling he was always at ease and in command. Maybe that was why she was so attracted to him. He didn't try to impress her. He didn't fondle her clumsily; he touched her with assurance.

After several dances in which Tyler politely refused to relinquish her to others, he escorted her from the dance floor to the punch bowl, and poured her a glass. He put an arm around her waist possessively and she leaned gratefully toward him, the memory of his lips, and now the feel of his body, causing her thoughts to stray. She was tired, but never too tired to be in his arms for another dance.

The conversation around her centered on what was happening in Colorado but she was not attending until a portly rancher by the name of Cyril Peterson drew her into the conversation by saying, "All this talk of Colorado makes me think of your father, Miss McVey. What's this I hear about him taking a herd of cattle up there this spring?"

Roseanne was familiar with the pompous Mr. Peterson who thought that if an idea hadn't come from his head then it was obviously a bad idea. Her father had never liked the man and neither did she. "Word travels fast, doesn't it?" She forced a pleasant smile but offered no more.

"Henry Grehan, one of your father's hired men, mentioned it a while back. He apparently felt that it was a stupid idea."

"What do you expect from a stupid man, Mr. Peterson? I hope you're not foolish enough to agree with Mr. Grehan. Daddy knows what he's doing," she assured him coolly, her smile gone now. "I'm sure that in a few years you all will be clamoring to get in his trail dust."

"Gold," another man muttered scornfully. "More money can be made off those fool miners themselves than what they ever dig out of those streams. They say those people up there will pay as high as fifty dollars a barrel for flour and two dollars for a dozen eggs. It amazes me why anybody would want to even get mixed up with the likes of people that have no more sense than that. Chances are, if your pa can get his herd to Denver, that crowd will be lame-brained enough to pay him a hundred dollars a head.''

"He won't lose," Tyler said. "Bill McVey knows what he's doing. He may lose a few cattle, but it's a gamble that's worth taking."

"Is that what you told him, Chanson?" A voice behind them asked icily. "Anybody who would believe a murderer is courtin' sorrow."

The group turned to see Henry Grehan, the short, stocky hired hand on William McVey's ranch. It was obvious he had had too much to drink.

Tyler stood calm despite the accusation, but Roseanne felt his sudden tenseness. He flicked contemptuous eyes over Grehan. "Just because a man is a murderer doesn't mean he's a liar, too."

Grehan, of course, had expected Chanson to deny it, to squirm a little, but Tyler was as much as admitting to the accusation. Now what could Grehan say? All eyes were on Tyler, naturally wondering if the man they had been conversing with so congenially was indeed a murderer.

When Grehan saw that he had created a stir, he continued cockily. "Apparently you boys haven't heard about our old neighbor's line of work lately?" He glanced at the others but avoided Tyler's cold, steady gaze. "Hear tell you take a dislike to somebody, you just hunt 'em down and kill 'em."

The others shifted uneasily as they looked at Tyler warily. Some of them remembered his family, some even remembered him, but Grehan's accusation gave them pause.

Tyler had worked alongside Henry Grehan now for nearly two months, and he had sensed the man's dislike for him, but he had never guessed the hatred ran so deeply. He wasn't sure why. He only knew that Henry was one of those men who found fault with everything. He and his two buddies had been hired because McVey had been short of help when some of his men left for the war. It was hard to get an honest day's work out of Grehan because he seemed to think he had McVey over a barrel. And it was true to a certain extent, because Bill needed the three of them now to get the herd to Denver. Otherwise he probably would have fired them long ago.

Tyler replied calmly. "If you believe what you just said, Henry, aren't you afraid I may take a disliking to you?"

Grehan felt chilly under Chanson's piercing eyes. Nervously he licked his lips. "Is that a threat, Chanson?"

Unwavering, Tyler still held Roseanne in the curve of his arm as though the discussion were of no importance. "No," he replied. "It was a question."

Grehan's eyes darted wildly, racing around the semicircle of men, looking for support; he saw nothing except curiosity. He was on his own. Vaguely he knew he should have kept his mouth shut, but the liquor always made him talk too much and too big. He stammered, "Well . . . it . . . it sounded like a . . . a threat to me. You all . . . heard him."

Tyler felt Roseanne's arm tighten around his waist as she pressed nearer to him. She spoke. "Henry, you're drunk. Why don't you go home."

Grehan pulled himself up straighter and tried to focus on her. How dare she order him around! "I don't take orders from the boss's daughter, although she does think she's almighty important." The words came out in a slobbery gush and he raised a heavy arm to wipe the spittle off his chin.

"It wasn't an order, Henry," Tyler cut in. "It was a smart suggestion."

"The place for a murdering renegade like you is in the grave," Grehan snarled. "There's no place for the likes of you in a civilized society. I ain't gonna let you lead Mr. McVey wrong. He can't see what you are because your pa was his friend. I'm challenging you to a gunfight, Chanson. It's the honest way to rid Texas of you."

The conversation had drawn other people. They all waited now, expectantly. Tyler didn't have a gun, although Grehan did, but even if someone loaned him a weapon, Grehan was too drunk for it to be a fair fight. Growing tired of the whole situation, Tyler replied soberly, "I've got no quarrel with you. If you want to kill someone, Grehan, why don't you join the army?"

"You refusing my challenge?" Grehan asked with a new smugness, thinking he had Chanson on the retreat.

Tyler wondered where Henry Grehan had heard about him, but he supposed it was only natural for things like that to travel like scent on the wind and become exaggerated. "Murderers don't duel, Henry. They shoot from the dark." Tyler turned his shoulder to the shorter man, dismissing him and his challenge.

A couple of Henry's friends came up behind him and tried to pull him away. "Come on, Henry, lay off him. You're spoiling the dance," one said.

Grehan jerked his arm free of the man's hand. "It's true. He's a damn murderer. He shouldn't be allowed to run around loose. He ought to be hanged!"

The ruckus had finally succeeded in drawing everyone's attention and stopping the music. "Get him out of here," Cyril Peterson said to Grehan's cronies. "Take him home and sober him up."

Screaming and shouting that Chanson had left a trail of blood from California to Texas, Grehan was finally dragged from the room. When the doors closed on him, everyone knew who Tyler Chanson was, and they were giving him a wide berth.

Gradually they went back to dancing but for Tyler the lightheartedness was gone. Even though he had murdered no one, he *had* hunted to kill, and would have killed if the law had not intervened. But it disturbed him that Grehan had cast a shadow on him and on the Chanson name.

Five of those men had died that day long ago and two had hung since, but their deaths had not alleviated the bitterness or washed away the blood and pain. It had only served as a thin thread of justice in a land where none had existed.

His senses had been honed to recognize the parasites of society and he had come to understand the godless men perhaps better than they understood themselves. He had learned the way to deal with them by reading their mannerisms and their eyes. He had seen their fear, which they tried to cover with bravado, and he knew how to use that fear to his advantage. There were only a few men who had no fear, and those were the ones to be reckoned with, for they killed with no qualms. They had little or no fear of dying; they simply did not believe it would happen to them.

Men like Cotton were born with the lust to kill. They possessed an inbred hatred for all, even for their own kind to a certain degree. The hatred and the lust motivated them, and little else. Maybe Tyler was no better than the men he hunted. They called it vigilante justice, but nevertheless he would see that each and every man who had been involved would pay for his crime. Then perhaps, when it was all said and done, he would pay for his.

Half an hour later, Tyler helped Roseanne with her shawl. She was exceedingly tired and, like him, her earlier exhilaration was gone, thanks to Henry Grehan's scene. The buggy was brought around and he helped her inside. Disregarding her objections, he bundled her up in the blanket. "You're hot from dancing. You'll catch pneumonia if you don't stay warm."

He climbed in next to her and shortly she was yawning and fighting droopy eyelids. Tyler smiled and placed an arm around her shoulders, drawing her head down against his chest. "Go ahead and sleep."

"Nonsense. We'll be at the hotel soon." But she found no strength to resist his gesture or his suggestion. Nestled in his embrace, she felt warm and secure.

"Sleep anyway," he said. "I won't mind."

She nodded, rubbing her cheek against his chest. In seconds she was asleep.

The next day the horses needed little guidance as they headed north out of San Antonio, and in the early afternoon quiet Tyler had some time to think. The McVey ranch lay along the banks of the Guadalupe River, protected by the hills and the trees, guarded by the guns of men and the mercy of God. It was a good ranch, a good land, but Tyler understood the restless needs of men like his father and William McVey. If no woman waited to warm a man's heart and his bed, then he could grow stale on the best of land. When that happened he needed the wind to his back, the sun on his shoulders, and a place in the far distance he could ride toward. That was why his father had gone to California, and he supposed it was why McVey was risking his cattle on an untried trail to Colorado.

Roseanne sat next to him and he liked the excuse to brush her shoulder. He admitted he not only enjoyed her company but he was finding it difficult to stay away from her. He had learned from her that women could get restless, too, and in a sense they needed the same freedoms as men. Personally, he would have liked to have her come along to Denver, but he knew his opinion was influenced by his growing personal interest in her. There were many dangers involved in the trip. No one knew that better than he did, and he would never encourage her to come or try to change McVey's decision. And, of course, there was still the one man he had to find. His mission of vengeance was starting to hang over him like a black cloud, interfering with his life for possibly the first time.

He had felt a new life in his heart while holding Roseanne in his arms, but his old life was not yet behind him. And, until it was, he knew he would have nothing to offer any woman.

Chapter 5

March–April 1862

THE HOPEFUL EXPECTATIONS FOR A Confederate takeover of Fort Union soon came to a head. The Union commander of the fort, Colonel Edward R. S. Canby, fearing this exact thing, sent some men to the abandoned Fort Craig on the Rio Grande along the Confederate line of advance. In the meantime, the Texas Mounted Rifles had been reinforced by General Sibley's troops, and on February 21, 1862, met and defeated Canby's troops at Valverde.

The Union survivors hastened from the battlefield to Fort Craig five miles away. Upon seeing the fort, Sibley thought the place too heavily armed with cannon to risk an attack. Most of the cannons were, in fact, merely painted logs. But the deception worked and Sibley moved onward to Fort Union. In March his troops occupied both Albuquerque and Santa Fe, but by not attacking Fort Craig, Sibley had given Canby sufficient time to summon reinforcements in the defense of Fort Union.

The Union regiment of volunteers from Colorado,

the so-called Pikes Peakers, got word of Sibley's advance and set out to aid Canby's troops who were now coming from Fort Craig. In late March, the forces met at both Apache Canyon and Glorieta Pass, south of the fort. One of the Union leaders raided Sibley's supply train, and destroyed seventy-three wagons and bayoneted the Confederates' entire herd of horses and mules. Sibley retreated, and with him went the Confederate threat to the mountain region, and the South's last chance for Colorado gold.

When the news reached the McVey ranch, the spring roundup was nearly over. Although it was a bad defeat for the Confederacy, McVey continued with his plans to take his herd on the cattle drive to Colorado.

The spring roundup took several weeks, usually starting in early March. The riders covered the ranch and outlying areas in wide circles of about five miles, gradually closing in and bringing the cattle to a designated area from where the branding, earmarking, and castrating took place. Ordinarily the steers and cull cows were all separated to be sold, while the cows, calves, and bulls were returned to the range. This year, however, cows and calves would be heading up the trail.

McVey was taking two thousand head to Colorado. He had three buyers; one who wanted a thousand head, the other two five hundred head each. It would be mixed stock since one buyer was interested in increasing his present herd, and the other two buyers were young men wanting to turn their gold dust into ranches.

As the drive drew near, Roseanne's tension increased. Hidden safely away in her closet now was nearly everything she felt she would need. She had gathered all her supplies in small quantities over a period of time. She now only needed to get a rifle and pistol. But that would have to come at the last minute, along with the selection of a packhorse, not only to carry her few things, but to serve as an extra mount should something happen to the gray.

As the time drew near, her fear and anxiety also increased, and as each day went by, she wondered if she could really go through with this, or if she should be sensible and stay safely at home. Yet, something urged her to continue with her plans, and she realized it wasn't the excitement or the adventure. Tyler had been right about that—it was miserable sleeping out in the rain and dodging Indian raids. The thing that drove her was the loneliness: week after week, month after month, so frequent these last few years because her father was always away. It had become her job to take her mother's place as *La Patrona*. And it was the last job on the ranch she wanted.

Now with the men, or at least most of them, helping with the roundup, Roseanne was already feeling restless and abandoned. Time weighed on her hands, and she paced the floor for lack of something better to do. And then, as if in answer to her thoughts, the door opened and she was caught wearing out the rug by Tyler.

He eyed her questioningly, his brown eyes playful as usual. "I see you're in need of something to do."

"Oh really? Actually I felt as though this was quite a good form of exercise for a woman."

He smiled. Wasn't it just like Roseanne to be facetious? He pulled his hat off and wiped his sweaty forehead with his bare arm. His shirt sleeves were rolled back, displaying deep brown skin. The dark hair on his head was wet and matted and he glanced toward the kitchen. "Do you have anything cold to drink?"

"I think we could find something." She led the way to the kitchen and spoke over her shoulder. "Is something wrong? Have you ran out of salt? Sugar? Possibly beans?"

"Why do I get the feeling that you don't really care?"

She shrugged and then sighed, giving in to her feelings. Suddenly she wanted to cry. "I'm just tired of pacing the rug, I suppose."

"Well good," he said, surprising her enough to have her stop and half-turn to stare at him in disbelief. He continued, "Because your father suggested I come back and bring you out to the roundup and let you spend the night. He felt that if you worked the cattle, it might get this foolish notion out of your head to go to Denver. The 'foolish' was his word, not mine, by the way."

Her eyes glowed and suddenly she threw her arms around his neck like a child. She kissed him several times on the cheek before she realized what she was doing. Surprise lit his eyes but the hands that had encircled her waist were slow in releasing their light hold. She didn't mind. Now that he was here her tension and loneliness had vanished. And, even better, she would be able to go back with him.

As quickly as she had lost her composure, she regained it, and the smile deepened on her face. She stepped away from him, found some lemonade Lolita had made, and thrust the pitcher into his hand in her haste.

"Help yourself. I'll go upstairs and get together a few things. I won't be long. Give me ten minutes."

He started to tell her to pack lightly, but before he could get the words out, she was gone, taking the stairs two at a time with her skirts hiked up. He enjoyed seeing her happy. She didn't need to know that it was he who had suggested she come, not McVey. He doubted the roundup and sleeping on the ground would change her mind about wanting to go on the cattle drive and seeing Denver, but it would give him a chance to spend more time with her before he had to leave. And as each day passed, he was becoming more reluctant to go—even for a few months.

From experience he knew it might turn out to be much longer; he still had the unfinished business of Walt Cotton to contend with and it was always there haunting him. He wished he could ask Roseanne to wait for him, but what did he have to offer her even if he did? And there was the possibility that she didn't even care for him in the way he had come to care for her.

He had never thought he would want to marry again; he never thought he could even love again. His life had fallen into a pattern of riding for endless days, doing menial jobs, following old leads and trails; of camping in deserts, on uncompromising mountains, in rowdy gold camps, and in the rain. He had never dwelled on what he would do when he had hunted down the last man. He had figured he could live his life roaming and raising cattle, but realistically, could a man grow old alone? Being with Roseanne made that question hard to answer. She soothed a need inside him and made him want to live again for himself and not just for those dead.

Roseanne mesmerized him with her sapphire eyes, eyes that contained no deception, only honesty; eyes that matched perfectly the necklace he bought for her. At the time it had struck him that the color was the same as her eyes and it was simply a gift for the young girl he remembered. But now it had come to mean more than that to him. It was a gift from his heart and one that he hoped she would cherish.

He wondered why she hadn't married, and he was glad she hadn't. He only hoped that a woman of her restless nature could wait for a man like him, a man with no promises he dared make, a man with no financial security to offer.

Then she raced down the stairs, ending his thoughts, bringing a smile to his lips. He took her bedroll and placed a hand on her back to guide her from the house. In minutes he had the gray caught and saddled. He tied her belongings behind the cantle and helped her mount, although she didn't really need his assistance. He noticed she was dressed in a simple skirt and blouse instead of one of the cumbersome riding habits. He liked this attire better. It allowed him to observe her figure without the concealing yards of material. . . .

When they reached the site of the roundup, Roseanne conversed a while with her father and then set out with Tyler and Diego into the brush. Her father was letting her go along, but with strict orders that she not tangle with any of the longhorns. She knew they could be vicious when cornered, but McVey knew his daughter could be just as bullheaded. She had been on roundups before, but always in the capacity of an onlooker, never as a cowboy.

As the afternoon wore on, the three of them herded back about twenty-five head to the roundup site. They had had no trouble aside from of the usual complications—a cow refusing to come out of the brush, or one that refused to be herded in the direction they desired. Roseanne proved herself to be a good hand more than once, and the gray a good cutting horse. The two worked together as a perfect team, almost as if they read each other's minds.

When the day's work was done they stood in line to load up their plates at the chuck wagon. Roseanne, Tyler, and her father found a place near one of the campfires and settled down wearily to eat. The cool night air felt good after the heat of the day. Before the stars popped out, laughter melted into the coming darkness. One vaquero began to sing in a voice that required no accompaniment.

"Well, my dear Roseanne," McVey said, smiling, a hopeful look giving away his innermost thoughts. "I presume you'll be ready to go back to the ranch tomorrow evening and leave this dirty work to the men."

Roseanne read his real intent even without looking at him. "No," she replied happily. "I was rather enjoying it, Dad. I'd stay a bit longer if you would approve."

There was a lengthy silence and Roseanne noticed her father's hand fidgeting with the fork as it hovered over his plate of stew. "I guess it wouldn't hurt anything, but you know how a woman's presence takes the men's minds off their work. They'll accept you on a visiting basis, but they won't like seeing you all the time. They don't want to share their work with a woman."

"I'm not trying to do their work," she replied and looked over at Tyler. "Does it bother you to have me around?"

He finished chewing the mouthful of beef and his eyes twinkled as his lips curved beneath the heavy moustache. He knew his answer was biased. ''Not at all.''

''See, Dad—''.

McVey cut her off with a weathered hand rising abruptly in the air. He pushed his battered felt hat back from his forehead. His brows came together in that stern, fatherly way of his. ''You're being difficult, Roseanne. Surely you can't want to ride behind two thousand head of rangy cattle for nearly three months just to see Denver. Good God, if it's Denver you want to see, I'll arrange a trip there when I return.''

''There's a war on, Dad. Hardly a practical time for pleasure trips. And it's not just Denver I want to see.'' She smiled teasingly and saw his feigned harshness weaken. ''It's everything in between!''

''You could see it some other time.''

She shrugged and turned to Tyler, intentionally changing the subject. ''I hear there are as many pro-Southerners in Denver as there are Yankees, even though the territory is now part of the Union.''

''I wouldn't doubt it, but I'll bet Gilpin's Pikes Peakers are feeling their oats about now after sending Sibley on the retreat. It may not have sounded like much of a battle, but getting possession of those goldfields would have been triumph for the Confederacy. It was quite a blow.''

McVey joined the conversation again with doubt in his eyes. ''I hope this doesn't affect our disposing of the herd. With feelings the way they are, those boys up there might not want to see any Southern cattle.''

Roseanne got worried. ''They can't stop your buyers from making a deal, can they?''

"I don't know," McVey said. "They could probably do just about any damn thing they wanted to. I'm
just hoping they'll all be beef hungry and have the
good sense to put their political emotions aside and let
their mouths water freely."

Around them the campfires opened small circles in
the night, drawing black profiles of the men as they
talked and laughed. Roseanne finished her food in silence, worrying over the chance her father was taking
now that war was displacing the normal movements of
their lives. Somehow the intensity of it made her
decision more imperative. The war had suddenly ac-
celerated life, and even though they were not actively
involved in the fighting, her feeling was one of urgency, haste, compulsiveness, even foolhardiness.
There were now no guarantees that things would be
the same tomorrow.

As soon as Tyler had finished eating, he laid out his
bedroll and then, a few feet away, laid out Roseanne's. McVey had gone to deposit their plates with
the cook and had stopped to talk to some of the vaqueros. Roseanne unpinned her hair and brushed it
quickly, not wanting to draw attention to herself. Tyler put sticks on the campfire then stretched out on top
of his bedroll. The idea of sleeping so close to him
made her nervous, but she got beneath her cover,
drawing it to her chin.

Like the others she would sleep in her clothes. Tomorrow they would be wrinkled, but that was the price
she paid for being here. She had to admit she preferred
the softness of her bed, the privacy of her room, and
the abundance of water to bathe with, but still she
could, and would, tolerate this. There was an adven-

ture here beneath the stars, an adventure she did not want to miss.

"Tyler," she said suddenly, softly. She looked over at him in the faint light and saw him push his hat back. The firelight caught in his eyes as he met her gaze. It was silly but that look made her heart pound harder.

"What is it, Roseanne?"

Now she wished she had kept her thoughts to herself. "It's just that with the war, everything seems so . . . . so temporary."

Silence stretched as he studied her and then she saw his hand reach across the space between them. She put her own out and met his. The strong, callused feel of his closing over hers warmed her body and she felt herself relaxing, feeling safe from those fears, feeling that her peaceful world would remain so.

He squeezed her hand gently. "I should be out there—fighting." It seemed the thought was almost to himself. "Still, there's Walt Cotton to find."

The fear returned. She wondered if he had noticed the sudden cold, clammy feeling running through her body. "Maybe the war won't last that long."

He smiled in the dark, but she didn't see it. He gazed up at the stars, somehow knowing that would be too good to be true. "I don't know—the whole thing is senseless—but war always is. They could have solved this thing if there hadn't been groups on both sides arousing hate and discontent, itching for a battle. The trouble is, those people who cry war are never the ones who actually have to fight the damn thing."

"Will you ever come back to Texas?" she asked softly.

The silence seemed too long and Roseanne felt a rush of heat; she was foolish for having ever asked the question. She wanted to pull her hand free of his, but he must have sensed that for his grip tightened.

Finally he said, "I can't see much sense in that, Roseanne—"

Her heart sank until she thought it would never come back up. She wondered if she would cry. But that was stupid. She wasn't in love with him. She just cared for him—like a friend. Then his whisper cut into her bruised thoughts.

"—not if you're going to be in Denver."

He was smiling at her, the white of his teeth sparkling in the faint light. So he was teasing her again. And what he had said about Denver—surely he couldn't know her plans.

"You *will* be in Denver, won't you?"

She stammered, lest she give herself away. "I . . . I don't know. I don't see how."

"Well, wherever you are, there's a good chance I'll see you again." He squeezed her hand again and then withdrew his, pulling his hat over his face. His voice came out muffled as he folded his hands over his chest. "You'd better get some sleep now. Morning comes all too quickly."

The fire at her feet was warm but without the feel of him she was cold. She nestled deeper under the blanket, rolled to her side and curled into a ball. Tyler was already breathing heavily. She closed her eyes but her mind was too active to sleep. She tried several times to get more comfortable. The ground was too hard. It was going to be a restless night.

By April the roundup was over and the cattle were ready for the trail. Roseanne sat on the porch railing and watched the drovers move the herd from the distant holding place and out into a serpentine column away from the ranch. The cattle were reluctant at first. It would take days for them to adjust to the trail. Soon enough the leaders would emerge and the other cattle would follow them. If the men were lucky, this herd would be cooperative and not stampede at the drop of every hat.

The yard was vacant. All the hired men who weren't going on the drive were seeing them off, helping to get the herd down the river a few miles. William McVey was at the head of the herd giving orders. The other men were taking their positions on either side, in the lead, or the rear.

She had said good-bye to her father, satisfied that he had no inkling of her plan to follow. She had wanted to say something to Tyler, something special, but there had been too many people about. He kissed her cheek and said he would see her again, but he had not said when and that troubled her for she had been hoping for more, something that indicated how he felt about her.

She searched for him and found him, working the cattle with ease. Then shortly, almost as if her thoughts had drawn him away, he left the herd and rode for the ranch on a lope. She stood up from the railing, hope rising in her heart.

He pulled up to the porch, swinging down from the saddle practically before the bay had come to a stop. The horse started grazing immediately on the tall shoots of grass around the wooden steps.

"What did you forget?" she laughed, straightening her skirt.

With no warning he reached for her hand and pulled her into his arms. "Only this." Before she could object, he drew her closer with one arm while his other hand cupped the back of her head. His unexpected kiss drew her ultimate response. Her hands slipped from his chest to his muscular back. She sank deeper into his embrace.

All too soon he lifted his head and studied her intently with eyes that were shadowed beneath the wide brim of his hat. Her breasts were pressed so tightly against his chest that Roseanne wondered if he could feel the erratic beat of her heart. It was a moment she wished could last forever. It was a moment that made her realize she was falling in love for the first time.

"Wish us luck," he said with a serious line to his mouth. "We're going to need it." He was thinking how his departure was so like the other one those many years ago, except that now she was a full-grown woman who aroused the desires that had been dormant in him for so long. He couldn't say so, but he had wished all along that McVey would change his mind and let her come. But, of course, it was too dangerous.

"I want to come with you," she stated as she tilted her head back to better meet his gaze.

A smile carved itself onto his mouth but the seriousness was still in his eyes. "Do you want to come with *me?*" he queried on a playful note. "Or did you mean with *us?*"

Actually it was both, but while she formulated the answer and wondered at his feelings for her, he laughed and said, "I think I know, Roseanne. It's adventure you want, a few kisses from a few strangers, perhaps some gold nuggets for your purse. I understand—and it's just as well."

"No. You're wrong, Tyler." A lump rose in her throat. Did she dare say what she felt? What if he simply laughed at her? But he *had* kissed her and it had been more than just a friendly good-bye. She looked into his dark eyes and saw expectancy and a caution that seemed to intensify as he waited for her to continue. "I want to see you again, Tyler. Will you honestly come back?"

His arms tightened on her again and his lips found hers, tenderly at first then demanding more as his kiss deepened. Again she succumbed to the easy arousal and was disappointed when he finally broke the kiss.

"Yes, I will come back to you, Roseanne. Promise me you'll wait. Promise me that you won't marry somebody while I'm away." He knew he shouldn't be asking that of her under the circumstances, but he found the words coming out anyway.

"Yes, Tyler. I will. I will," she whispered gladly.

"I have to go." He released her and, stepping off the porch, gathered his reins and swung into the saddle with only the aid of the saddle horn. He turned to her and touched the brim of his hat. The urgency in his eyes seemed to fit her own mood. And then he was gone.

Suddenly she was miserable again as she watched the wide span of his shoulders growing smaller and smaller in the distance. If only she could have confided in him that she was going to follow the herd, but if she had, he probably would have felt obligated to tell her father and she hadn't wanted to put him in that position.

And then she forced herself to brighten. She would see him on the drive, even though he wouldn't know she was there. And when they got to Denver she could be with him again. It would be over by then and her father would have nothing to say. The deed would be done.

It was time to go. She turned to the house and in seconds was in her room drawing out the supplies she had packed into saddlebags. The other larger things she had secretly hidden a quarter of a mile from the ranch, taking small portions to the hiding place each day. She changed from her dress to a skirt and blouse and then went to the kitchen.

"I'm going for a ride, Lolita."

Lolita smiled and plunged another dish into the dishpan. "Sí, señorita. I know it is hard for you to see him go. I saw him return." Her thin brows rose knowingly. "You will miss Señor Chanson, and he will miss you. I do not think friends kiss in such a fashion."

Roseanne blushed and turned for the door. "I'll be back this afternoon. I need to be alone for a while."

Lolita Alvarez went about her work smiling. It was good to see Roseanne attracted to Señor Chanson. Lolita had wondered if it would ever happen. Roseanne had just not been interested in any of her gentleman callers. They were nothing compared to the handsome Tyler Chanson. *Qué hombre!* If only she herself were twenty years younger and fifty pounds lighter! For Roseanna's sake, she hoped Señor Chanson would come back. He and Roseanna would make a good match indeed and make beautiful grandchildren for Señor McVey.

Roseanne went back to her room and double-checked her list. She found a piece of paper and wrote Lolita a quick note in Spanish. She glanced around the room, fingering the sapphire necklace around her neck. Lolita was singing in the kitchen, no doubt fixing something for the noon meal. She picked up the saddlebags and went to her father's study downstairs. His safe was unlocked and she took fifty dollars to see her through to Denver. She then took from his private collection a Spencer rifle and his old Paterson Colt revolver. She found the proper ammunition in the top drawer of his desk and dumped it all into her father's worn saddlebags, an old set he had not had the heart to throw away. She left the note on the table in the hall.

She slipped out to the barn and in minutes the gray was saddled and anxious to go. She tied her things to the saddle and then caught the packhorse. She climbed onto the Texas saddle and, leading the packhorse, headed out of the yard. The herd was well out of sight now. She planned to get her cache, load it onto the packhorse, and still be able to catch up.

She was a few yards past the house when the front door suddenly burst open and Lolita appeared on the veranda, her full bosom heaving in excitation. Roseanne gathered her reins tighter as the gray pranced in anticipation. She had no choice but to stop. Lolita exclaimed frantically in Spanish then reverted to English, waving the note Roseanne had left. Damn, but she hadn't expected the woman to find it so soon.

"Señorita!" Her voice was in a near sob and her face stricken. "You cannot do this. Your father—he will not like it. How can I stop you? Please—do not do this thing!"

The gray danced sideways, anxious to be gone. Roseanne looked down at Lolita as she tried to keep the gelding in check and keep the lead rope on the packhorse from becoming entangled with her mount. "I must go, Lolita. Please try to understand." And then she played upon Lolita's romanticism, but deep in her heart she knew it was true. "I must go with Tyler. I'm in love with him, Lolita."

Lolita broke out in fitful weeping, sobbing in Spanish so rapidly that Roseanne was barely able to decipher the words. Wiping at the tears streaming down her plump cheeks, she finally waved a useless hand and cried, "Then go, little one. I cannot keep you from the man you love!"

Suddenly Roseanne realized she would miss Lolita terribly. The woman had not only been a teacher and friend, but a mother as well. It was just as well that Lolita thought Tyler would be looking out for her. That way she wouldn't worry.

Roseanne released the tight hold on the reins and waved to Lolita. *"Hasta la vista!"*

Away from the ranch Roseanne crested a ridge and saw the longhorns strung out through the trees, a narrow strand of heated, shifting flesh. This was a venture that risked the life of every man and animal in her sight, yet William McVey had always told her a person could not live in a cocoon. Now she fully understood. She was taking the biggest chance of her entire life, and to say she wasn't afraid would be to say she was a fool.

She reined the gray from the road to the spot where she had her supplies hidden. Concealed by the thick trees, she changed from her skirt and blouse to the masculine clothing she had brought. They were sized for a teenage boy; she had told the clerk they were for one of the vaquero's sons. Still, they were a little large and helped camouflage her womanly shape; with the serape over her, no one would be the wiser. Next she wound her hair into a twist, covered it with the big

sombrero, then carefully rolled her riding clothes up
into small bundles to reduce wrinkles. She set about
loading the packhorse, and within the hour, her heart
pounding madly, she remounted the gray and took a
deep breath.

Around her the lush hills rolled gently, already making her homesick. She loved it here, but she had to see
something else to appreciate this more. Colorado
waited. And with it, its adventure, its uncertainty, its
newness.

Roseanne knew the route her father had chosen because she had carefully listened to his plans and
studied his maps. She had heard about the rivers, the
towns, the landmarks. She had drawn up her own
maps, copying his. They planned to strike a westerly
course until they hit the Pecos, then follow it north
through New Mexico, across the Canadian River, tip
the North Canadian and Cimarron into Colorado Territory, past Fountain City, Colorado City, and finally
into Denver.

As the day wore on, Roseanne had plenty of time to
think about what she was doing and how she would
survive in the weeks until they reached Denver. It was
still not too late to go back to the ranch. The cattle,
even though fresh, had gone but ten or twelve miles.
She could stay close to the herd while the trees and
rolling hills continued, but eventually the land would
give way to wasteland and she would have to drop farther and farther behind to keep from being detected.
No one knew for sure what problems the Indians might
pose, but this thought made her more than uneasy.

In the evening Roseanne set up camp on a secluded,
wooded knoll. Below her the longhorns milled until

they finally settled into a semblance of restfulness. They were a rangy breed, known for their perseverance. The longhorns were developed from crossing British cattle with Spanish cattle, mainly of the Andalusian stock. In appearance they were not handsome. They were a motley group of colors, a dusky sea of horns that were continually clashing. They were long-legged, raw-boned, narrow-hipped. Some had had many owners; their sides carried bold brands along with the familiar WM, and their ears were carved with various designs while dewlaps swung from their necks in time with their movements. They were wide between the eyes, wild in nature, coarse-haired and stubborn, thin and flat-sided. But they had hooves of steel, muscles of iron, and a strength that enabled them to endure the worst tests of nature and survive where no other creature could.

Roseanne was tired, hungry, and dusty. She had tried to stay clear of the clouds of dust made by eight thousand hooves, but it rose in the stagnant air and lingered, with no breeze to shift it. Now she longed for a good hot meal and a soft bed, but she had chosen this course and she would bear it.

Instead of giving in to the desire to rest, however, she gathered enough firewood for cooking and to last the night. When that was done, she found some jerky and curled up on her bedroll. She would build a fire later when her smoke would go undetected. The cattle were just below in a broad valley, but even with this proximity she didn't think she would be seen.

Darkness was hovering and she was thankful for that. She rose and walked to the top of the knoll. At the edge, she stretched out in the grass on her stomach and looked down at the herd and the men. Automatically she searched for Tyler and found him standing by the chuck wagon eating his evening meal. He stood out among the others, not only because of his height, but because of his charisma. Was it possible that only she noticed that characteristic in him?

Then, suddenly, as if he sensed being watched, he lifted his head and looked up toward the knoll where she lay. But he couldn't see her, she was positive of that. Nevertheless she scooted back deeper into the grass and the dusk. In minutes he was through with his food and sat his tin plate aside. He took up his reins and moved his horse out slowly around the cattle. The men would take turns night herding, talking and crooning to the cattle to keep them calm. The longhorns were easily excited into a stampede and something as innocent as lighting a match could send them on the run.

Roseanne crept back to her campsite. The small area was noticeably darker than it had been just moments before. She wrapped her arms around herself and shivered involuntarily. The gray looked at her and then went back to grazing. She moved closer to him, wishing childishly that she could sleep on his back. She patted his neck and moved reluctantly to her bedroll.

In the distance she heard the night calls of unknown birds. From the grass came the familiar sound of the cicadas. The dusk was slipping into darkness. She decided it was time to cook her meal and begin preparations for the early start in the morning.

She started the fire easily enough then nursed it into a self-supporting blaze. The flames could not be seen from below and what little smoke there was from the dry wood was dissipated by the tree branches just overhead. She set some dried beef to fry in tallow and in a small pot put a few dried apricots on to stew.

Even though she was hungry the meal settled into a lump in her stomach and her nerves prevented her from enjoying it. When she was finished, she quickly cleaned up the pans and put them aside for the morning's use. She double-checked the horses to make sure they were secure. Then, after piling more wood on the fire, she crawled beneath her blanket with the Colt and the Spencer as bed partners.

She tried to close her eyes but the snapping and crackling of night noises and the fire kept her awake. The fire lit the area, but made all else beyond its small perimeter black. She wondered if she should move away from the blaze to be a less noticeable target for whatever could be lurking out there. Perhaps she should put the fire out altogether. The men, the herd, the safety of numbers was so near, yet so far away.

She fingered the revolver and looked into the darkness and to the direction of a twig snapping beneath the thick bunches of trees. She couldn't see clearly after having stared into the fire. That important discovery was one she would have to remember. She listened. Silence. The gray blew and munched. She heard the occasional thump of a hoof, or the crack of a leg joint. She wished the moon would rise, but there was nothing but a smattering of stars. She closed her eyes and wished Tyler were nearby as he had been on the roundup. She didn't really think she would be able to sleep.

She awoke with a start, then came slowly to her senses. The fire was out. It was still dark. Something had set off an alarm in her head. She heard it again. Men talking, voices drifting up to her from far away.

There was a commotion, cattle bellowing. Morning was on the horizon, and it was now those dark preliminary minutes before the first graying of dawn. The drovers were preparing to move the herd out.

She got up hastily, a bit disorganized, disoriented. The men were probably already eating breakfast or would be soon. Did she have time to rebuild the fire and fix something to eat? She seriously doubted it, so she nervously ate some dried apricots and put some jerky in her pocket to chew on until later. She rolled up her belongings, scattered the fire's ashes, and readied the two horses. She was waiting on the ridge when the sky lightened and the herd stretched westward in its familiar sinuous column.

As the second day neared its end, Roseanne became greatly aware of her stiff joints and muscles from the many hours in the saddle. She also felt an empty tremor in her stomach and hoped the men would stop soon. She longed for a hot meal and wished her manly disguise would let her pass herself off at the chuck wagon as one of the hired hands, but she knew it wouldn't. Old Ramon Castillo, the cook, knew all the cowboys, and all the cowboys knew one another. She would be found out before she could get her plate loaded down. But she would have a hot meal tonight nevertheless. . . .

She fixed flapjacks and bacon and ate them with enthusiasm. When her plate was clean, she leaned back against the tree and groaned happily. Her stomach was full for the first time all day. When the food had settled somewhat she went about the nightly preparations and then returned to her bedroll, gladly stretched out on her side, and sipped the remaining coffee from her tin cup.

She was more relaxed than she had been the previous night, and she felt as though she was moving into a routine with her few duties. Her first nervousness was easing now. She was finally going on an adventure that she knew would probably last her a lifetime. She was not just a female onlooker whose world was a house and yard. Still, she was very much aware of the night sounds, and the possibility of encountering Indians—Comanches. She had heard frightening tales of what they did to captives.

She tossed the bitter coffee grounds into the grass and rinsed her cup out with some water she had placed on the fire earlier to warm for washing. She took a cloth and small towel from her bag and proceeded to wash the trail grime off her face and neck. When they reached the Llano River, hopefully in three days, she would take a full bath and wash her hair. But for now, this would have to do.

Suddenly both horses thrust their heads up, smelling the air with distended nostrils. The gray snorted nervously. Minutes passed until, the alarm forgotten, they both went back to eating. Yet Roseanne's heart continued to pound. She had the lingering feeling that someone was in the darkness watching her.

The minutes edged on, but the night was even quieter than usual. More reason for her suspicions? Time slipped away. How many minutes? Fifteen—twenty? She dared not move, but waited frozen in a disjointed wave of fear with her hand ready on her pistol.

Now, despite the need to stay awake, she was drifting off, completely against her will. Frantically she willed herself back to alertness only to have the wave take her mind again. She fought her drooping eyelids. She thought maybe she should get up and challenge the interloper, but her body would not answer to her command. Was she asleep? Dreaming? Finally she could fight no more, and unaware of the exact moment, lost consciousness.

The Llano River was a welcome sight. The herd had reached its banks just at sunset and plunged into its gentle waters, filled up, and had taken to grazing on the grassy banks and meadows nearby or shading up under the oak and cedar trees.

Roseanne moved about a quarter of a mile upstream from the cattle and set up camp in a thick grove of trees, just feet from the water's edge. Only five days on the trail and the slow procedure was already growing tiresome. Yet their journey had barely begun, and although the cattle were making excellent time through the hill country, it would be sometime in June before they reached Denver.

While she fixed her evening meal, the last of the sun's coralline glow faded beneath the pale, watercolor gray of twilight. Overhead the fluffy clouds hid the trace of the evening stars. The air was warm, and a bit muggy.

Roseanne eyed the Llano River, anxious to crawl into its refreshing waters. Her eyes darted around her campsite, leery, however, of the unseen presence, watching her, following her, waiting. She had felt it again last night, just as she was falling asleep. As on the other nights, nothing happened, but as usual, for the space of five minutes or so, she had felt the eyes from the dark.

She hastened her meal, not particular about its quality, only that it would fill her empty stomach and give her strength. The gray was eating peaceably along the water's edge, and she had watched him for signs of an intruder, for he sensed it before she did.

On the opposite side of the river, thick trees jutted skyward forming a black band of protection. Roseanne set her dirty dishes aside, found her soap and towel and hurried to the dark water. As she undressed, she saw the moon tipping the tops of the trees, the clouds alternately passing across its face. It was nice to have the light, but she cursed her luck that it should appear at this moment when she wanted complete darkness. Nevertheless, she finished undressing and waded quietly into the water. She temporarily abandoned the idea of a "quick" bath for the water was so refreshing and invited her to stretch out and loll in pleasure. She sank into peaceful oblivion.

The moon glistened on the water's dark surface, outlining the ripples in silver splendor. She did not see the man leaning casually against the cedar tree, enjoying the creamy white of her skin glowing in the moonlight. The strands of her long, dark hair gleamed black as they melted into the water like seaweed.

As she glided through the water, the exquisite form of her body tantalized the quiet observer on the river bank, until finally he slipped silently from his clothes and into the silvery water, creating only the slightest disturbance.

As he swam to the middle, the water separated behind him, fanning out into a shimmering "V" until it was finally dissolved into the gentle current of the Llano.

She made a graceful turn, and with head down, swam slowly and methodically toward him. He moved into her path. When she was nearly to him, he caught her shoulders and pulled her up out of the water. She gasped and tried to pull away, but when her eyes cleared, she looked up into his tender expression and her fright vanished.

The warmth of his hands burned into her bare flesh, his thumbs gently persuaded her senses to excitement. "What are you doing here, Tyler?" she asked weakly, fearful of the spell he was casting.

His dark brows rose in amusement. "I might ask you the same thing."

Chapter 6

April 1862

ROSEANNE TRIED TO SINK BACK INTO the water, embarrassed by her exposure and highly aware of the dark mat of his chest hair much too close to her breasts. Her black lashes fluttered in betrayal of her nervousness. What did he have in mind?

"Let go of me," she commanded evenly but ineffectively.

She had expected him to tease her as he always did, but instead his gaze was alarmingly intent. "I don't know if I care to."

Without being told, she knew he had been the one coming nightly to her campsite. He drew her an inch or two closer; she felt the dark hair on his chest titillate the tips of her breasts. She knew she should pull away, but his closeness, his raw masculinity and unmistakable male scent kept her hypnotized to the spot.

She glanced upward through cautious lashes and saw his head moving downward. She realized she was waiting in anticipation for the touch of his firm mouth over hers, and the seconds until contact seemed more like minutes. His moustache brushed the silky skin of her cheek as he laid a light kiss beneath her cheek-bone. Slowly his lips moved toward hers, tasting her flesh in their progress, until finally they closed over the petals of her mouth, demanding consummation. Tenderly his strong hands pulled her fragile body up against his chest as he enveloped her in his hot, compelling embrace.

His kiss started an easy fire inside her. She felt the sweet warmth grow into need. His lips, temporarily sated by hers, moved to roam over her face, satiny wet hair, and down the sensitive flesh of her neck. She quivered beneath his fiery touch as an entirely new set of sensations flowed through her body to join the other disturbing feelings that she had never experienced before. Eyes closed, she reveled in the glorious feel of him as his lips moved along her shoulder, then to her collarbone, and finally came to rest on the rise of her breast. She wasn't aware of the breath caught in her throat or her fingers gripping his shoulders. All she felt was the caress of his lips in complete intimacy.

Momentarily the spell was broken as he stood upright again to behold her face with muted passion, but the sensations continued to pile up endlessly inside her. Urgently she drew his head down to once more experience the taste of his lips on hers.

Then he lifted his head, and seeing his desire mirrored in her eyes, he slipped a strong arm behind her knees and quickly pulled her up out of the water and into his arms. In seconds he sat her on the bank and brought himself out of the water and by her side. Without the water to hide him, Roseanne saw the flawless form of his body and the hard heat of his passion.

Once again he picked her up, and walked the short distance to her bedroll. Lowering himself to his knees, he placed her on the blanket. He allowed his gaze to absorb the curves of her body, his view aided by the glow of the moon. She felt cool and vulnerable without the heat of his body touching hers. She lifted a hand and touched his arm. Silently he melted into her embrace, burying his lips in the softness of her wet hair.

His lips once again roamed every inch of her, bringing her back to the previous heights. Suddenly she felt as if she had an emptiness inside, one that only he could fill. Instinctively he sought to satisfy her need. At the initial pain she cried out, but his gentleness soon had her calling his name, a whisper in the night lost only to his ears.

Their joining carried her onto a spear of fire, higher and higher as if on eagle's wings to an ultimate satisfaction she had never experienced before. Finally, gloriously, he eased her back down from the flame and cooled her in the warm, rocking, rhythmic waves of lassitude.

Gradually she felt the weight of his body where he too had fallen, oblivious, from the heights. At the thought, he shifted knowingly and easily rolled to his side. He cradled her tenderly, lavishing her with kisses. She absorbed the salty taste of his skin with her own kisses and explored his body with a caressing, unhurried hand.

She smiled, contented, like a cat that has just been fed cream. She ran her hand down his leg, the coarse, curly hair teasing her fingertips. Beneath her hand she felt a strength that made her secure; every inch of him was hard-hewn just as she had known it would be.

Tyler lay on his side, keeping a hand around her waist. She sank her fingers into the dark hair on his chest and for the first time felt uneasy about looking into his eyes. What would he think of her now?

His hand rose to caress her cheek and the pressure on her chin forced her to look at him. She couldn't read his thoughts, his eyes were placid, dark pools glittering only with the light of the moon, just like the river that had incited their intercourse. She read a contentment in his relaxed features and in his purely satisfied body. Yet she feared his rejection now that it was over.

He sensed the content of her thoughts and he responded soothingly. "Don't let it trouble you, Roseanne. We did nothing wrong."

She tried to look away, embarrassed now by their naked bodies and the memory of the act, but his hand held her head steady, forcing her to face him and their lovemaking. Again she tried to move away, but he stopped her attempt by easily rolling her from her side to her back, taking the dominant position over her where he studied her intently.

Uncomfortable under his scrutiny, she inwardly squirmed. Finally she asked, "Aren't you wondering what I'm doing here?"

A smile curled his full lips. "No, not really." He paused, amused by the confusion in her eyes. "I expected as much from you, and I think I would have been disappointed if you hadn't met my expectations."

"How did you know I was here?"

"I've known you were following us from the first day."

"What!" She struggled to rise, but his immovable body kept her tightly in place. "Then it was you who has been sneaking around my camp at night."

"I had to make sure you were all right." He defended himself. "I'll admit your disguise was clever, but the gray tipped me off."

Her eyes narrowed in mounting anger. "If you knew I was here then why didn't you make your presence known? You've got no right spying on me!" Angrily she pushed herself up on her elbows, but the position only succeeded in thrusting her breasts into his chest, and arousing her inner sensations all over again. Quickly she lowered herself, aware that the movement had had the same effect on him.

"First," he explained, "I thought it would do you good to be alone, but I stayed close by so some Comanche wouldn't sneak off with you in the middle of the night. I wasn't spying on you. I didn't watch every move you made, for God's sake."

She visibly breathed a sigh of relief, but a new, more serious fear sprang to mind. "Did you tell Dad I was here?"

"Of course not."

Thankful of that, her thoughts slipped back to their lovemaking. A cautious glitter grew in her eyes. "Why did you decide to come out of hiding?"

"Who can resist the Llano after being in the dust of two thousand longhorns? It was only my intention to wash your back, but I guess you left your soap on the bank."

His noncommittal reply was a bit disappointing. He *had* sought her for physical gratification only. She had hoped for more. She bit her lip to keep it from quivering. "What will happen now? Will you tell Dad?"

He chuckled. "He doesn't need to know we made love."

"That's not what I meant," she replied indignantly

and saw his smile widen at her exasperation. "I meant—"

He laid a finger over her lips. "I know what you meant." He lowered his head, once again intent on the softness of her lips tempting him, and her body contours curved so perfectly to his. "I won't tell him you're here—not yet anyway." He noticed the light from the dying embers casting fluttering motions over her face and he knew he should put more wood on the fire, but he was drugged by the sweetness of her lips as surely as if they contained some secret intoxicating liquor.

He had not planned for this to happen. It had been his intention to keep their relationship honorable and eventually offer her the sanctity of marriage. But it *had* happened and it had been more than a momentary physical need for him. She had filled the void in his heart, given new meaning to his life, and made him realize he must have her for his own, forever.

"Do you need to get back to the herd?" Roseanne sensed some inner preoccupation in him, a coiled restlessness, and she wondered if now that he had what he wanted, he would turn his back on her. She had given in so easily—just like a harlot.

"No." He ran a hand along the silkiness of her shoulder, wondering what her feelings were for him now. Had they intensified as his had?

"Won't they wonder what's happened to you?"

"They're all sound asleep by now. Besides, your father knows I go where I please. His only concern is that I return to help him get his cattle to Denver."

Her heart pounded fearfully. She wanted him to stay, yet she knew it was foolish. He wouldn't love her if he didn't want to, even if she gave him her body. "Then what is it, Tyler?"

"You," he replied, banishing her fears for the moment. "I can't get enough of you." His mouth and hands roamed her body, leaving the burning tentacles of persuasive power to rock her reserve.

"Then stay," she whispered, deciding that she would try to get his love at any cost. "I don't want to spend the night alone."

Roseanne fell asleep in Tyler's arms sometime after midnight. Now he held her in loving remembrance of the physical communion that had developed unexpectedly between them. But had it been totally unexpected? The desire for it had been there right from the minute he had first seen her back in December. Still, something she had said troubled him. Had she wanted him to stay because she cared for him, or because she simply wanted companionship in this lonely place? He knew he could ask her, but he was afraid her answer might destroy this new feeling that he wished to savor.

His mind would not rest in the darkness, despite his physical exhaustion from riding all day, and it turned to other problems—namely the unfinished business with Walt Cotton. He couldn't let the man go free, but he couldn't let Roseanne go free either. Torn by the dilemma of what course he should take, he eased from her arms, found his pants, and slipped them on. He laid more sticks on the fire then pulled the cover up over her bare shoulder. She stirred and opened her eyes halfway, looking for him.

"Tyler?"

He stretched out next to her again, reassuring her with his immediate embrace. "I'm here, Roseanne."

He pulled her tightly against him and fondled the silky strands of her hair. Damn it. Why did he feel so tortured? Why did she have to have such a disconcerting effect on him?

Then he smiled helplessly to himself. Hadn't she always? Even as a child? And when he had seen her that day at the Guadalupe for the first time in thirteen years, it had all come back to him: the special feelings of adolescent protectiveness and fondness, culminating in mature physical desire and emotional closeness.

He had emptied himself body and soul into her. He felt a commitment to her. He had no willpower to rise from her arms. She had brought to life a part of him that he thought had long since died. No, he had no desire to leave her, now or ever.

The sun was thirty minutes into the sky when Roseanne woke. The events of the night before dominated her mind, but she wondered if she had dreamed it all because Tyler was gone. It was late; they would have moved the herd out by now. She would have to hurry to catch up.

She pushed back the cover and then wrapped it around her shoulders, looking for her clothes. Then she remembered that she had undressed by the river. She turned to the water and a smile cut into her sober expression.

Tyler was standing in the pool lathering his body with her bar of soap. Immediately a warmness rushed through her and a feeling of pleasant familiarity. He raised a hand and motioned for her to join him. "Come on in," he called.

She laughed and moved forward quickly. For the first time in years she felt truly happy. She couldn't deny she had noticed all the beauty of spring in the past five days, but this morning she saw everything with more clarity; the abundant purple blossoms of the laurel, the endless meadows of bluebonnets, the occasional red Indian paintbrush, the fields of coreopsis, and the blue-eyed grass.

When she stood at the water's edge, he said, "Come on. I'll wash your back."

"That was your intention last night," she lightly accused.

He nodded acknowledgment a bit sheepishly. "Well, this morning I promise."

She was uncomfortable to have him see her in full light but she dropped her protective cover and moved into the water. He allowed himself the pleasure of committing each lovely curve to memory. When she drew near to him, she felt a blush rising to her cheeks, but he took her hand and pulled her tight against his chest.

"You're more beautiful in the light of day." He kissed her possessively then reluctantly drew his head up. "I promised to wash your back"—he turned her about-face—"and I always keep my promises."

He lathered her back, but his scrubbing didn't end there. He soaped her shoulders, arms, and moved down her spine to her derriere and then down the length of her legs. At first she was extremely conscious of his intimate exploring of her body while she stood like a statue, feeling foolish. But slowly the slick, soapy touch began to work on her nerve ends, bringing together, in warm ripples of need, her desire and love.

Love? The easiness of the thought frightened her. Was she ready to fall in love with a man whose past remained questionable? A man whose sole purpose in life was to avenge the death of his family? She couldn't blame him for that, but did she really know him? Was it possible that he might enjoy killing as Henry Grehan had accused? Or was he the Tyler she thought she knew? It was hard to believe that there could be another side to him, a cold, ruthless side.

But she didn't want to think about that. She didn't want those frustrating thoughts to overshadow the explicit memories they had made last night and were making now. She closed her eyes and allowed his warm, caressing hands to blot out those pictures.

She leaned back against his chest, taking strength from his support. She felt his lips on her hair, kissing her softly, his breath tickling and teasing her senses. Then, seemingly unwilling, he removed his hands from her shoulders and slowly lathered the satin length of her hair. After he had helped her rinse it, he turned her in his arms and drew her close again.

"Love me, Roseanne," he whispered urgently. "Love me like you did last night."

He helped her from the water. Together they stretched the blanket out in the grass near the river. Tyler knelt on it and extended a hand to Roseanne. She melted into his arms. Then, slowly and lovingly, as he had done before, he made her his own.

Tyler watched her dress while he put his own clothes on. She was beautiful, even in men's clothes. "It was clever of you to think of dressing like a man."

"I thought it would be safer," she admitted.

"Oh, it is," he agreed, "but it didn't save you from me." His eyes danced mischievously.

"The only reason you knew it was me was because of the gray," she insisted.

He shrugged. "Just don't get too close to anybody. Even in men's clothes, you're unmistakably a woman."

She overlooked his bantering as she cinched the belt around her small waist. He would be leaving soon, and more than ever she didn't want to be alone. "Should I tell him, Tyler?"

"Your father?"

She nodded.

"He won't like it, Roseanne, but it's too late to send you back. He could take you to one of the military outposts, though, and arrange an escort home for you."

"No!" Her head shot up in alarm.

"Or,—" Tyler continued rather facetiously, "he could just take you home himself and catch up with the herd later."

"Damn," she muttered and moved to pack up her things. "I'm afraid to face him."

Tyler helped her pack, then picked up the blanket and saddle and threw them on the gray. "Because of last night?" he asked.

Roseanne looked away at the flowers, the river, and their bed of grass. "Partly. After all, if I show up in camp today he'll know you spent the night with me."

Tyler cinched up the saddle and let the fender fall. He turned to Roseanne. "I'm not ashamed of making love to you, Roseanne."

She met his stern expression. "And neither am I—ashamed of it." Her voice was laced with helplessness. "But to face Dad and have him know. I—" She whirled away, but he caught her shoulders and pulled her back around to face him.

"Have him know his little girl is now a woman?" He understood her concern. "He knows that already."

He pulled her into his arms and she willingly held him close one last time. As she listened to his heart thumping beneath her ear, she wondered how deep his feelings truly were for her. If he had only needed her body, she would be crushed, mortified. She could say something. She could ask for a love commitment, but she wouldn't put him on the spot and take the chance of hearing what she feared most.

Reluctantly she drew away from him. She said insouciantly, "Bring me some of Castillo's biscuits now and again, will you?"

His hands roughly kneaded her shoulders. "I don't want to see you out here riding alone any longer, Roseanne." His grip tightened, a muscle worked nervously along his jaw. "Up until now there hasn't been much danger, but we're moving into Indian country and I want you with me."

She remembered their first parting back at the ranch. She quipped, "With *me,* Tyler? Or with *us?*"

His tenseness wavered only slightly at her attempt to joke. "I'd feel a lot better if I could keep you in my sight at all times."

"But if I came to camp then you couldn't make love to me any more," she reminded him.

It was clearly something he had to consider, but finally he said, "I'd sacrifice that for your life."

He sounded so concerned. He was not making this separation easy for her. He acted as though he actually felt something for her, yet, like her, he wouldn't say the words.

She couldn't maintain the false front under the intense heat of his gaze. She looked at the buttons on his shirt because she couldn't look at him. "Give me a day or two, Tyler. Let me think about it. Dad won't be happy about this, and it wasn't my intention to let him find out I was anywhere near until we reached Denver."

"All right," he reluctantly consented, "but I don't like it. Now I'd better go saddle my horse before your father thinks I've been killed by Comanches."

"Can I give you a ride?"

"He's just over the hill in a meadow. You can walk with me. Then we'll ride together until the herd is in sight."

Tyler left Roseanne beneath a grove of trees and kicked the bay into a lope. In seconds he joined the herd and found McVey, who was riding lead.

"See you didn't get yourself killed," McVey said as the bay drew up alongside him. "I was beginning to wonder, though. How do things look?"

Tyler hated to lie to a man like William McVey. He needed to know his daughter was here. He needed to know of the dangers. But most of all, he needed to know so Tyler could have her close.

He lied, although it was a partial truth. "I didn't see any Indians."

"Good. So far so good."

"We'll see them, Bill," Tyler warned. "And I don't think it'll be long now. I'm sure they already know we're here."

McVey nodded. He had figured as much.

Several nights later, Tyler put in his watch early and then, with some of Castillo's biscuits, Roseanne's favorite, tucked in his saddlebags, he rode away from camp.

Her fire was small and fading; it was nearly midnight. She was asleep with her pistol beneath her slim hand. He stepped down from the bay, staking it by Roseanne's horse. He knelt down and placed a light kiss on her lips. It startled her awake but instinct told her it was him long before her blue eyes could focus on his dark face.

She sat up. "I meant to stay awake for you."

"It's just as well you didn't," he said. "It's nearly midnight. I couldn't get away tonight as early as I wanted to, but Castillo made biscuits so I brought you some."

He held the small bundle out and she thanked him for remembering her request. He stirred up the fire, added more wood, and quietly heated up the coffee. It was hot before Roseanne had finished eating. He poured them both a cup and sat hers on the ground. He cradled his own in his hands and studied her. "I want you to come back with me tomorrow."

Alarm widened the pupils in her eyes. There was a nervous silence. "Can't we wait a bit longer?"

"No," Tyler said firmly. "I saw Comanche sign today. They're trailing us at a distance. They probably know you're here, too."

She swallowed the biscuit that had suddenly gone extremely dry. She washed it down with the coffee. "Did you tell Dad?"

"About the Comanches, not about you."

His eyes were dark, disturbing, waiting for her response. She shifted uncomfortably. She looked away but saw nothing except the black humps of trees against the lighter darkness of the sky. "All right."

"You shouldn't have come, Roséanne," he said quietly, his intense gaze deepening. Then his raw features softened and he smiled faintly. "But I'm awfully glad you did."

Her smile disarmed him and he drew her into his embrace. The softness of her breasts pressed into his hardness and sent a pleasant shudder through his body. Once again he wondered if he should abandon his search for Cotton. Yet he knew if he did, it would always plague him, knowing the man had gotten away with murder. Still this increasing need for Roseanne was outweighing his bitter hostility, and taking precedence in his mind.

The campfire so near danced its warm reflections in her fervent eyes, hollowed her cheeks and accentuated the perfect bone structure of her face. He could easily fathom her thoughts for her eyes were lucid in the faint light of the lambent flame. He felt the kindling of his own fire and he knew she could turn it into a blaze.

She touched his lips with her fingertips and he kissed them. He took her hand and gripped it tightly against his chest. Her eyes closed and he kissed her face, her hair, her neck, taking a moment to revel in the beauty of her contented smile, and her long, black lashes lying softly on her delicate skin browned by the Texas sun. She sensed his observation and opened her eyes. He saw passion in their blue depths, the same passion pounding through his own body, beating at his insides like ocean waves beating a rocky coast. Her arms encircled his neck, drawing him closer. She wanted him as badly as he wanted her. And somehow, even without words, he felt a bond between them that would always make it so.

He held her tighter in his embrace. His lips sought

hers and were met by a concurrent hunger. They molded together into the curves of each other's bodies, locked in love.

After a time, Tyler pulled up the blanket and covered them, keeping Roseanne in the curve of his arm. She drifted off to sleep but Tyler lay awake, thinking about the intense, almost painful need he felt for union with Roseanne.

This need for Roseanne grew from some deep, hidden point within him that he realized he had never glimpsed before. He knew now that there were degrees of love, and he wondered if, like himself, she was just now discovering the full magnitude of a complete physical and mental joining. There had been no one else for her; he had taken her virginity. But he had loved before, and it was never like this. It scared him.

He pulled her closer. He never wanted to let her go, not even temporarily. Somehow he felt that if he did, he might never hold her again.

Chapter 7

April–May 1862

TYLER AND ROSEANNE CRESTED A hill and caught up to the herd. Below them, in a grassy meadow, the cattle churned in restless commotion. Beyond them, and to the west, the rolling hills once again undulated upward, and on those hills, moving slowly and cautiously, a dozen Comanches descended through the trees toward William McVey and his vaqueros.

With the Civil War taking most of the men and soldiers of Texas, only a few troops defended the scattered military outposts and thus the remaining settlers. The Comanches were virtually unopposed and turned central Texas into a disaster area, killing hundreds of settlers and burning their homes. Yet this success had been offset by the great losses the Comanche tribes suffered in the 1849 cholera epidemic brought through Texas by the hordes racing for California's gold. The Comanches also suffered from a low birthrate, a problem they chose to overcome by abducting young white women, then raffling them off to their young chiefs.

Yet the braves were matched, if not exceeded in

number, by McVey's vaqueros so their advance was seemingly friendly in nature. McVey moved to the front of the herd and waited for the Comanches, his riders close, tending to the milling longhorns. At the same time they were ready for a sign of impending attack.

Tyler quickly moved into cover at first sight of the Indians and he and Roseanne now hid in a thick stand of trees above the herd. Roseanne felt his tension and apparently his bay did too for it shifted nervously beneath him. He studied the scene below, debating what to do next. He was afraid to leave Roseanne there alone in case there were more Comanches about, but he was also afraid to take her into full view of the Indians, just in case they *weren't* aware of her presence.

Finally he decided. "Roseanne, put your hair up under your sombrero, put your serape on, follow next to me and then move around the herd slowly as if you were one of the cowboys."

She did as he suggested, no questions asked; she had no desire to be left alone.

Tyler moved his mount toward McVey, matching the pace of the Comanches, and reined in next to him. McVey kept his eyes on the braves now forming a line several hundred feet away. Their leader moved forward. McVey kept his eyes on him but spoke to Tyler. "They're a bit far south. Must be Kwahadi. Where you been?"

"Looking out after your best interests." He avoided upsetting McVey with the truth. "You're right about them being Kwahadi."

"Wonder what they want."

"Whatever it is, give it to 'em."

Simultaneously Tyler and McVey nudged their

horses. The animals moved forward slowly, sensing the tension of their riders, leery of the advancing red-man. Twenty feet from the Comanche, who had already brought his pony to a standstill, they pulled rein.

The Comanche spoke in broken English. "Many cattle. Where you take?"

"Colorado," McVey replied simply.

The Indian nodded his head, then raised one arm in an encompassing gesture of the land. "All this. Our land. White man take."

McVey's horse kicked its belly trying to chase away a fly. The bellowing longhorns and the creaking saddle leather beneath the shifting horses were all that broke the uneasy silence. Both Tyler and McVey wondered what kind of answer they could give to such an irrefutable statement.

"We go north to the gold mines. The men there need beef." McVey wasn't sure how much the Comanche understood, but he didn't know how else to tell him. He knew a little of the Comanche language but not enough to carry on much of a conversation.

"So do Indian. Our game"—he paused and looked out over the land and waved his hand futilely—"goes when white man comes."

McVey and Tyler knew he was building up to something. He looked at them intently. Then suddenly broke out in his native tongue. McVey couldn't follow the rapid speech, but was surprised when Tyler responded. The two of them continued back and forth. McVey knew they were negotiating. He figured the Indian wanted beef before his braves would let them pass. McVey could detect an occasional word, but by their tones alone and the anger flashing in the Indian's eyes, he knew a quarrel was ensuing. Finally, he said,

"What does he want, Tyler? If he wants a few beef, we can spare them."

Tyler kept his eyes on the brave, but the Indian spoke, answering William McVey's question. "Woman. I want woman."

Tyler was hoping to keep the Indian speaking in his own tongue, but he understood McVey's question and had responded. Now there was no way to avoid McVey finding out about Roseanne right now. Damn it. He should not have underestimated the Indians. He had known they had been watching them all for days.

Tyler answered in English so McVey could understand. "No, the woman is mine."

"I give you many horses for her. Pretty. Bring us many sons."

Tyler was adamant and secretly worried that he was going to have to kill this greedy Comanche brave. "My woman. My sons." He pointed to himself, his voice stern.

McVey's consternation came out in a blurt. "What in the hell are you two talking about, Tyler?"

Tyler studied the Indian's set jawline. "He wants Roseanne."

"What?" McVey spluttered. "But—"

"She's here, Bill. I didn't want you to find out quite like this. She's been following us."

"Jesus." He sounded sick. "How long?"

"Later. I'll tell you later. Now we just have to convince this gentleman here that Roseanne is worth more than his ponies."

The Indian caught a few of their words. "You trade woman. Give you many ponies."

"No."

The Indian's irritation mounted and he broke out in

his native tongue again. Tyler answered him and another negotiation was under way. Finally the Indian's eyes narrowed but they scrutinized Tyler thoroughly. Slowly he turned his horse around, twisting his neck back over his shoulder at Tyler, a cold, fearful look in his black eyes. Then suddenly he kicked his pony into a gallop.

"Tell the vaqueros to cut out fifty head of cattle." Tyler said.

"What about Roseanne?"

"I talked him out of her."

"How?" McVey wondered how he had miraculously managed that without a battle.

"I did. That's all that matters."

Tyler turned his horse back to the herd. McVey followed. A vaquero rode up next to them and McVey relayed the order. He and Tyler watched while the men cut out the cattle. It was some time before McVey spoke.

"All right, Tyler. How long have you known Roseanne was following us?"

He let out a breath. "For days," he said quietly, keeping his eyes on the cattle.

"And you didn't tell me. Why?"

"You could have taken her home, but it wouldn't have done any good. She had her mind made up she wasn't going to stay alone at the ranch any longer. She wants to see Denver and be part of the excitement. She would have found another way to get there."

McVey pushed his hat back and kneaded his forehead. "She must have been awful sick of things to take a chance like this. I should have paid more attention to her needs."

"Put yourself in her place, Bill."

He nodded. "Yes, I know. I've thought of it. I guess I was just hoping she'd find a man and get married and then—"

"And then you wouldn't have to worry about her any longer?"

"Don't be so damn crass."

"It's the truth. Damn it, Bill. Her time will come to settle down with a family. In the meantime, let her get that restlessness out of her system."

"And in the meantime she could get killed, too."

"She could get killed at your ranch in Texas."

"Why are you defending her?" Tyler was silent while he contemplated the answer to that question, but William McVey didn't wait for his answer. "Is that where you've been going at night?"

There was no concealing it. "Yes."

McVey was silent for several minutes, but he found himself easily accepting the implication. There was little he could do. In the distance the vaqueros cut and counted out the cattle. The Comanches waited patiently. "Will they be back for more?"

"I doubt it."

"They wanted Roseanne," McVey said. "I didn't think that Indian would settle for less."

"In *his* mind he didn't settle for less. A woman is of little consequence when you speak in terms of ponies or cattle. But he was no fool, I'll give him that. It took that many head to make the bastard happy. He knew better than to open up a battle over her. They were outnumbered."

Tyler sounded confident and McVey gave him a curious look and saw his faint smile. His own dry lips parted into a quizzical half-grin. "What did you say to him anyway, Tyler?"

"Well, I think he thought I was a little touched to refuse ten head of fine ponies for a woman. He couldn't quite understand that. Then I told him that if he came back and tried to steal her, I'd track him down, stake him out, cut off his greatest pride, and stuff it in his mouth for him to choke on."

McVey's lips twisted together tightly in an effort to keep from choking. He chuckled. "Speaking on their terms, huh?"

"It's the only way."

In the distance the vaqueros turned the cattle over to the Indians and the two men watched as the braves drove them off over the hill. Instantly the vaqueros let the herd of restless longhorns move ahead; to hold them too long in their nervous state could be asking for a stampede.

Then McVey saw his daughter, even in her disguise. He recognized the gray. He rested his arms over the saddle horn and watched her work the cattle along with the man. "You told the Indian she was your woman."

Tyler heard the question in McVey's statement. He replied quietly. "Yes, that's what I told him."

"And is it true?" William McVey asked the inevitable question.

Tyler pushed his hat off his forehead in a frustrated gesture, then almost immediately pulled it down again against the sun. "Yes, Bill," he continued in a low voice. "I care a great deal for Roseanne, for what little that may be worth to you."

McVey felt his insides shake, but the tension eased some at Tyler's concluding statement. He liked Tyler, and apparently his feelings for Roseanne were in the right place. He couldn't help but remember himself and Catharine when they had been young and first in love. Roseanne was a woman, Tyler a man. Therefore, they were both old enough to be responsible for their actions. Yet Tyler had made a commitment to find Walt Cotton.

"What about the man who led that gang in California?"

"If I cross his path again, I'll go after him, but I'm tired of following trails that have no tracks."

"I didn't think you would give it up so easily. Three months ago you were determined to find him."

Yes, he had been, but sometimes it seemed so long ago, other times just yesterday. Sometimes his vendetta seemed useless, sometimes it fired him. Now, however, his main need was to be near Roseanne. The strings of her love pulled on him stronger than the frayed strands of revenge.

"Of course I can't just forget it," Tyler replied.

"And what will it do to Roseanne if you get yourself killed?"

Tyler's patience gave out. He glared at McVey. "Any of us could get killed before we ever get to Denver."

"But it gets you quicker if you go looking for it."

Tyler thought McVey understood, but it was different now that Roseanne was involved. Tyler nudged his horse. "Come on. It's time you talked to your daughter."

Roseanne saw her father and Tyler riding toward her. The herd was moving once again, the vaqueros bordering the long line. Roseanne pulled the gray away from the herd. She moved slowly, reluctant to face her father, wondering if he would think of some way to send her back. She was a woman now, but he was still her father, and it was hard to disobey a man you had spent your entire life obeying. He had never been mean to her—quite to the contrary, he had doted on her, but she had the feeling from the strained expression on his face that now she had taken one step too far. Yet he could not, she told herself, stop her or make her go back. She was an adult. She could and would do as she pleased. He could tell her she was wrong, but he could tell her no more. She straightened her back and pulled the gray to a halt. Tyler moved past McVey and stopped his horse sideways, between them, like the staff of an arrow between the two points, pitting himself against neither one, but placing himself in the middle.

Roseanne acknowledged him. "Dad."

His voice was tight. "Roseanne." He wasn't happy that she was here, but he had to bear in mind what Tyler had told him. He could see now that he shouldn't have tried to stop her in the first place. She had grown her wings years ago, and now she had finally flown from the nest. He scanned her attire, the huge sombrero, the serape, the pants, the boots. From a distance, even the most discerning eye would not have been able to see the woman beneath the clothes. How then had the Comanches seen through her disguise?

"I may as well say this," McVey began resignedly. "I don't like the fact that you followed us, and I'm not happy with Tyler for keeping it a secret"—he laid his gaze on Chanson—"but I know now his reasons and I guess I can understand them. Now"—he pulled his horse around—"let's get going with the herd. It's still a long way to Colorado."

* * *

In the Sangre de Cristo Mountains of north central
New Mexico lie the headwaters of the Pecos River.
From there it flows seven hundred miles southward
until it empties into the Rio Grande. Four days from
the Devils they hit the Pecos and followed it northward. They would stay on its course until they passed
Fort Sumner.

For countless days they traveled. Two thousand cattle in endless motion. A dozen men, McVey, Tyler,
and Roseanne in saddles that never grew cold; Castillo
cooking in pots that barely got washed. Days too long;
short, restless nights; half-sleeps. The midnight witch-
ing hour when the cattle stirred, half-awakened by a
sixth sense that summoned them to be up as one day
merged into another. And then the mornings dis-
rupting the precious sleep; horses neighing and snort-
ing; longhorns bawling; bones and joints popping; the
crackle of fires; the rattle of pots and pans; sizzling
bacon; bitter coffee; and finally the chain harness
swinging against the chuck wagon wheels leading the
way from camp.

The cattle made good time up the Pecos. Soon they
had left behind the lush greenery of the hill country
and had moved into the arid regions of west Texas. It
was a different world, vivid in its contrast with its barren hills, dusty bluffs, infinite vastness, and naked
skies.

With no problems, they moved from Texas into
New Mexico Territory. On the edge of the Llano
Estacado, or Staked Plain, the broad Pecos valley
stretched westward for two hundred and fifty miles,
fringed by mesas, canyons, and cliffs. It was at the
southernmost edge of this joining that the herd

stopped at a place known as Red Bluff for their midday rest.

Roseanne was weary as she unsaddled her horse. Her father had thought she would stay with the chuck wagon, but she preferred the solitude of moving behind the longhorns, even if she spent most of her time eating dust. Besides, Ramon Castillo needed no one or wanted no one interfering with his cooking.

She swatted dust from her clothes until her tired arms gave up the futile attempt. She moved to the line at the chuck wagon and picked up a plate. The vaqueros all held her in the highest regard and made room for her. Most of them were her friends since she had been a child and they did not mind her presence at all. They enjoyed taking her under their wings, and they tried to give her the easiest jobs and keep her from danger. Yet they had gained a trust and respect for her, as they had her father, when they realized that she did not use her feminine wiles to get out of doing things, and she took the rotten jobs along with the rest of them with no complaints.

There were, however, several cowboys, Henry Grehan and his friends, who chose to make things difficult for her. If anything, they shirked their own duties to see if the boss's daughter could take the extra load or tolerate the behind-the-back snickers and the crude jokes about her and Tyler. They blamed her for McVey losing fifty head of cattle and insinuated that she wasn't worth the loss.

Grehan had brazenly made passes at her after the men had discovered Tyler had been spending nights in her camp, even though they couldn't have known the extent of the relationship. Roseanne had rebuffed his repulsive advances only to get more sneering comments about her character. She avoided him, being a bit afraid of him, not only because of what he said, but because he seemed to be able to see right through her clothes. But he was obviously intimidated by Tyler and was always careful not to say anything derogatory to her when Tyler, her father, or Diego were around.

In the depths of Grehan's colorless eyes was pure evil and cruelty. He seemed to carry venom for the sake of its taste, and she guessed that someday that venom would kill him.

As for her father, his first anger had quickly abated and now she knew he was enjoying her company, spending hours riding by her side, talking or just being in silent, relaxed company. She had to admit that she had grown much closer to him. She was seeing him as the man he was, not just as her father.

She glanced around now, wondering where Tyler was. He had been careful of her reputation and had only on occasion taken the privilege of stealing a few kisses. At night she unrolled her bedroll away from the others, and her father appointed himself her guardian, stretching his bedroll out ten feet or so from hers. Tyler stayed with the other men, although he had admitted to her privately that it was killing him to be so close to her and be able to do nothing about it. She felt the same way about him, but they were at least together and spent much of the day riding or eating together.

The line moved swiftly forward as Castillo dished up his specialty—frijoles and flour tortillas. Roseanne gladly accepted hers for she was exceedingly hungry, as always. She found a spot away from the others and settled onto the ground. In seconds, however, she was joined by Diego Padilla.

"May I join you, señorita?" he asked politely, displaying a large smile in his handsome, leather-tanned face.

"Of course, Diego," she consented, appreciating his friendship.

He lowered his slim frame easily to the ground and sat cross-legged. She guessed him to be in his forties, but his flashing black eyes seemed much younger. They ate in silence for several minutes but Diego was aware of Roseanne's continual searching eyes.

"He is with the herd, señorita. Some of us will trade him and the others off as soon as we have eaten." He smiled at her surprise that he should know her thoughts. He shrugged his shoulders as he worked the beans around onto his spoon. "Who else would you look for but Señor Chanson?"

She smiled, accepting his intuitiveness. She vaguely wondered, as she studied him, how he managed to keep his long, drooping moustache from getting covered with food, but he avoided it very neatly.

He felt her eyes and he said nonchalantly, "You wonder about me, don't you?"

"What do you mean?"

He pushed his sombrero back with his spoon then stuck the utensil back into his beans. "You wonder about me because I have always been just one of your papa's vaqueros, and now you are seeing me for the first time."

"I suppose you're right, Diego. This trail drive has given me more to think about than I was accustomed to."

"It is true, but you do not regret coming?"

"No, although I know some of the men aren't comfortable with me around."

He smiled broadly, then dipped his head forward in a slight chuckle, the sombrero covering his face from her view. "Yes, señorita," he looked back into the pools of her blue eyes and thought she was a very beautiful woman indeed. "The men have to watch their language when you are close by, but it is good for them. A woman's presence tends to encourage civilization in men."

"You don't wish I had stayed home, then?"

"Not I, señorita. I have always enjoyed the spring and the flowers and the warmth on my back, and I have always enjoyed the sight of a beautiful woman. She is much like the flowers. A bright spot in the desert." He complimented her graciously with his articulate English laced with its Spanish accent.

"Why have you always stayed with my father and never gone out on your own?" She was curious and hoped he wouldn't be offended by her rather bold question.

"Eh"—he waved his spoon in an inconsequential gesture—"I like to ride my horse. I like to spend all my days and nights beneath the sun and the stars. It is simple. I do not want the responsibility. I think I like to be free a little too much."

Roseanne laughed. "I think I understand, Diego."

"It is just as well that I am like this," he continued. "Men like your father are the leaders, the doers. Men like me were born to help, to follow men like him. It is the way the world balances out. The problems arise when men like Henry Grehan choose to revolt against men like your father. They do it because they are weak and they hate anyone with strength and power and position. They can only succeed in numbers. Alone they are worms on the ground—spineless. They blame their failures on others' successes, thinking they are being held down by the powerful foot of the Big Man, while all the time, it is their own inadequacies and weaknesses that keep them on their knees.''

Roseanne considered Diego's words. Was Grehan's hatred for her transmitted then from her father, and to Tyler because of her father's approval of him? Yes, it could be. And in Grehan's eyes Tyler was a murderer and therefore it made William McVey his cohort. It confirmed Grehan's belief that ''Big Men'' like her father took what they wanted, rather than working for it. It confirmed his belief that men like himself could only get ahead by going against all the William McVeys of the world.

''Tell me, Diego,'' Roseanne asked softly. ''Have you noticed Grehan's belligerence lately? Do you think he could cause my father some problems before we reach Colorado?''

Diego scooped up the last of his beans and wiped his plate clean with the flour tortilla. After he had consumed the bread and wiped his lips with the back of his hand he stood up and looked down at her. ''Who can say, Señorita Roseanna? But I think he is a man one should never turn his back on.''

Diego deposited his plate and cup at the chuck wagon, and then straddled his horse. She watched him move around the herd on an easy lope, a man born to the saddle, a man who wanted no other life. She finished her meal in silence, glad that she was no longer riding alone, eating dried beef and her own nasty coffee. She slept well at night now, and she did not fear every mile during the day. But now she thought of the seed Diego had planted in her mind about Grehan. Or maybe she had planted it and he had only watered it. Anyway it was beginning to grow.

She glanced to her left where a number of cowboys sat in the sparse grass eating, making small talk. Grehan was among them. Even while he ate, he seemed to harbor evil thoughts. There were men like him, men like those that had killed Tyler's family, men whose minds moved naturally from the ways of the light to the ways of the dark. Godless men who wanted it no other way.

Grehan looked up, sensing her gaze. She hurriedly looked away, but it was too late. With a crooked smile on his unpleasant face, he said something to his cronies, then stood up and moved toward her in a swaggering walk. She thought perhaps if she ignored him, he would go away or walk past her, but he stopped directly in front of her and leaned on one hip, assuming a cocky air. Finally she glanced upward but shriveled beneath his lubricious eyes.

"Finally regretting you tagged along on this trail drive?" he asked insolently.

She studied him a moment, wondering what he thought he could prove by making conversation with her. It was plain to see his intentions were not friendly like Padilla's. "Why should I regret it?"

"The only woman with a bunch of men." Somehow she heard a lascivious connotation in his tone. "Doesn't seem like you'd like the lack of privacy. After all, you should have stayed hid. That way you and Chanson could have kept on seeing each other intimately." He stressed the final word snidely.

"Your old man wouldn't have found out until Denver."

Roseanne had leaped to her feet midway through his narrative and by the time he had managed the last word her hand swung high and slapped him hard across his bearded face. Still she stung with red rage and she hit him again, only this time he grabbed her wrist and twisted it backward, threatening to snap it.

"What's the matter?" His lips curled wickedly as his gaze slid suggestively to her breasts. "Don't you like to hear the truth?"

"You scum!" She spat.

"Then it is the truth. We all wondered where Chanson was going nights, but when you showed up it was easy enough to guess. He's just like a wolf on the scent of blood. He could probably smell you miles away."

"Let go of me."

He ignored her hoarse command. "Why should I fall at your feet like all those spics do? You're nothing. You know what I think? I think you followed us because you wanted some action, and I don't mean Indians, gold, or shitty-assed longhorns. Chanson fell for you, but the rest of us won't. Of course"—he paused and bent her wrist back farther, forcing her up closer to him—"you might be interested in someone besides Chanson to satisfy your . . . er . . . needs."

Suddenly Grehan was pulled off his feet with a jerk. Tyler had him by the scruff of the neck and yanked him around. Before Grehan could react, Tyler sent a fist smashing square into his teeth. Roseanne heard them shatter and break, blood spurted, and Grehan's head snapped backward. He stumbled and tried to catch his balance. Tyler grabbed the front of his shirt

and brought him back up, sending another blow into
his jaw. His head sagged. Tyler hit him one more time
in the stomach and released him. He doubled over,
crumpled to his knees, weaved, then plunged forward
onto his face in the dirt, unconscious.

Tyler turned to the others who had risen now with
half-chewed food in their mouths which they hastily
swallowed, obviously with an effort. "I hope Grehan
is the only one of you who thinks that way. McVey
might fire you, but I'll kill you—any of you—if you do
anything besides your jobs."

One of the men felt he should defend himself.
"Well, that woman shouldn't have come along on this
drive." He spoke in a grating voice. "It's no place for
a woman. She's just asking for trouble. Who's to say
Grehan isn't right. Maybe she's just looking for trouble."

"She's here and she's going to Denver so you'd better get used to it. She's not complicating your lives or
your jobs in any way. She's carrying her own weight,
in case none of you noticed."

"Because of her we could have gotten ourselves
killed back in Texas with those Comanches."

"Well, you didn't get yourselves killed," Tyler replied unsympathetically.

"What's going on here?" William McVey entered
the conversation, quietly pulling his horse up within
earshot.

Grehan was slowly coming to, groveling for consciousness, spitting blood and bits of teeth. The others
dodged McVey's question. "Well?" McVey demanded.

"It's because of me." Roseanne spoke up.

"Is she right?" McVey looked down at them.

They hemmed and hawed, shuffled, ducked their heads. McVey had a notion to fire all of them, but he needed them to get the herd to Denver. He might be able to do it without them, but losing three men would short him, and extra guns were always welcome in case of Indian troubles. Finally he knew he would have to appease them. Two of them were good hands with the cattle, but somewhere down the line during this drive they were turning cold and malicious. He glanced down at Henry Grehan on the ground and without being told he knew he was the cause.

"I'll be honest with you, boys," he said. "I wasn't thrilled about my daughter coming along either, but she's here and she's helping move these cattle. Now the way I see it, she's not causing anybody any trouble. All of you just get back on your horses and get back to work."

He turned his horse, not waiting for any objections, and headed for the chuck wagon. The men did as they were told, having little other choice. Grehan finally found his senses and staggered after his friends. Tyler turned to Roseanne. He wanted to kill Grehan for touching her, for threatening her. It reminded him too much of the incident with Carlotta. Grehan was a man who might not live until they reached Denver.

Tyler took a step toward Roseanne. Most of the men had gone back to the herd, and he drew her into his arms and held her close for a long time. When he finally let go of her, he felt the embers blazing to fire inside him. "Talk to me while I eat?" he asked and slipped an arm around her small waist. Together they walked to the chuck wagon. Tyler filled his plate and Roseanne got a fresh cup of coffee. They settled themselves beneath a tree on the banks of the Pecos. The others were circling the cattle while they had their midday rest and water.

"If he causes trouble, we'll send him packing," Tyler said.

Roseanne knew her presence was causing problems for her father. However, she had thought things had been going smoothly up until now. Still she felt that the only ones who resented the boss's daughter intruding upon their male domain were Grehan and his buddies. The others had accepted her from the beginning.

"Maybe I should leave the drive when we get to Fort Sumner," she said resignedly.

Tyler looked over at her, surprise lighting his eyes. He hadn't expected her to give up so easily or give in just because of Grehan. "If you leave, then I will too," he replied adamantly.

"Dad needs you." Her tone held a hint of objection, but she was pleased that he wanted to stay with her.

"And I need you," he said softly, resting his hand on her leg.

Worried, she stood up and began pacing. Even though she wore men's clothing she was still attractive to him. Her long hair hung loose now, at least for the moment. Behind her the water made gurgling sounds and he remembered the night in the Llano beneath the moon and he fought to keep from taking her in his arms.

"Come and sit down, Roseanne." She stopped and looked dubiously at him. "Please."

She gave into his pleading eyes and sat down next to him again. He looked out over the water and the perfect sky, disturbed only by a few gauzy clouds. "I'm afraid Grehan will do something stupid because of me and then someone will get killed."

"Grehan is a stupid man. Can you expect anything else from the likes of him?"

"I'm serious, Tyler."

"And so am I." He hesitated over his dinner and his gaze stretched across the herd to Grehan. "If he touches you again, I'll kill him."

Roseanne heard the anger that he had physically expressed earlier. Was it that easy for him to kill a man? Or was he being overly cautious because of Carlotta? She began hesitantly, wondering if she should bring up the incident. "What happened to your wife . . . it's highly unlikely that it would happen again . . . to me."

Tyler had lost his appetite for Castillo's beans but he ate them anyway while he thought about what she said. Of course it was true. The odds were against it, but still it lingered in the back of his mind. He wondered again if he had only been fooling himself when he had thought he could settle down, knowing Walt Cotton was still alive somewhere. He had never mentioned the rape because it would not be a pleasant thing for her to hear, but maybe if she knew the truth then she would understand why he could not take men like Henry Grehan lightly.

Tyler finished the last of the frijoles. He sat the plate on the ground next to him. He glanced over his shoulder to see if anyone was watching, but only Castillo was in sight. Even McVey had gone ahead with the herd. He put an arm around Roseanne's shoulder and drew her near. "I'd better get back to the herd."

Roseanne could see he plainly didn't want to even think about the death of Carlotta, let alone talk about it. Suddenly she felt small, dwarfed by the shadow of a memory. "Yes, me too." She reluctantly glanced in the direction of the moving herd.

"You know," he said, his tone lighter now, "no one expects you to help drive the cattle. You could stay with the chuck wagon."

She shook her head. "After today I think there would be some people who *would* expect it and would probably get downright nasty if I decided to behave like a lady."

"They're getting paid for their work."

"Yes, but with the gold getting ever nearer, I imagine there are a good many of them wondering why they are working for twenty dollars a month when they could make their fortunes in the mines."

"Some of them may not go back to Texas. Gold has a way of getting next to people."

"But not you?" she said teasingly.

"I can't say I'm immune." He didn't wish for the conversation to go any further. He was interested only in her lips, which he now took in the provocative hold of his own. Their touch was too soft, too warm, too sweet. Hungrily he pressed his mouth to hers, slipping his tongue through her lips easily to sample the pleasant recesses there. Finally he pulled his head away, his conscience telling him he'd better stop.

He ran a finger longingly down her smooth cheek. "I think I should have kept you hidden. Sleeping without you is driving me crazy."

She thought of Carlotta again and wondered how she compared, where she fit in Tyler's heart. Then she admitted, "It's not fun for me either." She laid a hand lightly on his thigh and felt the steely muscles tense beneath her hand. "I lie awake and watch you near the fire, wishing I could be with you."

He took her hand in his and together they stood up. He drew her into his arms. "Meet me tonight, Rose-anne. I'll tell you where after supper."

She saw what she hoped was love in his eyes as his lips brushed hers. "Yes, Tyler," she replied. "I'll be waiting."

Chapter 8

May 1862

THE NIGHTS WERE STILL WARM BUT not like they had been in Texas. Roseanne shivered and nestled deeper in Tyler's arms. His naked body was hot and its heat helped to warm her. He pulled the blanket over her shoulder then beneath it his warm hands rubbed her skin to chase away the chill.

"We need a fire," he said absently as he moved his hand to brush away the dark strands of her hair that had fallen over her shoulder.

"The others would see."

He held her closer and she tilted her head back on his arm. "I should be going back," she said as she looked into his eyes.

"You've been tense since you met me tonight," he replied. "Have I lost my charm so quickly?" His tone was light, but deep inside he wondered.

She laughed softly. "No, that's not it at all." She wondered if she dared express this love she felt. Would she lose him if he thought she sought to put ties on him?

He held her for a few silent moments but the tense-

153

ness returned to her body. He broke into her personal battle of the mind and heart. "You're worried about what the others will think if they wake up and find us both gone," he said perceptively.

She put her head back against his chest. The curly, dark hair tickled her face. She rearranged the springy curls in a vain gesture, then admitted, "Yes, I guess so."

"Maybe it would be better if we didn't meet again this way," he offered, knowing how cruel men like Grehan could be, how inconsiderate.

His arms comforted her. She knew she belonged here, locked in his love, but the circumstances sent frustrating, confusing thoughts through her head. "I want to be with you, Tyler."

Her skin was like silk beneath his hand, and he realized that his own was calloused and rough but she didn't seem to notice. He wanted her with him forever, but not like this. He wanted a soft bed instead of the hard ground. He wanted her for his wife, not merely his lover. But he had no right to ask her to be his wife. He had nothing to offer her—no home, no security, and he had an unfinished job that would take him from her sooner or later for an indefinite length of time. So perhaps for now it was better not to say these things that were on his mind.

His hand gently tipped her head back until he could see into her eyes, sparkling from the silver reflections of the stars and gibbous moon. Slowly he bent his head until his lips closed over hers. He could give her no promises, but he could give her his love.

When they were camped a few miles away from Fort Sumner, McVey was approached by some men

from the garrison wanting cattle. McVey couldn't
spare many after the fifty he had given to the Indians,
but he gave them a few head. Tyler and Diego cut the
cattle away from the herd and went along to the military post to deliver them.

It was dark as they headed back to camp. About a
quarter of a mile from the herd, Tyler spotted what appeared to be a campfire in a dry wash. Diego saw it too
and simultaneously they reined their horses in.

"Could it be Indians, señor?" Diego asked.

"Possibly. I think I'll take a closer look."

"I will go with you."

Tyler and Diego circled the wash and came up on its
back side. They left their horses below the hill and
worked their way on foot closer to the campfire. They
saw two men, talking and drinking, not being any too
quiet.

"Why do you think they are here?" Diego asked.

"They could be drifters on their way to the goldfields."

"Yes," Diego replied slowly but even the one word
revealed his doubt. He continued, "Maybe I am just a
suspicious man by nature, or maybe I have learned to
be that way, but these men—they do not look like men
who want to dig for gold. They look like men who
would rather let someone else do the digging."

Tyler didn't like to prejudge people, but like Diego
Padilla, he had learned to tell the good from the bad
practically at first sight. "I think you may be right, Diego. But now I wonder if it's the goldfields they seek,
or if there's something closer that could be more interesting to them."

"Sí. That is what I am thinking. The cattle are not

far away. Maybe they mean to cause trouble for Señor McVey, no?''

Tyler considered it seriously. He knew it was a problem; outlaws would come upon a herd and would threaten to stampede it if the drovers didn't give them money or cattle in payment.

"What do we do?" Diego asked.

Tyler knew he could ride into their camp, sit for a cup of coffee, and casually inquire about the nature of their business or their destination, but something told him they would not take kindly to a nosy visitor. "I'm going to try and get closer, see if I can hear their conversation."

"Be careful amigo. If they hear you, they will shoot first and ask questions later."

Tyler glanced at Diego and saw concern etched into the familiar sagacious smile beneath his dark, drooping moustache. "Don't worry, Diego. I'm always careful."

Tyler moved down the hill into the wash. There was very little growth; the area was void of anything but brush and a few scraggly trees. The place the strangers sought shelter was about the best they could do under the circumstances, but it amounted to a "hollow" that could barely keep the wind off their heads. Tyler edged to within fifty feet of their campfire and used the darkness for cover. They seemed to have been drinking heavily because their voices carried plainly through the still night.

At first, their conversation gave him no insight into who they were or where they were going. After a silence between them, one spoke, and Tyler came to attention.

"That Gregory guy was supposed to meet us in Santa Fe. I wonder why he didn't show."

A deep voice came back through the night. "Cotton said Gregory might be avoiding the law and may have to go on to South Park if he ran into trouble."

"He probably got himself killed."

"He may still show."

"We don't even know him."

"Cotton does, and if he says he can be trusted then he can be."

"Yeah, but do we really need him?"

"It never hurts to have a good gun when you take a stage that's loaded with gold."

The men fell silent again. Tyler's adrenaline was flowing. *Cotton.* Could it be *Walt* Cotton? He waited, hoping to hear more, but the conversation shifted to another topic and then stopped altogether. One man rose and threw some sticks on the fire, then they both stretched out on their bedrolls. It was early yet, but they either wanted an early start in the morning or they had been riding hard and were tired.

Tyler made his way back to Diego.

"It is about time you have returned, amigo," Diego said. "I was beginning to wonder if the darkness had swallowed you. These men, what are they about?"

"They're on their way to the goldfields. They have a plan that they think will make them rich, specifically a stagecoach robbery."

"Ah," Diego said, nodding understandingly, "but what good is 'rich' to men who live to steal and kill? What do they do with the money? I tell you, Tyler. They spend it on whiskey and women."

Chanson nodded as they moved quietly to their horses. They did not step into their stirrups until they had put more distance between themselves and the two men.

"They had no interest in the cattle?" Diego inquired.

"None that they mentioned," Tyler replied. "They were obviously interested only in getting to Colorado."

After a time Diego glanced at Tyler and even in the dark he could sense the man's tenseness and the deep thoughts going on in his head. "What is it, amigo? Did these men have more to say?"

Tyler met Diego's shrewd eyes. "It was a name I heard. I think they may know the man I've been searching for."

"Will you follow them, then?" The information came as no surprise to the Mexican.

Tyler looked ahead at the dark trail. Up ahead they could hear the cattle bellowing. He had said he wouldn't hunt Cotton any longer, only if he crossed his path. He had wanted to ask Roseanne to marry him. But he needed to know if the man they spoke of was the one he sought. It would eat at him if he didn't follow this lead. "I don't want to, Diego, but I think I have to."

"It is the Señorita Roseanna that makes you unsure?"

Tyler nodded.

Diego could see the campfires ahead now and the occasional dark figure of a cowboy passing in front of the faint light. They would be at the camp in less than one hundred yards. "Do not worry about her, amigo. She will have her father to look out after her, and I will also see that no harm comes to her."

Tyler looked over at Diego Padilla, wondering

about him, yet knowing he was sincere. He could be trusted. Even more, he seemed to understand all that went on in a man's mind, whether he himself thought that way or not. "Thank you, Diego. This is something I have to do."

"Tell her. I think she will understand—although," he added skeptically, "she will be afraid you will get yourself killed."

Tyler chuckled. "You seem to understand women."

"Ah." He smiled broadly. "I do, amigo. I have had a few in my life. They are all different, but they are all the same."

McVey met them as they rode into camp; Roseanne was right behind him. He watched while they alighted and unsaddled their horses, then said, "What took you so long? We were beginning to worry."

Diego took Tyler's horse. "I will tend to him, amigo. Tell Señor McVey what you have found."

Tyler exchanged understanding glances with Padilla. "Thank you, Diego."

McVey, Tyler, and Roseanne went to one of the campfires and sat down. Tyler poured himself a cup of coffee and they settled around the warmth of the blaze. Tyler looked at Roseanne. She was so lovely. Could he really leave her now? "There were some men not far from here," he said. "We were afraid they might be cattle thieves, so I got close enough to listen to them. They are heading for the goldfields."

"Is that all?" McVey sounded relieved. "By the expression on your face I was afraid there was more." He turned to the pot and poured himself some coffee. Roseanne's gaze bore into him. If anyone could read his mind and his soul she could.

"There *is* more, Bill," Tyler added quietly, his eyes locking with Roseanne's.

Roseanne's eyes sparked in response and gradually smoldered into acceptance. It was as though she expected something such as this. But surely she couldn't know he would be leaving her at first light? She didn't even know what he was about to say. Or did she?

McVey had turned back around and Tyler felt his waiting gaze, but he spoke to Roseanne. "The men mentioned the name of the man I've been hunting. If I follow them, they could lead me to him."

McVey was quiet for a minute, watching the silent exchange between his daughter and Tyler Chanson. "I knew there would come a day when you'd find the trail again. I guess none of us expected it to be so soon," McVey said quietly, regretfully.

Roseanne stood up slowly, as though she were suddenly very tired. How could it have ended so soon? How could she have ever expected it to end otherwise? She moved into the darkness and melted into its protective blackness. Out of sight and out of his reach, she folded her arms over the pain obliterating all of the happiness that had just moments before flowed within her. She looked at the sky, thick with desert stars, and she wanted to laugh at her own foolishness. She should have known better. She should have seen that Tyler had no intentions of giving up his commitment to his first wife. She had hoped, dreamed, prayed, but she should have known better.

She felt the burning tears in her eyes and the tightening in her throat. No! She would not cry. She would never let him know how she felt. He had made no promises. He had uttered no words of love. She had only herself to blame for giving everything to him.

Still, why did he have to be so heartless? Surely he cared for her a bit—just a little bit? Was her judgment of his character and his feelings so totally in error?

Tyler watched Roseanne disappear beyond the light of the campfire. The moment he had hoped to put off forever had come much too quickly and unexpectedly. He put his coffee cup down although he had taken only a sip from it. He stood up and faced William McVey. "The sooner this is over the better."

McVey's eyes narrowed in consideration but he did not judge the decisions of other men. He would probably do the same thing if he had been in Tyler's shoes.

"I know I told you I'd help you get the cattle to Colorado," Tyler began.

McVey cut in. "If you don't follow this lead, you may not get another chance."

Tyler nodded glumly. He was tired of hunting Walt Cotton but he knew he could never rest knowing he could be so close. He turned and left the campfire. He had to talk to Roseanne. He had to make her understand. He had to let her know it did not change how he felt about her in any way.

She was standing by the river, her back to the camp and to him, looking out over the inky water. Its surface shimmered faintly with the silver reflection from the stars. He walked quietly up behind her and slid his arms around her, pulling her tight against his chest. "The Pecos has brought us a long way. We'll be leaving it soon."

She pushed his arms aside and stepped out of his reach. "Isn't this what you had in mind all along?" she asked vehemently.

He took a step toward her but she heard the sound of his boots in the gravel and she moved, once again, beyond him. Helplessly he replied, wondering how he could make her see, "No Roseanne, I didn't have this in mind. I don't want to leave you. I—"

She whirled on him, her dark eyes narrowed in anger and bitter pain. "I don't want to hear your excuses. Do you think I'm blind? I'm no fool, Tyler Chanson. You're leaving for good." She found a level of control for her outburst and she maintained it, tossing her head back in defiance. "But I suppose you were going to tell me that you love me and that you'll come back to me."

He could understand her hurt, but why wouldn't she listen to him? Why was she making it so difficult? He took the steps separating them and grabbed her shoulders, drawing her up off her feet, shaking her a bit as if he could jar some sense into her. He growled in his frustration. "Yes, damn it! That's what I was going to tell you, but I doubt you'd believe me now."

She laughed, a wretched little sound from deep in her throat. "Why should I believe you? How do I know you're not leaving because of me? Because you've had enough of me and this is the easy way out."

"You're wrong, Roseanne." He felt his anger mounting at her refusal to try and understand. "I do love you. I will come back to you."

"Ha!" She wrenched herself free of his grip. "If you loved me you wouldn't leave. You'd forget about your damn revenge and you'd stay here with me. It's just an excuse, Tyler, so you can get on your horse and go. Well go, damn it! I don't ever want to see you again!" She raced away from him and deeper into the night.

He wouldn't let her end it like this. She *would* listen

to him. He strode after her, caught her arm and jerked her roughly around and up against him. If she wouldn't listen to his words maybe she would respond to his touch.

"Leave me alone!" she hissed. "I've had my fill of you."

"Have you?" He grabbed the back of her head with his big hand in an iron grip. "I doubt that." She struggled as his mouth descended to hers and he felt her feeble kicks on his legs. But the heat that fused them together made jelly of her attempts and in seconds she was moaning beneath the power of his possession.

Suddenly she pushed herself away from him, stumbling backward off-balance. She caught herself, but he was coming closer to her again. "Leave me alone," she pleaded.

"Not until I'm done with you. Not until you hear me out."

She couldn't escape him so she stopped her retreat and waited for his inevitable touch. Even in her pain and anger, it could control her, but she fought an inward battle not to give in to him. He drew her, more gently, against his hard length, but she stood ramrod stiff, ungiving, unyielding.

He wrapped his hand around her hair and forced her to look up at him, being careful not to hurt her any more than necessary. "You will listen to me, Roseanne McVey, even if you choose not to believe me. You think I don't have to do this, but I do. Keane and Rayce and I have been hunting the men who killed our father and Kit and my wife for nearly eight years. To quit before the job is finished would make the entire quest pointless. What you and I have shared is something I don't want to forget—or leave behind—but if it's worth a gold nugget it'll be alive when I get back.''

For a moment she believed him and she understood him. But didn't he see what he'd done to her? He had made her a wanton, and he hadn't even offered marriage. She met his hard gaze. God, he could talk as sweet as he could love. He *wouldn't* come back. It was just words. He didn't mean any of it. If he did—if he really loved her—he wouldn't dream of leaving her. He would put the past behind him where it rightfully belonged.

She spoke, her hurt neatly covered with cold contempt. ''I won't wait for you, Tyler, so chase your damn nightmares. Live on your hate and your revenge. I don't believe you for one minute. You've been using me all along. Well, don't think yourself so clever because I've been using you too.''

He released her abruptly, stunned by her hateful words. Before he could stop her she was gone again—this time back to camp. He turned to the river. Why had she refused to believe him? Had he misjudged her emotions so completely? He had felt love in their union, and he could have sworn she did too. Why, weren't her feelings for him strong enough to make her wait for him?

Slowly he let out the air in his lungs that he had been unconsciously holding. The bay was waiting and so was a fresh lead. He walked back to camp and to his belongings. He saddled the bay quickly while William McVey stood by watching.

''Will we see you when this is all behind you?'' The older man asked as he helped tie Tyler's bedroll to the back of the saddle.

Tyler glanced through the night for the first time and

saw Roseanne curled up on her blankets in the distance. "I don't know, Bill."

McVey's eyes followed Chanson's gaze. "She didn't understand?"

Tyler shook his head.

McVey scuffed at some rocks with the toe of his boot and stuffed his hands in his pockets as Tyler boarded his horse. "Women, Ty." He tried to offer some explanation. "She probably just doesn't want to see you go."

"Maybe." He gathered the reins. The bay was eager to be off as it sensed tension and urgency in its master's movements. "I've got to go, Bill."

William McVey nodded his understanding and then touched the brim of his hat in farewell. Tyler nodded a silent good-bye as he looked down at his good friend, then he nudged the bay and it was off on a brisk walk into the darkness. A quarter of a mile from camp Tyler drew the horse up and untied his jacket from behind the cantle. He slipped it on and it alleviated the chill. He wasn't sure why, but suddenly the night had turned cold.

Chapter 9

May 1862

THEY LEFT THE PECOS, FOLLOWED the Canadian River northward, then cut toward the North Canadian and the Cimarron. Directly ahead was the Sierra Grande, a mountain that seemed an intruder among the rolling bare hills, skimpy grasslands, pointed buttes, and the sharp outcroppings of rock. Except for the evergreens that dotted the surface of the Sierra Grande and tumbled down into its canyons, there were no trees, brush, or bushes. The land was desolate.

The days since Fort Sumner had seemed as barren as this land. Roseanne's heart was a greater wasteland than that which surrounded her. She had never experienced so much intense pain, but despite her anguish and bitterness she couldn't help but wonder if Walt Cotton would eventually be the victor in this manhunt of Tyler's.

William McVey rode up alongside her, but it was a moment before she became aware of his presence. He spoke, dissipating her thoughts. "There's a storm brewing in the distance. The cattle could stampede

again. We're going to try and get them around the
north side of the mountain and bunch them there until
this blows over.''

Roseanne glanced over her shoulder and for the first
time saw the huge purple thunderhead building in the
distance. Its course was set directly for them. About a
week ago, the cattle had stampeded when an unthink-
ing Henry Grehan had fired his pistol to kill a rattle-
snake, and they had been jittery ever since. Now the
brewing storm was winding them up tighter. They didn't
need a second excuse to start running. This storm was
going to be a bad one, and it would not miss them.

On the north side of the mountain the area was more
heavily covered with evergreens. The illusion of a
wasteland disappeared. It was a perfect place to bed
the cattle; even the perfect place for a ranch. Not far
away rose an extinct volcano, and near it, traces of
volcanic rocks and outcroppings. In the distance to the
northeast, through an opening in two buttes, appeared
the first snowcapped mountains.

''Is that Colorado, Dad?''

''Those mountains are still days away, but yes, it is
Colorado.''

''I hope you've forgiven me for sneaking away and
following you,'' Roseanne said meekly. ''I've seen so
much. I wouldn't have missed it for the world.''

William McVey managed a weak smile as they
watched the vaqueros riding around the longhorns. ''I
tried to keep you confined because you were a woman,''
he finally admitted. ''This trip has made me realize that I
was wrong for doing that. A man should get to know his
daughters the same way he would his sons. He should
take the opportunity to work alongside them, to teach
them things. There may come a time when they will

need to know those things. Catharine never chose to get involved with the ranch, and I suppose I thought you should be the same way. I've enjoyed being with you on this trip, Roseanne, and although I've worried for your safety, I'm glad you came.''

Roseanne felt tears welling up in her eyes. Her father had never spoken to her in quite that way. He had never been one for putting his thinking into sentimental words. Action had been more his style. Hearing it somehow caused a lump to form in her throat. ''Thank you, Dad. I know I've been a source of trouble for you. I know you needed a bunch of boys to help run the ranch, but—''

''No buts, girl. Now it's time we got something to eat. When this storm moves in we're going to have our work cut out for us.''

They rode to the chuck wagon where Ramon Castillo had gone on ahead to fix a meal. They sat down side by side and ate in silence. Roseanne felt the bond between them growing. Overhead the dark clouds rolled across the Sierra Grande. Their ominous entrails boiled and churned in thunderous murmurings. Short flashes of yellow lightning darted everywhere over the cloud surfaces. No rain fell. The cattle bellowed nervously while the cowboys continually circled them, hoping to keep them calm with their assuring words and crooning songs, hoping to drown out the whistling wind and the rumblings in the clouds.

Night came prematurely but the storm was slow in leaving. The darkness seemed to intensify it. The thunder came in claps, the lightning in fiery trails of white fire splitting the black clouds into jagged sections, turning the land and all its objects into shadowed, livid forms.

Then suddenly, in a moment of calm, the longhorns bolted. Some mutual instinct brought them to their feet and set them on a wild, blind rush through the dark. They moved as one, in a frantic, panic-driven, surging mass of senseless hysteria. Beneath them the ground rumbled as loudly as the clouds overhead and shook as if victim to an earthquake.

All those in their bedrolls tumbled out and shot immediately to their horses. Those already astride set out with the herd, racing blindly, letting their horses have free rein since their eyesight and instinct was better. They could only pray their mounts wouldn't stumble; if they did, a fallen rider would be crushed instantly.

Roseanne was up with the others, disoriented at first, knowing the cattle were stampeding but wondering in which direction. Lightning lit the land and she caught a glimpse of the rampaging mass moving northeastward. Her father had leaped into the saddle with the others. Only she and Castillo remained behind.

In the darkness she could see bluish flames flickering over the lunging herd like small streaks of lightning. Some people said this was a phenomena of the imagination; others said it was a form of electricity caused by the friction of the animals' hairy bodies jammed together and their horns rubbing. It gave her an eerie feeling. She stood helplessly watching until the maniacal herd was too far away to see.

She turned to Castillo. "What will happen now?"

Lightning flashed and they both winced. Rain began to fall. "They will run until they cannot run any longer. Then the vaqueros will round them up, count the dead, bury the men, and we will go on toward Denver City."

Roseanne, of course, was stunned by his answer, but he had given her the bare truth. She had known already what would happen. She turned back to her bedroll and sat on it, drawing her knees up and encircling them with her arms. She had no choice but to wait.

Sometime in the night Roseanne fell asleep when the storm had finally lumbered away. With the sun came the sound of birds and small rodents scurrying about in the rocks and the trees. It was a sound she had been unable to hear with the herd continually bellowing and the cowboys continually singing or hooting. She came awake suddenly. The herd.

She jumped to her feet. Castillo was up, fixing breakfast, a worried expression making the creases in his weathered skin more prominent. To the east she could see no sign of the cattle or the men, and even Castillo could not keep his eyes from the horizon.

"The coffee is on, señorita. You may as well have some. I know you worry, but they should be returning soon. It will take a while to round them all up again. They will still be jittery, I think, so it will be a slow process. They may never find all of them."

Roseanne joined him at the chuck wagon and accepted the cup of coffee he handed to her. He took one himself while he absentmindedly attended to the food cooking in his Dutch ovens. Roseanne settled herself on a dead log and kept her eyes on the east. She studied the cinder cone in the distance for lack of something better to do, and wished Tyler were here with her, but almost immediately she was glad he wasn't. He would have gone off with the others after the suicidal longhorns and she would be wondering if he were lying somewhere out there, shredded to fragments from their sharp hooves. She shuddered. At that moment, she decided his chance of survival was better against Walt Cotton.

Finally, several hours later, a great portion of the herd was driven back. She waited until midafternoon but her father still had not returned, or Diego Padilla and several others. It was normal, the vaqueros told her. "Do not worry," Castillo urged. "They are out looking for cattle in the arroyos."

By afternoon she could stand no more and when some of the vaqueros left for another search she rode with them. By late afternoon they came upon Diego. He had twenty-odd head of jittery longhorns he was babying along by himself. He turned them over to three of the vaqueros and rode up to Roseanne.

"You are worried about your father, no?" he asked.

"Yes. Have you seen him?"

"I am afraid I have not, señorita."

"Do you have any idea how many men and cattle we've lost?"

"It is hard to say at this time. I have seen a few trampled head of longhorns and one cowboy, but I am afraid he was unrecognizable. We will know better when we all get back to camp tonight and count the heads. The cattle—we may never find them all."

Roseanne felt an unwarranted fear mount inside her. She tried to squelch it, but it only grew larger. Diego became her shadow for the rest of the day as they searched for her father in the vicinity of the stampede path. He forced her to go back to the camp at dusk and get something to eat. By nightfall she had still seen no sign of her father and she was exhausted from worry.

She built a fire and sat by it alone. She had shared it

with her father before, and Tyler had always been close by. Now she was completely alone. She glanced over the tired cowboys, some already asleep, others discussing the disastrous stampede of the longhorns, hoping they wouldn't run again. She saw Henry Grehan watching her and her skin began to crawl. She looked down at her pistol on the bedroll next to her. She wished it were in her hand, but to reach for it would tell Grehan she was afraid of him. Then she saw Diego Padilla walking toward her and warm relief rushed over her.

"May I join you, señorita?"

"Please, Diego. I wish you would."

He sat down cross-legged about two feet from her and drew his revolver from his holster. He immediately took to cleaning it with a rag that he extracted from his back pocket. "I think you are feeling very lonely."

She managed a weak smile, but he was looking at his gun and not at her. "Yes, Diego. I'm worried about Dad."

"And so am I. He should have come back. I think maybe he is hurt somewhere. We will need to find him tomorrow."

Roseanne spoke her fears in a tremulous voice. She had to talk to someone. "I think he's dead, Diego."

Diego was silent for torturous moments. Finally he replied in a very quiet voice. "I think you may be right, but we must not give up hope."

Roseanne didn't want to think of what it would mean if her father were dead. It would change everything, even their purpose for being here. It would change her life—her role—the "woman's" role she had long wanted to discard, but not under these circumstances.

Diego looked at the pools of moisture welling in her eyes and polished harder at his gun. McVey might be dead but he must reassure Roseanna otherwise until they knew for certain. "Do not worry needlessly."

"I can't help it," she said helplessly. "He could be thrown and lying out there with a broken leg or something."

"Do not give up on your father. He is a very strong man. He has survived where others did not."

"Yes, Diego, but we must all face death someday."

He nodded and finally put his pistol back into its holster. "Yes, señorita. It is true."

There was not much more to say. Finally, Roseanne fell asleep, Diego moved his bedroll to the opposite side of her fire. The other men appeared to be asleep also, but it did not matter. He had taken on the position as her guardian now that both her father and Chanson were gone and he would do the best he could. There were men here in this camp who were enemies. Being a man himself, he could easily get inside their thoughts. He had had associations with their kind many times before.

He was exhausted but he found sleep hard in coming. He listened to the men on night herd once again crooning to the cattle. They, too, were exhausted but they would be relieved of their duties to get a few hours of rest before dawn. He closed his eyes and hoped William McVey was not dead. For without him, Diego wondered if the longhorns would ever get to Colorado.

* * *

At first light, Roseanne was up. The storm had long since left, taking all its reminders. The sky was once again blue, the land had already soaked up the little moisture the clouds had dumped.

Roseanne saddled her horse then waited for Diego to join her. She had put him in charge and she watched him now, from over the top of her saddle, as he gave orders and directions. When the others had ridden off into their designated groups and search areas, Diego came back to her, leading his horse. As he neared, he took a small hand-rolled cigarette from his lips and tossed it to the ground, grinding it out with the toe of his boot.

"I see you are ready, señorita." He eyed her skeptically. "Are you sure you want to come?"

Roseanne knew what he was thinking. Was she strong enough to withstand the sight of what she might see if they found her father dead? She gathered her reins, setting her jaw firmly. She stuck a dainty foot into the stirrup and swung her leg over the gray's rump, settling down easily into the saddle. "Yes, Diego. It's harder for me to sit here in camp while everyone is out looking. I need to find him." And then, not waiting for Diego Padilla and not looking back, she nudged the gray out across the big, vast land.

Diego watched her for a few seconds, admiring the strength and determination for one so young, and female as well. Then he stepped into the saddle and hurried to catch up with her. They rode in silence, finding, after an hour or two, only a few stray head of cattle in a gully, which a vaquero would round up later. At midmorning Diego noticed vultures circling in the clear sky, their great wings dipping closer and closer to something hidden in an arroyo. Roseanne saw them too and her fears deepened.

They rode toward the arroyo, slowing their horses as they drew nearer, afraid of what they would find when they topped the rise. Simultaneously they drew their mounts to a stop when they spotted a dead horse below them, its legs crumpled beneath it as if it had been shot. Roseanne swallowed hard and fought the fear pounding her blood through her veins. It was her father's horse, but where was her father?

She pressed her knees into the gray's sides and Diego quickly reached across the short space separating them and encircled her reins in a brown hand, drawing the gray back up. His worried expression settled darkly onto her face as he tried to discern her feelings. "Perhaps you should wait here, Roseanna," he offered. "I will ride into the arroyo."

She shook her head stubbornly, her eyes on the dead animal below them. "Thank you, Diego, for trying to protect me, but we already know what we'll find. I think we've known from the very beginning. There's no delaying the inevitable."

Grimly Diego followed her into the draw. Roseanne stopped her horse within ten feet of the dead animal. Hope had welled momentarily but now it faded; on the other side of the horse she could see her father. There was no doubt that William McVey was dead.

She needed to be strong, she knew that, but she still couldn't quite believe it. Suddenly she leaped to the ground and ran to her father's side. Maybe, maybe he was still alive. She listened for a heartbeat, felt for a pulse. There was nothing. Uncontrollably she fell forward across his chest and weeped, cursed, and weeped.

After a time she became aware of Diego standing awkwardly over her. "It was lightning, señorita." Then she felt his hand pulling her upward to her feet and away from her father. "You must be strong now. You will have to take his place." She barely heard what Diego was saying, she only wanted to stay with her father; keep him near, keep him alive. She tried to pull away from Diego, but his grip was tight on her arm. Her father's figure was blurry through her tears as Diego dragged her away.

"No!" she screamed. "Let me stay with him. Please!"

Diego's voice took on a rough quality she had never heard before. "It is not possible, señorita. Your father is dead. You must accept it. Now you must get back on your horse. The vaqueros will bury your father. It must be done."

"No," she moaned weakly, but she knew it was true. Suddenly she wilted in Diego's grip, her composure completely gone. He caught her up and drew her into his arms. She fell against his strength gratefully and there, like a child, she cried uncontrollably. When she had exhausted her tears, dry sobs racked her body for a long time. Finally she pulled her back ramrod straight and stood on her own two feet. She did not look at her father again. She preferred to remember him as he had looked in life. She murmured a "thank you" to Diego then walked shakily to her horse and swung into the saddle. Diego watched her with sympathetic, moist black eyes. "I'd like to bury him beneath the Sierra Grande. Will you take him back there?"

He nodded somberly and Roseanne could see that he wanted to say something, but his condolences and his own sorrow were written plainly in his eyes. It was enough.

As she rode back to camp alone, the tears came again. She didn't want to believe he was really gone, but she had unconsciously prepared herself for this since the day before. She had thought about what his death would mean not only to her but to the men who worked for him, and getting these cattle to Denver. She knew she could tell Diego to assume authority, but she was rightfully in line for it. The cattle were her obligation now. And it had all come about because of war, restlessness, and gold. She wondered now if anything had been, or would be, gained by this trip. She and her father had grown closer. She and Tyler had found a lovers' haven. But now they were both gone and she was alone—alone in a harsh land with a group of hard men.

Chapter 10

May 1862

FROM HIS VANTAGE POINT ON THE mountain near Raton Pass, Tyler had a clear view behind and below him down the center of the pine-covered canyon. He saw the two men advancing slowly up the incline, stopping occasionally to let their horses rest. He had picked up their trail from the gully near Fort Sumner, had followed them for a while and then circled wide of them, moving ahead and leaving tracks they could easily detect. Now, out of a natural curiosity, they were following him just as he had hoped. He wanted them to think, from the conversation he had overheard that night with Padilla, that he was "Gregory"—the man who was supposed to join them.

He looked to the southeast, knowing the herd would be progressing slowly in that general direction, staying clear of Raton Pass. But they traveled much slower and the dust of their hooves could not be seen on the horizon.

He glanced at the evening sun. It would be dark in less than two hours. He nudged his horse and headed down the north side of the pass and into Colorado Territory. Shortly he found a stream running full from the spring runoff. He built a fire, set supper to cooking, and cleaned his guns by the warmth of the blaze. A breeze eased down from the mountains and with it a scent that made the bay's ears perk. Tyler reloaded his Colt revolver and his rifle. He replaced the handgun to the holster on his hip and left the rifle in easy reach. He stood, stirred the coals, and put the dark gray serape over his jacket. He knew the men were coming down off the mountain but it would be a while yet before they could see the fire. He wondered if they would camp close by as they had on the other nights, or would their curiosity bring them into the circle of the firelight.

Full darkness painted the dusky shadows and Tyler laid his bedroll in this darkness, away from the firelight. The quarter-moon was well into a partly cloudy sky when the bay's ears once again perked. Tyler moved from the bedroll deeper into the shadows, drawing his pistol, then he leaned patiently against a tree to wait. He could hear movement in the dark forest, twigs snapping, clicks of horseshoes on rocks, chinks of bridle rings.

Finally there was silence again, only the occasional thud of a stomping hoof on the rich soil. The riders were staying hidden, but Tyler had figured out their approximate location.

Then one spoke, hailing him. "Hey, stranger!" A baritone voice added, "Can we join you?"

Tyler slowly and carefully pulled himself up straighter. He purposefully cocked the trigger so they would hear it. He moved a few feet to his right, into the shadows of another tree, but he honestly doubted they could see him because he couldn't see them.

"Ride in," he replied. "Coffee's on."

They urged their horses into the flickering orange light. They sat astride for a few seconds, searching the darkness for him, then they dismounted. He moved into their view. They passed a hasty judgment over him then casually hunkered down next to the fire, making motions of warming their hands.

One spoke. "A bit chilly yet in these mountains."

"Coffee's hot. Help yourself." There was no friendliness in his voice, just a polite suspicion, which was the way he wanted it to sound.

The one with the baritone voice nodded his head toward the horses. "Get our coffee cups."

The younger of the two rose quickly, then checked his actions, making them slow and deliberate as he darted questioning eyes at Chanson. Tyler flicked a dark gaze over him then threatened, "Go ahead, but remember this Colt can be aimed at your head before you can blink."

The baritone leveled cautious but faintly amused eyes on Chanson. "Why so jumpy, friend? We're not the law."

"A man can never be too sure," he replied softly, easily deceiving them.

"You wouldn't be runnin' from the law, now would you?" the leader asked boldly.

Tyler allowed a silence to slip between them and he met the man's pale eyes. The youngest man was returning to the fire with the coffee cups. He handed one to his friend and the leader reached for the coffeepot, encircling the handle with his leather glove. Tyler watched him pour the hot liquid, then replied. "We all have our enemies."

His evasive reply gave them the answer they were seeking and the leader smiled wryly as he settled onto the ground with his coffee. "Headin' for the gold-fields?"

Tyler moved closer and folded himself Indian fash-ion a few feet from the fire. He had put his pistol back into his holster, but the rifle was stretched out in their direction on his bedroll just inches from his thigh. "That's where the money is."

The leader assessed Tyler's gear knowingly and quickly. "You don't appear to be heading to the goldfields to dig around in the dirt and wade in the water."

The man was feeling him out. It was something strangers did, for although the leader was brazen and straightforward, he would not come right out and ask a man's business if he had any inclination that it was suspicious. Tyler never flinched a muscle but inwardly he was pleased that his plan seemed to be working so far. Letting them approach him had made them less suspicious than if he had approached them. He wanted them to think he was on the same side of the law as they were.

A smile curved faintly beneath Tyler's dark mous-tache as he met the man's waiting gaze. "Pans and shovels are something that they sell abundantly in any gold town from here to California."

The leader's eyes narrowed and he licked his lips before he put the steaming cup of coffee to them. "That's true."

While the man sipped at his coffee, his friend did the same and Tyler poured one for himself and studied them covertly. He settled back, this time on his bed-roll, just out of the circle of light. "There's easy gold in Colorado Territory," he said, "if you know where to look for it." He had baited the hook and he saw their eyes flare in excitement and anticipation, but when he said no more they prodded him.

The leader said, "And you must know where there's a mother lode?"

Chanson smiled enigmatically, indicating that he held the secret for some immense treasure. "A friend of mine does. I'm on my way to meet him now over in South Park."

The leader's interest grew but Tyler knew that due to the code of the West the man wouldn't ask any pointed questions, respecting his privacy. So he would have to disclose the information without sounding too eager to do so.

"Have you ever been over in that South Park country?"

The leader nodded. "I've been through there. It's quite a coincidence, but we're headin' that way, too. We're meeting up with a man—a man by the name of Gregory." He eyed Tyler expectantly, waiting to see if it was possibly him.

Tyler's lips twitched with a hint of a smile. "Then you've found him, my friends."

"Why weren't you in Santa Fe?" the younger man asked, almost accusingly.

"I had to leave town in a hurry."

The leader, of a smoother temper, seemed to understand. "Is that something you do frequently?"

"It happens occasionally."

Finally the two men relaxed and introduced themselves. The older one, the leader, was John Samuelson. The younger one simply went by the name of Page. They made small talk around the fire, but didn't mention the plans they had made with Cotton. Tyler didn't mention it either for he knew he would have to tread carefully. He didn't know what was going on, but he couldn't let them be aware of that. He would just have to listen to their conversations and piece what he could together. First he had to find out if their Cotton and his were even the same man, for no given names had ever been mentioned. He knew he would be safe until the *real* Gregory showed up, if he did, but maybe by then he would have enough information about Cotton and his whereabouts that he wouldn't need these two any more.

Finally they decided to turn in. Tyler was the last to stretch out on his bedroll. He closed his eyes but feigned sleep until the others were snoring soundly. Even then he found sleep hard in coming, not because of them, but because his thoughts continually strayed to Roseanne. He missed having her in his arms. He longed for her with an intensity that was nearly painful. A taste of her love had made him realize just how alone a man could be. If only she could have understood that this was something he had to do. She could have said she'd wait for him as she had before. But she thought he had been using her. She had even said she had been using him, but he didn't believe that. She would have had no reason. He loved her, and she didn't believe him.

He cursed himself. He had lost her and it was his own fault. He could go back to her and try to reconcile, but he knew he would always be subconsciously searching for Cotton as long as the man was alive and free. Roseanne knew that too, and it was painfully

clear she didn't want him if he couldn't put the past behind him.

Walt Cotton stepped into the Louisiana Saloon and
surveyed the crowd with his habitual distrustful manner. The black coat he wore was unbuttoned and
pushed back behind the handle of the gleaming pistol
at his left hip. His hand strayed to it, hovering, but
there appeared no one inside with whom he had a reckoning.

He was sought by a few individuals as well as the
law in several states, and caution rode with him wherever he went. Relaxing the square shoulders that filled
out his coat, he moved his thin frame into the room.

He was to meet his partner here, a man with whom
he had done business in the Denver region for several
years. He was easy to spot at the bar, a tall blond man
dressed too fine for a place like this, but a man who
had made himself known and liked by nearly everyone
in Denver, a man who could fit in anywhere if he
chose to.

When Cotton joined Randolph Pierpont III at the
bar, the latter already had a bottle of whiskey and summoned the barkeeper for another glass. He poured
Cotton a drink and said, "I haven't heard of anything
going out that would be worth our time and the risk."

Cotton knew he spoke of gold shipments out of the
mountains en route to the mints for coining. Pierpont
was a prominent rancher in Denver, but he had made
himself wealthy with his "gold" enterprises. Pierpont's aspirations were high. The son of a rich Union
politician from Pennsylvania, Pierpont, too, was
working his way into the circles of political power in

Colorado Territory for the sole purpose of increasing his wealth even further.

"I hope something comes out soon. It's been a long spring." Cotton replied. "Things are slow up in Central City."

"I didn't think things were ever slow for you, my friend. Aren't you making interest on your money?"

One of Cotton's vices was gambling. He knew it, but he had no intention of stopping. "I get some, I lose some. There's not much else a man can do with it."

"It depends on where you want to go in your life. I've told you that. Invest it like I'm doing."

Pierpont, or "the Colonel," as he preferred to be called for all his "gold" dealings, was sharp, cunning, and careful. It was those qualities that made Cotton enjoy doing business with him. He had worked with his share of idiots and losers and loose-tongued drunks that gave away plans, names, and hideouts. With Pierpont, everything was professional and strictly business.

Cotton finished his first glass of whiskey and poured himself another. He looked straight ahead at the mirror over the bar; he seldom looked at the person he was speaking to. "I guess I don't have the ambition for that. I don't like work, but I don't like being broke either."

"I can fully understand that. I don't favor manual labor either. I really don't care what you do with your time or your money, my friend—you know that—just as long as it doesn't affect me in an adverse way." There was a warning quality in his voice but it quickly reverted to the congenial one he usually used. "Are things shaping up in South Park?"

"I haven't heard from Samuelson yet."

Pierpont pushed away from the bar. They had discussed all they needed to. He dug into his vest pocket for some coins and tossed them down to pay for the whiskey. "All right. Keep in touch."

With apathetic eyes, Cotton watched in the mirror until the doors closed behind the Colonel. Then with his one good hand he gathered up his shot glass and the bottle of whiskey, and turned to the room. His mouth quirked with the hint of a smile. There would be some idiot in here who would be willing to give up his gold in a friendly game of cards.

Below the riders stretched South Park, fabled hunting paradise of the Ute Indians, and natural passage through the mountains. The streams had once been full of beaver and fish, and the high, cool pastures had supported buffalo, deer, and elk. Now, most of the game had been driven deeper into the mountains by the thousands of miners. The lush meadows were pockmarked from diggings, scarred from the lusty desires of men, cluttered with haphazard, crude buildings that would someday tumble to ruin when the land had given up its gold.

Tyler, Samuelson, and Page rode through South Park to the gold camp called Buckskin Joe where Cotton had given the latter two instructions to wait until further word from him on the gold shipment they would take.

Along with the daily mail, passengers, and freight shipments coming out of the mountain gold camps, went shipments of gold dust. Since gold dust was difficult to measure and exchange for purchases, the miners usually brought it to local banks where it was exchanged for currency and coins. The dust was then shipped by stage line or freight wagon to the private mint in Denver, or it was melted down, transformed into bars for easier transportation, and shipped to a federal mint back East.

The shipping of dust was a booming business for stage lines and freight companies, and it was also a lucrative market for bandits. Tyler had learned that the man in charge of the planned gold heist was not the usual road agent. "The Colonel" had his connections all over the region and knew when sizable shipments of dust were going out from the mountains. He did not concern himself with anything petty. He made a heist only a few times a year, but he made sure it was worth his time. Each robbery, carefully planned in detail, would keep him free of suspicion and then he would return to Denver, calling his brief absences "business trips." His "front" business in Denver, as well as his real name, would not be disclosed to them, no doubt for his protection.

Tyler thought about what he was getting into as they rode into Buckskin Joe, which sprawled randomly in a meadow. The afternoon sun glanced off the prestigious Mosquito Range and brushed the town with summer warmth. The three brought their horses to a stop in front of a crude log building marked "Saloon." Across the street was the Grand Hotel, built on the same order as the saloon. Bordering the saloon was a general store on one side and a restaurant on the other. Tyler spotted a laundry and bathhouse down the street and knew that would be his first stop.

He was the last to step down from his horse, flinging his saddlebags over his shoulder. Samuelson and Page were walking up the steps to the saloon when they turned to see that he was heading in the opposite direction.

"Hey!" Page hollered "Where you going?"

Tyler looked back over his shoulder and ignored the accusing tone of the question. It had been apparent to him that Page didn't trust him. "I'm going to get rid of some of this trail grime."

Even Samuelson ran a suspicious eye over him, but decided he must be telling the truth since the laundry and wash area sign was in plain view. "Join us for a drink when you're done."

Hoping they wouldn't catch on to his true identity, Tyler walked to the bathhouse and stepped inside the crude building, which was strong with the odors of soap and lye, muggy from the steam and the ironing. Tattered curtains separated the desk from the work area, allowing him to see the washtubs and several young women scrubbing industriously at the piles of laundry. An older woman stood near a hot stove, sweat pouring off her brow as she mechanically alternated flat irons from the stove to the clothes. To his right was another door labeled, "bath area." He dropped his saddlebags onto the board that was held up on either end by a fifty-gallon barrel and served as a counter.

The older woman came to wait on him, took his clothes to be washed, his money, and led him to the bath area that was sectioned off by sheets for privacy. She and several of the young women filled the wooden tub with hot water. When they were gone, he folded his tall body into the tub, draped his legs over the side, and began scrubbing, working in time to the restlessness he was feeling.

It seemed to increase with each day that passed. It

was something new to him, but he knew it was because of his desire to be with Roseanne and to have his life settled and orderly. He knew she didn't fully understand his motives. Maybe he should have told her the truth—the truth about Carlotta being raped. Maybe she would have understood then why he had wanted to pick up on the lead about Cotton.

Cotton hadn't been involved in the rape—Tyler knew that much for sure. Cotton had been wounded and apparently taken away from the ranch by Tuttle and Ingram when Tyler's brother had returned. But still Cotton was the leader of the gang, and therefore, Tyler placed the blame for the incident on his shoulders more than anyone else's.

His thoughts shifted to the "partners" he had taken up with for the sake of finding Cotton. Samuelson was a quiet man, an intelligent man; a man who didn't fit the part of somebody's lackey; a man who didn't lower himself to petty crimes. Three of the men involved then—Samuelson, Cotton, the Colonel—were not common hoodlums, but men who had put much forethought into what they were planning to do.

It appeared, however, that Page and Gregory had been cut in simply as extra guns—guns that could possibly be eliminated after the heist to increase the total take for the other three. It was something Tyler would have to be wary of since he was posing as Gregory. He didn't care to be mixed up in dealings of this sort; he had never done anything like this before. But if it would take him to his quarry, then it might be worth the risk.

As for Cotton, he was a continually puzzling entity. Samuelson and Page didn't know where he was or where he stayed. "You know Cotton," Samuelson had said. "He's a peculiar man. He likes to be alone, although I've heard he used to prefer traveling with company. But since he lost the use of his arm, he's become bitter and unpredictable and even more calculating. Hear tell he's even obsessed with the notion of getting even with the man who crippled him. You can't second-guess Cotton. You just have to wait and see what he does."

The information had told Tyler for sure that he was on the track of *Walt* Cotton. It had been his bullet in California that had crippled the man, and this wasn't the first time he had heard about Cotton's eccentric behavior. It didn't surprise him that Cotton had sworn to get even with him someday. It was one more reason why he had to find Cotton *first*.

Chapter 11

June 1862

THE CATTLE MOVED PAST THE CI-marron and then past the Purgatoire. As they plodded their way closer to their destination, Roseanne dealt silently with her personal pain. With the emptiness crept a confusing ambivalent resentment, a shield for her predicament, a self-pity that she unconsciously tried to cover with a tough determination and callousness.

As the days progressed and Texas was ever farther behind them, the bitter resentment emerged. Why did it have to be William McVey who was dead? Why couldn't it have been Henry Grehan or even herself that the lightning had struck?

Grehan had started that first stampede because of his stupidity and carelessness, and indirectly that mistake had led to this more disastrous stampede. It might have happened anyway, who was to say, but her tortured mind preferred to lay the blame on him.

She had ten men left, plus herself and Castillo. They had lost well over a hundred head of cattle on this trip—fifty of which she was to blame. Luckily Denver wasn't far now, and hopefully there would be no more losses of any kind.

She looked westward at the mountains jutting up from the barren floor. Between two brown hills rose the Spanish Peaks, glistening blue, clinging to winter's snow just as she was clinging to her yesterdays. Tyler was in those mountains somewhere, possibly just beyond her sight. Had he found Cotton?

A cold breeze swirled around her but disappeared just as quickly. She shivered and glanced at the long string of cattle. They had been her father's life, her father's purpose. He had found satisfaction in seeing their numbers grow and in establishing the McVey ranch into a profitable enterprise. She had long wanted to prove that she, too, had the ability to make decisions. And now she would, although he would never see her. She knew she must not let her sorrow and her pain overcome her; she must continue on.

She pulled her back up straighter, and brushed impatiently at the dust filtering past the bandanna over her face. Ahead and skirting the cattle, the other drovers rode silently. A change had come over many of them since her father's death. When the men had buried him, they had worn tight-lipped expressions, almost as if his death did not faze them, but a closer examination revealed moist eyes, clenched jaws, and fingers tightly gripping the weathered brims of their hats as they held them in their hands.

Now, as they did their work automatically, they did not talk or laugh as freely. There was very little conversation around the campfires at night. One vaquero who had always sung to the cattle with his own lighthearted Spanish songs still did so, but the melodies and the words were now haunting laments.

Grehan and his two buddies had changed too; their cockiness was increasing and they did not hide the fact that they begrudged the job they had signed on to do. Many times they shirked their duties, leaving them for someone else.

Roseanne wondered if these changes were all due entirely to her father's death or if they had anything to do with her being in authority now. There was also the fact that the gold mines were near and causing a feverish excitement whenever talk shifted to that topic.

The closer they got to Denver and the neighboring mines, the more travelers they encountered. They were all connected in some way with the gold mines, although there had been a few army troops passing by on Indian detail. Word filtered through about the gold and the War between the States. Everyone was hungry for news, anxious to be away from the wearily moving herd. After talking with the travelers a restlessness always pervaded the men. Roseanne felt it herself, so it was no stranger to her eyes or her emotions.

During those brief encounters names were dropped; names like South Park, Tarryall, Clear Creek Canyon, Ute Pass, Red Rock Camp, Montana City, Chicago Bar, Idaho Springs. Names that meant nothing to Roseanne; places that even as they spoke were becoming nonexistent or were already a part of history.

They all added to the aura of the gold, the adventure, and the riches that surely awaited anyone who sought them in the giant mountains skirting the western horizon. Some of the names told of the gold that had been found, or they were directional devices to get to the mines. But the other names indicated that not only did gold flow freely here, but blood and sorrow as well. Dead Man's Gulch, Skull Creek, Troublesome,

Stringtown, Disappointment, River of Lost Souls, Cannibal Plateau, Last Chance.

The land was innocent in its reverent beauty, but the men who chose to rape it had easily removed their veneer of civilization and fought those who tried to maintain it. Men like Henry Grehan and his friends. With each new bit of news, the feverish wildness appeared in Grehan's eyes and Roseanne likened him to a caged dog on the verge of breaking free of his imagined bars.

Roseanne unsaddled the gray and dragged the heavy Texas saddle from his sweaty back and let it fall into a heap on the ground. She removed the bridle, replaced it with a halter, and then staked him out near Fountain Creek to feed. She picked up the saddle again and lugged it to a budding cottonwood tree where she had decided to sleep for the night. She turned it over and draped the bridle over the horn. Wearily she untied the dusty neck scarf and bent to the water's edge to moisten it.

Her body ached from the weeks in the saddle and she yearned for a warm, bubbly bath in a huge tub. She thought perhaps she might bathe in the creek and wash her hair when night came, but when she felt the icy water she quickly changed her mind and settled for wiping the dust from her face and neck and re-coiling her hair into a fresh bun.

She still wore her one suit of men's clothing—the baggy trousers cinched at the waist, the sweaty and wrinkled oversized shirt, the big sombrero, and the serape that offered warmth for the chilly parts of the day. She had washed her things a few times, hung them off the chuck wagon to dry, and worn her skirt and blouse, but it had been difficult sitting astride and keeping her

legs covered. Most of the men looked the other way if
any part of her legs was exposed, but Grehan openly
stared and gave her a lewd smile that filled her with
contempt and fear. He never concealed his lustful
thoughts and was always importuning her to give him
"favors" the way she had Tyler.

They were camped five miles north of Fountain City
and would be to Denver, hopefully, in five days. They
had one hundred miles left and it seemed a short distance after what they had behind them. To the west,
heavy gray clouds moved in over the Front Range of
the Rockies and the already chilly air had turned
colder. She didn't want rain, but maybe it would settle
the dust.

She relaxed beneath the cottonwood and watched
the clouds bubble into ever-changing patterns, only
threatening, for the rain, thunder, and lightning did not
materialize. After an hour the shapes had already begun to break up and the luminescent glow of the setting sun appeared on the snowy peaks of the
mountaintops.

The men formed a line at the chuck wagon but she
decided to wait until they were all seated before she
dished up her own plate. Then she would join Diego,
as she usually did, to discuss problems connected with
the drive or to simply sit in quiet companionship.

She leaned her head back against the tree and closed
her eyes. Things had taken such a turn, but it was
useless to curse the circumstances. She had taken over
for her father now and there was no walking out on
that responsibility, not that she wanted to, but after the
cattle were sold she would have to return to Texas
without him. He *was* the ranch, and now nothing there
would ever be the same.

She had tried to keep her mind solely on the herd, the problems of the drive and the decisions involved, but when she wasn't thinking of her father, her thoughts strayed to Tyler and how she had cut him down with her insane anger and disbelief. Now the things he had said returned to her guilty mind, and she questioned her hasty judgment of his sincerity.

"Señorita."

The voice startled her and she opened her eyes to see Diego standing over her with a plate of food. "The others will soon be going back for seconds and you will have nothing, I am afraid."

She straightened and he handed her the plate. She had not been hungry since her father had died, but she had tried to eat to keep up her strength. She met Diego's concerned eyes from beneath the wide brim of the sombrero. "Will you join me, Diego?"

"I think it is not my company you are wanting, Señorita Roseanna."

She couldn't help but smile. "Yes, I was thinking of him, but I would like your company."

"He will meet you when this job he has to do is behind him."

Roseanne was forever amazed at Diego's omniscience. "How did you know I meant Tyler and not my father?"

He shrugged and then settled down across from her. He pushed his sombrero back on his forehead, but he never took it off. Even when he slept it was placed over his face. She had never seen him without it. And she loved to listen to the educated flow of his language even though she knew he had had very little formal schooling.

He replied, "One can feel many emotions simultaneously, I have found. But love will surmount all the others.''

His words were so true, but he obviously didn't know she had spurned Tyler. He thought she was waiting for him, like any woman in love, with understanding and patience. He truly believed Tyler loved her and had all intentions of returning. She believed the opposite, that this ''discovery'' of Cotton might have simply been an excuse to leave her.

''Tell me, Diego,'' she said, seeking answers to her questions, ''did you hear these men speak of Cotton?''

Diego silently studied her. He was too keen not to know why she had asked. ''You do not believe Señor Chanson. I can see that. But I will tell you the truth. No, I did not hear the conversation, but I believe it is so.''

Roseanne nodded. His words only verified her suspicions, for surely if Tyler had loved her he would not have been drawn away so easily and so quickly. It might have been his intention from the very beginning never to return. Those words spoken on the veranda could have been said only to ease her foolish heart. But, even if Diego's perception was right, she had turned Tyler away forever anyway with her harsh, disbelieving words. He was a man of pride; he would not crawl back to her.

Diego swallowed the last bite of stew on his plate and washed it down with his coffee. Then he stood up, pausing to look down at her. She felt his irritation with her. ''Señor Chanson is a man of his word. I know this. Some men I could not be so sure about, but he is one to never doubt. He tells the truth about what he heard. This is all I can say to you.''

* * *

Roseanne woke with a start, groggy from lack of sleep. Thoughts of Tyler and Diego's words had kept her awake past midnight. She glanced at the sky. It was clear and, by the placement of the stars, about three in the morning. For a moment she lay quietly, listening to the sounds she had grown accustomed to, and consciously waited for the small, unusual noise that awakened her to sound again so she could identify it.

Then, suddenly, a thud and a stifled curse drew her attention to the chuck wagon not far away. Instantly her hand tightened around the revolver she kept by her side. Peering through the brush around her campsite, she watched in the dim light as the man leaned into the rear of the wagon, groping for something apparently out of reach inside. She thought perhaps it was Castillo, but it was too early for him to be up to start breakfast.

At that moment two mounted riders emerged from behind the wagon. They led a third horse, saddled and bridled. Her heart leaped. It was the gray! Frantically she wondered what she should do. All the men were asleep, including Diego just a few feet away. She searched for the men on night watch but they were not in sight. Yet the thieves must have anticipated no opposition for their guns were all holstered. The two on horseback seemed nervous as they glanced about and she wished she could see their faces more clearly in the dark.

The man in the wagon retrieved the saddlebags that contained the little bit of money her father had brought, increased by what she had "borrowed" from his safe in Texas, and turned to his friends with a gleeful grin. She stifled a gasp and then realized she shouldn't have been surprised. It was Henry Grehan. His actions and behavior had been leading up to something like this.

She had to stop them. Coming to her feet, she hastily pointed her pistol at them. At her movement Grehan whirled fearfully, made a move for his own gun and then halted, seeing the muzzle of hers pointed at his chest. Diego came awake at the slight disturbance, all signs of sleep gone. His mind leaped to action and his pistol into position.

"What is it, señorita?"

"It seems we've caught some thieves."

"Ah." It came clear to him and a satisfied smile slowly creased his face as he met Grehan's frightened, yet insolent eyes. "And you have caught them redhanded." He continued lightly, almost jokingly. "I have never liked you, amigo. Perhaps this will be a good time to kill you, eh?"

The whites of Grehan's eyes were prominent even in the faint light and shown with a fear that he tried to cover with bravado. Almost visibly he puffed his puny chest as if he could overcome his adversaries with self-assurance. "We're quitting this outfit and drawing our pay. We figure the money in these saddlebags will just about cover three months' wages for all of us. And if it doesn't, this fine gray horse will make up the difference."

Roseanne didn't care about the money, but she would fight for the gray, not only because a person's horse was the key to survival in this vast country, but because it had been a gift from her father. "You signed on to do a job, Henry. You've only got six days left, at the most. If it's gold you're getting anxious for, it'll still be there when you get to Denver. Don't be a fool. Think about what you're doing."

"I have, and I don't see where *you* will change my mind."

"You won't have my horse."

"Sounds like you're making a threat you'd better be able to back up."

Roseanne assessed the situation and she didn't like it. Behind her the other vaqueros had awakened and were now watching and waiting to see what she would do. It would be her decision because she was the boss. Even Diego was giving the choice to her. Grehan was trying to take her money, her horse, even her men, and he was not afraid of her or her threats. What would her father have done? What would the vaqueros expect her to do?

At her hesitation, Grehan laughed and tossed the saddlebags over the gray's saddle, somehow knowing that the final decision rested on her shoulders, knowing the vaqueros would not overstep her authority. He gathered the reins. The horse snorted and shied from him and he jerked at the bit cruelly, only making the horse more obstinate.

The deadly sound of a hammer clicking into place made him freeze in his tracks. He looked over his shoulder to see that it was Roseanne's gun, not Padilla's, that was threatening him. Obviously relieved, he laughed again. "You don't really think you scare me with that thing, do you? You couldn't even kill a rabbit if you was starving to death."

"Horse-stealing is a hanging offense, Henry. Think about what you're doing."

"I've thought about it for a long time. You won't stop me. Your Daddy might have, but you ain't got the guts." He drew the reins around the horse's neck despite its efforts to bolt away from him. He cussed it and tried to get a foot in the stirrup as the animal sidestepped at each attempt he made.

Her eyes narrowed with the contempt that had built up toward him, and the remembrance of all the vile things he had said to her. Now she wondered how she was going to stop him from taking the last thing that meant anything to her. She wouldn't beg him. She wouldn't plead. That's what he expected of a woman—of her.

"I'd be happy to be rid of you and your friends," she said. "You can even take the money as your wage, but leave the gray."

"You mean you're not going to kill me? Or hang me? Or even turn me over to the law?"

His ridicule hit a place deep inside her that caused her to boil with fury. She was realizing that being the boss of the McVey ranch required decisions that were distasteful, hasty, and possibly incorrect, but had to be made nevertheless. How could she have thought she was ready for this? But she couldn't show weakness or lack of control. If she lost respect now, it would be all over. Her father had had steel and now she must show hers if she was to continue in his steps, delegate his authority.

"The law will hang horse thieves, Henry. You won't get away with this. Get off the gray and you can go free. I won't turn you in."

He curled his mouth into a large sneer. "Big words, Miss McVey. Go ahead and turn me in. By the time you get to a sheriff to report me, I'll be long gone. Besides, ain't there something you're forgetting?" When she didn't respond he continued. "If you fire that pistol, you could start this herd to running again. Now do you want that? I'm sure these cowboys wouldn't appreciate it.''

She was fully aware of how easily the herd could run since they had done it twice before. But they were calm now and had been for days. It was a chance she would have to take, one Grehan didn't think she would. She moved her finger on the trigger. Her heart pounded. The others were waiting to see if she would stop him, waiting to see if a gunshot would cause another disaster. Grehan laughed and her finger tightened. The shock leaped into his eyes as a bullet tore into the stillness, ripping his hat from his head. He stared at the smoking pistol in disbelief. The other two men made a move for their guns but several hammers cocked into place in unison as Diego and the vaqueros came to her aid. The cattle did not stir.

''Get off the gray, Henry. You other two step down from your horses. Tie them up, Diego. They can walk behind the chuck wagon for the next one hundred miles and then they can rest up in the Denver jail while they await trial for attempted robbery.''

Diego grinned and chuckled deep in his throat. ''Ah, this is good, señorita. They will never try to steal anyone's horse again. They will learn what it is like to be afoot in this great land of ours.''

The three were hauled away and securely bound. When Diego returned, Roseanne was sitting on her bedroll, fingering the Colt Paterson that had been her father's.

''I've never had to shoot at anyone before, Diego, just cans and targets. It's not easy. I could have missed.''

''Maybe—but you didn't.''

"The herd could have run."

"*Sí*. But maybe they were just tired. We must all stand our ground at one time or another, señorita. Only the strong survive in a land such as this. They will think twice before they cross you again. Chances are they will never try."

"And if they do?" A harshness edged her voice as the impact of the incident settled into her brain.

"You cannot worry about that until it happens. Keep it in mind, but do not dwell on it," he replied knowledgeably.

"Is this the way we make enemies?"

"I am afraid so, señorita, but one man's power causes another man's hate. It has always been that way and it always will be that way. But remember, my young friend, while you have made a few enemies today, you have also made many friends. You have gained their respect and they will not turn their backs on you when you need them."

She licked her lips, suddenly realizing they were very dry. She rubbed her forehead where a tightness was forming.

Diego stood silently behind her. "Will you be all right, señorita?"

She noticed the other vaqueros had gone back to their bedrolls. They could probably get another hour's worth of sleep before daylight. "Yes," she replied, but wondered if that was a lie. "Go back to bed, Diego. I'm going to unsaddle the gray."

A few minutes later, when she had her horse unsaddled and tied securely, she walked some distance from the others. When she was out of sight and earshot, she sank to the ground in sudden exhaustion. The emotions she had held in check now flooded out uncontrollably in rapid, gasping sobs. They could be blamed on everything that had happened since she had left Texas.

Finally, as dawn painted the countryside in bleak shades of gray, she dried her tears and washed her face in the cold water of the stream. In the distance the herd was slowly stretching and getting ready for another day on the trail. The smell of Castillo's flapjacks drifted from the chuck wagon. The men were beginning to talk—no doubt about what had happened in the early morning hours.

The burden of being a woman alone and in authority would not be easy, but she had chosen her path and now she must follow it. But something troubled her even more than the weight of this new responsibility; something Grehan had said: "By the time you get the sheriff, I'll be long gone."

It had been that way with the murderers of Tyler's family, lawless men who knew they could escape their crimes. Therefore there were times when a person had to be his own judge in order to protect himself and his family. And so it was with Tyler. Cotton had escaped punishment for his crimes. If Tyler didn't find him, no one would. No lawman would care what one man did eight years ago in some other state.

Slowly Roseanne was beginning to understand why Tyler had had to leave her.

Chapter 12

June 1862

RANDOLPH PIERPONT III RODE HIS long-legged sorrel past the grazing, trail-weary cattle belonging to William McVey. He had made an agreement last fall to buy one thousand head and had received word yesterday from one of McVey's men that the cattle had arrived. Now, as he looked them over, he decided they had weathered the journey well and would be worth the price previously agreed on.

He pulled his horse up to a tired-looking Mexican cowboy and asked the whereabouts of McVey. The vaquero pointed to a small, slender person standing by the chuck wagon, drinking coffee with the reins of a big, powerful gray horse draped over his arm.

"That is not Señor McVey," the vaquero clarified, "but that is who you are to talk to."

Pierpont walked his horse the remaining distance and dismounted, readjusting his flat-brimmed felt hat atop his ashen blond hair. As a final gesture to assure his appearance was in order, he ran a hand over the blond moustache that he kept waxed and curled on the ends.

He approached the shoddy, small person that had been pointed out to him, thinking it could not possibly be someone of any importance or authority. He was slightly irritated that he could not speak directly to McVey or his trail boss.

"Excuse me," he halted his lanky frame by the cowboy in the scraggly, baggy attire while he continued to look over the top of the large sombrero, still searching for McVey. "I'm Randolph Pierpont, cattle buyer for a thousand head of these longhorns."

Roseanne had not seen his approach and now turned, eyeing him wearily. He was probably around thirty-five and handsome in a dandyish sort of way. His clothes appeared to be custom made, fitting him perfectly. The trousers were neatly pressed, almost to a painful degree, and the jacket rode gracefully over a neat, stiffly starched white shirt. Even his black boots gleamed despite the ride from town.

She became highly aware of her own appearance and wished she'd had time to change before he had arrived. Her trousers were soiled and covered with snags and tears. Her shirt was wrinkled and terribly dusty. But knowing she could remedy none of it now, she sighed and with a tired, brown hand pulled the sombrero from her tightly bunned hair.

Pierpont's thin-lipped mouth tightened as he stared down at her, dumbfounded. Quickly he scanned her entire form, no doubt checking for other signs of her sex.

She forced a smile and extended her hand. "I'm Roseanne McVey, standing in for my father. He was . . . killed in New Mexico." She wondered how she had managed that so unemotionally.

The shock was still on his face but he hastily found

his manners, jerked his own hat off, and pumped her hand with more enthusiasm. "I'm terribly sorry about your father, Miss McVey. How did it happen?"

With her hand still in his, Roseanne was noticeably aware of the texture of his. Even though it was tanned, it was probably softer than hers; she felt no roughness or callousness. It was strangely uncharacteristic of a rancher's hand.

"It was lightning," she replied, "during a stampede."

Again he murmured his condolences and stared at her with bright, incredulous blue eyes. She supposed he had never seen a woman in men's clothing before, at least not one in such shabbiness.

"I've heard Denver was nearly plunged into depression by your governor," she said on a light tone, opening the conversation.

"Yes, ma'am, but things are back to normal now."

"Good. Then there shouldn't be any problem with the terms you and my father agreed on." She continued before he could respond, "What do you think of the cattle?"

The longhorns had made themselves at home on the banks of the South Platte. Any weight they had lost on the drive was barely noticeable on their normally rangy, rawboned hides. "They seem to have made the trip in good shape." His glance rested on them only briefly before returning to her. "Did you lose many?"

"A little over a hundred, but we brought extras to compensate for any losses, so you should be able to meet your quota."

"A few head short is no problem," he said, seemingly more interested in her than the cattle.

"Will you be able to take your cattle tomorrow?" she asked.

His smile was friendly, charismatic, as he subtly avoided her question. "They look as tired as you, Miss McVey. Perhaps my coming out to meet you so soon was untimely. Could I make it up to you by escorting you to dinner tomorrow evening? We could discuss the terms of the deal then."

His invitation was tempting. She had wanted the experience of the cattle drive, but now she was ready for a hot bath, a soft bed, and some fine food. And he seemed a bit confused about the terms of the deal. "That's very kind of you, but there's no need to wait until then to discuss terms. My father already told me the price you and he agreed on."

"Well yes, but that was only tentative, you must understand. Didn't he tell you that?"

Her lips thinned as she ran shrewd eyes over him. Was he going to try to change the price now that he didn't have her father to deal with? She tried to temper her reply not to show her increasing anger. "My father said the terms were agreed upon. He wouldn't have brought the cattle up here on a tentative basis."

Pierpont's brow rose as his hands suddenly began rolling the hat he still held in his hands. She detected a trace of curtness in his reply. "Very well, Miss McVey. Then twenty-five dollars a head is agreeable?" When she nodded, he replaced his hat to his head. The moment of disturbing disagreement seemed to have already been forgotten. "And dinner? Will you accept my invitation?"

Her mouth curved into a faint smile of politeness. It crossed her mind to refuse, but a break from Castillo's cooking would be nice. "Yes, tomorrow night will be fine."

"Shall I escort you from here?"

"No, that won't be necessary. I'll be going into town and staying at a hotel."

"Very good, then we'll eat at the Tremont House—if that's agreeable?—about seven?"

She nodded. "Until then."

She watched him board his horse and ride away. Maybe now that he was gone, her nausea would leave too. Discussing the deal had made her extremely nervous. She was so afraid that something would go wrong and she hadn't cared at all for his attempt to nullify his previous deal with her father. She wondered if going back on one's word was a common trait of his.

Diego joined her. "Señor Pierpont—I think he is interested in you. No?"

Roseanne's eyes enlarged in amused shock. The idea hadn't occurred to her despite the dinner invitation. She had assumed it was only a business gesture. "Why I hardly think so, Diego. After all, I'm not much to look at right now."

"Maybe not, but he could not take his eyes from you."

"No wonder. I'm a terrible sight."

Diego's eyes twinkled. "Señorita, I think you are tired of the longhorns."

"No more than the rest of you."

"No, that is not true. You see, our work is to be with the cattle all the time. But I have talked to some of the vaqueros and we all agree that even though you have handled the drive very well and the problem with Grehan, you would be a much better boss if you would go into town for a few days, get a nice room, and put your dress back on.''

She smiled at his debonair way of telling her that her appearance was less than pleasant. ''Don't you like the way I'm dressed?'' she bantered.

He pushed his sombrero to the back of his head and ran his eyes over her doubtfully. Finally he said, ''It is not natural, señorita, if you will pardon me to say this. Women—their bodies—they were not molded to fit into—these pants.'' He extended a hand in a helpless gesture. ''It is very distracting, I am afraid. And besides, they are much too big for you.''

Roseanne laughed, a joyous note that sounded good even to her ears and brought a pleased smile to Diego. ''Ah, señorita,'' he continued. ''It is good to hear you laugh again. You should have done that for Señor Pierpont. Perhaps he would have given you a dollar or two a head more.''

''Diego! That is hardly a fair way to do business.''

''No, but your charms can be very persuasive, and a woman of power and mystery can do things and get things that a man could never dream of.''

''A woman in a man's world can also get trampled, Diego.''

''Perhaps,'' he admitted, *''if* she tries to act like a man. But if she doesn't—'' He shrugged his shoulders in that habitual manner and smiled more broadly.

''You are very perceptive, Diego. I see your point.''

''I am simply a man looking at this from a man's point of view. Perhaps some of it is merely wisdom that comes with old age and experience,'' he continued. ''Now, will you change your clothes and I will escort you into town. The men can stay here and tend to the cattle, and tomorrow we will dispose of the very tired Señor Grehan and his friends.''

A burden was lifted momentarily from her shoulders. "Thank you. I need to find the whereabouts of the other two buyers, too.''

"I will help you find them, señorita.''

Roseanne found a secluded spot and changed into her clean skirt and blouse. She didn't have a sidesaddle but possibly she could hire one for her stay in Denver. She would have to ride the Texas saddle for now, regardless of the looks it would draw.

Denver exceeded her expectations. She and Diego got directions to the Tremont House and as they rode, Roseanne studied the young town and noticed the changes it had already undergone. They were obvious even to a stranger, but Denver had the appearance of being more than just a boomtown. It had an air of stability despite some crude settlements. There were many new frame homes going up and brick buildings in various stages of construction. Some were fancied-up with wooden fretwork at the eaves and window glass. A few of the more pretentious homes had wooden shingles or rough-split shakes. Fancy curtains hung at the windows to add prestige and hominess.

To Roseanne, the busy atmosphere was tense with excitement, and she knew it must have been the same for those who had raced here in the spring of 1859, risking everything they owned, even their lives and their families for a chance at a big bonanza.

She took a room at the Tremont. Diego assigned himself as her personal guardian while in town, but she didn't mind having him to lean on and depend on.

He would not tell her what to do, but he would be there if she needed help or advice.

When she was in her room, Diego left to see if he could find the other two buyers. Roseanne unpacked the few things she had brought, called room service to have her clothes pressed, and ordered a bath with bubbles. She lathered and rinsed her hair several times, and then soaked until the water was cold. When she was finished, her clothes were returned and she donned a simple dress of lightweight cotton, realizing how good it felt next to her skin; she had nearly forgotten how it accentuated her curves. She brushed her hair dry and fixed it in an attractive style atop her head instead of the severe bun she had worn on the drive. She then picked up the disgusting garb she had worn for three months and gladly stuffed it into the garbage can.

Feeling refreshed, and very proud of getting the cattle to their destination, she decided she would look about town. The warm June sun filled her with a new determination and courage to face the unknown world alone. It was a perfect day to get acquainted with the town and shop for the items she needed to fill her scanty wardrobe. Hopefully, when she returned to her room, Diego would have found the other two buyers.

It was nearly dark when she returned to the Tremont. She had barely closed the door to her room when she heard a knock and Diego's familiar voice.

She opened the door and asked him inside, offering a chair, which he politely refused. "I cannot stay, but I have found one of the buyers, Señor Vincent Sell."

Roseanne noticed the quiet way he had spoken.

Something inside her tensed with an inexplicable alarm. "And?"

Hesitancy clouded his black eyes. For the first time Roseanne noticed he had a clean set of clothes on and had found a bathhouse somewhere. "He still wants the five hundred head, señorita, as he agreed, and he will pay you first thing tomorrow."

"I'm glad to hear that Diego," she replied, feeling that there was more. "What of the other buyer? Matthew Wray? Did you find him?"

Diego shook his head and let out a long sigh. "No. Señor Sell says that his partner was killed one night after leaving a saloon. He had some gold dust . . ."

Roseanne's eyes rolled upward and she released a discouraged sigh. Things had been going too smoothly to last. She turned away from Diego, placing a hand on her hip. "And I don't suppose Mr. Sell would be interested in buying his partner's half of the cattle?"

"He said he could possibly take an additional one hundred head."

"And that will still leave me with nearly four hundred head of longhorns to dispose of," she said glumly, her forehead crinkling with concern.

"Sí, but there are many ranchers in the area, and many more coming. It is a good place for cattle, and I know you will be able to find another buyer. Do not worry about the cattle. They can graze for a while."

Roseanne looked out the window at the busy street below. "I'm sure we can find someone who will be interested." But inside she wasn't so confident.

Diego turned to the door and stopped with his hand on the knob. "I will go now. I will be at one of the many saloons if you need me, señorita," he concluded with a smile that was meant to lift her spirits.

She chuckled, knowing she would never be able to find him if she *did* need him. "Enjoy yourself, Diego."

"It is my intention, Señorita Roseanna."

He closed the door and she sat down on the bed. Now, what was she going to do with four hundred head of longhorns?

The next day Vincent Sell paid her for six hundred head. He and two friends went out to the herd to cut them out and move them south toward his ranch. Randolph Pierpont and his men were also at the campsite preparing to move his longhorns away to the north, farther up the South Platte. The McVey Ranch was forty thousand dollars richer and now Roseanne had to decide how the money could be used to the best advantage.

She sat uncomfortably on a rented sidesaddle and watched the three separate herds, two going in opposite directions. It was a beautiful spot. There was plenty of good grass. In the western sky jutted the blue mountains, and in the east rolled the Great Plains. Diego had been right when he had said it was a good land for ranching; her father had even said that. Cattle would do well here. When Texas grasses were turning dry, these would be lush, tall, and green. This land was not overcrowded as it was becoming in Texas. Practically all this grazing land was unclaimed, virtually up for grabs to whoever could get it first.

Diego rode up to her on a lope and pulled his horse alongside hers, "I will escort you back into town now."

"I'll be all right, Diego. I can go alone."

"No, it is too dangerous." He reined his horse toward town.

Deciding there was no point in arguing, she followed. On the way he untied his lariat from his saddle and began twirling it above his head and then below his boots. As he twirled he talked, and the sun glinted off his silver spurs.

"Perhaps you should talk with Señor Pierpont about buying what is left of the herd. We have counted about three hundred fifty head. I think he can afford it. I have learned he is one of the biggest ranchers here. He has laid claim to thousands of acres to the northeast."

"He probably already knows about Wray being killed. If he had wanted the cattle he would have offered to buy them."

"But maybe he does not want to interfere with your plans. He has been busy this morning and he has been unable to speak with you."

"That's true. I'm having dinner with him tonight. I'll discuss it then."

"And señorita," Diego once again coiled the rope into his left hand. "If you don't mind me saying so, it would not be a bad idea to wear something more—"

"I think I get your point," she finished for him. "You're suggesting I charm the man. Very well. If men need to be charmed, then that is what I'll do."

He grinned. "It is only a suggestion, señorita."

In town, Diego saw Roseanne to the Tremont, then took her horse to the stable. In her room, Roseanne opened the closet and considered what Diego had said. Of course he was right. She would carry on her father's duties, but not as he would. She would not try to fill his shoes. She would wear her own shoes, use her own charms, and her feminine ways. Call them wiles if you will, she thought, but if it works that's all that matters. She had bought a new dress and she would wear it to meet Mr. Pierpont at seven.

Roseanne descended the carpeted stairs to the dining room, glancing at her reflection in the twelve-foot ornate-bordered mirror that stood on the opposite wall in the lobby. She wasn't feeling well this evening, a bit tired, but it didn't seem to show outwardly. Her skin was the color of rich cream, although her face showed a darker tone from the weeks on the trail. Her hair, fixed atop her head, accentuated the oval shape of her face, drawing attention to her cheekbones. The gown of ivory silk and lace fit snugly through the bodice and tight at the waist, conforming perfectly to her young yet ample figure. The skirt belled to the floor, covering stiff crinoline petticoats. Around her neck dangled the sapphire necklace, matching the blue of her eyes.

At the dining room entrance a finely clothed waiter escorted her to the table where Randolph Pierpont III immediately stood up at her approach and then helped her to be seated. He, too, was dressed in his best—a gray three-piece suit of expensive cloth. He looked even more dashing than the first time they had met. He greeted her warmly and with extensive flattery.

"Miss McVey, you are very lovely this evening. You hardly look as though you have just withstood a grueling cattle drive."

She murmured a thank you, pleased at his compliment, yet reminding herself he was a "suave" man and probably never let anything go unnoticed or unsaid where women were concerned. Yet his attention, no matter how bolstering, brought on an

unwanted, disturbing sadness deep inside her. Being
with him only made her miss Tyler more. And for just
a moment her mind fell into the past, when she was in
his strong and muscular arms. It was so easy to see
him: his lips, masculine and full, not pinched and thin;
his square jaw with a trace of stubble at the end of the
day; his eyes, showing all his deepest emotions or his
lightest moments; and his body, bold and hard and
muscled; his shoulders that she had loved to run her
hands over; the thick mat of coarse black chest hair
that felt contradictorily soft against her bare bosom.

"Roseanne?"

She was drawn back. "Pardon me?"

"You were far away," Pierpont smiled. "Would
you care to see the wine list?"

She noticed the waiter by their table, standing patiently. "No—no thank you. I'll leave the choice of
wine to you."

When he had taken the order, the waiter left menus
and departed.

Pierpont was too much of a gentleman to question
her daydreaming. "My hired hands turned the cattle
loose on my range today. I'm very satisfied. Perhaps
we can do more business in the future."

"Yes, perhaps we can."

"I heard one of your buyers was killed. Do you
have plans to dispose of the cattle?"

None of the rugged elements of Colorado Territory
seemed to have rubbed off on Randolph Pierpont
physically. Not that he was thin or weak, he was simply refined. Yet, if one were to look deeper, one
would see the intelligence, the aura of authority and
power, and the shrewdness that had no doubt made
him the rich man he was. And now he was combining

all his charm and talents, possibly to make another deal with her.

"Yes, he was. As for the cattle, I'll have to find another buyer."

The waiter brought their wine, allowed Pierpont to sample it, and then poured each of them a glassful. Pierpont suggested the roast wild duck from the menu and once again the waiter left them alone.

"If you're anxious to dispose of them, I could take them off your hands."

"For twenty-five dollars a head?"

He hesitated. "I was thinking more on the order of eighteen dollars. Some of the ones left aren't as top quality as the ones I cut out this morning."

She knew that even at eighteen dollars she could make a profit, but it disturbed her that he tried to make her believe those left were not prime stock. She knew better. He was definitely a businessman out to make the best possible deal for himself. But again, that was the key to success, and she couldn't fault him for trying.

"Thank you for your offer, Mr. Pierpont. I'm sure it will help me out of a bind. I will consider it and get back with you. Tell me," she continued, fingering her wineglass, "how do your cattle weather the cold winters I've heard about up here?"

He smiled, vaguely amused by her question. "Are you thinking of moving your operation to Colorado Territory?"

"Of course not." A short three-note laugh rose in her throat. In actuality it *had* occurred to her to have a small "extension" ranch where she could bring cattle from Texas's depressed economy, feed them out on these fine grasses, and then sell them here where the demand was greater. Perhaps the selling of two thousand head and the money earned had been an enticement, or an incentive, to keep the ranch operating with a profit. "I was just curious how things are done here," she said.

"The cattle are moved to the plains in the winter. The grass is hardy and abundant. They weather nicely and our losses have been minimal. But you may find our weather too bitter after living in Texas. Please don't misunderstand me," he hastened on. "You would be a lovely addition to our beautiful surroundings."

His words, always meant to charm, somehow fell short of sincerity.

After their meal, Roseanne listened as he talked about the war and the effect it was having on Denver. His information was fascinating and his animation kept her from getting bored. More than once he had her laughing over something that probably wasn't humorous at the time it occurred, but was when he related it.

"You should have been here last summer," he said. "Things have quieted down somewhat now that we're officially classified as Yanks, but when word first got to us that a war was on, there were some high tempers and bloody opinions. Why, all summer long they skirmished in the streets and the saloons. Most of it was just shouting, but every now and again a shot was fired, or there was a fistfight."

"Then about all the war has done to Denver is to raise some tempers?"

"There's a lot of feeling here just like any other place. But we're isolated, so it's a different situation. For example, last November some rebels were nearly caught trying to get off with a wagonload of gold for the Confederacy, but they escaped. You can bet the South has designs on our gold and California's too, but that battle down in New Mexico sent them retreating and, so far, there hasn't been another attempt. Jefferson Davis needed something to boost his shaky economy and something to entice foreign governments into loaning him money. But who knows, maybe he'll try another attack of some sort. And if he doesn't, there'll be plenty of rebels lying in wait for the gold to come out of the mountains so they can take it for the South.''

"I take it you are a Union man?"

Seriousness replaced his earlier gaiety. "I am from the North, Miss McVey. I came west during California's gold rush ten years ago. My father is a very wealthy and powerful man in Pennsyslvania. We never quite saw eye to eye. I hope this won't turn you against me—you being from the South.''

"Everyone is entitled to his beliefs, Mr. Pierpont. That is what is so confusing and painful about this war.''

"Do you have any relatives fighting?"

"No. Only neighbors, friends—boys I grew up with.''

Suddenly the tone of the conversation had darkened and she felt very sad and alone. She had no one fighting. She had no one at *all*. If only Tyler were . . . hastily she stood up, weaving as the wine went to her head. She gripped the edge of the table.

"Is something wrong?" Pierpont got to his feet.

"I'm sorry, Mr. Pierpont, but I really must go now.''

He didn't question her further. "I'll escort you to your room."

She allowed him to take her elbow for she was suddenly feeling very lightheaded and nauseated. She had only two glasses of wine, but she was not accustomed to liquor of any kind.

At her door, he sought her assurance that she would be all right, and hoped her abrupt departure wasn't due to something he had said.

She told him it hadn't and that she would be fine. She just needed to rest; she hadn't quite recovered from the drive. She looked up into his concerned eyes, remembering her manners. "Thank you for a lovely evening."

"Perhaps we can dine again before you leave Denver."

"Yes, perhaps."

"Good. I will stay in touch."

In her room she undressed and slid into bed where she stared at the dark ceiling. She felt better now; the queasiness had left her stomach. She hadn't felt well now for several days. The trip had undoubtedly been harder on her than she realized. Perhaps it was a good thing she would be staying in town a while to dispose of the cattle. She needed time to rest and to adjust to what she would be facing when she returned to Texas without her father.

Chapter 13

July–August 1862

A WEEK LATER ROSEANNE'S HEALTH had only worsened. She didn't want to draw attention to it so she tried to go on as usual. She still had not sold the cattle but she had not discarded Pierpont's offer either. He had left on a business trip and she intended to sell when he returned unless she found a buyer in the meantime who would give her a better price. She also knew, however, that even free of the cattle, she would not be able to return to Texas in her present condition. So, she left her room at the Tremont House early one morning and walked to the office of Dr. Benjamin Smith.

He was very young, in his early thirties, and he immediately welcomed her with a warm, robust greeting and a sparkle in his hazel eyes that showed he obviously enjoyed his work. "And what can I help you with today?" he asked as he offered her a chair in his small office.

She was nervous about discussing her problem; she had never really been sick before, but he was so attentive and concerned that she soon had told him everything and felt immediately relieved to be able to talk to someone.

He nodded, as though he had heard it all before, and then went to a small table where he had a few medical instruments. He talked while he checked her heart, pulse, eyes, ears, and so forth. He spoke of trivial town news and his personality glowed with the same excitement that was typical of Denver's atmosphere.

Finally he sat down opposite her and brushed at the brown hair that had fallen onto his forehead. "My dear, from the look in your eyes, I suspect you already know what is causing your problems." He waited for her response but when she only stared at him with frightened eyes, he continued lightly, "You're going to have a child, and after another month or so you will probably feel fine. However, I'd like you to come in and see me about once a month, and more frequently as your time draws near. From what you've told me, I suspect you'll have the baby around the end of January. Now, are there any questions I can answer for you?"

Roseanne tried to moisten her dry mouth. It *was* true then. She had suspected, but she had hoped it wasn't so. Not now. Not with Tyler gone. Not without marriage. Suddenly she felt worse. Dr. Smith saw her color fade and immediately insisted she lie down.

Suddenly everything whirled through her head. What was she going to do? She could not return to Texas in shame. And if she stayed here, her name would be tarnished. She would not be able to show her face in town. At the moment, the baby itself was the furthest thing from her mind.

Dr. Smith sat back down on his wooden chair, concern creasing his tanned, plain-featured face. ''Is something wrong, Mrs.—?''

''No—yes—'' She looked away, rubbing her head where a pain had begun. ''I don't know.'' She let her hand fall limply at her side. What *would* she do? How could she tell Diego and the others? And then she realized he had asked her name. She hadn't even told him. He didn't know she was single. He thought she was married. Of course, most people knew nothing about her. As for those who did— well, there would be no hiding the truth and her shame from the vaqueros.

''I'm sorry,'' she replied. ''I'm Roseanne . . . Chanson. I'm new in town. I've never had a . . . a . . . baby.''

The doctor propped his right leg over his left knee and rested his hands there. ''Don't be afraid, Roseanne. Having a baby is not easy—I won't lie to you— but you're a healthy woman and there is no reason why you shouldn't come through it all right and with a strong child. Your fears are not unwarranted and if you'll talk to me I'll try to alleviate them. And,'' he continued understandingly, ''if you don't care to talk right now you can come in any time and see me. Have your husband come with you.''

''I'm afraid that isn't possible.'' She hesitated and lied again, feeling uncomfortable with the deception. ''He's not here. He's in the mountains.''

''Well, the important thing right now is for you to rest and, if possible, get someone to help you until this sickness is over. I don't want you up and doing too much.''

"Well, you don't understand. I'm only visiting in Denver. I intended to return home to Texas shortly."

Wrinkles formed on his brow. "That may not be a good idea, Mrs. Chanson. A rough journey at this delicate stage of your pregnancy could cause you to miscarry. It might also be fatal to you it you were far from medical help. I really advise you against it. If at all possible, you should try to stay in Denver for a couple of months."

"But I came up here by horseback. I should be able to go back."

"You were simply lucky. You see, this is the time when a miscarriage generally happens if you are susceptible to having that problem. The bleeding is an indication that you could be. And, since this is your first child, we have no way of knowing how your body will react to the pregnancy."

Slowly she sat up, trying to sort out what she should do. He helped her to her feet and to the door.

"If you need anything, or have any more questions, please stop by my office, or send word and I'll come to where you're staying."

"I will," she replied with an effort and a numb feeling in her brain. "Thank you."

"Remember, at the first sign of bleeding, go to bed and get hold of me."

"Yes—yes, thank you."

Outside on the boardwalk, she took a deep breath and tried to imagine the child inside her. Tyler's child. If he were here, what would his reaction be? Would he stand by her? But it didn't really matter. He wasn't here. And the child was on its way; there was no going back in time. Deep inside, she felt a pain that pierced her heart. Not only had Tyler forsaken her, but he had left her with something that would never let her forget their bittersweet love.

In the hotel room she lay awake all night, wondering what she should do. If she tried to return to Texas, she could lose the child. Perhaps that was the solution, but immediately she felt guilty for even thinking it. The baby was a part of her and a part of the man she loved. But how could she cope with the shame?

Finally in the wee hours of the morning, she determined her course. She had let Benjamin Smith believe she was married. She could tell others that too. No one in Denver knew her, except for Randolph Pierpont, and she would think of something to explain her sudden new marital status to him.

She would stay in Denver, at least until the child was born. She would keep the cattle and do as other ranchers did—lay claim to the public land on the creek where they now grazed and start her extension ranch. By next spring perhaps she would return to Texas. That could be decided later.

She would dismiss all the vaqueros except Diego and two others, Salvador Olivares and Juan Mendez. The three would help her with the extension ranch and the others could return to Texas bearing her letter to Uncle Jack that would explain her father's death and her plans to stay in Colorado. She wouldn't mention her pregnancy in her letter. She could not even bring herself to disclose the news to those she knew so well. She knew she would have to sooner or later, but she decided it would be later. Texas was far away and so was Tyler. She might never see either one again.

Diego Padilla met Roseanne outside the Tremont House to escort her back to the herd. He had the horses saddled and waiting. He was still trying to accept the shocking news she had given him at breakfast. She was going to stay in Colorado—as an experiment, she said. She had asked if he would remain in her employ. Of course he had agreed; it would be interesting to set out on this new adventure with this courageous woman. And besides, he had told Tyler Chanson he would take care of her. All in all, it had a good effect on him. He had not wanted to return to Texas just yet. It would not be the same there without Señor McVey.

Once they were away from town, Diego spoke. "I do not know for sure, but I think this idea of yours is a good one."

"I believe it's a way to keep the ranch afloat. It's not necessarily a permanent arrangement."

"Things will get better in Texas when the war is over."

"I hope so, Diego."

There was a brief silence and then Diego continued in a thoughtful way. "The ranch, señorita—it is much work and worry for a man, maybe more for a woman."

"I'll manage, Diego. It's my livelihood now. I have no other way to support myself and my—" She sucked in her breath just in time and glanced Diego's way, but his eyes were intensely black which meant he was deep in thought and hadn't noticed her near slip.

"Let me say this, my young friend," he said. "You have men to help you. The vaqueros and I—we will shoulder the heaviness you cannot. All you need to do is tell us what you want and let us help you. When Señor Chanson returns he will take away all your burdens. Now, it is time we find a place to build your hacienda, no?''

Roseanne appreciated knowing the vaqueros would stand by her just as they had her father, but why did Diego keep saying Tyler was going to return? Did he know Tyler better than she did? It brought a feeble hope to her heart, but one she knew she could not live on. She continued to doubt his sincerity, believing instead that he had never meant to return to her, that it had been his plan from the beginning to leave on the cattle drive and never come back. His words had just been words, a way out for him without being cruel to her. It didn't matter that they had been lovers. There were men who used women for pleasure, made promises and pretty lies, and then left them crying when they had served their purpose.

Roseanne liked where they were camped, but she felt a spot farther south would serve her purpose better. She recalled seeing an abandoned place with some corrals and a one-room log cabin that could provide shelter for her until she could add on or have a larger dwelling built. It was a good location, not too far from Denver. To the west was the South Platte, Plum Creek, and the spread of the Rocky Mountains. Eastward ran Cherry Creek and the grasslands that flowed to the far horizon.

Within the week, Roseanne had drawn sketches for a house and presented them to a building contractor in town. She had designed the one-and-a-half-story house after her Texas home, but on a smaller scale. It would not be elaborate, but it would be comfortable and warm for winter. The log cabin would be fixed up before winter and serve as a bunkhouse for the vaqueros.

While the carpenters worked on the house, the vaqueros built outbuildings and more corrals. In her mind she was already calling it the WM ranch, and she watched with excitement as progress was made. Having a purpose helped her over the times of occasional sickness. She bought a used shay and stopped riding the gray. She stayed away from Denver as much as possible, sending one of the vaqueros after supplies.

However, when the house was nearly completed, a few weeks later, she knew she would have to go into town and buy a few necessary items to furnish it with. She rose from bed, noticing that although her clothes still fit, they were getting snug around the waist. It was August and she was about three months along in her pregnancy. She knew she could not conceal it much longer. Her reflection in her small hand mirror also told her that her skin was still a bit pale, and she hoped it would improve when the morning sickness stopped.

Outside, the carpenters were tumbling out of their bedrolls, complaining as usual. The aroma of fresh coffee drifted from the vaqueros' campfire through the open window of the log cabin. Juan had appointed himself cook for the three men and the other two didn't seem to mind. She couldn't help but wonder if they missed Texas and the other vaqueros. Did they miss her father the way she did?

Through her window she glanced at the nearly completed house so like her Texas home. Suddenly she felt her chest and throat tightening as tears threatened to undermine her control. Could she go on alone? Could she be the baroness of this ranch and the one in Texas, too? Was she being foolish and unrealistic?

She ate a small breakfast and felt a bit better, but as she went outside to hitch up the buggy, the strong aroma of the coffee sent her hurrying to the corral and away from the smell for fear of retching.

The gray came to her immediately and she took a few moments to rub his neck and talk to him. Diego left the campfire and joined her.

"He is restless from not having much exercise, I think."

Roseanne laughed. "I should think he would *like* a rest."

"You have not ridden him much. Perhaps if you bought a sidesaddle . . ."

She didn't want to tell him why she had bought the shay instead of the sidesaddle. She knew that decision had surprised him a bit. "Perhaps I'll try to find one today. I'm going into town to purchase a few things for the house."

"I will hitch up the buggy and ride with you."

"Thank you, Diego, but it isn't far. I can go alone if you have other things you'd rather do."

"Ah, señorita," he shook his head. "This is a wild country, I fear. There are many people about who could bring harm to you." He picked up his bridle and saddle and blanket from the fence and moved toward the corral. "I think you will have a better time in town if I do not have to worry about you."

After saddling his horse, he hitched her buggy, checked his guns, and in a matter of minutes they were leaving the ranch. They did not speak but companionably enjoyed the tranquillity of the warm summer morning. They had gone nearly a mile before Rose-

anne wondered whether he had guessed that the reason
she had been so anxious to make a home here was because of her pregnancy. It didn't matter; she would
have to tell him soon anyway.

Thinking of the child, her eyes strayed to the mountains rising up on their left. It had been over two
months since Tyler had gone. She wondered if he were
still alive and what had happened in his search for Cotton.

Diego's black eyes followed her interest and then
shifted from the peaks gilded by the morning sun to the
dark signs of worry and fatigue on her face. "You
have not looked well lately, señorita. Perhaps you are
letting this new venture of yours become too important."

She quickly denied any such thing. "I'm fine, and
what I'm doing *is* important to me. There's a lot to
think about and it's my responsibility now."

"Things will happen in time. It is best not to push
them. One must always be thinking, but you cannot
force things to come together. Do not worry needlessly. The hacienda is nearly completed and we will
have the other buildings done in plenty of time for
winter. We have nothing else to do, and this—it keeps
us out of trouble. No?"

She appreciated his encouragement and his concern
for her health. "Yes, it does keep you out of trouble. It
keeps you from getting rich, too. Don't tell me that
none of you have had dreams of searching for the gold
like everyone else?"

"*Sí,*" he confessed. "The men have looked for
gold in the stream, I think. But just looking keeps them
happy. They only *think* they would like to find some.
They are vaqueros at heart—not miners. Even your-

self, señorita—you have no desire to look for the gold.
It is not something that is for everyone.''

"Diego," she said suddenly, wanting to confide in
him but not knowing if she should.

"Yes, señorita?"

She took a breath and rushed on before she changed
her mind. "Do you think he is still alive? Tyler, I
mean.''

"Ah, I knew who you meant. And I will tell you
this. I think it is not easy to follow an outlaw's trail. It
is possible he has run into trouble, but I think you
should not concern yourself with his intentions."

"What do you mean?"

The Mexican continued. "I mean that you worry
needlessly, thinking he will choose not to return to
you. Unless he is so unfortunate as to be dead, you
should not doubt his love."

They were silent the rest of the way into town.
Roseanne became lost in her own thoughts and in the
things Diego had said. At the livery, Diego unhitched
her horse and they agreed to meet back there at three
o'clock. They parted and Roseanne first found a small
restaurant where she ordered tea. The warm liquid
made her feel stronger and better and eager to tackle
her long shopping list.

By noon she had most everything she had wanted to
get for the house and had made arrangements to have it
delivered to the ranch. She then stopped at a seam-
stress's shop and looked at some dress designs she
would need in the coming months to accommodate her
blossoming figure. After choosing several patterns and
cloth for dresses, plus some for warm winter apparel,
she returned to the small restaurant to order a late

lunch. The time had gotten away from her; she was due to meet Diego in an hour.

Suddenly, to her chagrin, Randolph Pierpont stepped through the door and strode directly to her table.

"Miss McVey, what a pleasant surprise! I was just coming from the bank when I saw you. I thought you had gone back to Texas."

"No—I—"

He placed a hand on the chair opposite hers. "May I join you?"

She could not refuse without being rude. She had hoped to avoid this meeting, but of course it had been inevitable now that she was staying in Denver.

With her consent, he folded his tall, lanky frame onto the chair and placed his hat on one corner of the table. He continued on a warm, friendly note. "I tried to find you when I returned from Central City. I even went to the campsite where your vaqueros were, but you had simply vanished."

"Well, actually," she began in explanation, "I decided to stay in Denver at least until spring." She went on to tell him about her plans for an extension ranch. "There's even the possibility that I'll have another herd brought up then if the market holds."

"Splendid! It will definitely be Denver's gain to have you here."

"How was your business trip, Mr. Pierpont?" she asked politely, wondering if now was the time to tell him she was "married."

"It went as I planned. However, I must leave again early next week, so I'm very glad you're still in town. The Apollo Hall is having a theatrical performance

Friday and Saturday nights, and I would love to have you attend with me.''

She had hoped his earlier dinner invitation had only been connected with their business deal. Perhaps it had been, but now his interest seemed to be going in a personal direction. She would definitely have to tell him now that she was not a free woman.

She looked at the tablecloth and the pattern of the fabric while she quickly thought of what she would say. Finally she met his waiting eyes. ''There is something I have neglected to tell you, Mr. Pierpont. I am a married woman. I will have to decline your invitation.''

He sat back in his chair and stared at her. ''But, Miss—''

She hastened on. ''Call me Roseanne, please. You see, I've gone by my maiden name because I was standing in for my father. I thought it would be less confusing and require fewer explanations. I hadn't planned on staying in Denver at the time so it didn't seem necessary to go into more detail.''

His silence was rather lengthy but finally he did recover. ''I'm sorry, of course, to hear that. It is always a disappointment to find a beautiful woman has already been taken, but it is understandable. I take it then that your husband is not here with you? Did he remain in Texas?''

''No. He came along but an unexpected event took him away.''

''I see.''

She was uncomfortable under the new censure of his eyes. ''I'm sorry to have to refuse your invitation.''

''Don't apologize. I fully understand. However, I

would still enjoy your company, if you don't think it improper of me to ask. I see no harm in sharing the evening as friends. Won't you reconsider?''

He was not a man to give up easily, and she supposed that was another reason why he was wealthy. "Very well, Mr. Pierpont. The theater would be a welcome change from work."

"Good. I'll come to your new home and pick you up Saturday afternoon."

"Thank you, that's most kind, but it won't be necessary. I'll be in town. You can pick me up at the Tremont."

Randolph Pierpont escorted Roseanne to the livery after their meal, and after he had left her, he realized he hadn't asked her married name. It was discouraging to hear she had a husband. He found her to be one of the most interesting women he had met since he came to Denver. He hadn't thought seriously of taking a wife before; there were plenty of women who could satisfy his needs, but they were not the kind a man married. He even had a regular over in the "district" that loved to see him—and his money—for he always paid her well. But he was a man of aspirations. He desired wealth and power, and the power came after wealth. Colorado Territory was young and budding and he foresaw a political future here for himself. It was a rich state and a man could get his share with careful planning and manipulation.

And that was where a wife came in. A man with a wife and family always drew more respect and favor from everyone. And a woman of Roseanne's caliber would have fit nicely into his lifestyle. She had many assets, simply not just beauty. She was well-to-do; she had the money from the cattle—his money—and a huge ranch in Texas that encompassed thousands of acres and livestock.

And now, just when he had found she would be staying in Denver, and just when he had begun to formulate his plans, she had dashed them by producing a husband. Of course there were other women, but none he knew with such property holdings and none quite so intriguing. Still, he was not a man to give up on an idea at the first sign of a problem. Sometimes a man had to *eliminate* the obstacles in his way. If a speculative venture was to be successful it required many hours of thinking and plotting and planning. All angles had to be considered. And if a man were determined, he would eventually get what he wanted.

Tyler had hired on to help an old man work his claim in the hills outside of town. For too long he had listened to the old man's opinions of the war, the "news" about the Indian raids in the region, and every tale of every rich gold claim since 1849 from California to Colorado. He had seen many a freighting wagon and stagecoach move out of South Park, carrying handsome shipments of gold dust to be melted into coins, and still no action from the Colonel in Denver. Therefore Tyler knew the Colonel was waiting for the shipment that would increase his wealth by more than a mere fraction. But the wait was getting tiresome and Tyler was getting restless.

He stepped into the saloon and saw Samuelson and Page standing at the bar with a nearly empty bottle of whiskey between them. Page was obviously drunk, and holding on to the bar for support. Samuelson, on the other hand, was in control of himself. Quiet and wary, he never let his guard down. In the time that had passed—over two months—Tyler's doubt increased as to whether Page was even supposed to come out of the robbery alive. It was evident that Samuelson had no tolerance for the younger man. With Tyler, posing as Gregory, Samuelson had simply maintained a distant watchful attitude.

Tyler stepped up to them and Samuelson poured him a drink. No words were exchanged; there was seldom small talk between them unless it led up to business. Tyler tossed the liquid down his throat, never letting it rest in his mouth. He didn't feel or taste its fire until it was in his stomach.

Samuelson filled their glasses again and then gave Tyler a nod that indicated he was to join him at a table. Samuelson took his glass and the bottle and told Page to stay at the bar. At a table in the corner, he drained his glass and refilled it, but Tyler wasn't interested in more.

"Gettin' tired of working that miner's claim?" Samuelson asked.

"I like to keep busy."

"Found any gold?"

"Enough."

"Well, it's time to move. I got word from Cotton. The Colonel's connection says there's a big one going out of here next Wednesday. Should be over two hundred grand. There's going to be four guards plus the driver, and the guards will be posing as passengers. It's going to be on a stage to be less conspicuous and it'll be hidden under the passenger seats."

Tyler wondered who the Colonel's connection was. He surely knew the details. Chances were, he was someone who worked in the bank where the gold was held until shipment. "How much does the Colonel's informant get?"

"He's cut in for a fair share. He can't lose a valuable man, so he has to make it worth the man's time. You aren't complaining, are you?"

"No, I just can't see splittin' it up too many ways."

"There's enough to go around."

"It'd be nice to reduce the recipients, though."

Tyler guessed Samuelson agreed with him, but the man wouldn't offer his opinion. His reticence seemed to come from practiced, methodical control, like the paddle on a steamboat that rolled in unbroken rhythm. Yet beneath the surface, just like the mighty Mississippi, his mind and soul lurked with deep, deathly currents.

"When is Cotton going to join us?"

Samuelson's eyes glinted and narrowed. "He'll meet us on Kenosha Pass—that's all I know."

"I don't suppose you know the Colonel's real name either?"

"No, I guess he prefers that we don't."

It wasn't the first time Tyler had tried to find out more information and gotten nothing. Samuelson had worked with Cotton before and if he didn't like the way things were done he apparently kept it to himself.

Samuelson poured himself another drink and proceeded to tell Tyler the plan for the robbery. It sounded foolproof. The Colonel had, indeed, put some thought into it to have it all come together perfectly. Now Tyler had to formulate his own plan for the confrontation with Walt Cotton. His restlessness was finally dissipating as the time for action neared. It would be over soon.

Samuelson went back to the bar and Tyler leaned his chair against the wall and crossed a booted foot over the opposite knee. If he was successful in catching Cotton he could get on with his life, a life that had to include Roseanne. Their separation was not final, as far as he was concerned. As he had promised, he would return to Texas, and to her.

Chapter 14

August 1862

SATURDAY, ROSEANNE PACKED THE few things she would need for her overnight stay in Denver. There were times when she still didn't feel well and today was one of those days. While Diego hitched up the buggy, her gaze strayed involuntarily to the blue Front Range of the Rockies. She had tried not to think of the precious moments Tyler and she had spent together on the drive, or how long he had been gone, but as always, in the silent loneliness of the night, the memories continued to rob her of sleep.

She straightened her back and thought about the ranch. She looked about the yard and at the evidence of progress being made daily. It was shaping up nicely. It was her life now and she would make the most of it. She would not betray her father's dreams or destroy all he had spent his entire life working for. Things were already looking up here in this young, wild land. There were many men with whom she could replace Tyler, but she was in no hurry to make another mistake.

She turned distractedly at the sound of Diego's voice, asking her a question. He repeated it. "Will that be all, señorita?"

She nodded and rubbed her head, feeling a trifle dizzy. She moved to the buggy and Diego helped her up. "Juan and Salvador will escort you into town," he said. "They would like to have some fun tonight. They have been working very hard."

"You won't be coming?" She was a bit disappointed that Diego would not be escorting her into town. If not for him, she would never have anyone to talk to, and the long, lonely days and nights were taking their toll on her. A night seldom went by that her dreams didn't turn into nightmares revolving progressively around her happy moments with Tyler, the shocking death of her father, and the incident with Henry Grehan. Only sometimes it wasn't Grehan, it was just a man with various faces, various names— Tuttle, Ingram, Cotton,—names she'd heard Tyler mention, faces her imagination conjured up.

Diego spoke again, drawing her back from her thoughts. "Yes, Diego?"

Concern deepened the leathery wrinkles on his face. "You go to town, Señorita Roseanna," he said, "but I do not think your heart is in it. Perhaps you should stay here at the ranch and rest. You worry too much about everything. There is no need to. The ranch is taking shape just as if your father were here. You are the boss, but let us carry some of the load for you. Your shoulders"—he smiled and shrugged—"they are too small to carry all that you put on them."

She attempted a smile at his concern, but it faded weakly from her colorless lips. "I'm afraid I have no choice, Diego. I told Mr. Pierpont I would accompany him to the theater.''

"It is easily explained. One of the vaqueros can get a message to him that you're not feeling well.''

Her shocked cerulean gaze leveled on the knowing black depths of his eyes. How had he known she was ill? Then her shoulders sagged and she glanced at the immense humps of the mountains again. She sighed tiredly. It was obvious; she should have known that. Of course Diego Padilla would recognize the change in her. There was very little that escaped him.

"I need to make new acquaintances," she replied stubbornly, trying not to look at Diego's black eyes shimmering with that golden, knowing glow.

"I think it is wise, señorita, but do not let Mr. Pierpont fall in love with you. But most of all, do not fool yourself.''

Her brow wrinkled as anger surfaced. "What do you mean, Diego? Mr. Pierpont is a gentleman. What would be the harm if he *did* fall in love with me?''

"Much harm, señorita, for everyone involved.''

She felt her emotions slipping from the hold she had kept on them. Tears flooded to the surface of her eyes and she fought to contain them, but they could not be stopped. She wiped at them angrily and lashed out at Diego. "Damn it! Why do you defend him? He is so caught up in his past that he throws away his future.''

Diego pushed his sombrero back from his forehead and wondered what he could do or say to comfort William McVey's strong, but sad and lonely daughter. He wished that things had not happened the way they had. He knew he was a poor substitute for the two men in

Roseanna's life that she needed the most. He could try to be her friend, but sometimes he wondered if he had failed at that, too.

"Why do I defend him, señorita?" He thought about it for a moment. "It is simple, really. He is a good man—even though he is terribly headstrong and determined." He shrugged again in that habitual, humble manner. "It is for this I defend him. He is one to be trusted. His word is as dependable as the sun each morning. He is a good man to have for a friend, but he is a bad man to have for an enemy." He paused a moment to consider his next words, then continued, "Patience is not a thing we are born with, señorita. It is not a thing of youth. Go and have fun tonight but do not let your impatience and your wounded pride make you forget what is in your heart."

He noticed her tears had stopped. She was a strong woman, indeed. These things she could overcome, but he hoped she would not allow them to make her become bitter. He had seen bitterness too many times. He had felt it himself and it was not a good thing. It could destroy a person. It could turn a constructive, happy life into shambles. It was the root of misery and personal devastation.

She did not look at Diego. "Juan and Salvador are coming."

Diego felt a heaviness in his own heart as he detected a coldness in her reply. He wondered if he had made her angry at him. It troubled him. "I'm coming into town toward evening," he said. "I'll ride back with you and the others in the morning."

She sighed heavily and turned to him, seeing her pettiness. "Good, Diego. You need to get away and enjoy yourself too."

He brightened and pulled his sombrero back down to shield the early morning sunlight from his eyes. "Enjoy yourself, señorita."

Roseanne watched him step easily into the saddle. She felt so tired. All she really wanted to do was go back inside and go to sleep. Of course she was fooling herself. Diego knew it. She didn't really want to spend the evening with Randolph Pierpont. She wanted Tyler's arms, his strength, and his love. But even if he did return someday, she wondered if she could take him back. He had hurt her so badly. She didn't want to open herself up to more sorrow.

"Are you ready, señorita?" A voice jarred her thoughts.

She looked up from the reins held limply in her hands and saw the vaqueros on either side of the buggy, sitting patiently astride their horses. "Yes," she quickly replied. "I was just making sure I hadn't forgotten anything." She took a better grip on the reins, then tapped them against the horse. With no further urging, the animal clipped off and away from the ranch on a gentle, easy gait.

It was a beautiful summer day. It was hard to believe that the winters could be as hard as people said they were. She thought she would have missed Texas, but she hadn't had the time to think about it. She definitely didn't miss the heat, but she did wonder how Uncle Jack, his wife, and Lolita were faring. She missed the presence of another woman on the ranch and sometimes, like today, she wished Lolita were here with her.

She liked it in Colorado. The vastness of the plains was a bit intimidating but the mountains easily lured one's inquisitiveness. Towering to the sky, they were a barrier, but also a body of strength and stability in a desolate land that otherwise stretched as far as the eye could see until it faded into hazy blueness in the sky. The land was harsh and rugged, but because of those very qualities it begged to be matched and conquered. She knew the gold was the incentive for people to come here, but the land contained a magic that would hold them long after the gold was gone.

The trip to town was a quiet one except for an occasional word between the vaqueros. Roseanne didn't mind; she didn't feel like talking and her silence allowed her to observe the countryside, to hear the calls of the birds, and the sounds of insects in the grass and air. She felt better now, almost normal again, and immediately she was able to take pleasure in the sun, the cloud-dotted sky, and the familiar noises of the squeaky buggy, the trotting horses, chinking bridles, and creaking saddles. It was a very pleasant day and maybe she would enjoy it after all.

The seven o'clock hour drew near and Roseanne looked at herself in the mirror. She wore a blue dress but not the silk her father had bought for her. The memories of Christmas day came back vividly to her mind. Her hand rose automatically to touch the necklace that hung perpetually around her neck. It seemed almost uneventful the way she and Tyler had fallen in love. It had been so simple and easy—as if it was meant to be from the moment they had seen each other there on the banks of the Guadalupe. And her father had been so alive with so many dreams. Those dreams—those plans—had gotten him killed, but he had always said that only death was a sure thing.

A knock sounded at the door, scattering her thoughts. It was Randolph Pierpont and she instantly felt the nausea in her stomach return. She took a deep breath and moved to unlock the door and greet him. "Good evening. How are you tonight, Mr. Pierpont?"

"Mr. Pierpont?" he mocked. "Isn't it time we were on a first name basis, Roseanne?"

"Yes, I suppose it is." She went to the chair to get her shawl to draw around her shoulders, but her action was disturbed by his hand on her arm, turning her around. Before she could react, he had taken the shawl and draped it over his arm. Almost simultaneously he drew her closer to him. Her defenses went up automatically and she slipped her hands onto his chest in an effort to push herself away from him. He felt her resistance and smiled, easing his hold on her, but not letting go entirely.

"Forgive me," he apologized, "but you are so beautiful, I couldn't resist."

"I'm a married woman, Mr. Pierpont." His touch was a source of irritation and she managed to free herself from his hands, taking back the shawl from the crook of his arm.

He said, "I suppose I doubted that you were really married—you don't wear a ring."

She looked away, lest he see the lie in her eyes, and made herself busy putting the shawl on again. "Rings are only trappings to satisfy society. Actually my husband gave me this necklace in preference to a ring." She fingered it for a moment, again feeling uncomfortable with her deception. She wanted some company—nothing more.

Randolph cocked his head to the side and studied her. "Where did you say your husband was?"

She didn't have to invent another lie or fake the worry that fringed her voice. "I don't believe I did say, but he's in the mountains. I'm not sure where. I haven't heard from him."

Pierpont stepped forward to comfort her, but she eluded his hands, easily stepping out of his reach. He halted and drew back. "I'm sorry, Roseanne. Is he engaged in the mining industry in some way?"

"No." She wanted to avoid any further discussion so she walked to the door. "We're going to miss the show, Randolph."

The play was a comedy and Roseanne thoroughly enjoyed it, but before the second act had ended she began to feel the heat from the crowded room. Her nausea returned and she became extremely dizzy. She knew she would have to leave but hated to draw everyone's attention to herself since they were at the front of the theater. Still, she had to get some air.

Turning to Randolph she whispered weakly, her head swimming. "I'm afraid I don't feel well. Will you excuse me?" She stood up quickly now, realizing she might faint. Being close to the aisle, she murmured a few "excuse me's" and hurried past the curious eyes to the exit. The door was so near yet seemed to get farther away with each step. The darkened room took on a light appearance and she reached out for the wall to steady herself. She knew she was going to faint now, but couldn't stop it. Slowly she crumpled to the floor into unconsciousness.

Pierpont had risen to follow her out, but hadn't been close enough to catch her fall. Now he hurried to her side and knelt next to her. Easily, and gallantly, he gathered her into his arms and assured those nearby that she was fine. She simply needed some air and would they let him through? Free of the crowd, he hurried down the stairs to the first floor of the Apollo and finally out into the cool evening air.

It was quite a long walk to the Tremont House but Roseanne was hardly a burden, and as he expected, she regained consciousness when he neared the end of the street. Immediately she began to protest being in his arms but he strode onward, ignoring her desire to be released.

"I can walk, Randolph. Really."

He refused to oblige until they were inside the lobby of the hotel. Then she gathered up her skirts and started to ascend the stairs to her room when suddenly the light-headedness returned and she clutched at the railing. She weaved, wondering aloud what in the world was wrong with her, but the words were barely out when once again she wilted, this time into Pierpont's waiting arms.

Pierpont hoisted her again against his chest and called over his shoulder at the gawking desk clerk. "Don't just stand there like an idiot! Get this woman a doctor."

The man obeyed the rude order, rushing out in search of the physician. Randolph carried Roseanne to her room and gently laid her on the bed. He rapidly went through her few belongings on the dresser but found no smelling salts, only a small bottle of perfume. Deciding that was better than nothing, he held it to her nose, but she did not respond. Deeply concerned now, he recapped it absently and sat down on the edge of the bed to wait for the doctor.

Roseanne was beautiful, but he noticed she was

much too pale. He studied the angles of her face and the classic features. Her hair had been curled on top of her head, but some strands had fallen in disarray on the white coverlet. Her breathing was shallow, but the rise and fall of her breasts was regular.

Even lacking color she was beautiful, and he wondered why she had consented to go out with him, being married. But she had, so what did it matter? Sometimes married women were the best. If she was lonely, he could surely take care of that.

Automatically his desires set him in motion and he bent, like a prince over a princess, and placed his lips over hers. He noticed a slight stirring and if he weren't mistaken, a vague response. A murmur rose to her throat and he thought she was regaining consciousness. He lifted his head an inch and caught one word as it slipped past her parted lips.

"Tyler."

In Roseanne's dreams, she could see him and even feel him. His lips on hers, the soft brush of his dark moustache against her tender skin. He had come back to her after all. How could she have doubted otherwise? She felt the lips again and gave into them, but then suddenly, she realized something was wrong. She struggled to come to the surface of her dream. The kiss wasn't Tyler's. It wasn't the right taste, feel, or scent.

"No," she mumbled and forced her eyelids open. A face was close to hers, but it wasn't the face of the man she loved. Gradually she focused and at the same time heard a door open and a voice that was vaguely familiar. The man in front of her came to clarity. It was Randolph Pierpont. She sighed and looked away, disappointed.

Randolph stood up and the other man came farther into the room. He spoke in that warm, robust voice she remembered, drawing her attention. It was Dr. Benjamin Smith.

He turned to Pierpont. "Are you her husband?"

Pierpont, caught off-guard, hesitated then stammered. "No, I—I—I'm just a friend. Her husband is away."

Smith seemed to think nothing of the questionable arrangement. "Then I'll have to ask you to leave so I can talk to her in private."

Pierpont obliged and when the door was closed snugly behind him, Smith walked to Roseanne. "So you are having some problems? Is this the first time you've fainted or felt like you might?"

"I've been light-headed, but this is the first time I've fainted. I'm sure it was simply due to the crowded theater."

Smith nodded. "Yes, you're probably right. It's not unusual for anyone to faint when they become overheated, and of course it is more likely in your condition."

He asked more questions and gave her another brief examination. "Everything appears to be just fine, Roseanne. You could probably return to Texas in your fifth month, although I still don't approve of it. Horseback poses too many risks, except for short distances. A wagon or a buggy would be much better."

She told him of her plans to stay in Denver at least until spring and he was greatly relieved. "I'm happy to hear that. It will surely eliminate the risk to the baby's life as well as your own."

He gathered up his things, reminded her to come to

his office again in a few weeks, and then bid her good-evening.

Randolph reentered her room and hurried to her side. "You had me quite concerned. What did the doctor say?"

Roseanne swung her legs over the edge of the bed opposite him and stood up, moving into a less vulnerable position. She knew now that he had kissed her when she had thought she was dreaming. It infuriated her that he would take such liberties with her in her helpless state. She began pacing the floor, nervously wishing he would leave. She turned her back to him and moved to the window. All she saw was the few streetlamps illuminating the blackness and glistening over Cherry Creek not far away.

She might as well tell him the truth. It would be obvious in a month or so anyway. But she couldn't—not yet. She pivoted and faced him. "It's nothing to be concerned with. The room was just stuffy, and the doctor tells me I'm simply overwrought from worrying about the ranch and grieving over my father's death."

He crossed the distance separating them. He took her hands in his and squeezed them sympathetically. "I should have known. You have been through so much and your husband being gone is of no help. You just need someone to lean on. Isn't there some way you can get word to your husband and tell him you need him?" His feigned interest in her marital separation did not fool her.

"No, I'm afraid not. I have no idea where he is."

"You never did tell me why you and your husband became separated."

Roseanne wondered if she should say more. It was really none of his business. Hopelessly she felt herself fall deeper and deeper into her lies. Finally she decided the truth would be of little interest to Randolph. "He had a score to settle with someone by the name of Walt Cotton."

With her back to Pierpont she missed the wild flash of alarm that whitened his face. Cotton. How was Roseanne's husband connected with Walt Cotton?

"What's your husband's name?" he asked offhandedly.

For a second Roseanne wondered if she should involve Tyler further. But she had carried the masquerade this far and he *was* the father of her child whether he liked it or not, whether he ever returned or not. "Tyler Chanson," she replied quietly.

Pierpont repeated the name several times in his brain to make sure he wouldn't forget it. He would have to get this information to Cotton. And suddenly it occurred to him that perhaps he had found a way to eliminate an obstacle—Roseanne's husband.

He moved to the door. "Well, my dear Roseanne," he said fondly, "I had better go and let you rest. But I am at your service if you need anything. Please don't forget that I will help you in any way I can, especially now since your husband isn't available to shoulder the problems of the ranch. I have to leave tomorrow on business again, but I'll contact you as soon as I return."

Actually she wished he wouldn't contact her. She had hoped that if he believed she was married, he would lose interest in seeing her, but it apparently had very little effect on him. Surely when he learned she was pregnant he would take his charm elsewhere.

She saw him to the door. "You've been most kind."

"Good night."

Roseanne closed the door softly and locked it, thankful to be alone at last with her problems and her misery.

Chapter 15

August 1862

RANDOLPH PIERPONT SADDLED HIS leggy thoroughbred and tied his saddlebags behind. Even though it was early morning, the August heat was already making him break out in a sticky sweat. His informant in Buckskin Joe had told him of a sizable gold shipment going out of South Park Wednesday morning en route to the mint in Denver.

It was time to strike out for Central City where Walt Cotton had gone and then ride for South Park where they would meet up with the others. Maybe they could pick up some easy gold along the way from some unsuspecting miner, but if Pierpont's plans worked out, the gold shipment would only be split four ways—between him, Cotton, Samuelson, and his friend in Buckskin Joe. Felice, Pierpont's regular woman in the red-light district, and the two extra guns in South Park, would only be excess baggage and there would be no return trip for them.

Pierpont glanced down the street and saw Felice hurrying down the boardwalk toward him, dressed in a simple brown riding skirt and jacket with her blonde hair pulled tightly in a bun, as per his instructions. He had been hard on her, insisting that she wash off her paint and leave the tight corset behind. She was overweight, but she was supposed to convincingly portray his wife.

He laughed inwardly. She couldn't cook. She couldn't sew. She was lazy and fearful of the unknown, but she could handle life in the "district" because it was easy and predictable. However, now in her late thirties, she wanted her own business. She was tired of working under a madam. It had been easy to convince her that when this was over she would have her establishment or anything else she desired.

She saw him and stepped up her pace. When she stopped in front of him, she was completely out of breath. "I hurried as fast as I could."

He wanted to keep her confidence going. He gave her his best smile. "You're the key to our success, Felice. You know we can't do this without you." That much was true. He saw nervousness in her eyes; it was finally occurring to her that this was no child's game. But she wouldn't back out. She wanted the money as much as he did—maybe even more.

Central City was expanding so much that it threatened to overshadow Denver in population and importance. It had become a gold camp in 1859, and like all the others, had been thrown together in an unorganized fashion. The hills surrounding it were stripped bare of trees, torn up by miners and equipment and by teams and wagons hauling logs for construction. Its embryo days had quickly given way to the birth of refinement, though, and in only a few years there was plenty of evidence of the wealth pouring out of the mountains. Unlike Denver, where very little actual gold had been found, Central City was in the heart of the goldfields.

Pierpont told Felice to stay in the hills and wait for him, then he descended down the slope to the main street. He knew he would find Cotton in their usual meeting place, the saloon across from the cheap hotel where he stayed. He could afford better, but Cotton was an odd combination of garishness and refinement.

As Pierpont stepped through the swinging doors, Cotton was in the middle of a card game, gambling as usual. Pierpont sauntered up to the bar to wait. When the card game was over, Cotton disengaged himself from the group at the table and joined him.

There was a lack of lines on Cotton's forty-year-old face, and Pierpont guessed it was because the man never smiled or laughed, even in the company of people he considered friends. He trusted no one, not even Pierpont, whom he had worked with now for several years. Because of Cotton's suspicious nature, Pierpont also knew it was a good idea for him not to trust Cotton too much either. The man was loyal only to himself. He had very little regard for life, and sometimes that included his own.

When they had drinks in front of them, Pierpont said, "Are you ready?"

"Been ready."

"Good. The woman is waiting outside of town."

"Can she be trusted?"

"As much as the others." Pierpont sipped at his whiskey and said, "Did you get word to Samuelson?"

"They'll be waiting at the pass. Samuelson's dependable."

"What about the other two? Page and Gregory?"

"We won't need them once the robbery is over,"
Cotton replied. "Extra guns are easy to find. There's
no sense cuttin' them in."

"My sentiments exactly."

"What about the woman? Does she mean anything
to you?"

Pierpont smiled. "Prostitutes are also easy to find."
He thought of a much more desirable woman—Roseanne—and he remembered what he had to tell Cotton.
"I hear there's a man by the name of Tyler Chanson
who's out looking for you. Says he's got a score to settle."

Cotton suddenly chuckled deep in his throat, but another belt of whiskey doused his amusements. His
eyes glinted in cold hatred. *"I've* got a score to settle
with *him."* Clumsily he propped his crippled right
hand on the bar. "He did this to me. He's hunted me
for too long. It's time I stopped him."

"He's here in the mountains looking for you."

"Where'd you hear that?"

"From his wife."

Cotton's eyes narrowed as he soaked up the information. "He's married again, then. Maybe she could
help me find him."

Pierpont stiffened and gripped his shot glass tighter.
"Leave her alone."

Cotton's black eyebrows rose as he looked directly
at Pierpont. "I take it she means something to you."

"She could—with her husband out of the way."

Cotton fingered the empty shot glass for a moment,
thinking. Finally he picked up the bottle and refilled it.
"I could help you if you help me."

"Meaning?"

"Find out from her where he is exactly and I'll track him down and kill him."

"She doesn't know where he is."

"Doesn't he keep in touch with her?"

"Apparently not."

"Maybe she just needs some persuasion."

"I said to leave her alone, Cotton. She doesn't know. She's got no reason to lie."

Cotton shrugged. "Okay, I'll leave her alone—for now."

"When this robbery is over, you'll have plenty of time to ask some questions."

"If we both want him dead, what will be your part?"

Pierpont knew that Cotton never did anything without a price. "I'll pay you ten thousand dollars for my part."

"Is that all she's worth to you?"

"Just because he's out of the way doesn't mean she'll come to me."

"At least you're not stupid."

"It's my top offer, Cotton."

"All right. I'll see what I can do when this robbery is over."

Chapter 16

August 1862

TYLER COMBED HIS DARK HAIR AND studied his reflection in the mirror. He wondered if Cotton would recognize him too soon, or if he would recognize him at all. He hadn't seen him since that day nearly eight years ago, and there were changes in his face, new lines, the old ones deepening, and age in his eyes. He was only thirty-three now, but the hard years had taken their toll on him, not physically so much as mentally.

He reached for the big black hat and positioned it on his head over the thick hair that needed cutting. He pulled it down low on his forehead to shade his eyes and to conceal his face even further. He worked at the hat brim, bending it down more in a place or two. Last, around his neck he tied the bandanna that he would be using to cover his face during the robbery. Satisfied, he reached for the Colt revolver that he had cleaned and loaded last night. He abandoned his reflection, picked up his bedroll and saddlebags, and exited the Grand Hotel.

Samuelson and Page were at the cafe having an

early breakfast. Their horses were standing outside, ready to go. The plan was set; they had only to follow it through. The Colonel and Cotton would stop the stagecoach at the pass, then Tyler, Samuelson, and Page would bring up the rear as reinforcements. It was all very easy, except that Tyler didn't like being involved in it. But if his own plans worked out, he wouldn't have to participate directly in it. His main concern was cornering Cotton.

He remembered when he had set out eight years ago, he had been angry and bloodthirsty. But now he just felt tired. It had become just a job that he had promised to do, a job that had long ago grown wearisome.

He walked to the livery, brushed and saddled the bay, tied his belongings behind the cantle, and put his rifle in the saddle holster. He paid the hostler and led his horse out into the dusty street and toward the cafe.

Samuelson and Page were just emerging from the cafe as he stopped in front of it. "See you're ready, Gregory," Page said.

"I've been ready for a long time."

Page smiled contemptuously. He had never cared much for Tyler. "You'll be rich by sundown—or you'll be dead."

Tyler shifted dark, threatening eyes toward him. "Maybe so, but don't count yourself too lucky yet."

The smirk faded from Page's face and a trace of fear replaced it. He turned to his horse and quickly gathered up the reins. He missed the stirrup the first time and glanced uneasily Tyler's way to see that he was still watching him with cold, unreadable eyes. Page put his foot into the stirrup again and this time was successful in gaining a footing. When he looked down from the top of his horse, his adversary was already on his bay, taking the lead out of town.

In the embryonic days of the mining camps in South Park, most of the traffic from Denver and the east traveled on the old Santa Fe road, east of the Front Range of the Rockies and up Ute Pass and into the park. As the region's population grew, however, a four-horse run with Concord coaches had been started. They took a more direct route over the old Indian trail across Kenosha Pass and into Denver. The line had stops in both Montgomery and Buckskin Joe, and carried mail, passengers, gold shipments, and commercial parcels.

Just south of Kenosha Pass, Tyler waited with Samuelson and Page. It was hot, even among the trees, but along with the shade they offered the necessary cover from the wary eyes of the guards aboard the stage. Then, in the stillness, they heard the distant creaking of wood against metal and the squeaking of wheels that moaned beneath their heavy burden.

Page's eyes lit up as he turned to Samuelson. "It's coming."

Samuelson grunted his acknowledgment but Page spoke up, facing their taciturn leader. "There's only five of them, Sam. I say we can take them here and now. We don't need the Colonel and Cotton."

Samuelson sat easily in the saddle, his arms resting over the saddlehorn. He didn't glance Page's way. He kept his eyes on the narrow mountain road. "You're dumber than I thought. There's only three of us. Those boys guarding this gold shipment aren't going to mess around. They'd just as soon scatter your guts all over these mountains as look at you. They see you pull up in the road and they'll just shoot you and ride on, never stopping. We need the others to pull this off.''

The sounds of the stage placed it just over the rise. Samuelson barked irritably, ''Here it comes.''

The stage burst into sight, swaying precariously on the bumpy road, the horses pulling it at a hard lope up the hill. In seconds it was gone, the dust filtering back through the trees onto them. They pulled their bandannas over their faces for protection to hide their identities. Simultaneously they nudged their horses and the anxious animals moved out through the trees, onto the road, and in controlled pursuit of the stage, now out of sight around a bend in the winding mountain road.

Pierpont checked his pocket watch and tucked it back into his vest pocket. ''It'll be coming along anytime now. Felice, you come with me.''

Felice nervously followed Pierpont into the center of the road, adrenaline flowing through her body. It was all so simple. They couldn't help but succeed. In just a few hours she was going to have more money than she had ever seen at one time in her entire life. Her eyes glowed with anticipation, gleamed with greed. She was scared, but it would be all over soon. Very soon.

Cotton moved into the trees, pulling his bandanna over his face. Pierpont stopped in the middle of the road and stepped down from his horse. He picked a spot about a hundred yards from where the stage would round the mountain. The stage would have no choice but to come to a halt when the driver saw the travelers in the road.

''Get off your horse,'' he told Felice. In the distance, he could hear the stage groaning up the incline.

The driver hollered. Felice leaped from the horse. He could tell she was scared. "Remember," he warned her, "your life depends on how well you perform."

Pierpont dropped his reins, covered his face with a bandanna and dropped to the ground face down. Felice slapped his horse's rump with her whip and it took off on a confused trot into a nearby meadow. She clung to the reins of her own mount as if they were the thread that would keep her from falling apart.

The stage swung around the narrow road. Felice immediately whirled to face it, waving her arms, looking as frightened as she really felt. The stage had no alternative but to stop, just as Pierpont had planned. A woman in distress would draw a crowd anytime and a hundred helping hands, especially if she were a voluptuous blonde.

"Whoa!" the driver hollered and wrestled with the racing team, successfully bringing it to a reluctant halt just feet from the frightened Felice.

Afraid of being trampled beneath the horses' hooves, Felice stepped from the center of the road until the stage stopped, then she hurried back to join Pierpont. "Please help me!" she called. "I'm so glad you came this way."

"What seems to be the problem, lady?" The driver hollered, apparently knowing no other tone of voice and obviously irked to have his run interrupted.

"It's my husband. His horse bolted and caught him unaware. He won't get up. I'm afraid he's hurt."

The driver rolled his eyes skyward in exasperation, muttered something about those "damn Eastern dandies." Then he said, "I'll take a look at him, ma'am."

When the driver had tied up the reins and stepped to

the ground, Page, Samuelson, and Tyler moved out of the trees, rifles aimed and ready.

The driver bent over Pierpont and simultaneously a handgun was shoved in his face. "Don't try anything funny, my friend," Pierpont said. "Tell your companions to toss all the gold dust out onto the grass. You're covered from all sides so you haven't got a prayer. Do as you're told, drop your guns and the gold bags, then get on down the road and don't look back."

The driver straightened and turned to his men. "Seems we've got a problem here, boys." His voice was nonchalant but they saw him glancing around them and cautiously, almost knowingly, they followed his gaze and saw the masked riders emerging from the trees all around them. "We're outnumbered. This fellow here wants you all to drop your rifles and toss the bags of dust onto the grass. I suggest you do it."

The men reluctantly gave in to the command. Like the driver, they were ashamed to have walked right into such an ambush. When the bags of gold dust were piled into a heap in the high mountain grass, they started the stage rolling again but without the vim and vigor of before.

When they were out of sight and the sounds of the creaking wheels had faded into the distance, the Colonel motioned the men to come forward. Tyler had watched it all with calm interest, glad no one had been killed. Now he moved forward, too, spotting Cotton—masked though he was. He saw his limp right arm and the rifle he carried in his left.

Tyler did not move to the gold with the others. Instead he skirted through the trees coming up behind Cotton, who, along with the rest, was moving nearer the sacks of precious gold dust. There was tension in the air, and a distrust circulating among them. The Colonel moved cautiously from the center of the road, the woman in hand. From the opposite side came Samuelson and Page.

Tyler drew closer and was now only about a hundred feet from Cotton, who had his back to him. The gold was all anyone could see. They all stopped within yards of the gold, forming an irregular circle around it. The Colonel had taken up his horses's reins and stood next to the animal, as if for protection. He drew the woman in front of him. Tyler noticed a strange fanatical gleam in his eyes.

Then Page happened to glance up and see Tyler across from him instead of behind him. For a moment he wore a frightened look of confusion. "What are you doing over there, Gregory?"

Hands moved to guns and all eyes shifted to Tyler. Cotton, too, turned to see Tyler and the rifle pointed at him. "Just watching to see who's going to get their share of the gold and who isn't." Then he spoke to Cotton, slowly removing the bandanna from his face. "Perhaps you remember me, Cotton."

A light dawned in Cotton's cold eyes and he swore. "Damn you, Chanson. I'm going to kill you once and for all."

He lunged forward and threw his rifle up. Tyler pulled back on the trigger and put a bullet into Cotton's good shoulder, sending him staggering backward into a tree. The action was all that was needed to ignite the others' previously unspoken intentions of reducing the number of gold recipients. But Tyler's eyes were still riveted on the surprised Walt Cotton, both of them ignoring the brief exchange that rendered Samuelson and Page both dead from each other's guns.

Cotton hesitated as he looked into the eyes of his tireless pursuer. Tyler had his gun pointed and aimed, but he was waiting for Cotton to make the move that would decide his own fate.

Cotton's voice was fearless despite the odds against him. "You just won't give up will you, Chanson? Well, this is where it ends for you."

He jerked his lax rifle up again and, as he fired at Tyler, he leaped to the side and behind a pile of brush. Tyler's bullet caught Cotton in the forearm but Tyler simultaneously felt a burning sensation in his shoulder. He wheeled the bay for cover but, from his left, a flash of metal in the sun caught his eye and instantaneously another bullet sank into his thigh. His reflexes brought the rifle to the opposite side to point it at this new source of bombardment. At the end of his sights was the Colonel.

Suddenly a new barrage of bullets came from the trees, but seemed aimed skyward. They were followed by four men—the guards from the stagecoach. They had apparently had guns hidden in the coach seats along with the gold dust. It was the one thing the Colonel had not anticipated. Being closest to the Colonel and the woman, the guards raced in and captured them.

Tyler kicked the bay and it darted into a nearby stand of thick pines and aspens. He leaned out over the horse's neck, letting the animal have his head to dodge tree limbs and leap fallen trees. He wondered if Cotton had gotten away. If the guards hadn't taken him, his search was still not over.

When the bay hit a clearing, Tyler opened him up

into a gallop and slowed him only when they entered
the trees again. Then he brought him to a halt, knowing the men on foot couldn't catch him now.

A darkness on the perimeters of his blurred vision
signaled unconsciousness, possibly even death if he
lost too much blood. He thought of Roseanne and
knew he had to find help if he ever wanted to see her
again.

Drawing all his strength and determination, he
clung to the saddle. Staying to the trees, he headed
down the mountain toward South Park. There would
be a doctor in one of the camps, or at least somebody
who could pass for one.

Tyler opened his eyes onto the faint, fragile light of
a coal-oil lantern. Its glow barely reached beyond the
table it sat on, but he could see in one dark corner of
the room a small wood stove, its surface covered with
several pots and pans. On the wall near it hung a dishpan and a remarkably clean drying towel. Boards had
been nailed up for shelves and there were various con-
tainers, cans, and odds and ends. Next to the shelves
was a small enclosed cupboard containing medicines
and other supplies. A broom was jammed into a
bracket on the wall near the table, but it had been used
so much there was very little left of it. The table itself
was covered with a faded, but clean, cotton cloth and
beside the lantern he now noticed a basin steaming
with water and next to it more clean cloths and several
surgical tools. It was a typical bachelor's quarters in a
mining camp, but it was astonishingly clean and obviously belonged to a doctor.

He heard a movement and searched beyond the
light. He saw the doctor, an older man wearing a black

vest and white shirt with the sleeves rolled up. It was all coming back to him now, and with the recollection of the robbery came the fiery pain of his wounds. He must have moved or unconsciously groaned because the doctor looked over at him.

"Glad to see you're awake," the man said congenially. "From the looks of things I think we'd better get to operating on you and get those bullets out. My name is Dr. H. C. Norton, short for Harry Charles." He drew a bottle of whiskey from his bag and shoved it at Tyler. "I'm going to prepare my things and in the meantime I suggest you drink this bottle of whiskey as fast as you can and as much as you can. If you're out cold I can work a lot more effectively."

Tyler knew all about whiskey as an anesthetic. He had used it before, but he also knew that the pain from the probing could put a man out faster. Nevertheless he obliged the paunchy doctor and uncorked the bottle. He struggled to a half-sitting position on his good side and let the liquor run down his throat.

He stopped after a few seconds, and said to the doctor, "I don't remember coming here."

"Small wonder. You were out cold. I really don't know how you stayed in the saddle, but your horse came wandering into town and some boys brought you over here."

The news of the attempted stage robbery was probably spreading over the region like wildfire, and he wondered if he would be connected with it. Both the Colonel and the woman had seen him and they were now under wraps. Even Cotton could identify him if he had been caught, too.

Weakness washed over him again and he lay back, staring at the three heavy log beams in the ceiling that

held up the roof of the cabin. The pain dug into him
and he wished Roseanne were there to comfort him, to
touch his hand, to kiss his lips, to just stand by him.
But he was back where he started. Alone. Suddenly he
wondered if this thing with Cotton would ever end.

"Drink up," the doctor prodded him.

Tyler collected his thoughts and put the bottle to his
lips again. "Well, am I going to live?" he asked sardonically, after another heavy slug, feeling sudden anger at the situation.

Norton's face was suddenly grim as he looked at
him seriously. "You will if you want to, young man. I
can dig out the bullets; the rest is up to you."

Chapter 17

September–November 1862

DIEGO PADILLA HURRIED BACK TO the ranch from town. There was mail for the Señorita Roseanna. It was a letter from Lolita in Texas. He dismounted before his horse had come to a stop, and as soon as his feet hit the dirt, he was hurrying up the stairs to the hacienda. The señorita was inside, out of the heat of the uncommonly warm September day.

He knocked several times, but there was no response and he immediately began to worry about her. She had told him in August that she was to have Señor Chanson's baby. It was what he had suspected all along and he had told her it was great news—which he sincerely thought it was, but the señorita had turned her head in shame. He knew she was very unhappy and alone and he hoped this letter would boost her spirits and give her new reason to face the coming days. She didn't believe Señor Chanson would ever come back, but Diego knew better. Diego knew this man loved Roseanna. If he stayed away, it was because he had not found Cotton yet.

He knocked again, but still no response. Maybe she

was asleep upstairs and couldn't hear his knock. He did not like to enter the house without being admitted, but this was one time he would make an exception. They did not receive many letters.

He opened the door quietly and uneasily stepped inside. The house was silent. From the living room he could hear the ticking of the clock she had bought to place over the huge stone fireplace. He moved from the foyer to the living room. The house was neat, not one thing out of place. He wondered how she kept it so nice even when she wasn't feeling well. Sometimes he wondered if she even ate regularly because she looked thinner than usual and tired. For this, he reasoned, she needed someone to help her.

There was no sign of her in the downstairs so he took a couple of steps up the staircase. "Señorita!" he called softly, then again louder. "Señorita! It is I, Diego. Are you up there? I have a letter for you. Señorita Roseanna!"

Roseanne had dozed off, but the urgent calling of her name from some distant corner of her dream brought her awake suddenly. It was Diego! She pushed herself from the bed, feeling momentarily light-headed. She was over the sickness now, but each afternoon she required a short nap. Dr. Benjamin Smith had assured her that she was doing fine, but he worried a bit that she was still rather thin. He had been fussing over her lately, as a matter of fact, even coming to the ranch about once a week.

He never failed to ask about her husband, showing his deep regret and concern over the situation, and he had more or less told her that Tyler could be dead and that she should be thinking about continuing her future without him. She didn't want to think about that possibility—that he was dead—but she already knew her future would be without him. He had been gone too long for her to think he would come back now.

She pushed the rumpled hair from her face and tried to smooth it the best she could. She hurried into the hallway and to the stairs. "I'm coming, Diego."

Diego moved back into the center of the huge living room and studied it while he waited. Señorita Roseanna had built the house exactly like the one William McVey had built in Texas, with only a few minor changes. This room—he liked it very much—was roomy like the great outdoors and comfortable like the well-worn seat of his saddle. It was not expensively decorated, but the furnishings were tasteful. The room opened its arms and drew one into a haven of protection and security, something similar to the arms of his María so many years ago. It was a welcome change from the bunkhouse and he still wondered, at times, why he had never made his own ranch and built his own grand hacienda.

Roseanne descended the stairs. "What is it, Diego?"

He extended the envelope toward her. "It is a letter, señorita. I thought you would want to read it right away. It was hand carried from San Antonio by some men coming to the goldfields."

Roseanne took the battered and soiled envelope, knowing that since the war Texas had virtually been cut off from the rest of the country. And if a person wanted to go north or send mail north from the state, he was left, as a general rule, to his own devices.

"How did these men find us?" she asked.

"The vaqueros told them where the ranch was."

"Are these men still here? I'd like to thank them."

"No, señorita. They have already gone on their way."

She wondered if the letter brought good news or bad. She moved to a chair and sat down and motioned to Diego. "Please sit down." She ran her finger beneath the seal and extracted the single sheet inside.

Diego settled himself uneasily into one of the high-backed chairs that huddled around the fireplace and pushed his sombrero to the back of his head.

Roseanne read the letter silently, occasionally making a comment about how things were at the ranch. Slowly the pleased glow in her eyes faded and was replaced by distress.

Diego saw it immediately. "What is it, señorita?"

Roseanne began reluctantly. "Lolita and Pablo are coming to Denver. Some of the vaqueros are going to see them safely here. There will be others in the party, too. Some people who have decided to"—she looked again at the letter, quoting—"to come to the 'richness of the Rocky Mountains.' According to the date, they have already left."

"Then this is good news, but tell me, did she say why they were doing this?"

Roseanne folded the letter up. "She said she and Pablo have very little to do now that both my father and I are gone. Uncle Jack and his wife are handling things. She thinks she can help me more here and hopes I won't be angry with her for making this decision. Apparently the vaqueros told her that Tyler was gone, too."

Diego's knowing eyes stayed on her. "But you are not happy about this?"

She glanced up at him then back at the letter in her hands. "It is the baby, I suppose."

"They must know sometime."

She nodded. "Yes, but maybe she won't want to stay here when she learns what I've done."

Diego stood up. "You misjudge her; you worry too much. She can help you very much. I am glad she has made this decision, señorita. Now I must go." He turned to leave but she stopped him. There was a serious inflection in her tone that bordered on uncertainty. He turned back to face her. "Yes, señorita?"

She paused, took a breath, then rushed on. "It's just *that*, Diego. It's the 'señorita.' " In frustration she tossed the letter into the chair he had vacated. When she looked back at him, a shimmer of tears tipped her black lashes. Concerned, he took a step toward her in a helpless gesture. "Diego," she sighed. "I can't be called 'señorita' any more." She moved her arms in agitated gesticulation. "I'm going to have a child." Her voice softened on the word. "I have lied to the doctor and a few others in town. I have told them that I'm married—that Tyler's my husband, but you already know that. Diego, you can't call me señorita any more."

He knew this, but it was a habit that went with her name. "Roseanna," he said simply, "I understand your grief, and I think that if Señor Chanson knew he was the father of your child he would come back to you right away. I think nothing could keep him from that. If he stays away it is because of something else, I think."

She gripped the back of the chair as if the touch of it could give her some inner strength. "Diego, I told Tyler never to come back. I told him I didn't want to see him again." In truth, she sometimes thought she might run into his arms if he walked through the door. Other times she felt angry and bitter toward him for leaving her alone and with his child. Despite her personal longings, she kept reminding herself that everything he had said could have been lies, even when he had said he loved her.

Diego's expression did not change, but his head cocked to one side and his eyes narrowed as a brow rose up in speculation. "And why did you tell him this?"

"Because I was angry! Because I believed that he really didn't love me, and I was hurt by what he had done to me. If he had loved me, he wouldn't have gone in the first place."

Diego moved to the door, then hesitated, his hand on the knob. He looked at Roseanne again from across the room. "This is a very foolish thing you have done, señora. I think you have not tried to understand the things in his mind and in his past. I know you want him to come back, but if you have said this to him then he will abide by your wishes. He is a man of pride. You have lost him, señora. He will not return."

The door closed behind him and Roseanne cursed him silently. She gripped the back of the chair so tightly that her knuckles turned white. Damn him for putting all the blame on her. Damn him for always being right.

Roseanne sat in her chair concentrating on the small stitches she was making in the nightgown for the baby's wardrobe. The late September evening was chilly and she had built a fire in the fireplace. She heard a knock on the door and, glad for a break from the strain of the fine work, put the cloth and needle aside and rose to answer it.

Outside stood Diego with a folded piece of paper in hand. His mouth moved into a grin under the drooping moustache. "I have just returned from town with your supplies and I will bring them in, but first"—he extended the paper to her—"you have another message from Señor Pierpont in the Denver jail. The sheriff —he saw me at the general store and brought it over.''

Roseanne took it with a frown on her face. Pierpont had been sending her these messages practically every week since he had been captured. Everyone knew now that the prominent Mr. Pierpont had been caught red-handed in an attempted gold heist in the mountains in August. It was also believed he had been engaged in this ''business'' for several years.

Roseanne wanted simply to toss the message into the fire. His notes all asked that she come to the jail and see him while he awaited trial. He was innocent, he said, and had to make her believe it. She had ignored all the notes. There was no reason to see him again; she was pregnant with Tyler's child and she had come to accept it, almost look forward to having the baby in her arms. She had never had a personal interest in Pierpont, anyway.

''I wonder what that man wants now.'' She impatiently unfolded the paper. ''I wish he would leave me alone.''

Diego replied in a quiet tone. ''Perhaps if he were to see you, señorita, he would no longer be interested in courting you. Maybe you *should* go to the jail.''

Roseanne's smile was wry. Diego was right. Her appearance would end Pierpont's interest in her and make him realize that she was more ''married'' than he would care for her to be. ''I told him I was married, but it seemed to make little difference. I'm getting tired of the deception. I don't know why I ever started it.''

''You were afraid—and as far as the townspeople are concerned, it is just as well. We do not think bad of you. You know your secret will spread no farther than the ranch.''

Her blue eyes were grateful as they met his black, sincere ones. "Thank you, Diego. I appreciate it more than you can know." Then remembering the letter, she began to read. Suddenly she gasped. "Diego! He says he has information about Tyler. He says . . . no—it can't be."

"What is it, señorita?" Diego stepped closer, his eyes riveted to the letter in her hands.

Suddenly her voice turned to quiet disbelief. "He says Tyler was involved in the robbery." She read on and when she was finished folded the message back up. "That's all he says. If I want to know more I'll have to go see him."

Diego was silent for a moment and Roseanne looked past him, her thoughts far away. "You must go see what he has to say about Señor Chanson," he said without doubt. "I will hitch up the buggy first thing in the morning. We will go into town."

Pierpont was lying on a worn-out cot in a jail cell in the sheriff's office. But despite the sparse and shabby surroundings, he still looked immaculate. His face had been freshly shaved; his hair was neatly cut and combed and his clothes were clean and unwrinkled. He leaped to his feet when he saw Roseanne, and then he took a step back as his eyes slid to her small, rounded stomach beneath the long, wool cape she wore.

"Roseanne." His voice could not conceal his shock.

"Yes," she replied. "You said you had news about Tyler."

Finally he pulled his eyes from her stomach to her face. He walked to the bars and wrapped his smooth hands around them. "I really wanted to see *you*, Roseanne."

Her irritation was growing. "Randolph, I came only to hear the news about Tyler. I hope you weren't lying just to get me here. As you can see, there's no future for us. I'm going to have Tyler's baby."

"Yes, I can see that. It is a bit of a surprise, but—"

"No buts," she replied tensely, twisting the strings of her cloth bag in her hands. "Please tell me what you know."

He moved away from the bars and began pacing the small room. She had no way of knowing what was running through his mind, but he glanced occasionally at her figure. After several minutes he stopped and looked intensely at her. "As I said in my letter, he was involved in the robbery. I heard one of the men shout his name. But there's more. He was shot several times. You should know that there is the possibility that he's dead."

Weakness flooded her; she gripped the bars for support. He couldn't be dead. He couldn't. And she recoiled inside to the idea of him being involved in such dishonesty, wondering if it was a side of him she hadn't seen, but yet believing that there had to be more to it than that. He must have had another reason for being there.

"He wasn't caught then?"

"I don't believe so. He rode away, but he was in a bad way. Chances are he never made it to a town."

"Have you told the authorities he was involved?"

Pierpont looked away again. Her question troubled him. He had kept silent, afraid that Chanson, who had apparently been posing as Gregory to get to Cotton, would know the particulars of the robbery and those involved, especially the leader, the Colonel. Chanson could turn information on *him* and tighten the noose even more around his neck. As it was now, it was his story against the guards. Cotton had gotten away and

Felice was on his side. Their story was that they had been traveling to South Park together when the robbers waylaid them and forced them to help stop the stage or be shot on the spot. No, he was afraid to turn Chanson in; it could work against him.

"I've kept silent for you, Roseanne, even though I've known there was little future for us. I want you to know that I will remain silent about his involvement. But if he is dead, you and I could . . ."

She turned her back on him, a strangled pain rising in her throat as she tried to keep back tears that wanted to fall. "Thank you for telling me."

"Roseanne, I wanted to talk to you. To convince you of my innocence. I can explain how I came to be there. I was just an innocent bystander. I was on my way to South Park on business and I—"

She had started for the door and the main part of the jail where the sheriff's office was. She was eager to be gone now, to think and to be alone with her thoughts and the feelings of pain welling up inside to choke her. Before she exited, however, she looked over her shoulder at Pierpont, wondering if he truly was innocent. But what concerned her more was whether Tyler was innocent. Whether Tyler was alive. "Convincing me is not important, Randolph. The jury are the only ones who matter now."

It was the end of October when Lolita and Pablo and the vaqueros arrived at the ranch on tired mounts. Roseanne was fixing a cup of tea when she saw them through the kitchen window. She sat her cup down hastily, splashing the contents over her hand and onto the counter, but she barely noticed the hot liquid. She was happy to see them but nervous about exposing her condition, so she left the house reluctantly.

"Lolita!" she called, raising her hand in greeting.

The travelers looked up and waved their own greetings in a mixture of English and Spanish. Even at the distance Roseanne could see the tired way they carried themselves.

Even at six months, the bulge in Roseanne's stomach was hardly noticeable in the loose dress she had made especially for her pregnancy. Yet, the very design itself drew Lolita's immediate attention to her form beneath. As Roseanne approached her, the older woman's eyes locked with hers. The vaqueros who had come along as guides and as protection seemed not to notice; they were too busy exchanging greetings and news with Diego, Juan, and Salvador.

Lolita came forward, looked deeply at Roseanne for a moment, and then put her arms around her. "Roseanna, Roseanna. It is so good to be here with you. Texas is my home, but I see that this Colorado is fine, too." She drew away and glanced at the mountains jutting up in the west, seemingly within arm's length. "The mountains—I have never seen anything so *grande*."

Seeing Lolita and Pablo with talk of Texas and now the grand mountains, reminded her of her father's death in New Mexico and his burial spot beneath the Sierra Grande. She had pushed it all so far away, obliterating it from her mind, believing that if she didn't think about it then it would somehow have never happened.

Lolita saw the tears glittering in Roseanne's eyes and felt her own forming. An understanding softened her sharp Mexican features. She held out her arms again and Roseanne sought their comfort as she had when she was a child. She bit her lower lip to keep from sobbing and succeeded only in allowing quiet tears to slip down her face.

"I'm glad you came, Lolita," she said and tried to laugh. She didn't want Lolita to know that her tears were more from the circumstances of her foolishness and the thought that Tyler could be dead, than from the arrival of her friends, although she was glad to see them. She forced herself to stand, once again, on her own two feet as she separated herself from Lolita. She stood back, wiped the tears away, and asked, "Tell me, how was your trip?"

Lolita sighed wearily but happily. "It is a very fine experience I will not long forget."

Roseanne smiled at Lolita's confused use of the English language then grasped the rough, brown hand in her own. "I'm so happy to see you. I hope you'll like it here. We've prepared your own private quarters, and tomorrow we'll celebrate your safe arrival with a barbecue."

Pablo stepped forward and removed his dusty hat, "We were all very saddened to hear about your father, but we see that you are his daughter for you have carried on his name and his dreams as he would have done."

His sincere sympathy brought tears to her eyes again. She murmured a "thank you" but was glad that William McVey could not see his illegitimate grandchild growing inside her.

Lolita, seeing Roseanne's distress, turned her away from the men. She spoke to her husband in Spanish and told him she was going to the house with Roseanna.

Inside, Lolita sat Roseanne on a chair and removed the scarf that protected her own raven black hair. She glanced around the house, taking in its similarity to the house in Texas and admiring Roseanne's choices in design and furnishings. Spotting a pot of water on the stove, she immediately fixed Roseanne a fresh cup of tea and also one for herself. "Here child," she said, setting it before Roseanne. "Seeing us again, I know, reminds you of your father's death."

Roseanne accepted the tea gratefully. "Lolita, you haven't been here ten minutes and already you're waiting on me."

"It is what I come for, Roseanna."

Roseanne stood up. "No, Lolita. I insist that you get unpacked and freshened up. We'll heat water for a bath and you can soak all afternoon if you like."

Lolita held up a hand and motioned for Roseanne to resume her seat. She drew her cup of tea forward and clamped it tightly in her hands. "The hot water I am looking forward to. These cold waters in Colorado were not meant for bathing—I think." She chuckled and then continued. "But for now I prefer the cup of tea. It has been a long ride. *Sí?*"

"Yes, Lolita," Roseanne agreed. "Yes, it has."

Lolita took a sip of the hot liquid and sighed with relief. "It is good to be off the horse. I think I will never get on one again." She rolled her eyes skyward and rubbed her fanny. "I ride on the wagon seat for a while, but it is no good either. I am getting too old and fat for such foolishness, I think."

Roseanne laughed. "You're hardly fat, Lolita."

"Ah." Her black eyes twinkled. "You would think so if you had seen me as a young girl. I was very pretty then, but the age"—she shrugged her shoulders—"it takes beauty away."

Roseanne laughed and realized she hadn't laughed right out loud for months. Lolita's company would definitely be good for her. She could feel an uplift in her spirits already, but she knew Lolita's questioning was about to begin.

"And now, Roseanna." Lolita leaned forward and rested her arms on the table. Her brow wrinkled into lines of worry and conern. Her lips thinned seriously. "What has happened to Tyler?"

Roseanne stood up so suddenly that her chair went over backwards and she doubled over with a sharp pain in her stomach. Immediately Lolita was at her side, picking up the chair and making her sit back down on it. "It's nothing," Roseanne assured her.

Lolita had waited a few minutes to be sure, before she continued, "Roseanna, you have gotten yourself in the family way. Have you also gotten yourself married? And where is Tyler? You have not written telling us these things, yet I know it is hard to get mail to Texas from here. One can find transportation going east and west, but I have discovered it is quite different to go north and south. The war and the Indians—they do not help matters."

Roseanne sighed and curled her slender hands around the warm cup. It was something to do. She began the explanation she had thought about for weeks. "No, Lolita, I'm not married. There are some people in town who think I am. I've told people I was Mrs. Chanson. I couldn't face the shame." She paused as she looked into her cup of tea, and then went on. "Tyler went in search of the last man who was involved in the killing of his father and brother. It's been six months now since he left. I have recently received information that he was wounded and could even be dead." She did not mention his involvement in the robbery; it would serve no purpose but to make him look bad.

She expected Lolita to burst into tears, but the excitable Lolita sat calmly across the table and studied her. "I have heard about what happened in California. It was his first wife they killed too."

"Yes." Roseanne looked again into the murky contents of her cup. "I don't know if his true intention was to come back, although he said he would. I hate to think it, Lolita, but I fear her memory may be stronger than my love."

Lolita's eyes narrowed, probing with intensity. Her lips twisted as if she had experienced an indignation. Her reply was stern. "Have you not discussed this with him?"

Roseanne thought about their times together. They had spent very little time talking, actually. No, she could not remember talking about his feelings for Carlotta. He had never even said he loved *her* until the night he had ridden off, and then she hadn't believed him. She believed he had only said those words to appease her wounded pride.

"We didn't discuss Carlotta."

"You did not discuss anything." Lolita sounded a bit disgusted, but her expression softened and she reached across the table to pat Roseanne's arm. "It is understandable. I think you were too much in love with each other to think of anything *but* each other. No?"

"I'm not sure, Lolita. We didn't have that much time together before he left."

Lolita drew her hand to her face and rubbed her chin thoughtfully. "I am here to take care of you, Roseanna, and now your child. The rest we can do little about; we must wait and see what happens."

* * *

Tyler brought the bay to attention, brushed him down quickly with a worn brush from his saddlebag and then, in seconds, had the blanket and saddle on his back, tightening up the cinch.

Slowly the last golden rays of the November sun unfolded behind the majestic peaks that formed the Continental Divide and the western horizon. In the dusk, his eyes strayed to his surroundings while his fingers automatically tied the leather strings around his bedroll behind the cantle.

Mingled indiscriminately among the miners' shacks here at South Park were numerous tepees pitched by the confused tribes of Indians who fought for the right to continue hunting here despite the hordes of interlopers. Their animosity had temporarily abated while they watched the white men dig and pan for the yellow metal in the water and attempted to understand the purpose.

Behind the small encampment, the golden glow fanned upward into the amethyst sky, backdropping the mountains and casting ghostly, purple-black shadows among the few pines left standing on the nearby hills.

It didn't matter that it would be dark before he was very far from town. It was time to leave. It had taken his wounds too long to heal, or maybe it had only seemed that way in his restlessness to be back searching for Walt Cotton. He had wanted to find out if Cotton had lived, and now he knew. After Doc Norton had told him, reluctantly, that he could ride, he had gone to camp after camp in the vicinity of the robbery and asked questions about a wounded man with a crippled right arm. Finally he had found the doctor who had helped Cotton.

The search had taken longer than Tyler had reckoned, and now the first signs of winter were evident in the high mountains. There was already snow on the ground and Tyler wanted to leave before it got worse.

He had worried for a while that he might be named as an accomplice in the robbery; now that fear had lessened, though his going had nothing to do with that.

During his recuperation he had had time to dwell on his pain, both physical and mental, and he had realized that the mental pain was far greater than the physical. He had ridden away from Roseanne seven months ago and the parting had become increasingly hard to bear. Cotton was still a free man, but Tyler had more important business he must deal with now. It was time to return to Texas, just as he had said he would, even if she had no desire to see him, even if she still had not forgiven him.

He had to try and win her love again, and her trust. Lives had been lost in the years past, loves had been lost. He could not afford to lose any more. He would look forward now. He was ready to put the past behind him.

Chapter 18

December 1862–January 1863

DR. BENJAMIN SMITH BUCKLED THE straps on his old, scuffed leather bag. "Everything is in order, Roseanne. You're doing fine."

The light from the midmorning sun streaked through the bedroom window, gilding Benjamin's light brown hair. Roseanne felt awkward now and very self-conscious about her increasingly cumbersome bulk. She moved to the door. "Will you join me for a cup of tea?"

She expected him to glance at the gold watch that was tucked inside his vest pocket, but instead he looked at her. There was that kindness that had always been in his blue eyes, but lately it had flamed with an intensity that almost made her squirm beneath his silent assessment.

"I'd like that," he replied, locking her gaze with his. "I don't have anything else to do right now, or anywhere else to go."

"Good." She led the way down the stairs and to the living room. "Please be seated," she offered. "I'll have Lolita fix some tea—or coffee, if you'd prefer."

"No, tea is fine."

She went to the kitchen and he settled himself into a chair where he could look out the tall, narrow windows into the yard. It was pleasant on this ranch, and in Roseanne's company. He rubbed his chin thoughtfully. It was wrong the way he was feeling about her. He had fought the growing desire, the pull toward her. She was another man's wife. She was going to have another man's child. Still, it did not detract from her beauty, or her desirability.

She came back into the room and he rose, helping her to the chair opposite him. He pulled out the makings for his pipe then halted in midair as he inquired, "Do you mind if I smoke?"

"Of course not. Please make yourself at home."

She watched him fill the pipe, tamp it, then clutch it between his even, perfect teeth. Benjamin was an easy man to look at, an easy man to be with. She enjoyed talking with him; he always made her feel comfortable and relaxed.

Those thoughts led her to think about Randolph Pierpont, Tyler, and the robbery. Pierpont had been found guilty, and he would be spending some time in jail. But it was agonizing wondering—and possibly spending the rest of her life never knowing—if Tyler had died from his wounds.

Roseanne was drawn back by the pleasant timbre of Ben's voice. He was watching her with those warm eyes and with a smile on his lips. "What keeps you so far away?"

She smiled and shrugged away the thoughts. "Just Mr. Pierpont, the man I sold Dad's cattle to."

"His being involved surprised everyone, I think. He seemed like such an upstanding citizen."

Lolita came in with the tea and placed it on the small table that sat between their chairs. When Roseanne declined her offer for anything else she left them alone once again.

Ben Smith noticed Roseanne's unusual quiet behavior and asked pointedly, "Roseanne, are you concerned that your husband is mixed up in something against the law?"

Her deep blue eyes flared in astonishment, but she did not reply. He nodded understandably and continued, "I thought as much. He's a renegade, isn't he, Roseanne? He's run off and left you, and God knows what he's doing. He probably has no intention whatsoever of ever coming back to you. He probably doesn't even care about your welfare—if he's still alive." He had come to his feet and was angrily pacing the floor, ignoring her murmurings that his accusations were not true. "For all you know he could have been a part of that holdup and he's one of the ones they buried."

It amazed Roseanne that he had guessed at least part of the truth, but his angry declaration surprised her even more. She felt her ire rising in Tyler's defense. Smith's words hurt her deeply, as if he had attacked her personally.

Ben tempered his outburst, suddenly aware that Roseanne had withdrawn even more. She looked pitiful, lost, and forlorn in the chair that was too big for her. Her hands were clasped tightly in her lap and she was staring at them as if they might produce some miracle relief from her anxieties.

He returned to her side and knelt down on one knee in front of her. He took her hands in his. "I'm sorry, Roseanne. I had no right to say those things. I have no idea what kind of man your husband is. It simply concerns me that his absence is putting you through so much pain. Please forgive me.''

"It's all right, Benjamin. Some of what you said was true." She disengaged her hands from his and stood up. She moved to the fireplace where a small, pleasant fire was chasing away the December chill. Almost immediately she felt his warm hands on her shoulders, offering solace. The rubbing action felt good on her tight nerves, but there was no fire in his touch, no flames to set her heart and soul to racing out of control.

"Roseanne." He gently turned her around to face him, keeping his hands on her shoulders. "I will be here when you need me."

He left her then, gathered up his things, and quietly let himself out of the house. From the window she saw him tie his bag to the pommel and pull his slender body easily to the saddle. She considered his words and now she knew his true feelings, feelings that went beyond a simple doctor-patient relationship.

The child inside her kicked suddenly and with such power that she felt like retaliating. It drew her attention back to its selfish existence and its father. Smiling, she placed her hand on the spot that was receiving the brunt of the energetic activity.

Lolita stepped into the living room, a scowl on her face that immediately softened when she saw Roseanne smiling. "Will you be wanting lunch soon?"

"Yes. I'll help you."

Lolita didn't move from her spot, but her black eyes narrowed. "I think this Dr. Smith forgets you are having another man's child, although"—she ran her eyes over Roseanne's blossoming figure—"I do not see how he could."

"Dr. Smith is merely a friend," Roseanne replied flatly.

Lolita nodded, as if to say that she knew better. "I wonder. Roseanna, what Señor Chanson would say if he knew."

Roseanne gritted her teeth. "Well, what he doesn't know won't hurt him. Remember, Lolita, he doesn't even know he is about to become a father, although I doubt it will be the first time."

"Roseanna!"

"Men are known to seek their pleasure where they can. As much as he's rambled, I'm sure he's planted a seed here or there," she said spitefully, inwardly hoping he hadn't.

"Possibly, but it counts only if it grows."

Roseanne walked past the Mexican woman and into the kitchen. "It's time we faced the truth. Tyler has been gone for months. If he were going to return, don't you think he would have by now? Please, I don't want to keep hearing that he will come back. He's probably dead. I have to look out for my future now." She whirled and glared at the older woman. "And if Dr. Benjamin Smith is part of that future, then so be it. For heaven's sake, I'm not in love with the man, but he would make a good father for the baby."

"So it is a father for the baby that you want," Lolita replied hotly. "But what will you do late at night in the bed of Dr. Smith when his touch turns you cold?"

Roseanne turned her back to Lolita, wishing she could close her ears to the truthful words she was being forced to hear. "You're wrong, Lolita. You're wrong."

Lolita shook her head in angry resignation. It was no use arguing with Roseanna. She was stubborn and strong willed and proud—and sometimes very foolish. Lolita could only hope that Tyler Chanson would ride into the yard soon, otherwise he would find Roseanna and his child in the house of another man.

Tyler stopped the bay and the packhorse atop the hill that overlooked the McVey Ranch. It was a welcome sight. He hadn't warmed up since the blizzard he had encountered in northern New Mexico. Now a cold, steady rain that had lasted for days put the chill deeper into his bones. The packhorse had a sore foot and both of the animals' ears were drooping, their tails tucked, and their backs humped against the wet cold.

Tyler loosened the reins and the bay moved forward, showing more interest now as they moved closer to the ranch. The horse lifted its head, perked its ears, and nickered in response to some other horses in a nearby pasture.

Tyler forgot his travel miseries as an apprehension built inside him. What if Roseanne refused to hear him out? To understand? He had been gone a terribly long time. And then a worse fear embedded itself inside him. What if she had married?

Suddenly some shouts went up as a vaquero emerged from the large barn door. His noise brought a few others from the various buildings where they were working. When Tyler reached the yard, they had joined him, with greetings and questions that he couldn't answer all at once. Jack McVey appeared on the house's porch and Tyler reined his animals that way. After he dismounted, a vaquero took his horses to the barn and the others hastened onto the porch out of the rain.

Jack spoke first. "It's a bad day for travelin'."

Tyler walked up the steps and shook hands with Jack in greeting. "It's been a bad *month* for travelin'. Blizzards in New Mexico, cold temperatures, and now this rain." Tyler removed his wet topcoat and tried to shake the rain from it. "Is Bill inside?"

A strange look passed over Jack's face and an intense silence slipped over the group standing by. Jack tucked his hands in his back pockets and shifted uncomfortably from one foot to the other. "I guess you didn't hear. Bill was killed on the drive by lightning."

Tyler was stunned. It took him a moment to absorb the news as he stared in disbelief at Jack McVey. And then a fear gripped him. "Roseanne? Is she all right?"

"She's fine—least she was the last time I heard."

Tyler's heart began to pound. "What do you mean?" He looked past Jack into the open door of the house. Jack's wife was inside. Suddenly it struck Tyler that things were not normal here. Jack and his wife had their own house. His wife had never spent much time in the main house.

"Come on in, Tyler," Jack said. "Get warm and into some dry clothes. I can see you've got some catchin' up to do."

Tyler stared into the fire, sitting in McVey's horsehair chair with his feet propped on the hearth. He had ridden a thousand miles only to find Roseanne had stayed in Denver.

Suddenly he felt like putting his fist through something. He could have been with her by now, but instead he was here alone in this house with all its memories, knowing it would be crazy and dangerous to head north now with winter settling into the mountains. He would have to wait until spring, at least until March.

He looked about the room. Jack and his wife had gone to bed. They had taken over the house until Roseanne returned—if she did. Jack didn't seem to mind that he had been handed this empire to run. Tyler had to remind himself it was not his business that Roseanne had given it up to Jack, even temporarily.

He stood up, and began pacing. The fire crackled in the late night stillness as it glowed in the darkness he had preferred over lighting a lamp. Why had she made such a hasty decision? Did it have anything to do with McVey's death? Did it have anything to do with Tyler leaving her? Or another man?

Tyler sat back down, feeling very tired. Depression and frustration filled him. Jack had no answers. The vaqueros who had gone on the drive returned with the news she had given them, and no explanations. He didn't want to think that she might have found another man, but it was so possible in a place like Denver where the men outnumbered the women and were, more times than not, single.

He pressed his head back against the chair and closed his eyes, which burned from staring at the fire. He had made some wrong decisions in his life, but leaving her to chase his past had been the biggest one of all.

The weeks passed and with each one came a visit from Benjamin Smith. He usually stayed for tea, dinner, or a quick lunch, depending on the time of day. As always, he was the perfect gentleman and there had been no more romantic implications unless they were in the warm way he watched her. Roseanne enjoyed his attention. In her condition, she needed the assurance that she was still attractive, the assurance that only a man could give.

Her time was near, and although she was frightened of the unknown, she was anxious to have it over with. She had all sorts of complaints and ailments. She couldn't sleep at night, for trying to find a comfortable position; the child's kicks were continuous, strong, and painful; she couldn't enjoy her food because everything gave her indigestion; it was hard to walk and her legs fell asleep when she sat because the weight of the baby cut off her circulation. But Ben said it was all normal.

She left her room and started down the stairs when suddenly she felt another sharp pain in her stomach. It was hard enough to send her groping for the banister and gasping in pain, but after it had subsided she continued down the stairs. It probably meant nothing. In the kitchen, Lolita had started breakfast so Roseanne went directly to the cupboard to set plates for the two of them. A couple of minutes later, however, she had another pain that doubled her over and chased the color from her face.

Lolita took her arm and immediately moved her toward the living room. "Lie down. I'll have Diego send one of the vaqueros for the doctor."

Roseanne could not dispute her orders; something told her it was time.

It seemed hours before Ben arrived, racing his horse into a froth beside Diego Padilla. He burst into the house without knocking and went directly to the couch. "How close are the pains, Roseanne? How long have they been going on?"

She tried to answer him but another wave tore at

her, flooding over her stomach and her back, forcing her into an arch against the onslaught of the agony. She had fought against screaming and the tears slid from her eyes. Her palms were gouged and nearly bloody from her fingernails.

Lolita answered the doctor's question. "The pains are maybe one minute apart. There is very little relief."

"I'll get her upstairs to her bed. Bring my bag, will you?"

As he placed her gently on the bed, another pain wrenched her body. He hung on to her hand until it had subsided, but he knew, by the crushing grip she had on his fingers, the full extent of her agony. He peeled his coat off and rolled up his sleeves. Lolita put the bag down and he asked her to get hot water. She left and he sat on the bed next to Roseanne.

She tried to acknowledge him with a smile but it was immediately twisted into a cry of pain, one that she could not suppress this time. He allowed her to take his hand again; he knew she needed something to hold on to. He had delivered many babies in his years, but he was nervous about this one. Nervous because it was Roseanne's, and he was tormented to see her in the pain that he knew she must suffer, the pain he could not stop.

Lolita brought the water she had heated at the first indication of labor. Benjamin scrubbed his hands thoroughly then asked her to bring what clean towels she had and a blanket to wrap the baby in. He returned to Roseanne's side and found she was watching him with frightened eyes.

He sat down on the edge of the bed, his own eyes tender and sympathetic. Although he couldn't know the pain, he knew it was tremendous. He had seen women die. He had seen babies die. He was a little frightened himself this time, but he knew there was no reason to be at this point. There was no indication that anything was irregular.

Lolita came back into the room and at Ben's request helped Roseanne into a gown. Then, Ben reentered the room, made a quick examination of Roseanne, and covered her with a sheet. He spoke to Lolita, never taking his eyes from Roseanne. For the moment she was resting again between contractions. "Lolita, would you fix a pot of coffee? It'll be a while by the looks of things. And would you bring some cold water for Roseanne?"

Lolita stood at the end of the large brass bed and wrung her hands, remembering the pain of the one child she had lost. "She is so small, Doctor. Will she be all right?"

Benjamin rested his hand on Roseanne's stomach and he felt the tightening of the next contraction practically before Roseanne did. It jerked her from her dozing, increasing in intensity until she fought the scream rising in her throat. The hand in hers was all that kept her on an even keel of sanity, otherwise she floated in a limbo of pain with nothing to cling to.

Benjamin felt her grip easing and he was thankful; it had been powerful enough to bring him to his knees. He answered Lolita. "She is small, but the baby's head is showing."

"Then it should be soon," Lolita replied hopefully.

"No." He unintentionally crushed her spirits. "I've seen labor go on for hours at this stage."

Hours ticked by on the hands of the desk clock in Roseanne's room. She was nearly too weak to push now when she needed her strength the most, but she was so numb from pain and weakness that Ben doubted she even knew who she was. Her eyes were glassy and she fell asleep immediately between each contraction. For the past three hours she had occasionally cried out and pleaded with him. "Do something. Please." But now she was so weak that even that thought had become lost somewhere in her tortured mind. She was aware only of the pain and she had seemed to accept that it would never come to an end.

Then suddenly she screamed a curse that made a chill run down his spine. The shriek scattered the chickens in the yard and brought Lolita on a high run from downstairs. By the time she came huffing into the room, Dr. Benjamin Smith was holding the baby in his hands. Lolita broke into tears of relief. "Thank God. Oh thank God, it's over."

Benjamin put the baby on Roseanne's stomach and turned to Lolita. "It's a boy."

He repeated the words to Roseanne and she acknowledged them with silent, exhausted eyes. The pain was over. She reached down and touched the warm, heavy, wet boy baby on her stomach and patted it feebly. Then her eyes closed involuntarily, but before she fell asleep, she had memorized the tiny little head covered with black hair, and she remembered the final pain that had threatened to destroy her.

Roseanne opened her eyes. The room was dark, lit only by one oil lamp. Within its glow, Ben slumped in a bedside chair, sleeping. Next to her in the small cradle lay the baby curled into a tight little ball on his stomach. He was washed, dressed, and perfectly content with his new world. The memory of the pain was still much too vivid, and she supposed it always would be, but she wanted to hold the child. It was hers. Hers alone. The love she had for Tyler, she would give to his son. If Tyler never returned, at least she would always have a part of him.

She tried to rise from the bed but fell back helplessly against the pillow. She was weaker than she had realized. The movement brought Ben to attention and he was on his feet and by her side with no sign that he had ever been asleep.

"Roseanne," he said softly. "You're awake. How do you feel?"

"Fine." She smiled weakly. She looked at the baby. "I want to hold him, Ben."

"Of course." He was glad that she was showing signs of improvement. He had been worried that something might go wrong, not that it couldn't even now, but her interest in the baby was a good sign.

Carefully he lifted the tiny bundle from the cradle against its wishes and placed it in the curve of her arm. It immediately fell back to sleep, obviously not interested in food or anything else.

Roseanne was concerned. "Why doesn't he want to eat?"

"Sometimes they don't for a while, but I'm sure he will pretty soon. What are you going to name him?"

She answered without hesitation. "William Tyler. For his grandfather and his father."

He watched her with the child. She was nervous, not knowing quite how to handle it, but he knew she would be a good mother. He turned suddenly and went for his coat. Damn her husband. If he weren't dead somewhere, then he ought to be. He gathered up his things but his gaze kept straying to Roseanne with her child. He was jealous. That was what was wrong with him. He was simply jealous that the both of them weren't his.

"I'd better go Roseanne, but I'll be back to check on you tomorrow."

She looked up from the baby, a soft glow showing in her face, but he remembered the pale lines of twisted pain that had been there earlier, the pain that could age a woman. She said, "Don't go now, Ben. It's dark and it's cold out there. If you don't have anything pressing just stay until morning. We have an extra bed, and you left word in town where you were, didn't you?"

He softened. He could not deny her any request she might make. There were no other babies due right away and the ranch wasn't so far from town that he couldn't be reached quickly in an emergency. He took a deep breath and let it out. Of course he would stay. He would stay forever if she would just give the word.

Chapter 19

April 1863

TYLER STEPPED FROM THE HOTEL with his few belongings over his shoulder. Outside, the wind blew fitfully down the streets, forcing him to lean into it and to pull his hat down tighter on his head. It had been a dry spring and the winds had continually lashed at the plains. It was a bad day for riding, but it was time for him to be moving and he would just have to put up with a skittish bay.

He rounded the corner to the livery stable and saw the hostler busy at work moving grain barrels into the barn. He wore an old threadbare coat that didn't look like it could turn much wind, but he seemed indifferent to the chilly April air.

Tyler stepped into the building and welcomed the immediate relief from the wind. The hostler barely looked up, but he recognized him. "It'll beat a man to death same as bein' in a fistfight," he said.

"Yes, it's a good day to stay inside," Tyler replied as he took his horse from the stall and proceeded to curry him down.

"Never seen the day I could do that, son." The hostler picked up a pitchfork and began shoveling out the bay's stall, already preparing it for another horse. "See you're headin' out," he continued. "You've had enough of this here town, I reckon. Ain't bad here. It's as good a place as any. Better'n some. You ever find that feller you was inquirin' 'bout?" The hostler shoveled in rhythmic motion, never glancing up but asking his questions as casually as he would the time of day.

Tyler had inquired about Cotton purely out of habit, but his real business lay up the road. He had spent too many lonely nights in Texas waiting for spring to get sidetracked now by any word of Cotton. It was time for a reckoning with the woman he loved.

He positioned the blanket on the bay's back and then threw the saddle up. "No, I haven't seen him."

"Used to ramble a lot when I was younger. Couldn't stay tied to one place. Always figured the grass was greener over the next hill, or I'd get to the end of the rainbow and find that pot of gold. Now, I just shovel muck, but in a way I guess it's my pot of gold. Where you headin' anyway? Reckon you'll find something better somewheres else?"

Tyler dropped the fender on the saddle and picked up his bedroll. He glanced over at the hostler who was watching him now and waiting patiently for his answer. "I'm going to Denver. I hear tell the streets there are paved with gold."

The old man shook his head and laughed. "Maybe so, son. Maybe so."

The dining room at the Tremont House was dimly lit for the evening meal and the room was filled to capacity. Roseanne sat at a center table with Benjamin

Smith and they chatted over unimportant matters while they waited for their meal to be served. Roseanne had regained her figure and had had a special dress made for the evening. She had gone out with Ben numerous times since the baby was born, but tonight was different. Two weeks ago Ben had stated his desire to marry her if they could find out whether Tyler was truly dead. With Roseanne's consent, he had hired someone to go into the mountains, in the vicinity of the robbery, to ask questions.

Lolita shrieked and ran into the kitchen howling when she had first heard the news of Ben's intention, then she had hotly denounced the idea when Roseanne belligerently said she was going to accept if—and she had hesitated with inner turmoil—if Tyler were dead.

"Lolita," she said, "it has been nearly a year since I saw Tyler and I've heard nothing from him. I don't want to think he's dead, but sometimes a person must face that which becomes evident. I can't spend my life waiting for a man who will never return. Ben is a good man and is willing to raise my son as his own. He has many good qualities."

She had sought words not only to convince Lolita, but to convince herself. Yet the more she talked, the more doubt arose in her mind. Quickly she had pushed it aside. She had to do something with her life; she had to forget Tyler. She had to settle it all permanently.

"But you don't love him," Lolita had insisted.

Roseanne denied this accusation. She did love Ben—in a platonic way.

She definitely didn't want a man who remotely reminded her of Tyler. She needed someone she could care about but not someone who could consume her body, heart, and soul. Ben provided a haven from emotion; being with him was like sailing a halcyon sea—there were no tumultuous waves to engulf her, no rocky shores to run aground on. It would be a peaceful relationship. Never again would she be powerless to the demands of the body and the heart.

Ben reached across the table, took Roseanne's hand and dissolved her faraway thoughts. ''Don't look so pensive,'' he said. ''This is a night to enjoy.''

She responded to his warm, gentle touch and reciprocated with a smile and a vow to give him her full attention. Tyler Chanson wasn't worth her thoughts, despite his monopoly of them. But, realistically, how could she forget him when every time she looked into the face of her son she saw his father?

The desk clerk at the Tremont House reached for a key. ''Room 10.'' Tyler moved to the register and picked up the pen. He had ridden past the ranch on his way to town. It looked very permanent and prosperous. He had been tempted to stop, but he wanted to spruce up a bit and buy some new clothes before he presented himself to her. It was late. He planned to rest up and go back to the ranch in the morning. It wasn't far.

In his search for Walt Cotton it had become his habit to idly scan the pages of the register while he signed his name. So it was because of this habitual wariness that his eye caught his own name, ''Chanson,'' and next to it, ''Roseanne.'' The pen halted in midair. It could only be his Roseanne. He stared at the name as if the ink could explain away the puzzling signature.

He finished signing his name then dropped the pen back into the center of the book. He took the key the desk clerk held out to him but his curiosity overwhelmed him. "Is Roseanne Chanson in this evening?"

The clerk twisted his head and read the name upside down. Just a few spaces below it was Tyler's name. The clerk looked back up into his bearded face. "Ah, yes. Mrs. Chanson stays here often. Is she a relative of yours?"

"Yes," he answered, covering his surprise at her marital status. "She is."

The clerk nodded. "Then you're in luck. She's in the dining room at this very moment.

Tyler folded his hand around the key. "Thank you."

As he moved to the entrance of the dining area, his heart picked up speed to the tune of an erratic tempo. He didn't have to search for her. She was in the center of the room with another man holding her hand. She was smiling at him as he talked to her in a very attentive way. The pale pink dress she wore was the latest fashion, high-collared with a ruffle that surrounded the neckline and curved around onto the bodice. It appeared as though she had taken pains to look her very best and he wondered, with an ache digging deep inside him, if this man was special to her.

A frown creased his face as anger swelled inside him and the shadow of jealousy clouded his thinking.

She was more beautiful than he remembered, and she was different somehow. Maybe it was only his imagination or the fact that a year had gone by, but she appeared older, more mature, and he wondered if the hardship of her father's death had brought this change in her.

In the dimly lit room a dark shadow filled the entrance and commanded Roseanne's attention. Despite

Ben's plans for their future, her gaze was drawn away from him and to the tall figure in the doorway. Suddenly, as if she had seen a ghost, she gasped and pulled her hand free of Ben's slack, unsuspecting grip. Even with the dusty black hat pulled low on his head, the heavy black beard concealing the greater portion of his face, and the clothes dusty from days of hard riding, there was no mistaking the man with the angry dark eyes that were riveted on her in narrowing, gleaming animosity.

She felt confusion, mixed with fear, love, and relief. She wanted to leap to her feet and run into his arms, but propriety kept her in her seat. Instead, all the questions of the past year tumbled through her mind again and she wanted only to hear the answers and to run her hands along his rough, bearded face.

But was he here because of her? Suddenly anger welled inside her. Or was he here still looking for Walt Cotton?

He was coming toward her and what would she say? What would she do? She had waited so long for this moment, hoping it would happen, and now she was mercly numb in the tangled knot of her mixed emotions. He had loved her. He had run off and left her. Damn him for it all. Damn him for the power he had over her mind and her body—even her life.

She released the air that had been held tightly in her chest. Ben turned in his chair to see what had caused her alarm and the fading color in her face. A man, resembling a ruffian, moved purposefully toward them. His eyes never faltered from the point of their interest—Roseanne.

Ben turned back to Roseanne and saw the helpless mixture of feelings crossing her face like a cloud passing over the sun. He did not have to be told; the stranger was Tyler Chanson.

He stood over the table, towering ominously like a black cloud of doom. When he spoke, his voice was deep, but loud enough only for them to hear. Roseanne's heart turned at the gentle, persuasive quality of it that stirred so many memories and so many feelings from their short powerful union.

"Roseanne," he greeted her blandly. "I see you haven't suffered for company in my absence." For the first time he removed his eyes from her and assessed her dinner companion openly. Then he extended a hand in introduction. "I'm Tyler Chanson."

He was minding his manners, but he wanted to pull her to her feet and into his arms. She was such a vision of beauty, but it was more than that that captured his heart. It, was everything about her; her honesty, her fire, her indomitability, her intelligence, and every little thing down to the silky feel of her fingers running over his skin.

But here she was with another man. All his plans and his words would have to be changed now. Suddenly he felt weak and he knew it was not because of the long, hard ride to get here.

Benjamin Smith came easily to his feet, but his legs felt like jelly. His entire life, his hopes and his dreams, were crumbling beneath him. He met Chanson's grip. "I'm Benjamin Smith, one of the doctors in town."

Roseanne held her breath and looked at her plate, hoping—no praying—that Ben wouldn't say anything about the child. This was not the time to tell Tyler he had a son. She wasn't even sure she wanted to tell him. The baby was hers. She didn't know if she wanted to share it with him. She felt somehow he had no right to it.

Still standing, Ben continued awkwardly when the introductions were over, looking first from Roseanne to Tyler. "It's been a long time since you've seen your wife. If you'll both excuse me, I'll leave you alone." He turned to Roseanne where his gaze fell fondly, lovingly. "It's been a pleasure, Roseanne. If you should need anything . . ."

Tyler pondered over the easy mention of Roseanne as his wife, but he remained silent. Roseanne met his questioning eyes, her head tilting proudly, daring him to deny it. Tyler had not missed the tenderness in Smith's eyes and he wondered to what extent their relationship had gone. The thought of Roseanne in his arms and in his bed induced him to a quiet rage, yet he had no one to blame but himself if it had happened.

He stopped the doctor's departure by a hand on the man's shoulder, forcing him back into his seat with subtle dominance. "No, please don't go, Mr. Smith." He looked into Roseanne's eyes for a clue that would tell him just what she felt for Smith. "You haven't completed your dinner." He was curious to find out why Roseanne had been posing as his wife, but it could wait until he had her alone. "I'm on my way to my room to get cleaned up. My wife can join me when she's finished."

Roseanne's eyes were lit by an unreadable brilliance; no doubt she was angry that he had shown up at such an inopportune time. He smiled down at her and reached out to cup her chin in his hand, the feel of her soft skin shocking his senses. He spoke only to her even though Smith could undoubtedly hear. "Enjoy your dinner, my dear," he said, his tone and his eyes containing a dangerous, romantic connotation. "But don't tarry too long."

He left them sitting uncomfortably at the table.

Benjamin watched him exit the dining room. Then he turned back to Roseanne. "Are you sure you wouldn't like to go with him now?"

Considering what would be expected of her in this situation, she was silent for several seconds. She wanted to talk to Tyler—or did she? She knew she would definitely have to explain why she was posing as his wife. But she didn't want to tell him about the child until she knew what his feelings were for her. The child could make him stay and she wanted him to do that only if he loved *her* as well. She needed time to think of what she would say, and what she wouldn't say.

"Don't go, Ben. I'm not sure what to do at the moment. I don't know if anything will change—I—" She averted her eyes to the doorway as she thought of Tyler and Ben and she searched for her true feelings toward both of them. Then, as if she had answered her own question, she shrugged and continued coldly and confidently. "Don't worry, Ben. Nothing's changed. I'm sure Tyler is only here temporarily. Settling down isn't first on his priority list."

Ben reached across the table for her hand, hesitant now that her husband had suddenly become more than a name. "You're just angry. He's your husband, the father to your child. You know I love you, but I won't stand between you and him."

Frightened that she might lose the one stable thing in her life, the security of Ben's love and devotion, she said as she gripped his hand, "He may not be back to stay, Ben. I can't let him hurt me any more."

Ben patted her hand and wished he weren't in the middle of this. He couldn't help but wonder how Roseanne really felt about her husband and how she really felt about him. She had never come right out and said, "I love you." Still he had been sure that he could make her happy and eventually she could have learned to love him. But now, he shook his head remorsefully, now he wasn't so sure. Things would have been so much simpler if Chanson had not returned.

Roseanne and Ben completed their meal in silence, then Roseanne rose dubiously. Ben was on his feet immediately. "I'll escort you to your husband's room."

"Thank you, but it isn't necessary."

Ben noted her nervousness and lack of color. "Roseanne," he said tenderly. "Are you sure you're going to be all right?"

"Of course." She attempted a smile.

He studied her skeptically. "I know the reason for your separation must have been unpleasant, but now—" He hesitated, wondering if he should continue. "You almost act as though you're afraid of the ruffian—excuse me— but he does look a bit like a ruffian," he apologized, seeing that his opinion of Chanson had struck a chord of amusement in her. Yet she did not deny or defend the description. Uneasily now he was compelled to finish. "Are you afraid of him for some reason?"

Yes, she was afraid of him. Afraid of how easily he could melt her heart and her pride and bend her to his will and make her admit that she needed him badly. Just thinking of their intimate moments together brought a crimson color to her cheeks and she hoped it wouldn't be too noticeable in the dim room.

"No, I'm not afraid of him," she replied quietly.

She placed her hand on Ben's forearm and considered their relationship. It had never gone beyond a kiss; silently she was thankful now that it hadn't. "I should go now, Ben, but I'll be speaking with you in the morning."

He caught her arm and detained her further, his blue eyes intense on her upturned face. "No, Roseanne. I think your husband is a very strong-willed man and I think he knows he'd be a fool to give you up. And now"—he shrugged as though he had already come to terms with the situation,—"now he has a son. If you need me, Roseanne, I'll be here." He dropped her arm and hurried from the room.

Roseanne collected herself and made her way slowly to the room that the desk clerk had told her was Tyler's.

Bravely she straightened her back and rapped on the door. From within she heard the rich timbre of his voice. "Come in."

Tensely, she opened the door and stepped inside. He was in the bathtub with water up to his chest and she tried to be irritated with him for allowing her to come in at such a time, but she remembered that they had never had anything to hide from each other. She moved farther into the room, keeping her distance and trying to keep her eyes from his broad, bare chest exposed above the water level.

Too well she remembered the hot feel of his skin on hers and how easily just his nearness, his touch, his kiss could ignite a sexual need for him that was almost shameful.

She moved farther until she was directly in front of him. With each movement he made lathering his body, the muscles rippled in his shoulders and arms.

She saw then, in the dim light of the room's one lamp, a ragged, flaming scar in his shoulder and she knew it was one of the wounds he had received in the robbery. She tried to be angry at him but deep inside she could not fully convince herself he would do such a thing for the sake of having the gold. Besides, she was not in a position to judge; she had been less than honest these last few months.

Knowing he had nearly died and the pain he must have experienced, she felt compassion well inside her. But with all her willpower she fought to keep from confessing how she had missed him, how she had needed him. He must not know these things if she were not the reason he was here.

"Dinner over so soon?" he mocked.

She moved back and sat on the one chair in the room. "Why did you come to Denver, Tyler?"

He rolled the bar of soap around in his hands then stuck one leg out of the tub and began to lather it, unconcerned at her presence. "Was Denver off-limits to me?"

She stood up again, agitated, and began pacing the floor in a tight little six-foot square. "Of course not, but weren't you afraid we'd meet again?"

"No," he replied more casually than he felt. "I know you never wanted to see me again, but how was I to know you were in Denver. Why *are* you still here?"

Of course, Roseanne reasoned, he would have had no way of knowing she had stayed here. He wouldn't even know about her father's death. How could she have been so stupid to even think he might have come back for her? He was here to hunt and to kill. He didn't care about her. Her heart was breaking and in her anguish she retaliated.

"Do you mean to tell me that after a whole year you weren't able to find your man? It seems to me that you should take some lessons on tracking from some old trappers, or maybe some Indians."

He shot her a sardonic glare then went back to scrubbing his feet. "I found Cotton, but he got away."

"And you're here looking for him."

He did not reply, but his thoughts were deep as they narrowed silently on her.

"It doesn't bother you that you just kill!" She threw her arms out in an agitated gesture. "And when Cotton's dead, then what? Will you find somebody else to kill? What will you do when it's all over? Is the taste of blood so strong in your mouth that you'll just keep on?" She had reached the edge of his tub. Her breathing was irregular and her eyes were sparking in rage. "Well, Tyler Chanson? Will you? And what will you do with all the blood on your hands? Will you ever be able to wash it off?"

Like a snake his arm darted out and his hand coiled around her slender arm, pulling her down with a power that nearly toppled her into the water. "We kill to stay alive," he growled. "And we kill to compensate for the justice that never takes place. They raped my wife, Roseanne." His voice was pitiless and cold. "They raped her, again and again. They killed the child she was carrying—*my* child. If I could make them suffer the way they made her suffer, believe me I would! But I don't kill just for the fun of it."

He released her with a shove and she staggered back against the bed, instantly rubbing her wrist where his iron hold had turned it red and fiery. The full extent of his desire for revenge finally came to her and she sat in stunned silence.

Angrily he reached for the towel and stood up, drawing it around him. He glared at her. For the first time she noticed the fresh, ragged scar on his thigh, no doubt another wound from the robbery.

"Does that answer all your questions?" he asked insolently, placing his hands loosely on his hips.

She swallowed hard. "I'm sorry. I didn't know . . ." She turned away, cringing at the thoughts of what his wife had experienced, visualizing what a horror it must have been for him to watch. "I'm sorry she was killed."

His voice was bitter. "They didn't kill her. She bled to death."

She looked at him disbelievingly at first, but she saw the angry memory written on his face. She felt uncomfortable, and inexplicably ashamed, so she moved to the door, but once again his hand encircled her arm, more gently this time, and he drew her around to face him. Beneath his fury, a calming curiosity struggled upward toward the surface, forcing those long ago memories to the background.

"Not so quick, *Mrs*. Chanson," he said softly. "I think you've got some explaining to do."

Chapter 20

April 1863

TYLER RELEASED HER ARM AND SHE moved away from him to the center of the room, turning her back to him. "All right. I'll explain everything to you, but only after you're dressed."

"It shouldn't bother you to see me half-dressed," he gibed, as he picked up his pants.

"Perhaps not," she answered, "but those days are over."

She heard movement behind her; the towel falling to the floor, the rustling of the rough cloth as it slipped over his legs, and his boots and socks going on. "How easily we forget love," he mocked her. "How long will it be before you discard your Benjamin Smith?"

She whirled on him just as he shrugged into his shirt. The muscles in his powerful arms and shoulders rippled beneath the movement and instantly her heart lurched upward just as it had all those months ago. He was a powerful man physically, but as her gaze locked with the lazy, dangerous light glowing in his dark eyes, Roseanne realized that his power over her was in his subtle ability to possess her, in the warm umber of his eyes, in the gentle touch of his lean hands, in the persuasive quality of his words, and in his familiarity with her body and the secret thoughts that only she should know. And even now, he knew what was on her mind. She looked away from his knowing eyes to the tanned, rugged hands methodically drawing the buttons across his chest.

For the space of thirty slow seconds her words were caught and forgotten in her throat. When the last button slipped through the hole she recalled her anger and dredged it forward and out. "Benjamin Smith has asked me to marry him."

Unmoved by her declaration, Tyler tucked the shirt into his pants then reached for a comb sitting on the bureau. He slid it through his wet, wavy hair. "From what I understand," he replied in a preoccupied tone, "you're married to me." He set the comb on the bureau and turned to her. His eyes bore intently into hers, demanding an explanation.

So she had been caught in her lie. Well, it didn't matter. They both knew they were not married and there was nothing he could do to stop her from marrying Ben. She tossed her head back defiantly. "It was convenient for me to be married. It keeps the wolves from the door."

His brow rose disbelievingly while his mouth quirked beneath the black moustache. "If you wanted to be married then why didn't you make up a name, or use someone who was dead. You wouldn't have had to worry about him coming back to alter your plans."

She turned her back to him. Yes, why hadn't she just fictionalized? Was it because she wanted her baby to carry its real father's name? Tyler had obviously been crushed by the loss of the other child eight years ago. It wasn't fair to withhold the truth about a son who was alive and well, but what if he tried to take Will from her, or stayed with her only because of Will?

"Well, Roseanne?" He stepped up behind her, but she moved away. "Why did you name me as your husband?"

His hand on her shoulder easily pulled her around. His eyes were on her lips. Frantically she fought to get away, but was motionless against his hypnotic gaze.

"Was it because you secretly wanted me to be your husband? Or was it because, in the carnal sense, I *am* your husband?"

Both hands were on her shoulders now. She was powerless against his strength as he slowly drew her up against his chest. Her hands curled into tight fists and she pressed them defensively and unconsciously against his brawn, but her eyes were on his lips and her mind was on his intent. Then, suddenly, his kiss consumed her mouth and for a glorious moment she fell into the dark abyss of possession. But remembering what he'd done to her, she struggled once again to the surface and writhed in his arms, pushing at his chest, severing the kiss before it could be completed. With all her strength she pushed herself away from him, the events of the past year tumbling back across her consciousness. He had left her alone to hurt and cry. He had left her carrying his child to suffer the sickness, the pain, the humiliation. "No!" she screamed at him, her face bursting with red fury. "You won't touch me again! I won't have another of your bastard sons! I won't! You just leave me alone. Get away from me. Don't ever touch me again."

Her outburst played out and she stared at him with

wide, wild eyes. She was panting in embarrassment at her lack of control and the startling realization of what she had furiously disclosed.

Only temporarily stunned, he moved forward deliberately like a mountain lion stalking its prey, closing in on her. His eyes narrowed. "My bastard son? What are you saying, Roseanne?"

He had her by the shoulders again, but his hands were as gentle and tender as she had recalled in her myriad dreams. At the moment all she wanted to do was fall into his arms and cry and seek the comfort that waited in his strength. But she wouldn't. No, she would never give in to him again without the sanctity of marriage.

He shook her slightly as his eyes pried into hers, looking for answers. "Tell me," he demanded, his voice grating with impatience. "Tell me about my son."

"Yes, you have a son. *We* have a son." She wrenched free of his grip and moved a safe distance away, waiting for his reaction.

Dubiously he stared at her slim figure, running the length of it and back, obviously questioning the validity of her story. "How old is he?"

"Add it up," she said. "The baby was born in January, at the end of the month. He's going on three months."

"Then that's why you used my name and why you stayed here in Denver." He nodded, understanding a little better now. "You were going to have my child and you didn't want anybody to know you weren't married."

"Of course." Her expression showed no hint of the

pain and humiliation she had suffered alone, but her voice was curt.

He wandered aimlessly about the room, deep in thought, jealous of Smith, angry at what he had missed. "Then Benjamin Smith thinks you're married? But tell me, how did you plan on marrying him if you were *supposed* to be married to me? Legally you can't do that. And I'm sure you didn't want to tell him that you were actually single and always have been."

She drew her back up straighter, but realized that there had been no sarcasm intended. She relaxed; she wouldn't need to defend herself. Quickly she told him how she had met Randolph Pierpont and what he had told her about Tyler's involvement in the robbery. "He said you could be dead. Ben hired a man to try and find out for sure."

Tyler's gaze pinpointed on her. "And did you hope I was so you could be 'free' to marry Smith?"

"Of course I didn't want you to be dead, but naturally I wanted to know if you were."

"Do you love this Smith guy?"

Roseanne met his dark gaze, wondering if he loved her as he had once said he did. So much hinged on that. She turned her back to him, unable to manage a reply. If only Tyler would say those words again. She might make herself believe them this time.

Seeing she wasn't going to give him an answer, Tyler continued. "What did you name my son?"

His immediate possession of the child disturbed her and she wavered nervously beneath the unexpected question. She faced him again. "William Tyler."

A flash of surprise shone in his eyes, but he was obviously pleased with the selection. Still his response was sarcastic. "I'm amazed you gave me any credit."

"Why shouldn't I? He *is* yours—unless, of course, you doubt that."

His eyes once again slid over her slim figure, either remembering their moments or doubting her story. "No, I don't doubt it, Roseanne. I want to see him."

Her nerves surged with alarm, but it subsided quickly; she could not deny him that. "Of course. He's in my room with Lolita tending him, but I'm sure he's asleep now. You'll have to wait until morning."

Tyler took her arm and pulled her toward the door. "No, I won't. I want to see him now—tonight."

In the hall he released her and she walked four doors down. "Keep your voice low if he's asleep."

Inside, the room was dimly lit by one lamp. Lolita was slumped in a chair asleep with her head thrown back and her mouth open. Next to her was a cradle, and inside the baby slept contentedly on his stomach.

Tyler left Roseanne's side, drawn to the baby by his curiosity and eagerness to see the son he had fathered. It was hard for him to believe this had happened, and now, as he looked tenderly down on the infant, he wished he had been here through the pregnancy and the child's birth. But it was obvious that since he hadn't, Roseanne held it against him mightily.

He couldn't see much of the baby except a head of black hair. Its face was turned to the side and its features and head shape were perfect, as far as he was concerned. Gingerly, a bit intimidated and awed by the tiny living being he had helped to create, he placed his hand on the baby's back, felt the warmness through the cotton gown and felt the steady, strong rise and fall of its breathing. The feel of the life, the recognition of his own blood, filtered from the child to the father and

Tyler knew he had to have his son, one way or the other.

Roseanne stood in the shadows near the door watching the silent, gentle exchange between father and child. Ambivalent feelings tormented her. On the one hand she was proud to see them together and to see that Tyler took great stock in William Tyler; on the other, she felt the strain of anger tearing at her heart that he could step in now and try to claim the child he had no right to. And last, she felt the threat that she might someday be pushed aside by the common male link that they would eventually share.

The child stirred, being drawn from sleep from the unfamiliar weight and warmth on his back. He fussed, but Tyler only hunkered down next to him and proceeded to finish waking him up. When his eyes were open he rolled him to his back and the infant stared at him with unconcern as he tried to find a fist to gnaw on.

Roseanne stepped forward now, perturbed at Tyler's pleased smile. "Now see what you've done." She stood over the cradle but she wasn't actually angry because it was the baby's feeding time anyway.

At the sound of Roseanne's voice, Lolita jerked awake, wiping at her eyes and pushing herself upright in confusion. She glanced around the room to get her bearings and she saw Roseanne by the cradle, then she saw the man kneeling down next to it, balancing his weight on the balls of his feet. She leaped to her feet. "Señor Chanson!"

The baby jumped, his face wrinkling in an attempt to cry that calmed when he heard the deep resonant voice of the stranger instantly soothing him, touching him once again with the warm, gentle pressure of a hand on his stomach.

Tyler stood up then and pivoted toward Lolita, a wide grin on his face. Lolita clutched her hands beneath her heart and sighed deeply, "Oh, Señor Chanson. You have come back. We thought surely you must be dead." Her eyes began to water and she dabbed at them. "But thank God. It is good to have you back." She turned to the child and smiled fondly down at him. "Your son. He is a handsome one, I think."

Tyler's gaze went back to his son also, for he found it hard to take his eyes from the fascinating little creature. "Yes," he replied proudly, "If I had known about William Tyler, I would have been back much sooner."

Roseanne's voice was cold, but her eyes revealed her hurt. "You would have known about him if you hadn't left in the first place."

"Yes, but how was I to know?"

It was a question that could not be answered so Roseanne simply looked away and back to the child. Finally Tyler said, "You know, this light isn't very good but I do believe he has your eyes, Roseanne."

It struck her as a compliment. "Yes," she replied. "That's what Ben seems to think, too."

Lolita's face clouded over and she inhaled sharply, but Tyler turned to her with the same smile he had been wearing since he laid eyes on his son. "Don't worry, Lolita," he said. "I know about Benjamin Smith's proposal to Roseanne. But"—and he turned to meet Roseanne's sulking expression—"she will be canceling her plans now that I'm back, alive and well."

Again Lolita seemed relieved. "Ah, that is good to hear, señor. Very good."

Roseanne bent to pick the baby up, wondering exactly what Tyler would do now. It appeared that he might stay, but if he did, it was obviously only because of his son. "You'll have to leave," she said. "It's the baby's feeding time."

Lolita gathered up her shawl and moved hastily to the door. "I will leave you two alone. I go to my room. *Adiós.*"

When the door closed behind her, Tyler held out his hands toward his son. "Let me hold him."

Roseanne instinctively held the child tighter but then reluctantly relinquished it into Tyler's large hands. He sat down on the edge of the bed and immediately began talking to the baby who responded with his own smiles and sounds. Angry and slightly jealous of their comradery, Roseanne tightly reminded him that it was the baby's feeding time.

"He's not complaining. Besides, I thought I'd stay to watch you feed him."

Roseanne flared. "You will not! You'll leave this room right now. You will not get the liberties of a husband, even though you are a father."

Tyler stood up and handed William Tyler to her. "If I recall, my dear Roseanne, this charade is yours. You invented it; you'll have to suffer the consequences. Unless, of course, you'd care to disclose to countless people that you gave birth to an illegitimate child. Why, I'll bet your Benjamin Smith wouldn't think so highly of you if he knew the truth."

"What you say is true," she said proudly but impudently. "But men bring women to shame, yet they are never the ones to pay for the crime."

"*I* brought *you* to shame? I think you'd better take some of the blame. You could have said 'no' at any given time. Don't make yourself into a victim, Roseanne." Now his tone was angry and curt. "One short year hasn't dimmed my memory. You helped conceive that child and you enjoyed every minute of it, so don't you try and make me feel guilty."

"Get out of here."

He walked to the door. "Even if you somehow manage to get yourself out of this "wedded" pickle you're in and actually marry Smith, you won't keep my son from me. Remember that, Roseanne."

Quietly the door opened and closed and the tears she had been suppressing finally slipped from her eyes one by one onto her cheeks to fall noiselessly onto the baby's gown. William Tyler stared up at her and smiled then turned his head to the familiar feel and smell of her breast and began searching for the source of his food.

Roseanne sat down on the edge of the bed, exhausted both mentally and physically. With one hand she wiped the tears away, but for the first time she wasn't able to stop them. Through her sobs, she spoke softly to the child as she often did. "Oh, what am I going to do? If only he had come here for me, not Walt Cotton! If only he would say that he loves me."

When the child had nursed all it wanted, Roseanne changed him and lay him down for another nap. She undressed, slipped on her nightgown, then crawled beneath the covers to lie awake, listening to the harsh April wind buffeting the town. It whispered and whistled and whined eerily through the spaces between the buildings. She couldn't fall asleep as easily as she usually did after a long, hard day. Instead she tossed and turned while her mind wrestled with and replayed the events that had brought her to where she was now. It was nearly one o'clock before she finally fell into a sleep as restless as her thoughts.

Tyler sat at a table in the saloon of the Apollo Hall and thought about things over a bottle of whiskey. Just how determined was Smith to marry Roseanne? How determined was *she* to marry *him?* Tyler poured himself another drink. He couldn't let another man raise his boy. He wasn't going to lose another child. But it was more than just the boy. His heart hurt to think that Roseanne wanted to marry someone else. She hadn't denied she loved Smith.

It was his fault for leaving her. Could it be that she truly never had loved him? That she had only used him, as she had said, needing him only for the moment and considering him an adventure the way she had considered the cattle drive?

Time ticked away and the bottle of whiskey was nearly half gone when Tyler felt a hardy smack on his back and a familiar Mexican voice. "So you have returned!" Diego Padilla pulled up a chair and sat his own bottle of whiskey next to Tyler's. His speech was a bit slurred and his breath strong with the smell of liquor, but he wasn't drunk—at least not any more than Tyler was.

"It is true," Diego continued, "I tell Roseanne not to worry. That you are not dead. That you will come back. She worries, but she pretends not to." His smile nearly covered his face. "She is here, señor. In town. You should be with her, not here filling your belly with this rotgut whiskey."

"I have been with her, Diego." He tried unsuccessfully to match Diego's jovial mood. "But she wasn't so happy to see me."

"She is just hurt, amigo. She has needed you, but how are you to know this?" He put the bottle of whiskey to his mouth and poured a large swallow down his throat.

Tyler was miserable. "You're going to have to answer some questions for me, Diego."

"Sí." Diego sat his bottle back down and pushed his sombrero to the back of his head. He settled comfortably into his chair. "There is much to talk about. Much catching up to do. I will tell you what has happened."

For over an hour, Diego and Tyler exchanged information, ignoring the wind roaring outside and scattering loose objects down the streets. The room was so noisy and full of cigarette and cigar smoke that they didn't notice anything amiss outside until a small, wiry man burst through the open doors.

"Fire! Fire!" he shouted frantically between gasps. "There's a fire down Blake Street! The whole town's gonna burn!"

Everybody got to their feet, forgetting their liquor and their cards. Someone ran up the stairs to warn those on the second floor. In seconds, everyone was thundering out of the Apollo. Two streets over they could see the smoke pouring from the Cherokee House on the southwest corner of Fifteenth and Blake streets. In the predawn hours the dark town was illuminated with an orange glow while the strong winds pulled and tossed the fire in every direction and onto any new source, hurtling the flames clear across streets and from roof to roof of the dry, combustible buildings.

Immediately every man in town volunteered to help

stave it off. Some were already tearing down buildings
to help stop its progress.

The fire was only two blocks away from the Apollo,
but it was also only two blocks away from the Tremont
House where Roseanne and William Tyler were
asleep. Tyler shouted above the roar of the wind and
pandemonium to Diego. "I'm going to get Roseanne
and the baby out of town! I'll be back as soon as I
know they're safe."

Diego ran to help fight the fire and Tyler headed for
the McGaa Street bridge that went over Cherry Creek
and to the Tremont House.

The desk clerk was asleep on his stool, his head
down on the counter. Tyler ran past him and headed up
the stairs, shouting as he went. "There's a fire at the
Cherokee House! Wake everybody up!" He didn't
wait for the clerk. He only paused to see that he had
put him into motion, then he headed for Roseanne's
room.

The door was locked. Without knocking and waiting
for her to get to the door, he drew his booted foot back
and sent it through the thin wood, splintering it in
every direction. Roseanne bolted upright but her
scream stopped in her throat when she saw him standing in the doorway with the pale light from the hallway
behind him, outlining his form.

He strode into the room and pulled her off the bed
before she could gather her wits and object. "Get a
robe on and get some things for the baby." He turned
to his son who was still sleeping peacefully despite the
intrusion. "There's a fire just down the street and with
this wind blowing the way it is the whole town of Denver could be cinders by morning."

Chapter 21

April 1863

SHE QUELLED HER FEAR AND DID AS he said. She tossed some things haphazardly into a bag by the light from the hall, stepped into her shoes, and glanced out the window toward Cherry Creek. The orange flames were dancing in the night, rising and falling through the dark sky.

Tyler had the child in his arms, cradle and all, and had moved to the door. "Come on. We'll get you out of town until we see what course this fire is going to take."

They stopped at Lolita's room but she was already gathering her few things together and she did not detain them. Without a word, the women moved past Tyler and into the hall, hurrying on silent, slippered feet into the chilly April evening. As they stepped into the street, someone pulled up with a buckboard already nearly full of women and children.

"Get in with us," the driver called. "We're taking them to the bluffs where they'll be safe."

Roseanne wanted to stay with Tyler; she felt safe with him, but he helped her into the wagon without a

328

word, and then Lolita. People made room for the small cradle and the baby who was sleeping through the commotion.

"Tyler." Roseanne looked down at him beseechingly. "What—"

He could see her fear and wished he could go with her, but he had to get back to the fire and he had to get his gear and his horse from the livery in case it were threatened. He laid a hand on her cheek. "You'll be all right. I'll be back to get you."

The driver tapped the horses and they hurried out of town. Tyler studied the direction of the fire but it was obviously out of control. As yet the livery was far enough away so the bay would be all right for a while. He hurried back across the bridge and ran down Blake Street.

Denver was a tinderbox town and most of the buildings on Larimer, McGaa, and Blake streets were built of logs or rough, unmilled clapboards sawn from pitch-filled native pine. The town was completely devoid of fire-fighting facilities as Tyler soon found out. Nine months ago a worried city council had made a resolution to equip their town with a volunteer hook-and-ladder company and two bucket brigades, but the cart and buckets were still on order and the idea of the fire department was still only on paper. It left the town helpless against the roaring inferno as it engulfed building after building and pushed the men back farther and farther down the streets. The only effective means they had to stop the blaze's onrush was to tear down the buildings in its path, destroying its fuel.

From her position on the bluffs, Roseanne watched with the other women as the fire ate Denver, piece by piece. They watched the men, small dark figures sil-

houetted against the churning, windswept orange
flames, as they fought the scorching heat and the
mighty destruction of the blaze.

At dawn, just a few hours later, the center of Denver
was a heap of black, smoldering timbers and ashes.
The fire hadn't crossed Cherry Creek, but some nota-
ble businesses had perished in its devastation; the
Cherokee House, Broadwell & Cook, the City Bak-
ery, the Elephant Corral, Daniels & Brown, W. S.
Cheesman, Ny & Company, Tritch Hardware—just to
name a few. The fire was a blow to the four-year-old
town, and the weary fire fighters, blackened by the
soot and wet with sweat, walked away to seek comfort
for their losses.

The first streaks of sunlight revealed what was left
of the city. Everyone on the bluffs had gone back into
town together.

Lolita turned to Roseanne and put an arm around her
as they assessed the damage to Denver City. Now with
the sun shining and the wind down, it all seemed like a
nightmare, but the reality was there in the charred
ruins before them.

William Tyler was fussing again; Roseanne
changed his diaper, aware that it was his feeding time
again. Roseanne wanted to go back to her room at the
Tremont, which was thankfully still standing. Lolita
offered to carry the baby's basket, and after Roseanne
bundled him up again, they started toward the hotel.

After just a few minutes they were met by Tyler and
Diego. They were tired and dirty, but relieved the
women of their burdens. The baby was hungry and
searching for a fist, but once in his father's arms and
free of Roseanne's scent, he quieted down and laughed

as he looked up into the blackened face of the bearded man.

Tyler's pride in the boy was evident and it was almost sad that he hadn't been around to see him sooner. Roseanne knew he would make a good father. Earlier she had thought she didn't want him if he stayed only for the sake of Will, but now, as she watched him and felt her love flowing for him, she decided that perhaps having him in that capacity was better than not having him at all.

When they arrived at the hotel, Tyler was met on the stairs by the manager, demanding payment for the broken door, and Roseanne went to Lolita's room to feed the baby.

Lolita looked out her window, but it didn't face the fire-blackened section of town. "I hope Señor Chanson hurries. I only want to get back to the ranch."

Roseanne was confronted with a new problem which hadn't even occurred to her before. Tyler knew nothing of what she was doing here. She would have to talk to him about it, since now he probably would be returning with her to the ranch. Everybody would be highly suspicious if he didn't. Besides, he would never let his son out of his sight.

Still, he hadn't found Cotton again, Roseanne remembered bitterly. He might pose as the doting father for a while, but one day he would get the itch, he would hear of a lead, and just as before he would leave. She must never forget that the trail of revenge was more important than the love he might find along the way. Therefore she must not give in to her need for him. Her love wasn't safe with him.

Then for the first time since the previous night she thought of Ben and wondered where he was and if he

were all right. She should go see him, but he was probably busy tending fire victims and exhausted from
being up all night along with the others. She could see
him later.

A knock sounded at the door, bringing her from her
thoughts. Lolita rushed to open it. Tyler was standing
there with his gear. "Are you ready to go?" he asked.

She looked up at him questioningly. "Do you know
about the ranch?"

He couldn't tell her that he had been to Texas looking for her; his wounded pride wouldn't let him con-
fess his feelings now that Smith was in the picture. He
wouldn't lay his soul bare to a woman who wanted to
marry another man. "Yes, Diego told me about it last
night, and also about your father's death. I'm sorry for
that, Roseanne."

He was sincere; she knew that. He and her father
had always gotten along well and had even become
good friends. She murmured a "thank you" feeling
sudden remorse as she thought about her father.
Quickly she gathered up the baby and led the way outside. Tyler helped her and Lolita into the buggy. They
left town with Diego following on horseback and Tyler's two horses tied behind the buggy.

With Lolita on the rear seat of the surrey, Tyler and
Roseanne sat uncomfortably silent, rubbing shoulders,
on the front seat. They were putting up a pretense for
the others, and they were too close not to think of the
relationship they had once had.

Finally Tyler glanced at her from the corner of his
eyes, turning his head only slightly. "I suppose
you've wondered exactly why I was involved in that
robbery."

"Yes, I have." She looked at him, liking the line of

his face and even the beard he still hadn't shaved. She also liked talking to him.

"I had a lead on Cotton," he said, and then continued, telling her the story.

"Then you weren't involved for the gold?"

His brown eyes locked with hers and for a moment he was lost in the blue depths as he had been so many times in the past and in his thoughts. "No."

Relieved, she looked ahead at the two-track road that led to the ranch. "I'm sorry you were shot, Tyler."

He directed his eyes back to the road, but his attention was still on her, sitting quietly with her hands in her lap. The gentle way she had said his name put a warm feeling inside him like that he had felt when they had been intimate. He felt a surge of longing. Maybe there was still hope for them.

At the ranch, they were met by the vaqueros who were very happy to see Tyler, but who also wanted to know about the great fire they had seen on the horizon. While they talked about it, Roseanne left the others and hurried, unnoticed, to the house and up the stairs to her room. She laid Will on the bed, and free of any restrictions, he began to kick and to play with his own hands, contented in his familiar surroundings.

She sat on the edge of the bed, watching his antics. When she heard the door open, she looked up expecting to see Lolita, but instead Tyler stood in the doorway with her belongings and the child's traveling bassinet. "Where do you want these things?"

She stood up, sudden anger sparking her eyes and her words. "Why didn't you knock?"

A sardonic smile curved his sensuous mouth and he moved into the room and dropped his burdens on the floor. "Why should I knock to enter my wife's room?"

"Because I'm not your wife!"

"Then I should tell Smith so you'd be free to marry him; that is, if he would still want you after hearing the truth."

She turned her back to him and folded her arms across her breasts. "You're playing this to the hilt, aren't you? You know you didn't have to come out here."

"What?" he gibed. "And let the cat out of the bag? I did it for you, Roseanne, to save your reputation. I thought you'd appreciate the effort."

She whirled around, raising an impotent fist at him. "Oh, you . . . you—"

"Bastard?" he taunted.

"Yes! Damn you for leaving me and running off when I was going to have your baby! Damn you for not being here to help me. Damn the pain you inflicted on me!"

Her anger sparked his defensiveness. He crossed the space between them in three steps. Glaring down at her, he grabbed her wrist. When she tried to ward him off, he grabbed the other wrist and hauled her roughly up against his chest. "I didn't know you were pregnant," he snapped. "Did you?"

"Well, no," she admitted sullenly.

"Then don't blame me for what you had to suffer alone. I would have been here if I'd known."

"I doubt it," she flung back belligerently. "You wouldn't have been able to leave your manhunt long enough to attend something so commonplace as the birth of your son."

His fingers bit into her arms until he saw her wince

from the pain, but he didn't loosen his grip. If anything, he applied more pressure. "I could have been
back here last fall but I recalled your parting words. I
didn't come back to Denver for your sake, Roseanne. I
came because there was no place else I hadn't looked
for a lead on Cotton." He didn't know why he was lying to her when he had so wanted to find her and marry
her, but he couldn't stop seeing her at that table, holding hands with Smith.

The first part of his speech had a calming effect on
her, but by the time he had completed it, she was furious again. "And now you're here not because of me,
either, but because of William Tyler."

"You bet your pretty little boots, honey." He released her and stood over his son who was watching
them with curious eyes. "You don't want me here, I
know that, Roseanne, but I have no intention of leaving, and I have no intention of giving up my son to
your Benjamin Smith. If you want to marry him, go
ahead, but you'll go without your child."

She swung at him, but he ducked her blow, taking it
instead on the shoulder. "You'll never have him. I
won't leave him. I bore him and I won't give him up
for anybody or anything—not you and not Ben Smith.
No man is worth that much to me! You'll never take
him from me. Never." Her voice had lowered to a
threat and her eyes warned him not to even try. He saw
the gleam of maternal instinct, like a female cougar
ready to defend her cub.

"It goes both ways, Roseanne. You'll never take
him from me either."

He stalked from the room, slamming the door. She
heard him take controlled yet hurried steps down the
hall and the stairs, and then she watched from the win-

dow as he came out of the house and crossed the yard to where everyone, including Lolita, was still talking.

The baby was watching her with mild interest. She bent and picked him up, then turned back to the window, continuing to watch Tyler who had already made himself at home. The vaqueros seemed to readily accept his presence as their new boss.

As her husband, Tyler was nominally the head of this ranch now, and that, too, wasn't fair since he hadn't been here to do any of the work or make any of the decisions. Yet, if she married Ben she would have to give all this up and move into his house in town, and that was something that had bothered her long before Tyler had appeared. The ranch was her life just as it had been her father's, and it would be a good place to raise William Tyler. She had never been sure if she could be content living in town with nothing more to occupy her than socials, teas, and town gossip. But now that problem was solved. The only way to keep her son was to stay here and continue with this ''marriage'' she had invented. She was relieved by this decision. But it would be so much better if things between her and Tyler could be the way she had always dreamed.

At exactly noon Lolita had the meal on, and just as Roseanne crossed the living room to the dining area, Tyler came in, automatically draping his hat and jacket on the hooks near the door. There was a tautness in the line of his mouth and a wariness in his eyes as if he were preparing to do battle with an enemy. ''Where do I go to wash up?''

She moved past him and answered over her shoulder aloofly, ''The kitchen will be fine.''

Her coolness grated on his nerves and he wanted to
give her a good spanking because she was acting like a
brat about the whole situation. He decided to give her
a little more time, for now. That wasn't to say he
wouldn't be forced to take some action sooner or later
to straighten out her thinking.

While Tyler washed, Roseanne helped Lolita put
the food on the table and dreaded having to sit through
the entire meal in his company.

To her surprise, he followed her to her place and
helped her with her chair before he went to the opposite end of the table to seat himself. It wasn't a big
table, so they were still too close for comfort. Roseanne dished up a helping of potatoes and refused to
look at him.

Tyler filled up his own plate and forced conversation. "Diego told me about the problem you had with
Henry Grehan on the drive. You handled it well."

Roseanne kept her eyes on her food and replied in-
differently, "It was nothing."

He gripped his fork tighter and gritted his teeth to
temper the anger she was trying to provoke in him. Finally he decided he wouldn't try to talk to her. The
meal was good, about the best he'd had for a long
time, so he diverted all his attention to his plate.

When he had had two helpings of everything, he declined dessert, wiped his mouth, excused himself from
the table and left the house quietly. Roseanne's forced
attempt to eat ended at his departure and she set her
fork down. She wondered what he was up to. He was
giving her the silent treatment now and she didn't care
for that.

Suddenly she felt very tired. Wearily she pushed
herself back from the table. She would take a nap. She

hadn't gotten enough sleep last night, but then Tyler hadn't gotten any.

By the end of the day the vaqueros had filled Tyler in on the operation of the WM ranch. It appeared that Roseanne had things running smoothly, and he was proud of her for making the best of a situation that could have been very painful and embarrassing for her.

Exhausted from the fire-fighting and having gotten absolutely no sleep the night before, he went to the house at suppertime feeling too tired to eat. He asked Lolita if she would just fix him a plate and bring it upstairs.

Since the house was on the same order as McVey's place in Texas, Tyler correctly guessed which was the spare room. It was clean but contained no personal items. He closed the door behind him, absently wondered if Roseanne were nursing the baby, then undressed and crawled between the covers. Before his head had settled into the pillow, he was asleep.

Lolita brought the plate shortly afterward and tapped on Roseanne's door. "Here is Señor Chanson's food that he requested. Would you like me to bring yours too so you can eat together?"

Roseanne wondered why Tyler had requested his meal in his room; no doubt to keep from having to sit at the table with her. She took the plate from Lolita. If he wanted to eat alone then she would let him. "No," she replied. "I'll be down shortly."

She went across the hall and rapped softly on the door to the guest room. There was no response, so juggling the tray in one hand, she let herself in. The curtains were drawn as usual, but the remainder of the daylight still filtered in through the center and fell across the bed where Tyler had obviously fallen asleep where he dropped.

She set the tray quietly on the small table next to the bed then studied the man who was still capable of drawing so many of her emotions to the surface. Tyler had said once that he loved her, but she had refused to believe that, hoping by denying it that she could keep herself safe from hurt, loneliness, and heartache. But it hadn't. And now she knew that her selfishness had alienated him, diminished his feelings for her. She thought of their bitter words. So much of what she had said she had not really meant. Had he? And if she did give in to him again with all her heart would he leave her, possibly to never return while she wondered if he had been killed somewhere along a dusty trail?

She studied the scar on his shoulder. He had been wounded in the search for Cotton. She looked at his other scars, the older ones. He had been through so much for the people he had lost so violently in California, and still he prosecuted the vow he had made all those years ago. He must have truly loved Carlotta, and Roseanne couldn't help but wonder if he would have done the same for her.

She had thought he would demand his conjugal rights in this absurd marriage farce and she had prepared all afternoon for what she would say and do, and what pieces of furniture she would push up against the door should he decide to break it down. But now her silly fears were unwarranted. She was even a bit disappointed. Tonight would be another lonely night. But it would be worse, because tonight she would be alone when she really didn't need to be.

* * *

Tyler awoke in the night and was unable to go back to sleep. The food by his bed was cold, and he had no appetite anyway. He needed Roseanne, but he wouldn't force himself on her. He could only hope that eventually they would solve their problems and go back to the love he remembered.

Starting a ranch here had taken courage on her part and immense faith in her ability to make it work. It required great insight into ranching, and the foresight to take advantage of a lucrative, growing market that hadn't, as of yet, been overrun. He admired her intelligence and business sense. He planned to stand behind her and work to improve what she had begun. If they could bring another herd to Colorado, it would make more grazing room on the Texas ranch and bring in operating money for both ranches.

He hoped Roseanne wouldn't resent his efforts to help her. She would learn that his true desire was for them to work together, and to love together. He had no intention of leaving. If she wanted to be free of him, she would have to be the one to go.

Chapter 22

May–June 1863

IN THE SPACE OF JUST A WEEK, ROSE-
anne had grown accustomed to Tyler's comings and
goings in the house and she had come to anticipate him
at those specified times. He stayed out most of the day
except for meals, which he took quickly and silently.
After supper he played with Will on the big rug in the
center of the living room and then went outside until
he retired to his own room. He spoke very seldom to
Roseanne and usually only when it was required. He
stayed away from her room except to see his son or
take him to and from bed.

Roseanne found the situation increasingly frustrating. She knew this arrangement couldn't go on indefi-
nitely and the fuse inside her was burning. It was
childish, but she had wanted to be the one to shun him,
but he had deftly turned the tables on her.

There wasn't much for her to do any more, either.
The vaqueros were beginning to turn to Tyler for ranch
supervision since he was with them all the time. Lolita
handled the housework and needed very little help.
Roseanne found that she was usually in the Mexican

woman's way. When William Tyler was asleep, she usually paced the floor, roving aimlessly from one room to the other.

So she had taken to riding to ease the restlessness, although Tyler frowned on her going out alone because of the increasing Indian problems in the area. He never failed to warn her not to go far. His warnings, however, simply increased her determination.

She pulled her riding gloves on and crossed the living room for her hat. "I'm going riding, Lolita!" she called into the kitchen. "Will is asleep. I'll be back to feed him."

She heard Lolita's acknowledgment, then she stepped out into the early May sunshine. She tightened the string that went beneath her chin and walked quickly to the corral. The gray was easy to catch because he enjoyed the rides as much as she did. In minutes he was saddled and heading toward Denver on an easy, rocking-chair lope.

She breathed freely once out of the yard, glad that she hadn't seen Tyler and subsequently been warned or detained by him. It pleased her a little that he was concerned about her, yet he never offered to ride along with her. She smiled cynically to herself. It would actually be to his advantage if she did get killed by Indians. Then he could have his son, a ranch, and he would be free of her.

From the west, she saw a lone rider cutting across on a path for Denver. He spotted her too and suddenly waved. She pulled the gray to a dancing halt and waited as the rider drew nearer. It was Ben Smith. Delighted she waved and gave the gray his head as she rode to meet him. She hadn't seen or spoke to him since the fire over two weeks ago.

He pulled his horse up alongside hers. "What brings you out this way?" He was glad to see her alone.

"Just riding. And you?" She glanced at the black bag tied to his saddle.

"Mrs. Conroy just had her fifth baby. She gave birth before I got there. Everything's fine—both mother and daughter." While the gray danced beneath her constricting rein, Ben's horse stuck its nose in the spring grass. He gave it its head and folded his hands over the saddle horn. "How are things going for you, Roseanne?" Concern was in his eyes, sadness, and even hope.

Roseanne grew tired of fighting the gray's energy so she dismounted. Seeing that they weren't going anywhere, the horse relaxed and began eating. She hesitated, wondering just how much she should tell Ben, but her moment of silence and her unhappy expression were all he needed to draw his own conclusions.

He swung to the ground and took her hand, drawing her a step or two closer. "Things are not good, are they?"

Roseanne became painfully aware of her hands in his, and for the first time, noticed the smoothness of his. But they were the hands of a doctor, she reasoned. In vain she tried to conjure up some significant feelings toward him outside those of friendship. She wondered how she had ever thought she could tolerate his touch as a husband and for a lifetime. Lolita had been right, of course.

She pulled her hands free of his and fought the urge to wipe them on her riding skirt. "Things are just fine." She forced a smile as she lied.

His eyes drilled into her as if he could see into her thoughts. "I don't believe you, Roseanne."

She turned away, nervously running the leather reins through her slender fingers. Overhead a hawk circled, looking for its next meal, and in the distance the Rockies stood their silent, perpetual guard. Softly she replied, accepting the decision of her future, "If I want to keep my son, Ben, I have no choice but to stay with his father. Tyler has made it very clear that if I leave I go without my baby."

Ben flared with incredible disbelief. "He would deny you your happiness—even deny himself happiness?" When she did not respond, realization dawned and suddenly it all became clear to him. "I see, Roseanne," he continued tightly. "The truth of the matter is that you love him more than you do me, and rather than coming right out and telling me, you are making up this lie instead."

His accusation brought her head up sharply. "It's not a lie!" But then what was the use of denying it? She saw no sense in arguing with Ben. It wouldn't get them anywhere and the truth of the matter was that she didn't love Ben. She wondered how she could have been blind to it before.

She gathered her reins and in a second was back in the saddle. "I've got to be going now." She rested a warm gaze on him; she would always have a certain fondness for him. He had been there when she needed him. She didn't want to hurt him, but she saw no other choice.

He reached up and took her reins, detaining her. "Roseanne." His tone was apologetic. "I know I'm being selfish, but I hope you won't blame me. You know I love you. For your sake, I hope your husband loves you just half as much.''

He released the reins and she nudged the gray into a lope, wanting to put distance between them as quickly as possible. *Half as much?* Could you weigh love, divide it, multiply it? All she knew was that it could be compared in terms of more or less, in degrees of hot, cold, tepid. It could nurture, or it could destroy. But how could one be absolutely sure that a fiery desire was the equivalent of love, or whether it was simply a lusty need that could, also, like love, lead to devastation and despair?

Tyler crested the knoll on a lope but drew his horse up abruptly when he saw the two riders below. He first thought they were Indians, but that notion was quickly discarded. Even at the distance he recognized one of the figures as being a woman. Then he recognized the big gray horse she had quickly mounted. The rest was just a matter of simple mathematics. The man was Benjamin Smith, of course. He had wondered where she went on her daily rides alone, but he had never thought to follow her. He hadn't even known she had gone out today. Seeing her had been purely accidental, but it erased any illusions he had been harboring as it clearly put everything into black-and-white.

He had hoped that with time they might find what they had once had. He thought perhaps if he just stayed away from her that she would eventually come to terms with her anger and be ready for a reconciliation. Now he could see he had been foolish. It was Ben Smith she wanted. The child was the only tie that bound her to him. Now he knew he needed something more.

He followed her to the ranch and rode into the yard just as she was unsaddling her horse. He came up beside her and swung down. "Have you ever been into the mountains?" he asked casually as he undid the rigging on his own saddle and flung the works over the pole fence next to hers.

The fact that he had spoken to her for no apparent reason drew her interest, but she hid it successfully behind a cool mask of reserve. She looked to the mountains. There had been thousands of times that she had wanted to see what was beyond the Front Range, but she had only gone once with the vaqueros after a few stray cattle.

"Yes," she replied, telling him about it, "but I didn't get to see much. From here those mountains simply look like a wall, but inside them, it is a world all its own." She stopped herself, wondering why she had been so extensive in her reply when a simple "yes" would have been sufficient.

He leaned against the bay's shoulder, listening attentively while the horse cropped at the trampled spears of grass growing around the corral posts. "Why don't you and I go for a ride tomorrow? We could leave early and spend the day."

His offer to share company made her wary, but it also pleased her. She really needed to get away for a day. "What about Will?"

"Can't you work something out with Lolita to give him a bottle and some cow's milk for just one or two feedings?" he asked lightly.

"Well, I guess I could," she conceded reluctantly.

"Then it's settled." He took her horse's reins and led them both into the corral. He quickly stripped their headgear off, draped it over a post, and then joined her. Together they went to the house.

It was early afternoon and Lolita was surprised to see Tyler, and more surprised to see the two of them come in together. They hadn't gotten along, yet she was wise to the look of love they both had in their eyes. She had long hoped they would settle their problem and get married.

Tyler hung his hat near the door, calling, "Don't fix anything for me tonight, Lolita. I have some business to attend to in town."

He left the room and ascended the stairs. Curious as to what his business was, Roseanne followed him up the stairs and into his room. "What takes you to town?" She noticed he had taken out one of his better shirts and pants.

"I thought I'd go into town with Diego for a few hours."

"Oh." She released a sigh of vague disappointment, and turned to leave.

"Would you like to come with us?"

She stopped and looked over at him, her curvaceous mouth an oblique line of agitation. "I doubt I would fit into your plans."

"We could work them around you," he offered. "Diego will probably drink, but you and I could take in the theater if you'd like."

She wouldn't interfere with their plans for a night on the town. Suddenly she wished she hadn't agreed to go riding with him tomorrow. He probably asked only so she would excuse his carousing tonight. She wondered if his rounds would include some lady friend.

"No." She pretended indifference. "Perhaps some other time."

* * *

It was well after midnight and Tyler still hadn't returned. Had he forgotten their early morning engagement? Or had he even any intentions of keeping it? She wadded the pillow up and then punched it in an effort to make it softer, but it couldn't comfort her head or her mind. She had no right to be jealous of his night ramblings or his seeking comfort in the arms of another woman. After all, he wasn't getting any loving kindness from her. But on the other hand, why should she give him anything when she wasn't his wife? She had been foolish once; she wouldn't be again.

As on many other nights she lay awake unconsciously comparing him to the other men she had known. Ben had spoken of love in halves, and she had thought of it in degrees. There was no comparing her love or her need for Tyler to anyone that had gone before or would likely come after. She had denied her sexual needs except for those short-lived nights with him, and now as she watched him each day, watched him work, eat, and play with their son, she recalled just one year ago when they had loved so naturally and uninhibitedly. She yearned to have him satisfy her again, both emotionally and physically.

She was finding it harder and harder to remain angry at him for his desertion of her. She knew she had been wrong. She knew it was something he had to do, just as well as she knew that he would leave again to find Cotton when that day came. But in the meantime, she reasoned, shouldn't she take what she so desperately needed, and what only he had been able to give her?

Perhaps he was turning to another woman, and she had lost him for good. What if he only lingered because he would never give up his son?

She tossed again, kicked at the blankets then almost immediately pulled them back up as the chilly night air rushed over her. She clamped her lids tightly together but pictures of him in another woman's arms kept flashing painfully across her mind. Damn it, she was jealous. She didn't want to admit it, but the very thought of another woman in his passionate embrace, beneath his persuasive hands and lips, tortured her more than even the birth of William Tyler.

Then, loud against the quiet of the night, she heard the faint clip-clopping of horses' hooves on the dirt road, moving at a regulated gait. Hastily she wiped her tears away with her fingertips and glanced at the clock. It was now nearly two o' clock. The moon was full and she slipped from bed to the window. It was Tyler and Diego. She watched them unsaddle their mounts in the moonlight then part ways. A few minutes later, she heard Tyler's footsteps as he tried to move quietly up the stairs. He came down the hall, stopping at her door. Her heart began to beat wildly. She should have locked it. He was probably drunk. She didn't want him to touch her while he had the smell of another woman on him. Then she heard the footsteps move away, another door opening and closing, the boots hitting the hardwood floor, the faint creak of springs, and finally, a disappointing silence.

Tyler was there at the breakfast table looking no worse for the wear because of his late night when Roseanne stepped into the dining area, dressed for their ride. He got up from his chair and came around to seat her. "I see you didn't forget our ride," he commented.

"Nor you. As late as you were getting in, I thought you might not have wanted to rise so early."

"You shouldn't have waited up for me," he said with a mocking smile.

Unobtrusively she ran her gaze over him, deliberately looking for a clue that would tell her whether he had been with another woman last night. He had shaved his beard for the occasion. He looked more relaxed than usual, more content. There was a particular satisfied glow in his eyes that hadn't been there before. It was enough to give her the answer she sought. Hurt, she found it increasingly difficult to be civil or to even to eat.

Tyler noticed the way she shoved her food around on her plate, taking only an occasional small bite. He was finished and he wiped his mouth on the napkin. "Lolita is packing us a lunch, but that's still a long way off. You'd better eat up."

It was her way out. She set her fork down. "I really don't think I feel up to going. I don't feel very good this morning."

Suspicion and jealousy leaped inside him. He had had a hunch she would try to back out of this. She probably had plans to meet Ben Smith again, for what purpose he couldn't figure, unless it was a few stolen kisses. Inside he was boiling. This had gone far enough. He stood up, moved around the table, and gently took her arm and pulled her to her feet.

"In that case, my dear," he replied sardonically, "you'd better go back to bed and stay there all day. I wouldn't want to see you coming down with something."

Without a word of warning, he easily picked her up and strode toward the stairs. Immediately she struggled against him, kicking her feet in the air. "I don't need to go to bed."

He held her tighter and took the stairs two at a time. "Perhaps you do," he chided. "Much more than you realize."

"Let me down! Do you hear me?" She was intensely aware of his strength and her helplessness.

He pushed open her bedroom door. "Of course I hear you." Unceremoniously he dumped her onto the bed then walked back to the door and locked it. When he turned to face her, she was struggling to a sitting position eyeing him like a cornered animal, looking for an escape. He moved forward; she pushed herself up against the brass rails.

"What's the idea of this, Tyler?" She made a move to get off the bed but he stopped her, taking her shoulders, drawing her upward toward his body, then slowly pressing her back onto the cover.

He paused, the muscle in his jaw tensing as though he fought against some inner turmoil. "You said you weren't up to riding," he said through clenched teeth. "I just wanted to make sure you didn't do any. With me or anybody else."

He leaned over her, holding her snugly immobile in his iron grip. His gaze wandered restlessly over her features. His eyes glowed with the lambent flame that Roseanne recognized. She picked up the scent of soap combined with the special scent of his skin that charged her senses into awareness of his maleness.

A pleasant, inviting warmth invaded her body. Her nerve endings came alive and along with them her desire. Motionless, she watched him watching her, watched his eyes roam her face and come to rest on her lips. Paralyzed under his spell, she waited as his mouth slowly descended to hers. Waited until he possessed her lips with a ravenous mastery, and then she gladly plummeted into a golden swirl of pleasure. But suddenly, she was drawn back upward as his kiss hardened and lips pressed angrily into hers cruelly. He pulled free of her with an effort, and breathing heavily and raggedly, he glared down at her.

"Well?" he demanded. "Were you able to think for even a second that it was your Benjamin Smith?"

The words stung and she struggled to be free of him. "Damn you," she sobbed, then forced strength into her voice. "Why did you do that? Why?"

He stood up, bringing her with him, and then he moved a few feet away and began pacing the floor. "Isn't that where you were going again today? To meet him? You probably had it all figured out that once I was out working you could sneak off and I'd never know the difference."

"I assume you saw me with Ben yesterday?" she asked boldly. He didn't answer but the frostiness in his eyes gave her the answer. She forced a stilted laugh. "Well, for your information, I didn't *plan* to meet him. I simply ran into him. But I don't see why you should care. I don't see why it should concern you in the slightest after last night."

The lines in his brow deepened. "What exactly do you mean by that?"

"You go into town to another woman's arms and then you have the audacity to treat me like I've committed a cardinal sin by simply talking to Ben Smith."

"Ha!" he laughed. "I wish I *had* been in another woman's arms, because my dear, loving wife doesn't seem to have any."

"I'm not your wife!" she shouted, her arms straight and tense at her sides, her fists clenched.

He turned and stalked to the door. "Then, in that case, allow me to spread the word."

In a flurry she was across the room, imploring him. "Don't, Tyler. Please."

"I'm tired of this charade, Roseanne. There's going to be some changes made or I *will* tell Smith and everyone else in town."

Quickly she weighed her alternatives. "All right." She moved into the center of the room again, rubbing her forehead to chase away the pain that had started there. "What kind of blackmail do you have in mind for me this time?"

He didn't care for her choice of words but he ignored it. Instead he reached into his shirt pocket and extracted a small box. He handed it to her. Curiously, but hesitantly, she accepted it. "If you're going to be my wife then you'll wear my ring. Open it, Roseanne. That's why I went into town yesterday."

Inside the box, nestled on a small piece of black velvet, was a cluster of diamonds and sapphires mounted on a gold band. The largest diamond stood boldly higher than the others, and huddled around it were six smaller diamonds and three blinking sapphires. Roseanne caught her breath at its exquisite beauty, knowing without a doubt that Tyler had bought the most elaborate and most expensive ring in all of Denver City. She also thought it extraordinary that the ring contained sapphires just like the necklace he had given her.

Unable to resist, she picked it out of its velvety bed and slipped it onto her finger. It fit perfectly. It was so beautiful that it was an effort for her to remember its actual meaning and to pull herself back to the hard reality of the situation.

She looked up at Tyler. ''It's beautiful.'' That much she couldn't deny. ''But for our purposes a simple gold band would have been sufficient.''

He took her hand in his and took the ring off. He placed it back into its little box and back into his shirt pocket. ''Not exactly, Roseanne. I want you to be my wife in every sense of the word. That means no more clandestine meetings with Ben Smith—or anybody else. It also means seeing a preacher, carrying my name *legally,* and sharing my bed—or yours, whichever you prefer. The decision is up to you. You either become my wife before a preacher, or I tell the world that we're not married and that Will is illegitimate.''

He drove a hard bargain, but from the determined look in his eyes she knew he meant business. There was no reasoning with him. ''It's not me you want,'' she argued. ''It's the child and an outlet for your desires.''

''As you mentioned earlier, I can always get that satisfied in town, but if we're going to be forced to live together because of Will, then we may as well do it legally as man and wife and make the best of it. And Roseanne''—he placed his hand beneath her chin, making her look up into his eyes—''if I recall, you and I could make a cold night warm not many months ago. You must know by now that it can get mighty cold up here in Colorado.''

She felt her heart thudding unmercifully against her breasts at the warm touch of his hands, and she wondered if he could see the blood surging there, feel it pumping in her neck just beneath his fingers, giving away the feelings that were gathering speed and threatening to run away with her ability to think straight. If only he weren't so close, but his arm had come around her waist, holding her in a captive position.

"What will you choose" he prodded insolently, his gaze lazily assessing her indecision. "Shame or respectability?" When still she didn't answer, he continued. "A woman who gives birth to an illegitimate baby has a hard row to hoe, Roseanne, as you're well aware. You'd have plenty of male suitors, I'll grant you that, but they would be on your doorstep for all the wrong reasons. And your Benjamin Smith would probably pretend he never knew you."

"He's not *my* Benjamin Smith, and I wish you'd quit referring to him that way." She made an effort to get free of his arms but he had her securely in his possession.

Wasn't this what she had wanted since she had met him? Yet it was a bittersweet victory. He wanted Will, not her.

She turned from him, feeling worse than if he had never asked her to be his wife. "You give me little choice, Tyler. When is this wedding to take place?"

He had hoped for a different response from her. He had hoped to see a glimmer of satisfaction. Perhaps he had been too rough with her. He never would have exposed her to the town, but he had to do something or lose her to Smith. "Immediately, of course," he replied, feeling anything but happy at his accomplishment. "Just as soon as you can have a wedding dress made."

Three weeks later the house was decorated and arranged for the ceremony, reception, and dance that would follow. It had been explained to those acquaintances from town that she and Tyler had been married on the trail, so no one questioned the fancy wedding party. Those who knew the truth were happy to see the two of them finally united.

Roseanne did not wear the smile of a bride, however, as she waited in her room dressed in the off-white silk wedding dress. She looked at her reflection in the full-length mirror as Lolita's fingers deftly worked the tiny pearl buttons that went up the back. On the upper bodice, around the neckline and onto her bosom, the cloth was drawn into intricate tucks and held in place by individual pearls. The tucking was edged with wide, gathered lace that joined in a ''V'' and continued down the center to the waistline. From there the skirt rode Roseanne's hips and fell freely in shimmering folds to the floor, concealing a minimum number of petticoats.

After Lolita had buttoned the dress, she fussed a moment with Roseanne's hair, making sure nothing was out of place. ''You are a beautiful bride indeed, Roseanna.'' She scrutinized Roseanne and allowed her observations to go deeper. ''Still, you do not smile as a bride should, and this troubles me. I thought you had long wanted this day.''

''I have, Lolita.'' Roseanne turned away from the mirror and moved to the window.

''Then why can you not smile?''

Roseanne watched the activity in the yard. The vaqueros were already celebrating with some bottles of liquor they had purchased in town. The guests were arriving; the preacher, Roseanne's dressmaker, and the few others she had come to know. ''There won't be many people—none of my old friends and acquaintances from Texas. Not my father.''

"Ah, this is the cause of your sadness."

Roseanne turned and her skirts rustled with the movement, the pleasant scent of her perfume drifted through the air. "No, it isn't, Lolita. It's Tyler. I don't know if he loves me."

Confusion crossed the older woman's face. "I do not understand, Roseanna. You and he—you were in love. You have a child. He has asked you to marry him. What is this doubt you are feeling?"

"We've had some problems since he left last year. I was not very understanding. It has changed things. Now"—she looked out the window again, pulling the curtains back farther,—"I think he's only marrying me because of Will."

"Why don't you tell him how you feel, Roseanna," Lolita advised. "I have been married many years and I know it is not good for two people to be guessing what the other one is thinking. The truth can hurt you no more than the wondering."

Roseanne stared at Lolita for a moment. It sounded so simple. She *had* never told Tyler she loved him. Surely he must doubt her the way she doubted him. And if he couldn't respond then Lolita was right. She would be hurt no more than she was by not knowing.

Suddenly she moved to the dresser, opened the top drawer, and withdrew a sheet of paper from inside. She found her pen and ink and began to write. It only took a moment and then she folded the paper in quarters and handed it to Lolita.

"The ceremony will start soon, Lolita. Will you take this to Tyler? And then return, please, to tell me his reaction."

* * *

Downstairs Tyler waited in a black suit and tie and white shirt. Nervously he awaited Roseanne's signal to commence the ceremony. He was finally going to marry the woman he loved, but he had to convince her that he *did* love her and that the child they shared was only part of the reason he had insisted on this marriage. Would she ever trust him again after he had let her down that once?

Then he saw Lolita hurrying down the stairs in her finest dress. Her expression was anxious and he feared that Roseanne had changed her mind.

Lolita came to him and spoke quietly, drawing him away from the others. "Señor, Roseanna has asked that I give you this. She is waiting for your reply."

He took the note and unfolded it, dreading what was inside. His eyes skimmed the brief contents, and he smiled. Slowly his smile changed to a grin and suddenly he tossed his head back and released a short hoot that drew the attention of some of the guests. But it didn't matter to him. When he looked at Lolita again his eyes were joyous with a happiness that had not been there since he had come to the ranch to stay.

Suddenly he placed his hands on Lolita's shoulders and squeezed their ample roundness. "Tell her my answer is the same—no, I'll tell her myself."

His long strides took him across the room in seconds. He was on the stairs when Lolita exclaimed. "But Señor Chanson, you are not to see the bride yet. It is—" Her words fell only on the ears of the guests for, taking the stairs two and three at a time Tyler had already reached the second floor.

At Roseanne's door, Tyler contained himself enough to stop and knock. When she opened the door, he saw apprehension in her eyes as she searched his face for a reaction to her note. He reached for her hand, feeling the feminine fragility of it, yet knowing the strength the fine bones belied. She was a vision of loveliness in the expensive wedding gown, but his attention focused on the beauty of her face and the woman he knew her to be. He gently drew her to him until he could feel the soft thrust of her breasts against his chest. While one hand circled her waist pressing her hips to his, the other caressed her cheek.

It was an effort to keep his intense emotions under control when all he wanted to do was take her to the bed and lay bare his love to its fullest extent. "Roseanne," he whispered hoarsely, his throat tightening in his pure joy and in his need of her, "I love you so much. There's so much I need to tell you, *should* have told you, but my foolish pride . . . I was so jealous of Smith, thinking you loved him and not me. I would have done anything to get you to marry me and I guess I did. I used Will as the excuse when"—he ran a hand over the curve of her lips as he hesitated, absorbing all about her he loved—"when I have wanted you for my wife from the very beginning." He told her of his journey to Texas to keep his promise, only to find she was in Denver all the while.

"Oh, Tyler." Roseanne slipped her arms around him, so happy and relieved to hear his confession and to know—and believe—how much he truly loved her. "I'm sorry, too, for all the misunderstandings. I was just so hurt. I thought for sure that you didn't really love me, that you had only used me."

"My sweet Roseanne."

His lips were about to taste the long-awaited satisfaction of hers when Lolita huffed down the hall, her skirts held high in her haste. "Tyler Chanson! You are not to see the bride before the wedding. It is bad luck."

Tyler smiled down at Roseanne, reluctantly delaying the sweet taste of her lips until later, silently accepting the Mexican woman's wish to uphold tradition. He withdrew to the stairs, looking down at the plump older woman, a smile now widening his lips and a twinkle easing the seriousness in his eyes. "Very well, Señora Alvarez, but I don't believe that nonsense about bad luck. Roseanne and I have had all the bad luck we're going to." He looked back over his shoulder at the woman who would soon be his in every way. Her beauty continually stunned him. He wanted to hold her so badly it left an ache in his chest that was nearly unbearable. His love for Roseanne overflowed in the eyes that met hers. "Nothing will ever separate us again. *Nothing.*"

When Roseanne came down the stairs with Lolita behind her, a hush went over the small group in the room. Her gown was exquisite, her beauty astounding, but it now came from deep within and from a love that could finally be expressed.

She paused for only a second on the landing, then she moved confidently toward Tyler, her eyes linked with his. He held out his hand and she slipped hers inside. He drew her up next to him, holding tight to her hand and putting his arm possessively around her small waist.

The preacher opened his book and began to speak loudly so all could hear. "We are gathered here today to join this man and this woman in the bonds of holy matrimony . . ."

Tyler felt Roseanne leaning toward him, her shoulder brushing his arm, her fingers curling through his. He glanced down at her. She tilted her head and met the muted softness of the love laid bare in the brown depths of his eyes. She gladly returned it with her own unspoken promise. All doubts between them vanished.

They repeated their vows fervently, and Tyler slipped the ring onto Roseanne's finger. The preacher concluded, ''. . . what God hath joined together, let no man put asunder.''

Chapter 23

June 1863

SMOKE SPIRALED FROM DENVER CITY for days, but the people wasted no time in rebuilding. Construction was in full swing when Walt Cotton rode slowly into town.

He halted his horse at a general store and swung to the ground. Inside, the owner was unboxing a new load of supplies and systematically putting them away on the shelves. Over the door the bell tinkled and he turned to greet his customer.

"I need some things," Cotton said as his cold gaze roved over the items stacked to the ceiling and cluttering the floor space.

The store owner picked out the things Cotton wanted and then tallied them up. "That's four dollars and five cents, sir."

Cotton counted out his coins and put the rest back into his vest pocket. "You wouldn't happen to know if there's a Tyler Chanson about these parts, would you? He's a friend of mine from California and the last I heard he had a ranch around here."

The proprietor put Cotton's supplies in a cloth bag

and nodded his head in time with his hand movements. "Yes, sir. As a matter of fact, you're in luck. He and his wife have a ranch south of town. You can't miss it. Just had them a son about six months ago, I hear. Also hear they're having a big party out there tonight."

Cotton smiled faintly as he pulled the string on the cloth bag with his good hand and his teeth, and turned for the door. "Thank you kindly for the information."

Cotton tied the sack behind his saddle, swung himself up, and headed south.

He had recuperated from his wounds and had lain low to see if Pierpont would squeal on him. But he would give Pierpont no quarter in a trial and the Colonel knew it. Apparently he kept his mouth shut; the law was not looking for him.

Now he was looking for Chanson. He had had some wild notions that day he rode onto that ranch in California with his gang. Who would have guessed that things would have turned out the way they had? He had long wanted to get even with Chanson for making him a cripple. He did promise Pierpont he wouldn't bother Chanson's wife, but Pierpont was out of the picture now, safely tucked away in jail. She would be the best way to get to Chanson. The odds were on his side; he had the element of surprise. Chanson had sought his revenge for nearly nine years. Now it was time to turn the tables.

Tyler closed the door on the last guest. "Did you ever think they would all leave?" He turned to Roseanne. Like him, she was happy but tired. "Do your feet hurt?" he joked. "It feels like we never stopped dancing."

"It reminded me of the night we danced in San Antonio, only tonight was much better."

He pulled her into his arms again, liking the way she felt there against his chest. "I was beginning to think this would never happen," he whispered against her hair. "Why did you give me that note at the last minute?"

Her arms moved farther around his back and caressed the muscles hidden beneath the black suit coat. She nestled deeper into his embrace, happy and secure now with his love. "It was something Lolita said about honesty between two people. I didn't want to marry you if you were only doing it because of Will."

"Will was part of it, Roseanne, but you were the bigger part. We should always be honest with each other. I never want to wonder about your love again."

"Nor I about yours."

They held each other in a tender embrace, contented to finally be together after so long apart. Then Tyler shifted, and brought her into his arms, easily carrying her. As he moved from lamp to lamp, Roseanne blew them out. In the dark, in the house lit only by the light from the kitchen, and the moonlight streaming in through the windows, he carried her up the dark stairs. In Roseanne's room he sat her on the bed and settled next to her. A quick surveillance, even in the dark, showed him that the baby's crib was gone.

Roseanne answered his unspoken question. "I had Lolita move it to the spare room when it was time for Will to go to bed tonight."

"So that is his room from now on?" Tyler's eyes lit up with a pleased twinkle. "I always believed that anything a father could pass down to his son was a good thing."

She laughed and placed a hand on his chest. He put an arm across her in a protective gesture that made her feel more secure and warm than she had since the night he left over a year ago.

The twinkle in Tyler's eyes was replaced by seriousness. "I couldn't bear the thought of you with that Smith guy, but I didn't know how I could ever convince you that I loved you. And I was so afraid that you'd never forgive me for leaving you. I can see it was wrong to let the past rule my life so completely. I hope you will forgive me for all of it, Roseanne."

She ran a hand along his cheek, liking the angles of his face with no beard to hide them. "It was foolish of me not to try to understand what you had to do. It was even more foolish of me to not believe you when you said you loved me."

"Yes," he agreed, his brown eyes sparkling again. *"That* part was exceedingly foolish. But I'm through with Walt Cotton. I won't search for him any more. My place is with you and Will, building our life together. Tomorrow we'll start by going into Denver for a few days and having a real honeymoon."

She protested that going to Denver wasn't necessary to satisfy her, but he placed a finger gently on her lips and followed it with a kiss that captured her, subdued her, and laid her back against the pillows. After a time, the warm mastery of his lips moved from her receptive mouth to the smoothness of her face, following its every contour, its every hollow. His kiss teased at her hair, her ear, then moved seductively into the sensitive curve of her neck.

Beneath his stimulus she came alive. Inside her a dormant ember sparked under the new kindling. Hungrily she slid her hands inside his jacket to explore the flesh that she longed to know again.

Then he sat up, drawing her with him. She curled her legs beneath her as his fingers patiently undid each and every tiny button on the back of her dress, while his lips wandered on their unending renewal of long ago pleasures. When the last button gave beneath his fingers, he carefully slid the silky material off her shoulders. The creaminess of her skin taunted his memory, his desire, and his lips to taste the perfumed, exposed contours of her body. Gradually the dress slid over her breasts, off her arms and his mouth followed each new revelation. Finally he laid her back, slipped the dress completely off and carefully draped it over the chair in the corner. He stood up and unhurriedly removed his suit coat, shirt, and boots.

She watched his movements in the dim glow of the lamp. Yearning to touch him as he had touched her, she stood up and ran her hands over the solid flesh of his chest, the muscles in his shoulders, arms, and back, and traced the manly curve of his mouth with her own. Gladly she ascertained that there was nothing soft about him, unless it was possibly the silky hair at the nape of his neck, entwined in her fingers.

He drew her tightly into his arms as if he hoped to draw her into his body, forever near his heart. The kiss was interrupted as he lowered his head onto the dark, soft strands of her hair, whispering against her ear, "I love you, Roseanne. Finally I can show you how much."

The need inside him was painfully strong. She could feel his passion in every taut muscle in his body. But she knew she could ease his overpowering desire. He was a man no one could own, but in her arms he would willingly turn his soul over to her. But she didn't want his soul, only his love.

"Tyler," she whispered, despairingly as a painful realization pushed at her heart. "I don't think there are words to tell you just how much I love you. I've missed you, longed for you, secretly loved you. So secretly, in fact, that I insisted on keeping it from myself."

Her new declaration of love brought a thankful moan from deep inside him and he held her tighter. Against his chest she could hear the quickening of his heartbeat and the increasing, rapid rise and fall of his breathing. "Do you remember, Roseanne, how I told you I longed to have a soft bed where we could lay together all night and make love?"

She nodded. "Yes, but we had some good times even without it."

"We did," he agreed. Then he straightened and loosened her corset. Suddenly he became impatient with her trappings. "You never wore this thing before. Damn it, Roseanne." He pulled her against him again and kissed her hard and quick. Then he whispered against her mouth, "Take off that silly corset. You never did need it. I want you, Roseanne," he whispered. "I want you now."

Quickly they removed the remainder of their clothes and carelessly let them fall to the floor. Tyler moved her backward toward the bed, pulled back the covers, then tucked an arm behind her legs and laid her down. He stretched out next to her, warming her with his body, his kisses, his hands, bringing her back once again to the heady heights of arousal.

Roseanne thought for a fleeting moment of the joy a man and woman could bring to each other. A joy she

had never known until Tyler had showed her that
lovemaking was not a one-sided thing. From her he
took, but he gave so much more in return, and between
them flowed a delicate yet enduring tie that made their
love that much more enjoyable, beautiful, and natural.

He moved over her and she welcomed him in the
possessive embrace of her satiny legs. A swelling in-
sistence engulfed them that soared above all mind and
matter. When it summited, they drifted downward in a
radiant wave of tumultuous flame, fusing them together in the ultimate union, consummating their
emotional commitment to each other in a lustrous, un-
earthly afterglow.

A sixth sense told Roseanne that she was alone in
the bed, but the faint rustling sounds a few feet away
assured her that she was not alone in the hotel room.
She rolled on her back and brushed the hair from her
face. The room was aglow with the morning sun filtering in through the white, lacy curtains. The shade had
been opened and Tyler stood in front of the window,
tucking his shirt into his pants and looking out.

"Is the honeymoon over?" she quipped, stretching
languorously.

He smiled down at her then sat on the edge of the
bed. "Hardly." He chuckled. "I'm sure we can pick
it up again tonight, but it's time we went home." He
ran a finger along her cheek then followed it with a
kiss, thinking it felt good to *have* a home again. He
smiled as he continued, "I need to get back to work. If
we don't return soon, all the hired help will think
we've died and gone to heaven."

Roseanne sat up on the bed, kneeling behind him
and wrapping her arms around his broad shoulders.

"Very well." She laid a series of kisses to his neck. "I'll get dressed."

He pulled her onto his lap, loving the feel of her against him. "You are a temptress who knows all too well a man's weaknesses." His lips sought hers again, never tiring of their taste or the pleasure he derived from touching them. From the next room they heard a faint whimpering and they automatically separated. "Will's wanting breakfast." Tyler voiced Roseanne's thoughts. "You get dressed and I'll go get him. Lolita probably has him dressed and ready for the day."

Roseanne reached for her robe at the foot of the bed. "Lolita will probably be glad to get back to the ranch and to Pablo. Maybe it wasn't fair of me to ask her to come." Worry lines creased her forehead.

"It was Lolita's idea to come and care for Will, remember? She's excited about us getting married, and besides, you can't say you've neglected your duties to him. He's still getting his share from you."

He watched her dress, minus the cumbersome corset. "I'm proud of our son, Roseanne," he continued a few minutes later, "and I'm proud of you for all you went through alone." He drew her into his arms for a long moment, thankful that his life at last was the way he wanted it to be. Then, keeping an arm over her shoulders, he led her to the door. "Let's let Will know we haven't forgotten him."

Tyler pulled the surrey up to the ranch house and helped the women out. When he had taken everything inside, he went upstairs, changed and joined Roseanne in the foyer.

"What will you be doing today?" she asked.

"Unless the vaqueros have taken the initiative, I

want to brand some late calves that are grazing on the south range,'' he said as he took his hat from the peg.

"Will you be back at noon?'' Roseanne juggled Will in her arms while he squirmed energetically.

"I doubt it, but we'll be here by six this evening.'' He kissed the baby and then her, hoping night would come quickly so he could be with her again. "I'd better go.''

"All right.'' She hated to see him leave and wished she could go with him. It was a good day for riding, but she felt she had better stay home and help Lolita with the laundry and get the house straightened up from the wedding.

Tyler stepped out onto the wooden porch, feeling the heat. "It's going to be an awfully hot day for branding, but it won't get done by my just thinking about it.'' He smiled down at her, feeling the contentment of their union settle comfortably over him. "Until tonight,'' he promised.

She felt selfish, not wanting to give him up for even a short while. He moved out across the yard. "Tyler,'' she called suddenly. He turned around, concerned over her altered tone of voice. She quickly eased his mind. "Nothing, honey,'' she said. "I just wanted to say 'I love you.' ''

They silently exchanged their secrets, their understandings, their promises, their love. Then she watched him walk across the yard and disappear inside the barn. Will began to fuss and she went back into the house. "You're lucky to have a father like him,'' she told the baby as she sat in the rocking chair to soothe him. "It won't be long before he'll be taking you everywhere with him. I don't doubt for a minute that you'll follow in his footsteps. He loves you. And now I know he loves me, too.''

It was unseasonably hot for early June and hordes of mosquitoes were out along the creek, but Walt Cotton seemed not to notice either the heat or the bugs. Stretched out on his stomach in the tall grass, he held a pair of binoculars to his eyes with his good hand, balancing himself on his lame arm.

Chanson and his wife had been gone for several days but now they were back and Chanson was leaving. It was all going to work out just as he planned.

He lifted the binoculars from his eyes and studied the ranch without them. He watched Chanson saddle his horse and leave. There were only two men and two women left behind. He tried to readjust his position to see better when his right arm collapsed beneath him. He gritted his teeth at the painful truth of his deformity, ready to demand payment of the man who had caused it.

The sun went behind a white, billowy cloud and gave some temporary relief from the heat. Cotton put the binoculars back to his eyes, and didn't notice.

Shortly after Will had had his lunch, Roseanne put him in his basket and set it out on the porch so he could enjoy some of the warm weather. Loaded down with a bucket of wet clothes she headed for the clothesline. The ranch yard was silent. Tyler, Juan, and Diego had gone to brand the new calves. Salvador and Pablo stayed behind to work with some new, unbroken colts, and to be available in case Indians came by hunting trouble and scalps.

Roseanne looked up from the line and saw a lone

rider coming in from the west. Distracted, she finished hanging the diaper and watched him ride into the yard and come to a stop twenty feet away from her.

"Howdy, ma'am," he said. "Wonder if I could water my horse?"

The sun was behind him and his face was shaded by the brim of his hat. She didn't recognize him, but a lot of travelers passed by en route to and from the gold-fields so she thought little of his request.

"Of course," she replied, going back to her work. "The trough is right over there."

He kicked his horse but it moved reluctantly, and Roseanne suddenly realized he couldn't have come into the yard just to water his horse. There was no need to. The creek was just over yonder, and the animal was obviously not thirsty.

He turned his horse back to her and then stopped in the same place as before, idly watching her with eyes that unnerved her. She worked steadily, ignoring him, hoping her unfriendliness would make him leave.

"Hear tell this is the Chanson ranch."

She forced a clothespin over the thick cotton of a diaper. "Yes, it is."

She abandoned the clothes finally and stepped to the side until she could see his face fully. There was a strange glow in his eyes, otherwise he might have been handsome. She nervously wished she had thought to prop her rifle nearby, but it hadn't crossed her mind today. "What do you want? Are you looking for work or something?" She tried to cover her inexplicable, growing fear of this man.

He crossed his hands over the saddle horn and she noticed one arm seemed loose, limp, out of control. Her heart began to pound and she met his cold eyes, hoping he wouldn't see the new fear surging inside her.

"My name is Walt Cotton, and I've come to see Tyler Chanson."

She reached for the porch railing to steady herself as she stared at him. Desperately now, she wished she had her rifle in hand, or that one of the vaqueros would come to the rescue. But they had no way of knowing anything was amiss. From a distance it looked like she was having a friendly conversation with a traveler.

Inwardly she quivered, knowing what he was capable of, and knowing she must tread carefully and try not to show fear. Men like him were never predictable. Calmly, as if she did not recognize the name, she said. "I'll give him your message. Can I tell him where you'll be?"

He smiled, slowly and deliberately, as though her innocent words struck some secret point of amusement inside him. "Oh, he'll find me. I can make sure he will."

Then, in an unlinking action, he straightened in the saddle, and pulled his gun from his hip holster. Roseanne's heart pulsed in her ears until she could hardly hear. He was going to kill her. He was going to make sure Tyler came after him. Then, suddenly, she realized that he couldn't kill her if he wanted his message relayed. He smiled down at her, a sickening smirk that drew his lips back. His gun moved toward the porch. Instantly she knew his intent.

Fear overpowered her, pounding in her brain, but her reflexes moved her. She rushed toward the porch and Will's basket. She heard the cocking of the trigger. My God, she could never get there in time! Will! She heard the deafening roar of the revolver, saw the bullet rip into the basket, splintering it. She screamed, followed by convulsive, helpless sounds coming from her throat as she ran. Then she heard the gun again, but she was there now. She raced in front of it. She reached for the basket, covering it with her body. She felt the bullet hit her and throw both her and the basket across the wooden porch. She fell screaming into darkness. It sucked her downward in fear, helplessness, pain, and in incredible hatred. She grabbed her child into her arms. Suddenly everything went black.

Cotton cursed. He hadn't wanted the woman dead. She was his security. He killed the child to fire Chanson's vengeance. But maybe it wouldn't matter if she *was* dead as long as Chanson believed she was alive and would come after her.

Suddenly a Mexican woman rushed onto the porch, saw Roseanne and screamed. From the corral, the two men appeared with pistols drawn. Cotton pointed his weapon at the woman.

"If you don't want to see her dead, drop your guns," he said to the men.

The vaqueros stopped short and reluctantly obliged as they kept worried eyes on the stranger.

"You," Cotton waved his gun at Salvador, "come over here and pick up Chanson's wife. Put her over the horse's neck. I'm taking her with me."

Salvador was reluctant, but when Cotton instantly pointed the gun at Lolita again, he moved toward the porch and picked up Roseanne's body. Her wound appeared to be only in her upper arm. He felt shallow breathing and was relieved that she was still alive. He glanced at the baby. It stared up at him with large, fearful blue eyes, but it made no sound. There was

much blood on him, but he guessed it was from Roseanne's wound.

"Hurry up!" Cotton ordered.

Salvador stepped up his pace and carefully draped
the unconscious Roseanne limply over the horse's
neck.

"Now," Cotton said. "Tell Chanson my name is
Cotton and I have his wife. If he wants to see her alive
again, he will meet me at Manitou Springs and he will
come alone. Tell him he'd better hurry; his wife may
not live long in her condition."

He reined his horse away from the house and was
nearly out of the yard when Pablo dropped to the
ground for his gun. Cotton saw the movement and
whirled his horse, at the same time aiming his gun and
firing. Pablo dropped and Lolita screamed again, not
knowing whether to take up the child or rush to her
husband.

"I mean what I say," Cotton said as he held both
pistol and reins in one hand, and balanced Roseanne
across the horse's neck with his lame one. Then, with
no more interference, he left the yard.

Tyler looked up from the branding iron and saw
Salvador racing toward him from down a long hill. He
dropped the iron back onto the fire and ran for the bay
without being told something was wrong. The way the
cowboy was riding meant there was trouble at the
ranch. His heart pounded as questions raced through
his mind. Had Indians attacked? Was Roseanne all
right?

Juan and Diego, too, were going for their horses.
Salvador shouted in Spanish as he pulled his horse up
alongside Tyler's. Then, excitedly, and not very suc-

cessfully, he converted to broken English. "Your wife, señor, a stranger has come to the ranch and shot her." The Mexican was nearly sobbing now and reaching for breath as if he had run the entire way on foot. He hurried on. "But she is alive. The stranger's name was Cotton, but he has taken her with him. And your son—he has also been hurt. Come quickly."

Tyler kicked the bay into a run and in seconds it was taking the meadow in long, consuming strides. The horse was in a lather when he pulled into the yard. He hit the ground on a run and raced up the steps. Suddenly he was very afraid. Salvador had said she was alive but she was wounded. How badly was she hurt? As he stepped into the foyer where he had said goodbye to her this morning, it came to him that happiness was always short-lived. He had learned that long ago. He should have remembered it.

Inside, Ben Smith was sitting on the edge of the sofa, bending over Pablo. Next to him was his black bag with bandages and medicines spilling out of it. He wondered how Smith had gotten here before him—unless he had come to see Roseanne. He ran a hand over his agonized face, sickened at what he had caused by simply seeking justice.

Smith saw him and his face twisted into contempt. "Pablo will probably live and so will your son, but it's hard to say about Roseanne if she doesn't get medical attention soon." The doctor's skillful hands cleaned the wound, applied antiseptic, then bandaged it as he continued talking. "It amazes me how people like you can lead such charmed lives. Maybe you know what this is all about, but my guess is it's all because of you." He completed his work, pulled the covers up to Pablo's neck and stood up.

"I've looked at your son," he continued, rolling down his sleeves. "Lolita is cleaning him up now." As he put his jacket back on, he lambasted Tyler more. "You've caused Roseanne nothing but pain and trouble. I guess you know that." He bent and angrily stuffed his medical supplies back into his bag. "God knows why she loves you, and now she could be dying."

Smith made a move to leave the room but Tyler grabbed him by the shoulder. "What about Will?" Tyler didn't need Smith's lecture; he knew the blame was all his.

"He's upstairs. His leg was creased by a bullet. He's lucky—he must take after you."

Smith left and Tyler hurried upstairs. Will was whimpering as Lolita wrapped a gauze bandage around his small fragile leg. He moved to the bed, his insides turning over, burning tears stinging the back of his eyes.

Lolita looked at him. "Your son is all right, señor. And the doctor says Pablo is, too."

"What happened, Lolita?"

"I am not sure. I hear two gunshots and screaming, much screaming. I come running, but the man—he aims his gun at me." Her voice caught, but she quickly controlled it as she carefully finished up the bandage on Will's leg. She told Tyler what the man had said and how he had taken Roseanne. "But Salvador said she was breathing when he picked her up. The wound was in her arm. I think she was unconscious from fear of Will being dead."

Tyler sat on the bed next to his son and the boy looked up at him. Finally Will smiled and it tore into Tyler's heart. He took the small hand that waved in the air and gently leaned down and kissed its baby softness. Then he shot to his feet, and picked up the gun belt hanging on the back of a chair near the door. When he turned to Lolita his eyes flared with fiery hatred.

"You go alone, señor, to Manitou Springs," Lolita said. "You must be careful. This man—he will be ready for you. He may even have other men with him. Perhaps you should take Diego—get the sheriff maybe."

"He said to come alone or he would kill her. I can't take a chance. He'll do what he says." He strapped on his gun and tied it to his leg. Then he looked up at Lolita with a deep pain written in his eyes. "Lolita, why was Ben Smith here?"

At first his question confused her. "To help Pablo and your son, of course."

"No. I mean, he couldn't have gotten here before me unless he was already here."

Understanding relieved her expression. "Ah, señor. He was nearby. He had gone to Mrs. Conroy's to check on her new baby, which has been sick. He heard the gunshots. He came right away. Señor"—Lolita's eyes softened—"you worry needlessly. Your Roseanna, she loves you very much. Now go to her. Bring her back to us. Please. I will take care of your son."

But his mind was still troubled. "How can you not blame me for what has happened?"

"I understand. Now that is all I will say. *Go.*"

Chapter 24

June 1863

 ROSEANNE CAME AWAKE WITH A scream in her throat. Darkness surrounded her and a chilly breeze pushed at her groggy head. In front of her was a fire and next to it the dark silhouette of a man she did not recognize hunkered over a cup of coffee.

Suddenly everything came back to her and a wail rose in her throat. She started to rise, knowing she had to get back to Will, but an intense burning in her shoulder and arm raked her body, and stopped her.

The man turned his head toward her. "You'd best not move around too much if you don't want to bleed to death."

She stared at him, still trying to gather her wits. The voice was so cold and heartless. And then she remembered. He was Cotton. "My baby. I have to get back to him. Why am I here!"

He didn't answer, just sat and stared at her. Then he took another drink of the coffee. Finally he spoke. "You're here as my hostage—just to make sure your husband shows up. I'm going to kill him and you're my key to success."

As the pieces fit together in her confused mind, she wanted to sink back into the world of unconsciousness where she wouldn't have to think or face realities. He was going to kill Tyler; he might have already killed her baby. The pain of uncertainty, of thinking the worst, was greater than the pain throbbing in her arm. She knew she couldn't bear to live now without Tyler and their son.

Her eyes narrowed as she studied Cotton's profile. Now she fully understood Tyler's need to see this man brought to justice. He had no respect for life, probably not even his own. And she knew that when Tyler caught up with them, Cotton wouldn't give him a fair chance. He would probably be waiting in ambush. If only there were something she could do to increase Tyler's odds, to warn him.

Suddenly Cotton stood up and looked down at her, as if he had read her mind. From his back pocket he pulled a length of thin rope. "Now that you're conscious, I'll have to tie you up. I wouldn't want you trying something foolish."

Her heart sank. What could she do now?

Tyler rode hard but cautiously, following a blatant trail that skirted Plum Creek through rolling hills and grasslands. To his right, peaks piled upon peaks as the Rocky Mountains stretched westward, finally fading into the hazy blue of the sky. To the east, buttes and bluffs cropped out on the sloping hills. As he neared the city, the plains met the mountains, and the blue-green pines stretched down to enclose it and draw it into the arms of the towering mountains.

By dusk, the clouds gradually increased, rolling over the mountaintops in heavy, gray waves, fluctuating across the sunset. Just as the last light fell into the valley, Tyler unsaddled his horse on the banks of Fountain Creek. The water shone silver-gray in the reflection of the clouds, its surface gleaming in metallic ripples and catching what was left of the light.

He staked the bay near the water, set up camp, and put coffee on. He had no appetite. He was mentally tired, wondering if Roseanne was all right and trying to think of what sort of confrontation Cotton had planned for him. He stretched out on his bedroll near the fire, but he lay awake wishing he could go on even in the darkness. He tucked his hands under his head while he looked at the stars that appeared and disappeared behind the moving, dark masses of clouds. He had made good time, but Cotton had a couple of hours lead on him. Yet, riding double, he must be pushing his horse hard to maintain that lead and get to the springs in time to set up his ambush. Tyler wondered why he had chosen the springs, why he hadn't just bushwhacked him from some distant hill, but one could never second-guess Cotton. He probably had a reason; he probably wanted to make sure he was successful in killing Tyler.

He knew he could probably overtake Cotton before he reached the springs, but perhaps it would be better and safer to play his hand there. He could assess the situation and try to make sure Roseanne wouldn't be hurt. He felt desperation and anxiety seize him again, but he knew he must remain levelheaded and think things through. It would not help Roseanne if he went blundering into this.

The ripple of the water tumbling over the rocks drifted across the night, reminding him of her laughter. The hardness of his bed reminded him of that first night they made love by the Llano River. He closed his eyes and tried to sleep. He would need to be alert tomorrow to save her life as well as his own. But sleep wouldn't come and he watched the stars' progress across the sky until they were chased away by the morning light.

A low butte ridged with trees crested the east bank of Fountain Creek and the settlement of Colorado Springs. Scraping the western sky was Pikes Peak, its lower regions overgrown with aspen, poplar, birch, and pine. Higher up it was blotched with piles of conic rocks and the morning sun glinted off patches of snow.

Tyler's gaze shifted from the peak to the narrow confines of the red rock canyon that led to Manitou Springs. High overhead and all around him, sharp, irregular formations of red rock erupted in the steep, rugged terrain. Cotton's bullet could come from anyplace and his escape would be difficult in the narrow canyon.

He moved forward slowly, eyes continually scanning the walls that rose on either side of him. When he found a relatively sheltered cove in some trees he decided to hide his horse and proceed on foot so he could find better cover.

Cotton sat patiently by the fire, calmly cooking bacon, lost in his brooding thoughts. He had her hands tied in front of her. Her arm throbbed, the pain rippling outward to enclose her entire body. She was feverish and knew the wound was becoming infected.

"Guess you're wondering if he's going to come and rescue you," Cotton said suddenly.

Roseanne wasn't worried that he wouldn't show.

She was only worried that he would be killed. Cotton, on the other hand, seemed to be voicing his own concern. Cotton was a strange, quiet man. He had said very little to her and anything she had said had seemed to drift into his ears meaninglessly. He seldom responded. Now he stared at the bacon, not really expecting her to reply to his statement. He watched the meat cook, although she guessed his thoughts were in some secret corner of his mind, plotting how he would kill Tyler.

He looked at her again. "It'll be over soon. He'll be coming."

Roseanne leaned back on the rock he had propped her against. She was burning up, yet the sweat on her skin turned cold in the mountain air. She closed her eyes, wishing for a blanket. She tried not to think of Will—but when she did, she tried to think positively. As for Tyler, she kept reminding herself that he could take care of himself, he would not do something stupid. If only she knew what Cotton had planned, maybe she could do something to help Tyler.

Her thoughts drifted to him and the days they had just spent together. It wasn't fair, now that they had just found love and happiness, that it should be taken from them. Cotton had ruined Tyler's life once before; now he was planning to do it again. But he was going about it in a strange way, cooking bacon as if there were no doubt tomorrow would come. He was taking no precautions. He was sitting out in plain sight.

She closed her eyes and listened to the wind soughing through the pines, never resting. Sometimes it could be foreboding, sometimes comforting. And there was the vaguely ghostlike movement of unseen creatures. Or was it the Manitou, the Indians' Great

Spirit, pausing by the springs to ensure victory to those who would appease it with offerings?

Suddenly Cotton stood up, reaching for his revolver. Roseanne's eyes popped open as she watched him kick out the fire and search the trees. "He's coming."

Fear soared inside her. She glanced into the increasing brightness of the sky. It was extremely hard to see in the glaring midmorning sun. She had to warn him. Suddenly she screamed, "Tyler! He's here!"

Cotton hauled her roughly to her feet, unheeding of her wound. "Shut up! I'll kill you cold!" He put his crippled hand over her mouth, his gun in her back, and pulled her backward. "Move into the brush. Don't try anything."

Roseanne's terror escalated. If only she could do something to warn Tyler where Cotton was hiding. She tried to scream from deep in her throat, but Cotton's gun pressed into her shoulder, gouging the wound and bringing a pain so excruciating she thought she would crumble in agony.

"Don't try to protect him. I don't have a quarrel with you, but I don't care whether you live or die. I'll kill you if you try anything."

She nodded and he moved the gun lower into her back. Her head swam and she fought the urge to give into her increasing weakness. A twig snapped far away and tears suddenly sprang to her eyes. What was she going to do? Was it her fate to watch Tyler die?

Tyler looked up the narrow draw at the sound of her scream. His view was blocked by heavy brush along the creek that flowed from the springs. There was a trail that followed the water, but it went through underbrush and willows. He couldn't advance without being heard.

Finally the canyon opened up. On the right bank of the stream, a few feet above it, was a white, flat rock with a round hole. Water bubbled from it, along with escaping gas. A few yards farther was another spring, the true soda spring. Tyler studied the narrow thicket of shrubbery bordering the stream. He could smell smoke, and finally, in the bright light he saw it wisping upward in a white coil. A huge currant bush overhung the spring which was at the foot of the timbered mountains in a small recess. Cotton was hiding there with Roseanne, and it would seem he was using the bush for concealment. He moved in a few feet closer, expecting to get gunfire, but all was still.

The basin of the spring was filled with the Indians' wampum, their colorful beads of polished shell tied into strands, belts, and sashes. There were pieces of red cloth floating on water that looked nearly blue in the morning sun, and beneath the surface he saw knives, their blades reflecting dully in the clear water. On the trees hung more pieces of brightly colored cloth, moccasins, strips of deerskins and "sign" of the Indians' war dances, their offerings to the "Manitu" in exchange for his approbation.

And then Cotton stepped from behind the bush with Roseanne in front of him. Her hands were tied, her arm was bloody, and her eyes revealed to him all her fear and a silent pleading. Cotton had his bad arm around her neck. His revolver, in the other hand, pressed into her side.

"Come out from hiding," Cotton said unemotionally. "I'll kill her if you don't."

Tyler was relieved to see Roseanne was alive. The

dried blood on her dress told him that her wound wasn't bleeding. He had gotten to her in time, but she was not out of danger. Infection was, no doubt, setting in.

He did as Cotton demanded and stepped in view with his rifle in hand, poised in Cotton's direction. He watched the man closely, waiting for him to make his move and praying he would do no more harm to Roseanne.

"Did you come alone?" Cotton demanded.

"Would I tell you if I hadn't?" Tyler retorted.

"For your wife's sake, I hope you have."

"You can only guess at that, can't you? I have the advantage over you, Cotton. I *know* you're alone."

"Don't be so sure."

Roseanne shook her head to try and tell Tyler that Cotton was lying, but Cotton's gun dug deeper into her back. His lame arm encircled her neck tighter to keep her in check, but she realized with a sudden rush of hope that there was little strength in it.

"Let her go," Tyler said. "She's served her purpose for you."

Roseanne sensed the waiting tenseness in Tyler. He was poised on the edge of the spring, like a cougar waiting for just the right moment to pounce, with a cold fury held tightly in control.

Cotton's voice was without sympathy, just as it had been nine years ago during that first confrontation. "I could have shot you in the dark, Chanson, but it would have been too easy and not very satisfying. I thought, instead, I'd see just how much you loved this woman. See if her life means more to you than your own."

A cry rose in Roseanne's throat only to be squelched by Cotton's gun digging deeper into her back. Her eyes flared with desperation as they locked with Tyler's. She saw his love evident there and she knew he would do whatever Cotton asked. Frantically she tried to break free of Cotton's grip but his gun rising to her wound stopped her with the excruciating pain.

"Throw down the rifle, Chanson, if you want her to live."

Rage assailed Tyler, nearly blinding him. Cotton was asking him to lay down his defenses so he could kill him in cold blood. Yet, what choice did he have? It was him or Roseanne.

The hammer on Cotton's gun clicked back into firing position. "Throw it down, Chanson! Unless you're so cowardly you'd rather see a woman die in your place."

Roseanne pleaded with her eyes and with sounds from her throat, but Tyler's rifle hit the ground with a thud. Her heart began to pound violently, resounding in her ears until it almost deafened her.

Cotton's only outward sign of pleasure at being in full command did not show on his face, but rather edged into his words with a gloating quality. "Now, pull your revolver from your holster and toss it down, too."

Slowly Tyler withdrew the gun, but hesitated. His anger burned at being stripped of his weapons, and at being rendered powerless to this man he so despised. He refused to think of dying, he only wanted his chance at Cotton.

Suddenly Roseanne rammed her elbow back into Cotton's stomach and pulled free of his crippled arm. "No!" she screamed. "Tyler, don't do it!" Purposefully she tangled her feet and her skirts into Cotton's legs tripping them both. She fell to the ground, unable to stop her own fall. The pain nearly made her lose consciousness. Cotton was thrown off-balance and went down to his hands and knees. Simultaneously, Tyler leaped to the left and pulled up his pistol, leveling it on Cotton.

"Drop your gun, Cotton! It's over."

Cotton sneered at him and the crazed look deepened in his eyes. With his good hand, he pushed himself upright until he was balancing on his knees. He looked at Tyler with calculating eyes and then suddenly he jerked his gun up. The mountain reverberated with the report of a single bullet, echoing like several. The smoke from the gun wafted into Tyler's nostrils, and across the springs of the Manitou, Walt Cotton lay still. His gun fell from his grip, catching on his index finger, dangling for a moment, before falling to the ground.

When the shock had turned once again to stillness, Roseanne struggled to rise. In seconds Tyler's arms were around her, pulling her up and into the protective haven of his embrace. He held her for a length of time that was not measured, and she listened to the rapid beat of his heart slow to a normal pace beneath her ear.

She glanced at Cotton, fearful he might rise up and threaten them again, but the whites of his eyes shone upward to the cloudless sky. He was dead.

Slowly the fury cleared from her head. She felt the soothing warmth of the sun in contrary calmness to the hysterical pounding of her pulse. The green bulk of the trees in the steep ravine swayed to a gentle breeze. Her breathing slowed and she closed her eyes and fought unconsciousness. She heard a voice that momentarily brought her back, but it slid from her mind like a figment of her imagination. She couldn't be sure if it had even been real.

She heard the voice again, calling her name. "Roseanne." And then he lowered himself to the ground and her with him, keeping her on his lap. He removed the rope from her hands while she kept her head on his chest, reassured by the sound of life thumping inside.

"Roseanne, I love you."

"I know—enough to die for me. Oh, Tyler!" Her hand went to his cheek. "You shouldn't have let him force you to throw away your guns. I knew—I *know* you love me. You didn't have to prove it. We could have found another way."

"And what was that? That you would die for me? Never."

Suddenly needing him as she never had, she drew his head to hers and with a muted moan sought his lips as if they could ease the terror still overwhelming her. He wrapped her gently in his arms, being careful of her wound. She shuddered in relief and finally buried her face in his shirt and fought back tears that marked a release from their ordeal.

"It's all right, my love," he said softly against her cheek, taking her once again into his arms as he came to his feet. "Now, I have to get you home."

"Tyler," her hand tightened on his arm as her eyes and her voice beseeched him, fearful of asking what she knew she must ask. "Is Will all right? God, please say that he is."

Tyler's lips touched her forehead. The tenseness eased from his face. "He's fine, Roseanne. Just fine."

From over Roseanne's head, he looked at the dead man in the grass. It had started with this man, so naturally it should end with this man. Now Tyler could feel the claims of his past disintegrate in Roseanne's soothing, warm embrace. In her hands was a subtle, soft strength and comfort that had breathed new meaning into his life. Now he was free to love his wife and his son.

He bent his head to possess her lips again with the perpetual promise of his love. "It's over," he whispered against her cheek. "Nothing will separate us again."

With Roseanne held tightly in his arms, Tyler took the first step from the canyon. Overhead, the sun blazed in the Colorado sky with unspoken promises for the future. From the distance, a bird reclaimed the mountain with his cheery call; and from the depths of the tall, thick grasses, the earth reclaimed the godless.

This is the special design logo
that will call your attention
to Avon authors who
show exceptional
promise in

THE AVON ROMANCE

the roman
area. Ea
month a new nov
will be feature

SURRENDER THE HEART Jean Nash   89622-2/$2.95 US/$3.75 C
Set in New York and Paris at the beginning of the twentieth century, beauti
fashion designer Adrian Marlowe is threatened by bankruptcy and must tu
to the darkly handsome "Prince of Wall Street" for help.

Other Avon Romances by Jean Nash:

   FOREVER, MY LOVE   84780-9/$2.

RIBBONS OF SILVER Katherine Myers   89602-8/$2.95 US/$3.75 C
Kenna, a defiant young Scottish beauty, is married by proxy to a wealt
American and is drawn into a plot of danger, jealousy and passion when t
stranger she married captures her heart.

Other Avon Romances by Katherine Myers:

   DARK SOLDIER   82214-8/$2.
   WINTER FLAME   87148-3/$2.

PASSION'S TORMENT Virginia Pade   89681-8/$2.95 US/$3.75 C
In order to escape prosecution for a crime she didn't commit, a young Engli
beauty deceives an American sea captain into marriage—only to find
tormented past has made him vow never to love again.

Other Avon Romances by Virginia Pade:

   WHEN LOVE REMAINS   82610-0/$2.